For a long time Adam had been interested in
the meaning of life. He had no doubt
that there was a purpose to it all,
and, hopefully, a destination,
but he had never really
considered the ways
and means of

D0469209

Getting There

*And then, one day. . .*

Books by Michael J. Roads

Published by H. J. Kramer, Tiburon, California

*The "WORLDS BEYOND" Quartet:*
*TALKING WITH NATURE*
*JOURNEY INTO NATURE*
*JOURNEY INTO ONENESS*
*INTO A TIMELESS REALM*

*SIMPLE IS POWERFUL*

Published by Hampton Roads Publishing Company,
Charlottesville, Virginia

The *"BEYOND SELF"* Trilogy
*GETTING THERE*
*\*NEW BEGINNINGS*
*\*GOING BEYOND*
[*Forthcoming]

# MICHAEL ROADS

# Getting There

## a novel

HAMPTON ROADS
PUBLISHING COMPANY, INC.

Cover design by Marjoram Productions
Cover art by Susan Jones

For information write:
Hampton Roads Publishing Company, Inc.
134 Burgess Lane
Charlottesville, VA 22902

Or call: 804-296-2772
FAX: 804-296-5096
e-mail: hrpc@hrpub.com
Web site: http://www.hrpub.com

If you are unable to order this book from your local
bookseller, you may order directly from the publisher.
Quantity discounts for organizations are available.
Call 1-800-766-8009, toll-free.

Library of Congress Catalog Card Number: 98-71593

ISBN 1-57174-104-6

10 9 8 7 6 5 4 3 2

Printed on acid-free paper in the United States

To my beloved wife, Treenie, a rare and wonderful
lady who is definitely "Awake."


*How unjust to themselves are those who*
*turn their backs to the sun, and see naught*
*except the shadows of their physical selves*
*upon the earth.*

—Kahlil Gibran

# Acknowledgements

Allow me to quote two sentences from a letter written to me by my excellent editor, Robert S. Friedman: "Dear Michael, I tried hard to find something wrong with the book, so that I could at least say to myself that I did a good job as editor. I failed miserably."

Bob, let me say only that you did not fail miserably. You proved yourself to be free of "editor-ego" by allowing the book to pass through unscathed. By your suggestion of practically all the italics, I know that your "heart" was in the book. Sincerely, I thank you.

To my beloved wife, Treenie, again, my most sincere thanks for you always being so wonderfully you. You gave me Amber. Thank you.

I would also like to thank my agent, Marilyn McGuire, for so easily "fitting the bill." When Treenie and I first met her at the airport, I breathed a sigh of relief, and recognition; she was one of "us."

And, to who I AM, for *all* I am, thank you.

# $One$

I limped along the shoreline, my left leg slightly numb and uncooperative. Pain is a mean companion, and my mood was sour as I gazed across the waves gently lapping the beach.

My footsteps were sinking deeply into the yielding white sand as I walked slowly along the sunny Queensland beach on the Sunshine Coast. Remote and deserted, this was how I like my beaches. Small white waves scurried over the surface of the blue sea, each one a miracle of perfection as it busily chased after its predecessor.

I had long been a lover of the natural world, and this lonely, unspoilt beach called to me again and again. Lips compressed in a grimace, yet another stab of pain reminded me that walking in soft sand was no longer a wise recreation. Today was one of my defiant days—a day when I said to hell with it all, and did it anyway.

Lying down to ease the throbbing ache, I squinted out to sea. I sighed deeply, my mind wandering back to the accident that had left me with this unwanted legacy. It had seemed so little at the time, so mild an incident that it hardly rated attention. I had been building a shed, and was ready to lay the main roof beam in place. The main beam was heavy, very heavy, but I was strong and capable. Too strong, I realized, as I looked back over the years. I had tried to manhandle the huge beam into position by myself, and in the moment of success, there was a clear sound as though a soft handclap, and a disc ruptured in my stretched and vulnerable lower spine. Since then, pain had continually dogged my footsteps.

The sun was very warm and I semidozed for a while, my mind quiet. Maybe half an hour had passed when, unthinking, and purely on premonition, I suddenly sat up. Like the touch of a mild electric shock, a weird sensation tingled through my whole body. Despite the heat, I shivered.

I enjoyed being alone on the beach, losing myself in daydreams and specu-lation. To me, life was a mystery—a vast unfathomable unknown that we humans seem to be very poor at dealing with. Life defeats so many people. My thoughts were just heading along a familiar track when I spotted the dead osprey. Unaccountably, I shivered again.

I knew what it was instantly; I know my birds. Sometimes called a sea eagle, or a fish hawk, it is neither of these, for the osprey is a distinct species. It lay like a dirty buff-colored scarf on the edge of the waves, its wings undulating gently as the tide lapped it.

Walking the dozen or so yards over to it, I squatted down and picked it up. Forlorn and pathetic in death, it had probably been dead about a day, its splendor gone. Never again to swoop in silent mastery, it was a fallen hero of the skies, its eyelids closed over sunken eyes, its breastbone a sharp wet wedge. Surprisingly, it had not yet been gnawed or nibbled by the crabs, but I knew that once it began to stink they would be quickly attracted.

I stood up, holding the osprey. They were not really uncommon birds. I had spent many hours on the coast watching their aerial acrobatics as they snatched a fish from the waves. The osprey was a bird I admired. However, its beauty lost, this bird was dead. Of that there was no doubt; as cold as the ocean, it was soaking wet, limp, and lifeless. I considered giving it a burial in the sand, then silently laughed at my morbid, sentimental foolishness.

"May I see it?"

The voice did more than startle me. I jumped so sharply and violently that I stumbled, jarring my back and nearly falling headlong at the sharp surge of pain. An angry retort leapt to my tongue, but I bit it back, taking a deep breath as I struggled to regain my composure. "Er . . . yes, why not," I growled with ill will.

A rather plump adolescent boy stood in front of me. Fair-haired, his face was round, pleasant, while his eyes, wide and very open, were fixed on mine. He had a look of vague surprise on his face, his roly-poly figure unruly in long, dark green shorts, and a glaring orange T-shirt that sagged nearly to his knees.

As our eyes locked and held, I felt uncomfortable. Despite his lack of any physical attraction, the kid had some undefinable quality, or presence, that I had never before encountered in anyone, especially in a boy, and I was somewhat disconcerted. Teenagers generally have a slightly defensive attitude, lacking the assurance of an adult. This boy was different. He looked a slob, yet his eyes held mine without the slightest self-effacement. His eyes seemed a complete mismatch to his body, for they were clear, hard, and penetrating. I felt as though he were looking both through me, and deeply into me.

My arms jerked as I clumsily offered him the osprey, and it fell onto the sand between us. It lay limp as a rag, unmoving, as we looked down at it. Neither of us made any attempt to pick it up.

"Just a dead osprey," I said, trying to fill the silence and ease my startled discomfort at his abrupt and unexpected appearance. Mild electric tingles were sweeping over me again, further adding to my confusion.

"Er . . . how the hell did you get here? The beach was empty when I picked up the bird . . . then suddenly, you're standing here."

"Obviously you didn't notice me coming," the boy said dismissively.

Subject closed; that was the wave of feeling that I received with his words, and despite knowing in my gut that I had not made an error, I felt strangely powerless to act against it, or even argue with him.

Casually, the boy bent down and picked up the dead osprey. He held it by its breast, its head facing forward as though he held a model airplane. For long moments he stared at it thoughtfully, his eyes narrowing at some inner, silent speculation, then, to my angry consternation, he suddenly started running along the beach, the bird's wings grotesquely flapping up and down as he jogged along, the osprey held high above his head.

Despite being plump, he ran swiftly, moving over the white sand like a very fast lightweight. Shocked by his callousness, he was well away from me before I could react.

"Hey! You rotten kid. Come back here."

Angry, I chased after him, managing a fast limping jog as I determined to tell him off. Dead the osprey might be, but it was still a creature of nature and worthy of respect.

Rather than run away, the boy had swiftly run in a large circle and was coming straight back toward me—when my world of normality came to an abrupt and shocking end.

My eyes wide with disbelief, I watched as he drew back his arm and launched the osprey impossibly high into the air. I gaped in shock as its wings opened and caught the breeze, and as it whirled higher and higher, a harsh shriek of triumph escaped its beak.

My whole reality overwhelmed, I sank down onto the sand, my legs abruptly weakened by this stark impossibility. On my knees, I watched, dumbfounded, as the osprey swooped down, down, toward the boy, deliberately brushing his

11

outstretched hand with a wing tip as it swept past on a smacking rush of air. I watched as the osprey flew high, ever higher, seeming to vanish as it flew into the dazzling light of the sun. An involuntary moan was torn from me as I clutched at my sanity. The boy jogged over to me, concern in his eyes.

"Are you okay?" he asked.

"How?" I gasped. "How?"

The boy smiled, his eyes crinkling, his mouth wide and generous. "Why? That's the real question. Not how."

Staring at him stupidly, I blinked owlishly as I tried to consider his words. "Why! What the hell has why got to do with it? How? That's what I need to know."

Squatting next to me, the boy smiled, our eyes now on a level. His whole energy was disconcerting, for I could feel power radiating from him, a power that was unknown to me.

"The how of it may be difficult for you to grasp. It's the why that matters," he insisted.

The strange surreal quality that had begun at the boy's appearance persisted. I felt that I was out of step with time, that everything had the consistency of an unrelenting dream.

"I must be asleep, dreaming," I declared.

The boy nodded solemnly. "That's exactly why I'm here."

I squinted at him, then, with strong deliberation, I slapped my own cheek, hard. It hurt.

"I'm not asleep," I protested.

"Oh, but you are," the boy said, looking amused.

Deadlocked, we stared at each other, before the boy giggled. There was something infectious about his chuckle, or maybe it held a compulsion, but it drew me in like a fish, trembling and gasping.

As I began to laugh, the shock of what I had witnessed receded slightly, and gradually my laughter became more real, more genuine. But as the laughter quickly died, I quietly wept. Adding to my confusion, the tears were almost wrenched out of me. I felt emotionally shocked. What I had witnessed was just too much to contain. Dead birds do not fly, not under any circumstances—but this one had!

My embarrassment did not help either, but as I caught the boy's eyes, I knew that he understood. Damn it, I even got the feeling that he had deliberately provoked this whole emotional outburst. When, finally, the tears had come to an end, I looked at him, holding his gaze. I looked into eyes of cerulean blue, impossibly old eyes in such a young face.

With a lot of effort, I managed to smile. "Okay. Tell me why. Then, perhaps, how. And who are you?"

The boy held out his hand. "I'm Selph."

"Sel . . . ! How do you spell it?"

"S-e-l-p-h."

I shook his hand. "Selph who? Or, who Selph?"

"Nothing else. Just Selph."

"That's silly. You must have more than one name."

"Why? Does it matter?"

"Well, you've got to be Selph somebody, or somebody Selph. I'd like to know."

"Why do I have to be Selph somebody, or even Selph anybody? What's wrong with Selph?"

I felt thoroughly confused. There was no deference from this kid, none of the adolescent conceding to the greater age and life experience of an adult.

"Okay, if you don't want to tell me that's your business. My name's Adam."

He smiled knowingly. "Yeah, I know. Adam Frederick Sebastion Baker, to be precise."

That shook me. I never told my full name to anyone. Only my separated wife, Amber; my sister, Kate; and my parents would know. "How do you know that?" I demanded. "How do you know me? I've never met you before."

"Does that mean I shouldn't know you?"

I groaned aloud. "Christ! Can't you talk sense? For God's sake, everything you say leads in circles. Who the hell are you?"

"I'm your teacher!"

My mouth fell open as I goggled at him. "You're what?"

He rose to his feet with a smooth, unnatural ease, offering me his hand. "I'm your long-awaited savior," he said mockingly, bowing low before me.

Slapping his hand away, I was speechless with rage. For long moments I sat and swore.

"Does that help?" he asked seriously.

Confused, angry, and reactive, I shouted at him. "Get the hell out of here and leave me alone."

"Is that what you really want?" he asked.

His tone and manner had changed from one of banter and provocation to one of deadly seriousness, and I was suddenly unsure. What in the hell is going on? Who is this kid?

"I don't know," I groaned. "I'm confused as hell."

"All this reaction and trauma simply because you're out of your comfort zone. Relax man. Loosen up. You watch a simple miracle, and zap . . . you go to pieces."

He squatted in front of me, talking as though I were the kid, and he some mature adult.

"Please," I said weakly, "just tell me what the hell is going on."

He offered me his hand once more. "Come on, let's walk along the beach. I'll explain it to you, then you can decide."

"Decide what?"

He grinned. "I haven't explained yet."

Defeated, I sighed. Taking his outstretched hand, I allowed him to help me to my feet.

"That's the first hurdle dealt with," he said.

"What do you mean? What hurdle?"

Selph squinted up into the sky, as though he might be looking for the osprey, then gave me a serious look. "I mean you don't like being helped. You take offense easily. You really don't like people. You act as though your back problem is the end of the world, and you blame your wife for leaving you. On top of all that, you . . ."

"Just who the hell do you think you are?" I shouted angrily, cutting him off.

"I already told you."

"No, you didn't. You told me your name is Selph. That doesn't tell me a thing."

His eyes were stern, incongruous in his round, soft face.

"And you like to play games. You can't face your own reality. You don't like yourself much, do you?"

I stared back at him, unable to answer. I was way out of my depth. This fat kid was touching onto everything in me that I most despised. He seemed to be able to see right into me. How? I thought of the dead osprey. How could he have possibly made it fly? Was it an illusion?

I sighed again, deeply. The unknown was too great. I didn't even know how to think it out. Nothing he did or said conformed to my everyday reality. What was it he had said? He was my teacher! Ridiculous!

He was uncompromising. "If you remember, I told you who I am, but that confronts you too much. So, you tell me who I am. Let's see if you can face it."

I stared miserably at the sand, the words stuck in my throat. How could a kid be my teacher? If such a person were to come into my life, surely it would not be a fat kid!

"I can't hear you," he said in a singsong voice.

Anger bubbled in my gut, but I was achingly aware of how inappropriate it was. Anger had become a permanent resident in my stomach, aching when I was tense or upset. Like now, for instance.

I swallowed hard, the words coming out in a low rush.

"You said that you're my teacher."

He nodded. "I did indeed."

We walked side by side for nearly a mile, neither of us speaking. I was aware of his silence. Somehow, it was more than silence; it was as though he weren't there. It felt like I was walking with a ghost. I had the distinct impression of being alone, despite his obvious physical presence. My mind was strangely numb as I tried to grapple with all that was happening. Nothing conformed. The osprey incident should not be possible, yet I had clearly seen it happen. How could a stranger—and a kid, at that—know about Amber and me? Neither of us had talked about what had happened. How could he know that I don't like people? And he knew about my back injury! How?

I glanced at him out the corner of my eye. Apart from his eyes, and his powerful energy field, he looked just like any other overweight fifteen-year-old kid, a bit plump and shapeless in those ridiculous long shorts and that garish T-shirt. As for a teacher! Gee, what could he teach me, older and more experienced?

"How did you do that osprey trick?" I asked.

Selph stopped suddenly, his hands on his hips as he gave me a vexed stare. "Why do you persist in asking damn fool questions that you wouldn't under-stand even if I answered them? The question you should be asking is why?"

In that moment, I knew that he was in control. Either I played it his way, or there was no game. "Okay, you win. Tell me *why* you brought a dead osprey to life and caused it to fly again." The question made me sound like a lunatic.

"I did it to attract your attention."

I goggled at him. "Well, you sure as hell succeeded! But why?"

He smiled disarmingly. "Because, as your teacher, I decided to establish my credentials with a spectacular and undeniable flourish."

My mouth hanging open, I managed to spit out a few uncoordinated words. "Ah . . . er . . . but . . . what."

His face was open and guileless. "Would you have believed me if I had approached you and told you that I am your long-awaited cosmic teacher?"

"I'm not sure I believe you now," I muttered.

"That's the decision you have to make," Selph replied seriously. "You have just witnessed a miracle, impossible by any normal standards. So, either you accept me as your teacher and we get on with it, or just say the word and I'm out of here."

"Supposing I was . . ."

"No supposing, no avoidance," Selph cut in sharply. "I want either a yes, I am ready to expand and grow, yearning to know my truth, or no, I prefer to stagnate and wallow in self-pity."

"How old are you?" I asked abruptly.

"How old do you think?"

I shrugged. "About fifteen."

"Fifteen it is," he grinned.

I realized that whatever age I suggested he would have agreed, but there was little I could do about it. For a fifteen-year-old kid, he came across as brusque, curt, and painfully blunt. I smiled inwardly. This was the way I treated most people. He was beating me at my own game. I looked back over the years of my seeking a greater truth. There was no question that I had longed for a teacher to come into my life; it had been my focus for years . . . but a fat kid! It did not make sense. And yet, there *was* the osprey! He was right. If I had not seen that, there is no way I would even vaguely consider him as my teacher. So what the hell! What had I to lose? Nothing. I could cut loose anytime I wanted. This wasn't a binding commitment. I could see how he shaped up, and if he was no good, tell him to get lost, osprey or no osprey.

"Okay," I said condescendingly, "I'll give it a go."

He faced me squarely, and suddenly it was difficult to see him as a fat kid. The sun was behind him, causing his features to be lost, his definition blurred in light.

"Not good enough," he replied calmly. "I'm about to withdraw the offer." His voice rose powerfully, not in volume, but with a penetrating intensity. "I need a total commitment from you, nothing less. Your casual, slack, and arrogant attitude is not good enough. I am the response to your soul's longing, and you adopt a 'try it and run' attitude." He shook his head. "Not good enough by half."

Turning on his heels, Selph walked away from me.

I stared after him, stunned and guilty, when I noticed something that sent chills up and down my spine. There was no shadow with Selph. A quick glance confirmed that my shadow was clearly apparent on the white sand, but Selph was shadowless. In that moment, I knew beyond any doubt that Selph was far more than he appeared.

"Wait," I shouted. "WAIT!" But he took no notice. I ran limping after him, shouting, but in some strange way his walk left me far behind. As hard as I could go, I trailed further and further behind—then he vanished.

I sank down to the sand, overwhelmed by my stupidity. How could I be such an idiot? I now knew that Selph had told me the truth. How it could happen I had no idea, but my years of longing had somehow brought a teacher to me. And I had just turned him away. I shook my head in disbelief. I must be the world's biggest imbecile. He had no shadow, for God's sake! For some reason, that clinched it. Bringing the osprey to life was stunningly miraculous, but no shadow! It suggested light to me, light beyond shadow. And I had turned him away!

"Oh shit! Shit!" I sat and swore in sheer frustration, a lamentation from the soul. That Selph would be demanding as a teacher was obvious, but I longed for his return. Who he was, where he came from, or how or why—none of that mattered any longer, and now it was too late. I cursed myself for a fool. My God, if anyone needed a teacher, I did. In my musings on life, I had come to the point where all the evidence indicates that we lack the essential skills of living naturally. We lack some profound knowledge, some vast insight that would enable us to do it better. If there is *a* truth, then we know nothing of it. Religions profess to know it, uttering endless rhetoric about the subject, but the leaders of these religions suffer from the same anxieties, fears, and personal problems that the person in the street has to cope with. There is no indication in their personal lives that they live in a superior way. I was unconvinced that life was intended to be the vast, mind-numbing, gut-wrenching, soul-destroying process of elimination it has become, but all the evidence indicates that this is our everyday reality. I had not yet come up with a solution, but I felt sure that somewhere, one must exist. A teacher would have the solution, and I had just turned him away. I groaned in misery and despair.

As a consultant, I could plan my days in any way I wanted, within reason. Some of my time was spent studying, and I had read many books on spiritual, esoteric, and philosophical matters, but it made little real difference. I had

17

some knowledge in my head, but very little came through into my day-to-day reality. I understood such concepts as "oneness," but so little of it rubbed off on me. Reading words like "wholeness" is easy, but what the hell did it really mean? How could so many separate things, people, and the vast diversity of nature possibly be "one?" I knew the theory, and it really excited me, but the reality remained distant and unobtainable. Applying such a concept in everyday life defeated me. And that's what I wanted. I wanted to experience an inner peace, and know the real meaning of life. I wanted it so bad, it hurt. And now, just when a cosmic teacher had come into my life, I had turned him, and all that he offered, away.

"OH SHIT! YOU STUPID BLOODY CRETIN. STUPID. STUPID. STUPID," I screamed hopelessly into the sea breeze.

Sitting slumped on the beach, I stared blindly out to sea for another couple of hours, hoping against hope that Selph would come back. I thought about how he had appeared so suddenly when I found the dead osprey. He had vanished just as quickly. It had seemed as though he just walked away from me, but even though I had immediately run after him, I was left far behind. Who was he? What was he? The implications of Selph being shadowless were stunning, yet when he had walked beside me I had felt that I was alone. A body that allowed light to pass through it. I shook my head. This was beyond anything I could understand. I was way, way out of my depth. And he was gone forever.

Finally, still angry at my own stupidity, I got up from the beach and commenced the long walk back to my car. I was so engrossed in my own thoughts that I saw nothing of the natural beauty I usually enjoy so much. Normally I would be watching the pied oystercatchers as they ran along the shoreline before me, their bright, orange-red beaks glinting wet in the sun, or marveling at the terns, diving as shards of white crystal elegance into the sea, emerging with a small fish taken from the abundant shoals. Like dead leaves blowing in the wind, small sandpipers raced along the beach on twinkling feet, but I was blind to everything except my own stubborn foolishness. Fervently I prayed for just one more chance. Just one opportunity to make amends.

As I reached my green Nissan Pulsar car, I knew that I had blown it. Miracles do not happen more than once in a person's life. I had thrown away the chance of a lifetime simply because I could not accept another person the way they were—however odd. I bit my lip. That was why Amber had left me. I was forever trying to change her; something I had not really faced until now. I was much better at blaming than I was at accepting responsibility.

Reaching into my pockets for my car keys, my eyes were caught by a bright orange T-shirt stretched out on the backseat. I stared in amazement, utterly delighted, embarrassed as tears sprang to my eyes. Selph lay there, sprawled out and fast asleep, audibly snoring.

My mind raced, words churning to the surface as I tried to snatch the car door open. It was locked! I swallowed nervously as I quietly unlocked the door by the driving seat. How did he get in? How? How? How? Selph was one big question that I now realized I could not ask! He was an enigma. Either I accepted him on his terms, or he would simply leave. One blue eye opened as Selph looked up at me.

"Let's go home, I'm hungry." He sat up, opening the door to emerge with a small sigh. "Good car for sleeping in, even if a bit cramped."

"I thought you had left me forever," I said. "I'm sorry I was so truculent. Why did you stay?"

"When the student is ready . . . and all that jazz. You are ready, but you're sure reactive. However, let's get one thing clear, right now. We do this my way. Next time I leave, it will be for real. I'm not attached to you, or to being your teacher. Forget all your questions, because I'm all about experience. Questions are a mind game, and the rules of play are separation. So, do you accept me with a total commitment, or do I cut loose?"

I did not hesitate. "I accept, and . . . thank you."

Ducking into the passenger's seat, Selph patted the driver's place. "Okay, Adam, let's go home and eat."

We drove in silence for a way, but there were a few details I had to know. "Er, are you planning to come and live with me?"

"Yep. That's the general idea. Any problem with that?"

"Oh, no, none at all. It's quite okay."

"Hey look," Selph shouted. "There's a McDonald's." He was visibly excited. "Let's drive in and get some burgers."

I opened my mouth to protest, but closed it quickly. I hate burgers, but if he wanted one that was okay by me.

Turning off the road, I swung the car past the pink-flowering camellia bushes that lined the driveway. Pulling up next to a row of cars, within moments we were walking into the noisy restaurant as the automatic doors opened for us. I winced. Too many people, too much plastic, too much noise, and I do not like junk food. Selph had no such qualms, he was already at the counter.

"Shall I order one for you, Adam?" he asked.

"Er, okay."

"Two with the works," Selph told the petite blonde girl who awaited his order. He smacked his lips eagerly.

I pulled out my wallet, but Selph waved me away. "You grab a table and chairs. This is my treat."

Perched on a plastic seat, facing a plastic table, I waited for Selph. At this moment he was more like a twelve-year-old than a teenager. He was almost drooling as he waited for the burgers. I shook my head in disbelief. It was weird! This was the same person who had just performed a miracle—my teacher! Had I been conned? I watched him as he paid for the burgers, before threading his way past the other tables to the corner I had chosen. It was all he could do to restrain from eating as he walked.

Plonking my burger in front of me, Selph smiled at me brightly. "Great grub, Adam."

Grunting noncommittally, I picked up the burger and took a bite. Yuk! There was nothing wrong with the food. I just did not like burgers. And "the works" just made it so much worse.

Selph was definitely happy. Already halfway through his burger, he was chewing with an overstuffed mouth looking blissed out. What I was looking at and what I knew of him just did not add up.

"You're enjoying that, aren't you?" I said smiling.

He grinned back. "A whole lot more than you are. Tell me, why are you eating a burger with the works?"

He was chuckling at me, a picture of boyish adolescent innocence, but I had the distinct feeling that a trap was looming. What should I tell him?

"Er, I'm eating it to keep you company."

"You could keep me company just as well with a cup of coffee, or with something else on the menu. Why did you agree to a burger? You hate burgers, especially with the works. So tell me, why are you eating it?"

"How did you know that I hate burgers?" I gaped.

His smile was all innocence. "I'm your teacher, remember? I know all about you. Why are you eating burger?"

My temper heated a couple of degrees. "You tell me why I'm eating it if you know all about me," I muttered angrily.

"Okay. You're eating the burger to gain my approval. You're eating a burger because I am. You're surrendering your reality for mine, even though my reality of enjoying a burger doesn't honor you. How's that?"

There was a long pause as I searched my mind for some plausible evasion. I swallowed uncomfortably. The trouble was he was exactly right. I did some fast and frantic thinking.

"Well, that's almost right, but . . ."

"I'm exactly right," he cut in, "and you know it. You're scratching around for an excuse like a hen scratching for worms." He grinned engagingly. "Be honest. In eating that burger you are not being true to yourself, are you?"

"No," I said glumly.

"That's the lesson," he beamed. "Willy Shake-a-speare said it, 'to thine own self, be true.' Easily said, even easier to disregard."

I cringed at the massacre of Shakespeare's name, but had to concede his truth.

"You don't need my approval, or anybody else's. Honor yourself by being true to you. Always."

Taking the last huge bite of his burger, he stuffed it into his mouth. "Hungry business, being a teacher of profound truths," he mumbled, as onion and crumbs fell from his lips.

Dismissing my look of distaste with easy nonchalance, he continued. "It really disgusts you to see me stuffing burger into my mouth, and you make all sorts of judgments. Not only that, but it really gets under your skin. It irritates you, bothers you. Cosmic teachers don't do things like that, do they? But fifteen-year-old boys do."

Grinning, he sat back, knowing that the tomato relish smeared over his upper lip, along with the grease around his mouth, all aggravated me.

Biting down on my anger, and all the cutting remarks I could make, I sat and fumed. A couple of families close by were staring at Selph, and I could see that they were commenting on his lack of manners. I felt embarrassed by what was happening.

"Adam, life is a burger in McDonald's. This is life right now, not some cosmic fantasy or deep esoteric truth. This is where we are, this is where it's at. Do you get it?"

I shook my head wearily. "In all honesty, no. There are such things as manners, and decorum. And they can be used. To me, grossly stuffing food into your mouth proves absolutely nothing. What do you think the people around us are thinking? How about setting a good example to kids?"

Selph sighed, shaking his head sadly. "Manners are taught by parents at home, not table watching in McDonald's." He spread his hands out, indicating the people who were furtively watching him. "What these people think of me is up to them. If they want to condemn me for what they perceive as inappropriate behavior, so be it. This is your lesson, not theirs."

"I fail to see it."

Selph looked up at the ceiling, sighed, and got up. Going to the counter, he spoke to the little blonde. A few minutes passed and he was back, carrying a tray with two coffees and another burger. Sitting down, he held the burger before him.

"Watch," he said

I stared dumbfounded as he pushed the whole burger into his mouth in one smooth easy movement, swallowing it in one large gulp. Impossible! But he did it. He did not squeeze it smaller, or compress it. He simply put a burger that was far larger than his mouth into his mouth, and swallowed it without any chewing or biting. It was like seeing someone pour a pint of water into a half-pint glass.

"Does that offend you?" he asked.

I shrugged. "I've never seen anybody do such a thing before. I didn't even know it was possible. But in all truth, no, I'm not offended."

"Did it embarrass you?"

"No."

He beamed. "Why not? *That* was gross."

Puzzled, I shook my head. "I agree, it was totally gross, but it wasn't offensive. I don't know why, but it didn't offend me."

"I'll tell you why. That simple gross act was outside your conditioning, your training. It shouldn't be possible, so it was beyond your parameters of right and wrong behavior. So you didn't react. You were forced into a different perspective, where you don't have your judgments concreted into place."

"Yes, that makes sense," I nodded.

"So you were comfortable with that grossness, but embarrassed by the more familiar grossness. Right?"

I nodded again. "It sounds crazy when you put it like that, but I have to agree."

"Great," he beamed. "So stretch beyond your old parameters. Let go of old conditioning. You don't need it. You don't have to agree with gross behavior, or even like it, but you do need to reach a space where it doesn't affect you. Disapprove if you like, but release it as well."

His pudgy face was innocent as he slurped into his coffee, deliberately making it sound like a pig at a trough. He then picked up my untouched coffee, and effortlessly poured the whole mug of very hot liquid down his throat without appearing to swallow.

I shook my head in astonishment, then, catching the eye of a nearby table watcher, I grinned. As they blushed, jerking away from eye contact, my grin grew even wider.

"I see what you mean," I said to Selph.

He looked at me inquiringly, his face its usual mixture of bland innocence. "Ready to go?"

# Two

Selph was quiet on the journey home, staring around at the countryside with apparent enjoyment and fascination. I lived a few miles inland from the sea, so we did not have far to go. We turned into my garden, driving under a canopy of forest trees for a hundred and fifty meters until we reached the house. A fairly big house, it had been built with a low roofed profile, making it easier to weather the cyclones that rip along our subtropical coast in the wet season.

"Is this familiar to you?" I asked Selph, as we climbed out of the car. "Do you have any luggage anywhere?"

He gave me a sidelong glance, his expressive chubby face registering approval as he looked around. "I can't think why or how I should be familiar with this," he replied. "And no, I don't have any luggage. I travel light." He giggled, as though at some private joke.

"Well, you appear to know all about me," I said defensively, "I thought that might include where I live. How will you manage for clothes, and personal items?"

He shrugged. "No problem. If I need any, I'll use yours. I'm sure you won't mind."

I took a deep breath as he followed me indoors. Just what was I letting myself in for? I was still not too sure about whether he was just a fat, uncouth, rather miraculous slob, or a teacher from . . . wherever!

Selph was walking round the swimming pool while I got the coffee percolator going. It was gurgling pleasantly when I heard a tremendous splash. The kitchen window looked out over the pool and I could see Selph swimming vigorously. He had taken off the dreadful orange T-shirt, and his long green shorts, but as he came out of the water, I noticed that he was wearing boxer shorts. In keeping with his character, they were white, with bright pink-panthers all over them.

"Do you want a coffee?" I called through the window.

Slightly flabby, he looked like any normal school kid.

"Please, and a chocolate biscuit or three."

We sat at the table by the pool, each in a recliner.

"Great place you've got here," Selph commented. By direct contrast to his performance at McDonald's, he was eating his chocolate biscuits as daintily as any aristocrat, and quietly sipping at his mug of coffee.

Not speaking, I nodded. It was a great place all right, but without Amber it felt empty and deserted. Only in the garden could I find any consolation. Amber had enjoyed the garden, but it was always my domain. She had organized the house and office, everything flowing smoothly while I worked as an eco-farming consultant. The garden was my place of recreation and exercise, and I love fish ponds and plants. We had a big garden—a couple of acres—although most of it was light forest. Our home was set on a low mountain ridge, offering excellent views, even though the trees tended to shut us in. Looking out over the valley, a curtain of gray-green leaves created an ever-shifting screen through which we could peer, yet it offered us all the privacy I so enjoyed.

I sighed. It was about two years since Amber had left me, and I had never recovered from the devastating sense of loss. I had made a small shift from totally blaming her, to realizing that I was not an easy person to live with. Maybe Selph could help change that. I thought back to our bizarre meeting on the beach, reviewing the incident with the osprey. I suppose it *had* happened. My lips pursed as I nodded thoughtfully. Yes. No doubt about it. My mind moved along, recalling the conversation that had followed. At one stage I had mentioned that I must be asleep, dreaming, and Selph had nodded, saying, "That's why I'm here." Then I had slapped my cheek, stating that I was not asleep. Selph had strongly denied that, saying, "Oh, but you are." I frowned; what did he mean?

I glanced at him to find that he was observing me. He smiled encouragingly. "I find this whole situation very strange," I said. "I never really dreamed that a teacher would come into my life, never truly expected it. And never in my most far-out fantasies did I expect . . ."

"A fat kid to waltz into your life on the wings of a miracle," finished Selph.

"Something like that," I said lamely.

We were quiet for a while. "How did you do it?" I asked tentatively.

He looked at me seriously. "We each have a power within us that we can tap into. Everybody has it. You could call it the power of miracles. In me, this power is very highly developed. In you, and most other people, it's practically dormant. But, it *is* there."

"How come it's so developed in you?"

He looked thoughtful "Let's just concern ourselves in your own development. When you know *who* you are, you will know me, and all these personal questions will be obsolete."

"What did you mean on the beach when you said that I'm asleep? You put great emphasis on it at the time."

Selph closed his eyes, but rather than shut me out, it seemed as though he drew me in. In that moment I felt very close to him.

"Adam, you are asleep, along with most of humanity. You live a shared dream known as a consensus reality. This dream is fabricated and woven from the mass illusions of life. It has become so powerful, so hypnotic, that you now fight to maintain it, even though it holds you all as prisoners. The basis of the dream is mass self-deceit, and by its very nature it holds you enslaved."

My gut felt hollow and empty as he spoke, for I knew that he spoke the truth. I had known this for years.

"How do we get out of the dream?"

His eyes opened, and for long moments twin orbs of blue space pierced me through and through.

"The dream holds people collectively, but there is no collective way out. Each person is on a journey, and their destination is Truth. The journey is an individual one, each finding his or her truth in their own way."

So where do I find this . . . Truth?"

"Within yourself."

"It always comes down to this, doesn't it?" I sighed. "No simple cosmic recipes, no quick fix, just an inner searching that is almost guaranteed to make you an outcast, considered by the many as living on the lunatic fringe."

Nodding his head, he grinned. "Yep! It's always been that way. The many, as you call them, are the very heart of consensus reality, while the seekers of truth are an indirect threat to the status quo. The few threaten the comfort of the many."

"But the many aren't comfortable," I protested. "They are acutely uncomfortable, forever struggling to be more comfortable."

Selph's eyes held a fleeting sadness. "That's part of the paradox. The dream will always be uncomfortable; it has to be, for it is the fabrication of deceit. People deceive themselves, struggling to stay within discomfort while trying to become more comfortable. They attempt to do this by acquiring more material goodies. More appliances, more cars, more status: toys, all fodder for self-deceit."

"We deserve better than that," I said sadly.

"Indeed you do, but first you have to see through the deceit. You have to see that spending all your energy to go nowhere is counterproductive. Each person deserves the very best that life can offer."

Staring at Selph as he talked, I marveled at the incongruity of hearing this wisdom and insight come from the lips of an adolescent boy. But more than ever, I knew that he was deceiving me. Whatever or whoever Selph was I had no idea, but his apparent age and personality was a mask that I had to learn to disregard.

"Who are you, hiding behind that mask?" I murmured.

"Who are *you*, hiding behind that mask?" he countered.

I smiled sadly. "There's the difference. You know who you are, and the facade is a game. I don't know who I am, and the mask is killing me."

"That's more true than you realize. It is. That's why I'm here. I told you before, I am the response to your inner cry for help. This also is true. It is the birthright of every human being to live in the golden castle of abundance on the peak of the mountains of beauty. But what happens instead?" He looked at me expectantly.

I shrugged. "I don't know. We are pretty rotten at mountain climbing, I guess."

He shook his head. "No. It's only the few who attempt the climb. No. You settle for a rathole at the base of the mountain, and you measure success by the number of toys you can collect and store in that meager space. Your birthright is freedom, but you chase the acquisition of possessions by way of compensation."

"And it can never compensate," I added.

"Never," he agreed.

"And the trouble is, not only have we lost sight of the mountain, we have forgotten that it exists."

"That's about the sum of it," he nodded

❖  ❖  ❖

Later, I showed Selph into the spare bedroom, and gave him a tour of the house.

"Welcome to my rathole," I said depreciatingly.

Selph looked at me with a frown. "I hear frustration, self-condemnation, guilt, and self-pity all wrapped up together in that remark. It doesn't honor you, but thinking it and saying it will make it your reality."

"You're right, but I've decided that I'm going to be honest around you. My life is a mess, and I'm not going to pretend that everything is okay. My marriage is a rathole, and my relationship with my Dad is only marginally better. Oddly enough, I get on well with Mum and my sister, Kate."

"How about your relationship with yourself?"

"Another rathole," I lamented despairingly.

"This is where it all begins," Selph said. "When you honor who you are, then you honor all else in life. Honoring yourself is the masonry of the castle."

"I had better learn to lay building blocks then," I said flippantly.

"On the contrary," Selph said seriously. "You cannot build the castle with blocks of anything. Conversely, you build the castle by removing the blocks that have already been laid and concreted in place."

Taking a deep breath, I released it slowly. "Christ! Is there any chance for me? I must have spent all my life building a dungeon in which I'm now imprisoned. How do I get out? What do I do? I've read the books and learned nothing. Am I stupid, or what?"

"Not stupid, Adam, just conditioned. Your beliefs shape your thinking, and your thinking creates your own particular rathole, or dungeon. To read about Truth is conceptual, to *live* it is to experience its reality. That's what you and I are going to do. We can discuss issues like this, and that's a fair learning process, but it all has to be lived. That's where I come in. I'm going to open doors that you may choose to walk through."

I was surprised. This was the first time Selph had given a real indication of what he would do. What doors? Did he mean opportunities?

"I'm not sure I understand."

"You will, when it's appropriate."

That sounded ominous. "I hope you've got plenty of time," I said. "You could be with me for the rest of my life. There's nothing to indicate that I learn quickly."

Selph smiled. "Not exactly light and joy at the moment, are we. And as for time . . ." He waved his hands in easy dismissal, bowing before me. "Teacher knows what he is all about, don't you worry."

We did not talk much for the rest of the day. I plunged into a deep gloom, while Selph seemed to deliberately avoid me. Our conversation had given me a glimpse of just how much I did not know—and we had hardly started! Thinking about it depressed me, and I could not stop the thoughts.

Despite gaining the insight that there was more to Selph than a fifteen-year-old boy, I was stunned when he produced an incredible three-course dinner. He called me in from the garden, where I had been sharing my gloom with the fish pond. I am not sure that the fish wanted a share, but I invariably ended up by the fish pond in the garden when things got on top of me. Somehow, it always seemed to help.

His voice had startled me when he called. "Adam."

"What?" I shouted back.

"Dinner."

"Oh, God," I groaned to myself, "now I've got to cook for him."

"Coming," I called back, cringing at the thought of cooking when I felt so depressed. I was getting fed up with this teacher idea already, especially if I had to cook for him and generally look after him.

I smelt the aroma as soon as I entered the house. He had set the dining table for three, and I looked at him with an amazed and puzzled frown.

"You never fail to surprise me. You can cook?"

"That's for you to decide," Selph said, indicating a chair. I sat down, staring at the three-place setting.

"Why three? There's only two of us."

For a while he said nothing, serving up a savory soup of tomato and herbs. We ate in silence, dipping crisp homemade crouton fingers into the soup, and nibbling on the soggy ends. I glanced at the empty place setting, trying to figure it out. Was someone else invited? Surely we would have waited for them? Was there someone here I could not see? With an oddity like Selph around, who knows!

The soup finished, Selph served up baked schnapper, one of the very tasty Australian fish. Cooked to perfection it was accompanied by steamed broccoli, young carrots, and baby potatoes. All this was offered with a superb parsley white sauce. I knew that he had taken the ingredients from my fridge and freezer, but it surprised me that Selph had far surpassed my own reasonable skills at cooking.

"My God, Selph, where did you learn to cook like this? How many more hidden talents do you have?" I pointed to the third empty plate. "And why set the third place?"

He smiled benignly, looking anything but a fifteen-year-old boy. "My natural genius knows many outlets, this is but one of them. As for the third place . . ." He paused, looking at the empty plate as though just seeing it for the first time, "... this is to honor the new you. This is to give recognition to the potential you. A potential that has been unfed, uncared for, and basically ignored until now."

He held up a tall slim glass of water, indicating for me to do likewise. "Here's to your unlimited potential."

Solemnly drinking the toast, I was aware that something both very new and rare was taking place in my life. Where it was all going to lead me I was not sure, but every judgment I had made of Selph was always proved to be unworthy of him. I was finally getting to the point where I was committed. I had thought my commitment was made earlier, but like a fickle breeze, I swirled and eddied around, finding it difficult to be sure and clear.

Sometime later, Selph sat by the pool, gazing over the still water at the glowing silver orb of the moon as it appeared among the gently rustling leaves of the gum trees. I stood near the open window at the kitchen sink, washing the plates and dishes. Selph had offered to help, but after such a fine meal, I felt it was the least I could do. Besides, I don't mind washing dishes. It can be quite therapeutic.

Selph was in easy conversation range, and I had an observation I wanted to share for feedback. "You have mentioned honor quite a number of times. You've said words to the effect that I don't honor myself, and I get the impression that you consider this to be important. Could you expand on your meaning of honor?"

He was silent for a while, but I felt comfortable with this. I was content to wait, for the whole atmosphere was one of peace and quiet.Once again I had the inner sense that Selph was not really fully there, even though I could physically see him. I was adjusting to this strange contradiction, even though I did not understand it. My gloom had disappeared with the meal, and as much as is possible for me, I was at peace with life.

Selph stirred finally, as though coming back from some distant place. He stretched, yawning. "What does honor mean to you, Adam?" he countered.

Grinning at the way he countered my question, I thought about honor. "I guess it is about keeping my word. A bit like the Cub Scouts; I promise on my honor, et cetera."

Nodding slightly, Selph asked, "How about the vows of marriage? Does that involve honor?"

The peace was shattered as I felt a rush of blood to my gut. Damn it, yes. On a surge of guilt I could see Amber as she sobbed on what was to be our last evening together. "Are you so angry, Adam, that you can no longer honor me, or yourself?" she had asked poignantly. The memory brought tears to my eyes. She had looked so utterly beautiful, yet so torn apart. She knew then that she would have to leave me. I bit my inner lip as tension mounted. As I looked back into the past, it seemed that I had been powerless to prevent myself from sabotaging our marriage—a marriage that I had wanted more than anything in my life. Was there any honor in my actions of the past, as a marriage partner, or in me as a person? The answer was obvious, but not easy to face.

"I neither honored our marriage, nor Amber," I muttered in a low, choking whisper.

"And this is the first time you've faced it."

It was true. Why I should face it now, I did not know, but it was true. I could see it clearly now. I had been so fouled up in my head that Amber's innocence and joy had overwhelmed and threatened me. Inadvertently, I had tried to maneuver her into my space of misery, rather than learn to find my way into her natural joy of life. God! What an idiot. Now, I had lost it all, my marriage and Amber. The feeling in my gut was back, but it had changed. Always before I had felt the clutch and tension of anger, but this was the hollow emptiness of despair.

"Yes," I whispered huskily. "This is the first time I have been able to acknowledge it. My lack of honor has wrecked two lives."

Turning away, I left the last plate undried, stumbling to my bedroom. Pierced by shafts and arrows of undiluted guilt, I fell onto the bed with a soft moan of defeat. It might have been hours or minutes that I lay there, before I became aware of Selph standing in the doorway. For long seconds I had the impression of someone ancient beyond time, before his words rearranged the image.

"The process has begun, Adam. Clear your mind . . . and sleep."

My mind reared up in protest, wanting to scream aloud its pain and anguish, but it seemed that a soft blanket of oblivion was pulled over me, and everything faded out.

❖   ❖   ❖

The early morning sun shining through my open window woke me at six o'clock. A good time to be up and about. I lay for a while thinking about my revelations of last night. I could easily recollect facing the reality of how I had sabotaged my marriage, and of facing my unrealized lack of honor, but the guilt and shame I had felt so strongly last night now seemed to evade me.

Dressing slowly, I pulled on khaki shorts and a sleeveless red T-shirt. Walking down the hallway, I looked through the open door of the spare room to see if Selph was awake. There was no sign of him. Crossing the room to the bed, I found that it had not been slept in. My own particular way of bedmaking had not been touched. Frowning thoughtfully, I continued on to the kitchen to prepare breakfast.

A splash drew me to the large window. Selph was skinny-dipping in the pool. He saw me, and waved. "Hi, Adam. Sleep well?"

"I slept like the dead," I called back. "And you?"

"Oh, I had a great night."

I walked out to the poolside. This was going to be interesting. "So where did you have a great night's sleep? It sure wasn't in your bed. That I do know."

Unperturbed, Selph smiled at me. "Did I mention sleep, or being in bed?"

Caught out by my own smartness, I tried to bluster my way through. "But . . . a great night implies that you slept well."

He chuckled around a mouthful of water. "Poppycock! I told you I had a great night, and I did. Where and how I spent it is none of your business. You've got enough on your plate as it is, without trying to keep tabs on me."

Swallowing my indignation, I retreated from his laughter. Trouble is, he was right. I had more than enough to cope with just trying to sort myself out. Grinning wryly, I put the water on for some rolled oats and rolled barley porridge, while scouring my mind for some smart reply.

"I suppose you do eat porridge?" I asked sarcastically.

"Only if it has rolled barley in it," he called back.

My jaw hung open as I stared at the saucepan of boiling water. How the hell could he know that? Nobody else that I knew added rolled barley to oatmeal porridge. Gee! The mystery of Selph deepened. He really *did* know me. I made the porridge, taking it off the boil, and after allowing time for it to soak and swell, I called out to Selph.

Sitting at the breakfast nook in the large kitchen, we ate in silence, although my mind was anything but quiet. When I offered him home-baked bread, toasted, he eagerly accepted. Watching the toaster, I put another question to him.

"Selph . . . how could you possibly know about the rolled barley? And all that you know about Amber and me? Who are you? Where do you come from?"

He buttered his toast, declining the marmalade. Looking pensive, his blonde hair a wet halo of light around his head as it caught the slanting rays of the early morning sun, he turned to me.

"In the simplest possible terms, I *know* you. I won't explain this, for eventually you will *know* what I mean. Equally, to tell you who I am and where I am from will mean nothing until the timing is right."

I shook my head. "I hear your words, but I don't understand a single thing that you are saying."

He nodded sadly. "Don't I know it."

"I don't understand how I can learn from a teacher whom I don't understand," I said seriously.

Selph threw his head back, laughing like any average kid. "Sure beats me," he giggled.

"Look, this is serious. I want to learn about the meaning of life. Accepting you was not easy. Ask any adult how they would feel if they had to learn about life from a kid. It's ridiculous. But if I don't understand what you are talking about . . . ?" I broke off, shrugging helplessly.

"Bypass the handicap," Selph said, still chuckling.

I goggled at him. "What handicap?"

"The need to understand. That's a handicap."

I groaned. "This is bloody absurd. I don't even understand what you're talking about again. How, in all that is merciful, can understanding be a handicap?"

"Simply because right now you are handicapped by not understanding. Therefore, understanding is a handicap."

Throwing up my hands in sheer frustration, I stormed outside in anger. I didn't slip, nor did I trip, but with no choice at all, I fell headfirst into the pool.

"Cool off, Adam," Selph called out, as I came up gasping. He pushed me! He was nowhere near me, but I felt him push me into the pool. My God! What sort of teacher had I somehow invoked?

I did cool off. Although suitable for swimming, the water had a chill to it, and after staying in for ten minutes, I was well and truly cooled off.

Selph had the coffee percolating by the time I had changed my clothes, and we sat in the poolside recliners.

"You pushed me, Selph. I don't understand how that's possible when you were still sitting in the house, but I definitely felt you push me in."

"Do you trust your perceptions?" he asked.

I thought about it carefully. "Yes, I do, but I would still like it confirmed. You did push me, didn't you?"

He nodded. "I sure did. And it took quite a strong push to do it. You stand unusually firmly on your feet. So, do you understand? Or, can you trust your acceptance of what happened, and go beyond the need to understand?"

I shook my head in pure admiration. "Gee, are all cosmic teachers as tricky as you? I finally get it. Some things are not understandable by everyday standards. Yet, that is where most of our understanding is based. The need to understand is a habit. Understanding how a car engine works may be sensible and applicable by all normal standards, but trying to understand experiences that do not conform to a consensus reality is just continuing the habit."

Selph smiled, a look of pleasure on his open face.

"That's part of it, and well said. Listen carefully to another part, without trying to understand. Understanding is based in your mind. The mind needs to understand. However, your mind is always based in the past or the future. The mind is *never* based in the moment. The moment is where freedom IS; a state of inexplicable joy and peace."

He paused, waiting for me. "Listen. Because the mind is never based in the moment, joy and peace are both beyond our understanding, but not beyond our experiencing. A master of two thousand years ago spoke of 'the peace that passeth understanding.' He knew that peace can be experienced, but not understood. Peace is not fodder for the mind, it is the food of the soul. For as long as you need and want to understand the meaning of life, it will evade you. Experience the mystery of life, even contemplate it, but don't allow yourself to become enslaved by the habitual need to understand, for understanding a greater reality is not appropriate." He paused. "There's more."

"Wait." I sat with my eyes closed, attempting to just absorb it. "No more," I said softly. "Just let me be with this."

Some subtle nuance of feeling changed as Selph left me, and I knew that this was something else that I did not understand. But I felt it, and I knew that I could trust the feeling. All this was new for me. As I sat contemplating my feelings, without intellectually chasing an explanation so that I would understand, I felt a new feeling of lightness and freedom. Trust! I had to trust myself without any need of explanation. How much of my need to understand was based in not trusting myself? Understanding somehow bypassed my trusting myself. For me, understanding had become a prerequisite to acceptance. But accepting an experience needed neither understanding nor proof. It was enough to experience, and to simply trust myself and the experience without explanations or understanding.

I sat in the recliner by the pool for quite a long time, gently nursing a whole new realm of contemplation. I was now able to accept Selph without any explanation, knowing that it was okay. The incongruity of an apparent youth teaching me about life's deeper issues was still a tremendous challenge, an outrageous disparity with all that is normal, but I suspect it needed to be this way, for me. I am not quite sure why, but this is the way it is! Either I trusted the situation, or I didn't. I thought about it for a while, until, with some surprise, I realized that it was me I needed to trust and accept, rather than Selph. It occurred to me that for the first time in my life, this was possible. I hoped that if I were put to the test, I would be able to continue finding that trust.

Calling out to Selph, I spent the next ten minutes looking for him, but he seemed to have vanished. The thought crossed my mind that if I were to talk about him to a friend, I had not a single shred of evidence that he had ever been to my home. Where did he disappear to? Come to that, where did he appear from? I shrugged; forget it!

Grabbing a pen and paper, I wrote him a quick note, letting him know that, due to previous arrangements, I was going to visit my parents, and would be home late the next day. I even added the phone number where he could reach me, but I suspected that would be the last thing he needed. I even felt that the note was not necessary, but I wrote it anyway.

My overnight case was permanently packed, so it took me only a few minutes to be ready. Starting the engine of my Nissan Pulsar, I headed off into the Bush. It seems that any place in Australia that is away from the cities, towns, suburbia, and people is known as the Bush. Generally, the Bush is inland, and invariably thick with flies whose only purpose in life seems to be to cluster around your eyes and mouth. Anywhere off the beaten track, with or without trees, is generalized as Bush country.

I was driving into the fringe of the Great Divide. Also known as Bush country, this is a low, eroded mountain range dividing the coastal strip of soft, lush, easy-living land from the vast inland regions of desert, heat, and human endurance. The outback, sometimes called the Back of Beyond, describes the inland regions well. It was not unusual in some of the more harsh areas for a child to reach three or even five years of age without ever seeing rain. So hot and dry a person could dehydrate and die within hours, it was not a place for the unprepared. Among a surprisingly large range of animals, birds, and reptiles, this huge area was home to the big, flightless emu, large mobs of kangaroo, and where there was more scrub, the thickset wallaroo abounded, sturdy cousin to the kangaroo.

However, this was not my destination. I was heading for the cattle country just inland from the coastal strip. Dry, when compared with the coastal strip where I lived, it was, nevertheless, much greener and with a far higher rainfall than the immense outback. Greener, that is, under normal conditions. An exceptionally long drought held vast regions in a grip of cruel devastation, and as I drove along I was shocked at how badly the land was drying out. Further inland, cattle and sheep were dying in many thousands, their sun-dried carcasses a mute testimony to the unforgiving impact of a hostile environment—so hostile, even the kangaroos were dying. Lulled into a false sense of security by huge stock dams offering that most rare and precious of inland commodities—water, the tough kangaroos had multiplied into unprecedented numbers, all dependent on water for survival. Now the water had gone, evaporating in the scorching heat. Each water hole had become a crazy paving of dried-out mud, a cruel morass of suffering and misery for the desperate and dying animals that depended on it.

An intuitive and experienced farmer, Dad had sold off a lot of his cattle before the drought had truly settled in, keeping only the nucleus of his Braford breeding stock. He loved his cattle, and I knew this drought was hurting him. But that was also true of many other farmers. It was more than simply a drought that created the hardship; it was also the despair of watching a lifetime's devotion to breeding the best livestock possible slowly waste away, starving to death. And powerless to prevent it.

It took a little under four hours of fast, but steady driving to reach Fred's Retreat. My father, Fred Baker, was a reclusive man, and his property had long ago picked up the local name that reflected its owner. If it could be read, a termite-riddled and collapsed signpost near the entrance declared in bleached and faded letters this property to be "Glendale," but few people, if any, remembered or cared.

Following the dusty, winding track across a kilometer of their parched land, I was shocked at how fast the farm system was collapsing. I also felt bitter. Following a violent row over management practices, Dad had told me to get off his farm property, spelling the end to our short and turbulent partnership. Looking around me now, I saw all the environmental evidence that was proving me right in my more enlightened approach to the land, but I knew for certain that there was no way Fred Baker would ever concede that he could be wrong.

The last fifty meters was through Mum's garden. Strongly fenced, creating a tiny oasis free from cattle and sheep, even this was drought-ravaged, the normally bright green, somehow perky and defiant lawns, now brown, withered, and sad. All the water she could spare was saved for the rose bed, Mum's pride and joy. She had about six hundred massed hybrid tea roses, creating an unforgettable visual and fragrant effect in such an unlikely, and unexpected, setting. Bred for Queensland conditions, they were planted in color groups of a dozen. After studying many books on European rose gardens, Mum had designed her rose beds to create a sepia effect, ranging from yellows to ambers, from oranges to reds, and on into pinks and whites. The effect was stunning, never failing to elicit comment from her visiting friends. Despite our shared love of roses, Mum and I managed to disagree about them, for while I also liked multicolored floribunda roses, Mum emphatically declared them to be nothing but blatant impostors.

Driving past the roses slowly, I wound the window down, the air-conditioning turned off. The fragrance in the cool of late evening was a natural tonic. It never failed to amaze me that Dad actually encouraged and indulged Mum's passion for roses; it seemed so out of character for him.

I pulled up in front of the big timber home. Typical of the older style Queenslander, it was surrounded on all sides by wide verandahs, with a high, steeply pitched roof. This allowed for rooms with very high ceilings, thus hot air could rise and disperse. In the past this had not always been brilliantly successful, but in our times of efficient modern insulation combined with hot air displacement ventilators, it now proved to be an excellent system.

My mother was on her way out of the house to greet me before I even managed to get out of the car. A lean, gray-haired, friendly woman, she looked tired, and I knew that the unrelenting heat was taking its toll. A chatterbox, she was talking non-stop as soon as I had hugged and kissed her, giving me the latest news about life on the farm.

"Myrtle," a voice called from within the house, and I knew that Dad was as demanding as ever. "Have you put the kettle on?"

"Can't you manage that, Dad?" I shouted back.

"Now, now. Let it be, dear. You know what your father's like when he's tired. I'll put the kettle on."

"Don't I just," I muttered. "Don't I just."

Swallowing my anger, I followed Mum into the large airy kitchen. Although they spent the long dark evenings of winter in the living room, the kitchen was the overall center of the house—the place of decisions, the scene of most dramas, the hub of indoor activity . . . and arguments!

Dad was seated at the large, Tasmanian blackwood table, his elbows on the stained and mellow wood as he eyed me up and down.

"Do you want something, or is this a social visit?"

Looking at Mum helplessly, I shook my head in mock astonishment. "What a greeting!"

My voice going deep and thick as I attempted to control my anger, I turned to him, glaring fiercely. "I used to live here, remember? I'm your son. You're my father. Sons do call in and see their beloved parents from time to time without wanting or needing anything. Is that too much for you to understand?"

My outburst was not without result, but Dad simply went red and angry without saying a thing. I groaned. This meant the cold, silent treatment. At times like this, I was pleased that Mum was a chatterbox, for she filled in the awkward spaces with a torrent of words generally designed to heal, while Dad and I, for the most part, just sat and glowered at each other.

I tried not to react to Dad, I really did, but I had reacted before I could even begin to get it together. I was glad that Selph was not with me. I had the feeling that it would be me he would disapprove of, not Dad.

We had a cold salad dinner, with Mum's assorted homemade pickles, mango chutney, and various cold meats, all taken from the massive refrigerator that dominated the room. Harsh outdoors it may be, but in the house my parents enjoyed good food in copious amounts. Not that you would think so to look at them. Taller than my mother, Dad was also lean and rangy—a strong man capable of almost endless physical work. Grim and gray-eyed, he was a dour man who struggled to find humor in anything. Although he did not lack affection in his deep, innermost nature, it was so deeply buried that he might as well have been devoid of feelings. All in all, Dad was a clever, complicated man, highly respected in the local community, but with almost no close friends. He neither drank nor socialized; he was a loner, yet intuitively, I suspect that this was not from choice. He was a victim of himself and his circumstances, trapped, and isolated from other people. Mum was just about the opposite.

She was kind, friendly, and outgoing. She knew everyone in the whole district, and most of them knew her. When she smiled at you, her warm brown eyes made you feel special, and you knew she really cared. Cars filled with bright-eyed kids and smiling parents seemed to arrive endlessly at home, but always it was Mum they were visiting. Looking serious, Dad would hover uneasily on the fringe of activity, never involved, but more interested than he cared to admit.

How their relationship worked is a mystery, but I do know that they genuinely loved each other. Maybe that is all it took, for them. I used to think that love was enough for any married couple, but it was not so for Amber and me. I reckon Mum is supertolerant. To be fair, no matter how difficult Dad is, that is his way, rather than his intention. Trouble is, that does not help me when we are involved in a fracas. The only person outside the family who ever reached him, finding her way into his heart, was Amber. When Amber left me, Dad was mortified with anger and pain. I had learned then that he loved and accepted Amber as his other daughter. He ranted and raged at me, blaming me even more than I blamed him and her. I shuddered at the memory. God, what a mess that had been. However, it had become apparent that he had never forgiven me, for I had deprived him of one of the very few people whom he loved and felt close to, and most importantly for him, he could show it. Dad also got on well with my sister, Kate. At thirty-four, she was a couple of years older than me, and very tolerant by nature. I suspect that she inherited all the genetic tolerance that was available, for I seem to be a bit short in that department.

People say that Dad and I are alike, but I'm damned if I can see it. I reckon we are poles apart. Kate has the gift of people. Obviously inherited from Mum, along with the tolerance, Kate is an attractive, easygoing brunette, with an enormous circle of friends. Recently married to an immigrant doctor from Europe named Bruno Strickland, she lived in Brisbane, and to the great delight of Mum, and, I suspect, Dad, they were expecting their first baby in another seven months, or so. To be honest, I couldn't wait to be Uncle Adam!

The meal was unhurried, and I listened attentively to Mum's chatter about Kate and Bruno. I liked Bruno; Dad accepted him. Maybe like would come later. I tried to draw Dad into the conversation, hoping he would ignore our earlier clash, but he remained withdrawn, merely grunting with brief monosyllabic replies. I sighed. Nothing unusual about this.

The drought was the main topic of conversation, and finally Dad allowed himself to be drawn in. He told me about his neighbors, who, way back at the beginning of the drought, had laughed at him for selling a large number of his cattle, pouring scorn on his concern about the drought. "We ain't had a long 'un for over fifteen years, Fred. What makes you think this 'un will be so bad? It takes too long to breed good stock, an' we ain't selling. Hang in there, Fred, else you'll regret it."

I watched Dad as he told the story. "'Never underestimate the climate,' I told them. 'No matter what we do, or how good our livestock, we are only here at the mercy and whims of the climate. It can make or break us.'

"They laughed at me," he said softly. "They told me I was a sour old pessimist." He looked glum. "I think maybe I am, but I was right about the drought. I had a bad feeling about it right from the very beginning."

Now, nearly three years later, it was they who were sadly regretting it. Dad got no pleasure from this. It hurt him equally as he saw their cattle first lose condition, then gradually waste away to walking, stumbling skeletons. Because the drought was of such a long duration, hay stocks had become seriously depleted, along with the grain and other forms of supplementary feed. We all knew that when this drought finally ended, many farmers would be wiped out, financially ruined. All they would be able to do is sell their farms, their homes, their livelihood, and probably remain deeply in debt at the end of it all.

We were all quiet for a while, feeling pain and pity for the men and women of the land. Australian farming conditions were invariably feast or famine, but it never ceased to shock and hurt, and somewhere along the line, everybody suffered.

With all the care and sensitivity I could muster, I leaned over to Dad and placed one hand on his shoulder.

"Dad, will you please come with me to see Joe's place? The drought is hurting him also, but please, just come and see the difference."

For long moments Dad just sat there, and I thought that he might finally relent, but no. Shrugging off my hand, he got up from the table.

"Can't sit here all night. I've got another busy day tomorrow."

I sat back with a sigh. Oh well, what did I expect?

"Good night, Dad. See you in the morning."

Mum fixed her soft brown eyes on me. "So how are things with Joe and Joyce? I haven't seen them in ages."

For the next hour, I described their farming situation to my mother, being careful not to exaggerate. Joe and Joyce Steadman were my first clients when I began as an eco-farming consultant just over four years ago. They had liked the idea from the word go, generously allowing me to experiment on their land when I was uncertain, and implementing all the changes that I had recommended. Although they were over two hundred kilometers from Mum and Dad's place, it was very similar in land condition, with an almost identical annual rainfall. We had quickly developed a strong friendship, and although I had never considered myself as children oriented, I also enjoyed their four children. Mattie, at fifteen, was the oldest, a serious and responsible girl, followed by three boys: John at ten years, Jimmy at seven, and the youngest red-haired handful, Liam, at four.

Slowly, facing resistance from the very conservative farmers, I had built up a consultancy of clients. Most of them were younger and more open to change, but there were a number of older farmers, who, seeing their land's fertility in a steady decline, decided to give me a go.

From day one, I loved it. The principle of eco-farming was simple: enrich the soil and replenish its depleted humus. All fertility was based on using natural fertilizers. We used no chemicals, nor did we need them. Generally, it took three years for the ecosystem to adjust, but the results were, without exception, positive. If you have a healthy, vitally alive soil, then the plants that grow in it will be healthy, and the animals that graze those plants will also continue the legacy of health—nature's way.

Most of my clients were graziers, although I now had quite a few who were grain and crop growers. When I started with Joe and Joyce, we had redesigned their farm, turning all low-lying land into water catchment ponds. Previously, this land had all been drained, forcing it to shed its water. Where possible, we had linked the ponds with streams, so that the water could literally flow around the farm. Only last week I had spent a couple of days with these, my favorite clients, and Joe was ecstatic over the difference between his farm and those around him. As with so many innovators, Joe and Joyce had been ridiculed in the early days, but now they were putting more clients my way than I could cope with. Mum listened to my story without interruption, smiling proudly, and enjoying my obvious enthusiasm.

"Do you reckon Dad will ever embrace eco-farming?"

Mum pursed her lips, looking thoughtful. "I don't know dear, I just don't know. He's a stubborn man, but he isn't stupid. If you can ever get him over to Joe's place, who knows what might happen."

I grinned at her, then hugged her. "That would have to be the biggest 'if' in the world."

By mutual consent, we both headed for bed. I had a room in the house always ready for me, with my own clothes and personal toiletry, so it was not long before I was lying in bed, looking through the bedroom window at the stars in the clear night sky. My last coherent thought was 'wish it would rain,' and I was asleep.

I spent the next morning with Dad. He showed me over all the property, as we assessed the drought damage to his pastures. I carefully avoided any mention of Joe and Joyce's farm, or anything remotely connected to eco-farming. In fact, we both enjoyed ourselves, managing to go the whole morning without any arguing or quarrelling.

I left for the four-hour drive home about midafternoon. Mum waved me good-bye, while Dad solemnly hovered in the background as usual, unable to quite manage a wave.

As I drove along, I reflected somewhat sadly on how carefully we had all avoided any mention of Amber. My thoughts were random snatches at the past, all mixed and intermingled with memories of Amber, but I was wide awake and alert, only too aware of the danger of falling asleep at the driving wheel.

Reaching Donkey Creek, I drove very slowly over the old wooden bridge. It was at least ten meters above the steep, rock-lined creek, and, almost stopping, I peered down to see if there was any water left in the creek. Green, turgid, and stagnant, the last remnants formed a series of large puddles. I frowned in consternation. I had never before seen this creek get anywhere near dried out.

I was in no hurry. This was a remote and lonely road, and the traffic on the narrow bridge was controlled to one way at a time only. As I looked back at the road, ready to increase speed, I had one instant's shocked impression of a huge truck hovering right over the top of me . . . a terrible wrenching sensation . . . then oblivion.

# $\mathcal{T}hree$

It seemed that I had been walking for a long time, but I wasn't really getting anywhere. Around me, the tunnel was a pale silver, and although I had no idea how I got here, I knew that I had to reach the Light that always seemed to be some way ahead. Glancing back the way I had come, the tunnel stretched back endlessly into gloomy darkness. My whole focus was to reach the Light; that wonderful, white intensity that shone with such promise and hope.

I walked on, my pace brisk, until gradually the Light was so bright that the tunnel had become brilliant silver. The intensity of feeling I held for the Light was beyond anything of my experience. I could feel its energy pulsing all around me. I smiled, for I sensed a promise of such proportions within the Light that I couldn't wait to reach it. I was filled with, and consumed, by an intense longing to simply reach the Light.

Beginning to jog, my feet scarcely touched the ground, but as I ran with no discomfort or pain, I vaguely and disorientedly tried to comprehend the mystery of what was happening to me. Everything was unclear, lost and shrouded in uncertainty.

Faster I ran, and faster, but it made no difference to my approach to the Light. I did not seem to be getting there any quicker. Stopping suddenly, I began a very slow walk, and with no real surprise I realized that I was advancing on the Light at the same speed as when running. Baffled, I stopped, staring into the blazing Light ahead of me. I could feel questions within me, but they were too distant to grasp, too distant to be of any real importance. All that mattered was that I reach the Light.

Even the Light was mystery, for it now blazed brighter than a sun, yet I could look right into it with no discomfort or distress. Intense beyond measure, it had no glare.

And the closer I got, the stronger was the overwhelming intensity of love. Not just love, but an all-encompassing, uplifting, transcendent, LOVE. I knew, without knowing how I knew, that the Love and Light were one. Maybe the Light was an expressive, visible, outpouring of LOVE. Maybe it was all that and more, I don't know. I only knew that I wanted to run into that Light more than I had ever wanted anything in my life. Steadily, I continued.

I was close, very close, when suddenly Selph came walking out of the Light toward me. One moment nothing, next moment he stood before me, spilling out of the Light. I stopped and stared, gasping my surprise.

Still wearing his ghastly orange T-shirt and the long baggy green shorts, he looked me in the eyes. He grinned then, that engaging grin that always preceded his friendly banter.

"Hello, Adam."

Speechless, I shook my head in wonderment.

"Where are you going?"

Opening my mouth to reply, I hesitated, lost in surging uncertainty. "Er, I'm not sure. Into the Light, I think."

He just looked at me.

"Where am I, Selph? What is that Light? And how did you get here?"

He turned around, and putting an arm casually across my shoulder, we faced the Light together.

"Do you see that Door?"

I gasped. Now that he mentioned it, I could see a Door. It appeared that the Light was behind it, although clearly the Door could not hold back the Light. It seemed that the Light was almost consuming the Door, so bright and powerful it shone. "I never noticed the Door before," I said. "The Light is so bright that everything else is overwhelmed."

Selph nodded. "It surely is bright."

I frowned, trying to focus on what was happening.

"Where am I, Selph?"

"Adam, you stand at the threshold of a physical and nonphysical reality. You stand at the point between life and death, between the corporeal and incorporeal reality."

Insight blossomed. "My God! You mean I'm dead?"

He nodded toward the Door. "You are if you go through there. Or at least, it's what people call death."

"Do you mean to tell me that death is a step into the Light? Nothing in my religion ever indicated that."

"You have to experience death to know its truth. The very few enlightened ones discover this, but for most people, it's a personal, one-way ticket."

"Are you suggesting that by knowing death you can go through that Door and come back again at will?"

"Yes, but I do mean *knowing* its truth, not simply by experiencing death. You can do that and remain unaware."

"Well, that's where I'm going," I said determinedly. "I just know that it must be somewhere very special on the other side of that Door."

"You're right," he nodded. "It is."

"And that really is death?" I asked incredulously.

"Only your fear has ever implied that death is bad."

"Selph, what *is* going on? I feel more alive than I've felt in a long time, but where is this place? How did I get here? And where did you come from?"

The arm over my shoulders firmly turned me around, and I saw a small coffee lounge just off the silvery tunnel.

"That wasn't there a moment ago," I gasped.

Selph nodded thoughtfully. "No, it wasn't, but it's a good place to chat while I show you a few details that may interest you. Come on."

He led me over to a small wood table with a couple of comfortable padded chairs. Snapping his fingers softly, a smiling girl dressed in a smart, gray-and-white-checkered outfit was there to take our order.

"What will you have?" she asked me.

"Two cappuccinos, please," I replied automatically.

I turned to Selph, as the girl walked away. "How did this place get here?"

"I put it here."

The girl was back with two big mugs of frothy cappuccino before I could think of what to say. Selph picked up his mug, and took a long, deep drink. As he put the mug down, I noticed it was still full, frothy and steaming.

He grinned. *"That's* bottomless!"

I wasn't really thirsty at all, but when I tried my cappuccino it tasted incredibly full-bodied and rich.

"Wow! That's the best coffee ever."

"Yeah, a heavenly brew," Selph chuckled.

It was the weirdest thing, drinking a mug of coffee that continued to stay full, hot, and frothy.

Selph pointed to the wall of the coffeehouse. "There's the answer to some of your questions. Sit back, relax, and take it all in."

With a wave of his hand, the whitewashed wall had become a large movie screen, and we were watching the most personal and horrifying movie I had ever seen.

I watched *me* driving my green Nissan Pulsar across the high, narrow bridge at Donkey Creek. I saw myself peering through the lowered window, staring down at the last few pools of water in the creek. Despite the drought, it was something I always did, simply because I love creeks and rivers. I watched as a huge truck loaded with precious hay for the drought-stricken farmers came tearing onto the bridge from the opposite direction, completely ignoring the red light that warned him to keep off the bridge.

And I watched in shock and horror as I saw the truck, braking desperately, but far too late, ram into my Nissan. The car flipped up into the air, smashing through the side rails of the bridge as though through kindling, before somersaulting twice to land with a shattering crash on its side in the creek bed ten meters below.

The truck almost followed, jackknifing across the bridge and smashing out a further section of wooden side rails before coming to a shuddering halt, a quarter of the truck hanging over and off the bridge.

The movie scene changed, showing the inside of the car. Watching, I was abruptly weeping, for I saw myself crunched in a twisted heap behind the driving wheel. Blood trickled in a thick red stream from my mouth, and I could see that the steering column was buried in my chest cavity. My legs, arms, shoulders . . . everything, looked displaced and broken.

Weeping in shock and horror, I remembered now that last awful moment. "You're wrong, Selph. I must be dead. Nobody could survive that."

The sympathy and love I felt from Selph in that moment was tangible. He nodded at the wall.

Looking again, I watched the movie continue.

The truck driver staggered out of his cab, white and shaken. Taking one look down into the creek, he swore, then turned and ran. For a moment I felt a surge of anger, but as I watched, I realized what he was doing. The tiny township of Donkey Creek Bend was about five kilometers back along the dusty, unsealed road. To his credit, that man ran as though pursued by the devil, not stopping until he arrived in a lather of sweat and fear at the one and only service station.

Gasping out his story, it seemed that the whole township was suddenly galvanized into action. I realized, as I watched, that mine was not the first vehicle to go over the edge, and on a surge of insight, I knew that none had ever survived that long drop.

For me, the rest passed in a blur as they opened up the car with the "jaws of life" and took me out. I gasped anew at my mangled body. I was practically scalped by a jagged lump of broken window, and every limb seemed to be pointing in the wrong direction. I shuddered.

"How can I be there, and here?"

Selph pursed his lips as he carefully considered his words. "You—the essential you—is here, alive and aware. The physical you died briefly, but is now in a deep coma in a Brisbane hospital, and not expected to live. You have multiple fractures to both of your legs, both arms, and your pelvis. Your left hip is shattered, and both shoulders are broken. You have a ruptured spleen and liver, bruised kidneys, and a lot of internal damage. You have several very bad lacerations; you were nearly scalped, and one hand almost severed. One eye is cut, your nose is smashed, eight ribs are broken, your lungs have been punctured, and you lost a huge amount of blood." He looked grave. "Unfortunately, your spine suffered more damage. You have a few cracked vertebrae, with massive bruising to most of your body. The blessing is that your spine was not broken."

Unable to prevent it, I sat and cried for what seemed a long time. Finally, picking up my paper serviette on the table, I blew my nose and wiped my eyes. Yet even as I did this, I realized that it was habit. I was not congested from crying the way I would have been when physical. I held up my hands, staring hard at them.

"I look the same as always, although I feel lighter and far more energetic. How can I be alive . . . and dead?"

"I've told you clearly, you are not dead. If, or when, you die, you will continue just like this, for a while."

"Then what? And how did you get here?"

"Reality is not as fixed for me as it is for most people. I can walk between worlds, travel beyond linear time, and cause miracles to take place. I live and express a higher Truth. As for what happens if you die, that's irrelevant for the time being. Right now you are faced with having to make a decision."

"What decision?"

"About life and death. Are you going to make the struggle to physically live, or will you let go, surrendering your body to death. The end of Adam Frederick Sebastion Baker. This is a major decision in your life."

"What do you think I should do?"

"I think *you* must decide. After all, it's your life."

I picked up my full, steaming mug of frothy cappuccino and sipped thoughtfully. "Are all the cafes like this over here?"

Selph grinned at me. "This isn't 'over here.' Call it a way station between realities. When you make your decision, all this will change. This coffeehouse is my creative reality, especially tailored for you, but very soon you will have to continue creating your own reality."

"Is the pain in my physical body really bad?" I asked tentatively. I didn't really want to know.

Selph's eyes met mine. "Beyond anything you can yet imagine," he said seriously.

I felt a numbing dread. "Oh God! With both my legs broken and my body smashed, I could be crippled for life."

"It's your reality," Selph said softly, gently. "How you live with that body is determined by you."

"But if I'm crippled, I'm crippled," I protested. "I can't alter that, or change it, just by wanting to."

"Adam, why did I come into your life?"

Staring at him thoughtfully, I wondered what had happened to the fifteen-year-old. He appeared ageless, glowing with an inner light.

"You said that the timing was right for you to come."

"So why do you think I came just when I did?"

I gaped at him in fresh shock as his meaning became apparent. "You knew this was going to happen?" I gasped in protest. "But you couldn't. You would never let me suffer this if you knew about it beforehand. You would warn me . . ." I choked off the words as I saw the regret in his expression.

"Wouldn't you?" I said.

"It's your life, Adam, and your life is your creation. The essential you is an immortal Being of Light, all humanity is, while the physical world is a place where we learn the lessons of manifestation. You are into drama. If it doesn't hurt or shock, you disregard it, learning nothing. This time, in a typically dramatic fashion, you have set yourself up for a massive learning curve. In fact, you may have overdone it. It is not yet certain that your physical body can survive, no matter what you want."

With a sudden insight, I had another question. "Could you survive in that body?"

He nodded. "Yes. I could heal it."

"Well then, you can heal me," I said happily. "You can do for me what you did for that osprey. That will solve our problem, and I can get back to our lessons."

Selph shook his head sadly. "I can't do that. The . . ."

"What do you mean, can't?" I cut in. "Surely if you can work a miracle for a bird, you can do the same for me!"

Leaning his elbows on the table, his chin resting on the back of his hands, Selph stared at me gravely, his eyes so intense it seemed that I could see through his eye sockets into the endless blue of the sky.

"Okay, I'll rephrase it. I won't do that. The osprey was expressing nature in a defined statement of behavior, and I did not interfere with that process. You, on the other hand, are creating and expressing your own unique reality, and for me to simply heal you would be a direct violation of your creativity."

"Easily fixed," I shouted. "I give you my permission."

Regarding me with ageless patience, Selph continued. "It doesn't work that way. You want me to bail you out, and in some ways I would like to do just that. But if I did, I would dishonor you."

I shook my head in exasperation. "What about Jesus? He healed people without asking their permission. He raised the dead. Did that dishonor them?" I glared in triumph.

"You're wrong," Selph said softly. "Every person the Master healed, it was with their soul's consent. And even then, he didn't heal them; he made it possible for them to heal themselves. He raised no one from the dead, but with the soul's permission, he made it possible for a few people to again express their immortality through their physical body. He knew that death is an impostor."

"But I've given you permission," I insisted.

He smiled ruefully. "I hear two messages. I hear Adam, the identity, asking me to heal his physical body, and I hear the soul, who you are, telling me to stand back while you make your decision of whether to enter the Light, or return to the physical body of pain."

"Damn, you don't make it easy, do you?" I growled.

"On the contrary," Selph said quietly, and with a great depth of feeling. "It is *you* who doesn't make it easy. Adam, your lessons don't begin again when this episode is resolved; this is a continuity of your lessons. You are right in the thick of it, and whether you physically live or die, the lessons will continue."

Sipping on the unique coffee, I tried for a joke. "If I go back, can I have the formula for these bottomless coffee mugs? I could make a fortune."

It was a weak effort, and neither of us smiled. On impulse, I got up and walked out of the cafe. I wanted to check if that Light was still shining at the end of this strange tunnel I had been walking along.

Undiminished, the Light pulsed out stronger than ever, and as soon as I faced it again I felt irresistibly drawn to it. I glanced sideways at Selph. "I've decided. I'm going into that Light."

"Are you sure? Once you go into that light, Adam ends. Who you are will continue, but as far as any physical reality is concerned, it's finito for Adam."

Puzzled, I stared into his eyes. "But, who am I?"

"That's what I came to help you find out."

"If I go into the Light, will you still help me?"

"No. But there are others who will."

"And if I return to my body, you will help?"

"I will help you to help yourself."

Looking back at the Light, I swear it beckoned to me, so compelling was it. "I can feel the Light calling me. It feels as though I should go and join with it."

"That's because your physical body is going through another crisis. This time, as soon as your decision is truly and consciously made, your body will either die, or live, according to your choice."

"Are you saying that it's my choice to live or die?"

"No. The essential you never dies. I'm saying that every person chooses the moment they release their physical body. Your spiritual body continues."

I waved my arms. "And this is a spiritual body?"

Selph nodded. "It's a body-of-light. As you probably know, even your physical body is composed of light, but it has a density that takes on a physical manifestation. Your spiritual body is of a different dimension of light."

"I would have to be stupid to go back to a body filled with pain and suffering, when I can continue like this."

Selph nodded. "So, is this your decision?"

Frowning, I glanced back to the coffeehouse. "I really don't know. I'm strongly attracted by the Light, there is just so much Love, but if I join with it that means I'll be quitting my physical life, and that feels like failure. I never dreamed that anyone could be confronted with a decision like this. It would have been far easier if I had been killed outright. My choice would have been made."

"But, Adam, this is your reality. You created it this way. This is your drama, your choice. It's not a matter of choosing life or death; be clear about that. The essential you is ageless and deathless. This is a choice of timing and direction. Your potential has many probability patterns. One of them is staying with the body, and growing through the experience you have created. Another is to surrender the body and lose that potential, but to create new potential in another incarnation at another time."

"So reincarnation is a fact?"

"Only inasmuch as the essential you continues, taking on new identities and lessons on a physical plane. You do not die and are then reborn. Who you are was not born, and who you are can never die."

I sighed. "I don't know what to do. I just don't know. I don't like quitting my body, but I shudder at the thought of all that pain and suffering. What . . . ?"

I was spun around as though by a gust of wind, and drawn toward the Light. My feet scarcely on the ground, I was drawn ever closer. "Selph! What's happening?"

"Your physical body is failing, and an emergency operation will soon be taking place. It looks as though you have made your choice."

"No! Not yet. Don't rush me."

Selph took my arm, leading me away from the overpowering influence of the Light and back into the little coffeehouse.

"You will have to be quick, Adam, there's not much time left. Take this one last look at the physical you, and decide."

Sipping that delightful brew, I stared at the wall as it again became a movie screen. I was looking into a single room, where my heavily bandaged body lay inert, connected to numerous tubes in my mouth, nostrils, and arms. But it was not my body that I stared at in such shocked surprise—it was Amber.

Her auburn hair a mass of dark golden waves, her head was bent over my face as she whispered to me. "Adam, come back. Please, please don't die. I love you, Adam. I love you, my darling. I always have and I always will. Come back, Adam, and we'll work it out. Adam, darling Adam, I never asked for a divorce because I have never stopped loving you. Adam, please don't die."

In a low despairing monotone, her voice droned softly on, while I watched the screen in shocked amazement. "My God, I had no idea," I muttered.

"That doesn't surprise me," Selph replied. "You can be as thick as a plank where people are concerned. Amber has always loved you. To be honest, it's her love for you that is part of the equation that brought me into your life."

I stared at him, appalled. "What do you mean?"

"Forget it," Selph said briskly. "Choose now, or your choice is made."

A nurse had just entered the room, and glancing at the electronic gadget above my bed, was shouting for help. A sobbing Amber was rushed away, and an emergency was declared.

I stared at Amber longingly, shaken by her grief. What wouldn't I give for another chance to be with her. She was my life.

"I'll go back," I said impulsively. "I choose to continue in my physical reality."

# Four

How much time passed I will never know, but there came a moment, when, like a hammering steamroller, a wave of terrible pain crashed into me, and I groaned aloud. For a few, brief, terrifying moments, I hung on to consciousness, while the unbelievable pain gripped every part of my body.

Jumping to her feet, Amber raced out of the room.

"He's awake. He's awake," she shouted excitedly. "He's going to live, I just know it."

As her words faded away, I felt everything slipping, and happily, I dived into oblivion.

When I next felt the return of physical consciousness, I tried to open my eyes. This proved to be difficult, as I became aware that my head and left eye were swaddled in bandages. My right eye, however, fluttered open, and I stared around me, unable to move. Everything was blurred for a few minutes, but as my focus gradually returned, and I could see, I was almost startled to be gazing into the tear-rimmed eyes of my mother. She looked older, more haggard than usual, and was staring at me with a breathless, slightly stunned look on her face.

"Adam? Adam?" Her voice was subdued, and filled with questioning. "Can you hear me? Can you see me? Oh God, Adam, please speak to me."

I tried to force some words into my mouth, but I could not. As I took a breath to speak, a blast of pain hit me in the chest like a thousand splinters of glass, and I softly moaned as the shock forced my breath away.

I heard her calling my name once more, before it all slipped away. I welcomed oblivion. It was deep, peaceful, and without pain. If time happened, I was unaware of it. I became semiconscious, was blasted by pain, and slipped away. I had an inner awareness that I still walked the line between life and death, but I also knew that I had made my choice, and that I would live. There were moments when I longed for the Light to consume me, but it had gone. I was overwhelmed by stark physicality: its pain, suffering, and loss.

There were moments when I had a vague awareness that I was being prepared for an operation, but if or when I was anesthetized eluded me. I so easily slipped in and out of consciousness that I had no idea whether it was induced or not.

Once, when I was struggling toward consciousness, I was sure that my good eye opened, and I could see the room that I was lying in. Then it got confusing, because there appeared to be what I can only describe as a glowing form of very pale golden light close by my bed. In volume it was maybe two or three times the size of a human, and I had the strangest feeling that I could claim it. For long moments I struggled to understand what it was, then it slowly faded away as I lost consciousness.

With my increasing activity, my left eye slowly but surely turned to molten fire, and in the delirium of pain I wondered if it would burn its way clear through my skull. I think I lost it for a while, as the pain in my chest and eye mixed and merged with the pain of my limbs, and I seemed to be floating in some other place. Compared with this unremitting agony, what I had previously called pain in my lower back had been no more than a mere twinge, a slight aggravation.

With no idea of how long a period of time was passing, I floated horrifyingly in and blessedly out of consciousness. I only knew that staying alive required that I continue to focus on living. Often I could not understand why I needed to live, and in those moments I could feel everything slipping away. Invariably, I would then recall seeing Amber, and would remember why I wanted to live. While I was lucid, I practiced visualizing her face, the way I had seen her as she cried for me next to my bed.

For a long time it seemed that I drifted in and out of consciousness. Once again in a moment of lucidity I saw the glowing golden presence near my bed, and again it seemed that I should claim it, or that I should recognize it, but as before, it all slipped away as I struggled to grasp what it meant.

During all this time, the pain in my left eye was very gradually, but very definitely receding. For me, just to lose one source of pain was a major benefit.

One day, disjointed and distant, I could hear voices.

"I can't take . . . more. He has been . . . coma for nearly . . . month. Poor Dad . . . frantic."

I pondered on the words. Someone was in a coma, someone who knew Dad. I wondered who it could be. I hoped they were not hurt. Hurt! I hurt. Oh! God!

It's me. A month. God! Dad, worried about me! Frantic? About me? Gosh! He does care after all. How was I to know? For the first time it occurred to me just how much of a facade he presented, hiding himself and his true feelings.

Awareness came fast and smoothly, as though I rode a roller coaster down a steep slope covered in a dense, thick fog, and out into bright sunlight.

"He's focusing."

With those words, the sun went out, and with instant clarity I realized that someone had been shining a torch into my right eye.

"Of course I am," I muttered around the tubes and pipes in my mouth.

"ADAM! Oh God, Adam."

The shout that greeted my words set my head ringing, causing a rush of nausea. I squeezed my eye shut, tight.

"Keep your voice down, Mrs. Baker, please. He heard you. I got the impression it hurt. Very few people survive injuries like his, and quietness is absolutely essential."

Very astute doctor, this one. Despite the pain, I knew that I was in capable hands.

His voice, hardly more than a whisper, came to me clearly, and I knew his lips were close to my ear.

"Relax, Adam, and listen. You have been in a deep coma. I know that you have felt very bad pain, but if you had been sedated or drugged in any way, you would have died. Are you in much pain now? Wink your right eye, if you are."

An enormous sense of relief swept over me. I had so much pain I hardly knew how to survive, now it would all be ended. A quick prick of the needle, and pain-free peace.

And then, on the heels of that relief, came a clear and intense knowing. This is where it all began. Selph had told me that we each create our own reality. He had told me that I was right in it—now, not when the pain and suffering had ended. I could have a drug-induced reality of no pain, or maybe I could find my own way through and beyond the pain. Maybe I could create my reality myself, a reality without this agony of pain and suffering.

Even as I thought about it, I knew clearly that this is where it begins. I knew that Selph would help me, but I also had to help myself. It did not begin when I was up and about, it began the moment I chose to live. I was no more crippled now than I had been before the truck hit me; it was just much more physically apparent.

"Adam, can you hear me? Wink if you are in pain."

I kept my right eye tight shut as a fresh wave of pain flashed through my left eye, while chomping and chewing like a pit-bull terrier into the cavity of my chest.

"I'm really not sure what is happening, Mrs. Baker. I'm certain that he is conscious, but he has not responded to my suggestion. I cannot believe that he is not in serious pain, but I am highly reluctant to use any drugs on this man."

"You must do what you think is best, Doctor."

"Thank you, Mrs. Baker. When you chose me as you son's specialist, you did so knowing that I am unconventional in my approach. You were influenced by your son's abhorrence of both orthodox agriculture and medicine. He is probably now paying the price in pain, but this is not necessarily a bad thing. Come, we must let Adam sleep. In view of this new development, we have things to discuss."

I felt them depart, rather than heard them, but I had the satisfaction of knowing that I was in good hands. Squeezing my eyes against the agony of my body, I wondered what I had let myself in for.

❖   ❖   ❖

I was asleep, dreaming, of that I was certain. Although I was aware of pain, it was a distant murmur, lost in the beauty and tranquillity of the river. With startling clarity, I could hear the trilling songs of birds, while a nearby tree was smothered in fragrant pink blooms. I knew I was asleep, because none of this conformed to any normal reality. It was more real, more powerful, overloading my senses with an overexpressive abundance I had never experienced before. To be honest, it was almost a Disney dream, overemphasized to the point that it was slightly comical.

The river, for instance, was clear and sparkling as though ignited by light, while the tree disappeared beneath a vast overflowing wealth of pink flowers just too real to be realistic! And the bird-song, definitely Disney! Without doubt, this was a dream, and I liked it.

In my dream, I was walking along the riverbank, watching the swirl of rising fish in the deep, calm pools, listening to the chuckling water as it raced across the shallows, and as I strolled along, I was basking in warm, mellow sunshine. Euphoric stuff, the substance of the very best dreams. Even so, I was somewhat surprised when I saw in front of me what appeared as a huge bubble, completely spanning the river.

Approaching it, I stopped. Tentatively, I reached out to touch the delicate bubble, expecting it to burst. As my fingers slid over its resilient surface, I could feel its enduring and flexible strength, while its surface was a beautiful swirling reflection of the colors of a rainbow.

Placing the flat of my hand on the bubble, I pushed hard, testing its strength, but to my surprise my hand slid smoothly through it, rapidly followed by the rest of my body as, caught off balance, I staggered forward.

I was now inside the bubble.

Grinning, I recalled how monkeys are often led to trap themselves, employing the prompting of their curiosity. How different was this? If it were a trap, I had just walked in. But I did not feel trapped. I felt more alive and empowered than ever before. Following an impulse, I walked toward the middle of the bubble, which took me out to the center of the river. Most curious, the bubble was indeed a wondrous sphere, for I remained on a level surface as I walked on transparent, multicolored light across to the middle of the river.

Definitely the stuff of dreams. I stood inside a bubble at the very center of the river. I could see fish flashing silver under my feet, the water only the skin of a bubble beneath me. Staring in wonder, I stood spellbound. This was the finest and most lucid dream I had ever experienced.

"I'm glad you like it."

How Selph managed to get into my dream, I have no idea, but he was not only in the dream, he was in the bubble.

"My gosh! How did you get here?"

Ignoring my question, he indicated the river and the huge bubble."Pretty good, huh?"

A suspicion crept into my mind. "Er, is this your dream, or mine?"

Sitting down, cross-legged, Selph indicated for me to do likewise. Physically sitting cross-legged hurts my knee joints, so I hesitated. Then, knowing that this was a dream, I tried it. Wow! It was both easy and comfortable.

"This is not so much a dream, as a shared reality," Selph began. "Physically you are asleep, dreaming, but you are fully conscious and aware on a nonphysical level. I intend to teach you how to get into this reality while physically awake. At . . ."

"But why?" I cut in.

He scowled at me. "Don't butt in. Physically, you are in considerable trouble, and I'm aware that your doctor has not drugged you to relieve the pain. This is not chance; it's a reality of your own making."

"I know. I made that choice while I was conscious."

"Adam, you still don't get it. Your reality designed it so your mother would choose a doctor who would not drug you even before you were aware you could make that choice."

"Are you saying that I'm creating my reality even while I'm not aware that I'm creating my reality?"

"You got it. Every living, breathing, moment of your life you are creating your own reality. Each person is doing this all the time, and generally totally unaware of the creative process they are involved in."

"So I created the accident . . . and the agony?"

Selph nodded emphatically. "Absolutely right. But when you view life in those terms, there are no accidents. There is only purpose. Your purpose is obvious . . . drama. Drama catches your attention. A purposeful accident with horrific injuries and all its agony is powerful drama."

"If I were to believe this, I would also have to accept that I must be mad."

"No Adam, not mad, just conditioned. Over eons humanity has become so conditioned to pain and suffering that it has become a serious and malignant addiction."

"I hope that isn't true."

"I'm sorry to assure you that it is. Do you know what happens when you have a so-called accident? You look for a person or cause to blame. By blaming either a situation or another person, you are able to abdicate from any personal responsibility. This both prolongs the suffering and further concretizes the conditioning. And so it continues."

"Is there any way out of all this?"

"Of course. If you were to always assume responsibility for any so-called accident you are involved in and, without judgment, study your *thoughts* and the *events* leading up to it, you would invariably find the cause within yourself. You could then begin to correct the self-destructive thoughts and behavior patterns that continually lead to your downfall."

"But in my case the truck rammed into me. I'm not responsible for what the truck driver did. He's at fault. The blame is his. How can I create his reality?"

"Adam, nobody can do anything to you without your inner permission. This permission is always on a soul level, where the lessons for all people involved match up, each in their own way. You are not consciously or intellectually aware of this hidden agreement, but it is there, always."

"Even in a war?"

"Particularly in a war."

"I don't get it. How can you have hidden agreements with so many different people?"

"By knowing that there is no one outside of who you are. Who you are contains All That Is."

"I don't get it."

"I know you don't. That's why I'm in your life right now. When you do get it, you will be Awake to who you are."

"But why isn't this common knowledge? If you're right, why don't we approach life and accidents in a different way, so we can get out of this repetitive cycle?"

"Because it's far easier to blame."

"Yeah, and we don't always blame the other person," I said glumly. "We also blame ourselves."

"Which is every bit as destructive as blaming someone else. Judgment and blame were not born from intelligence."

He smiled at me brightly. "So are you ready to accept responsibility for the predicament you are now in?"

I nodded, filled with a deep certainty. But I did have one niggling question.

"How do I know that what you are telling me is true?"

He looked at me thoughtfully. "There are several ways, or none at all, depending on you. Search your heart instead of your mind. If your heart resonates to what I have told you, then you should recognize its truth. If it doesn't then either you are not ready for this truth, or you are divorced from your own deeper feelings.

"Another way involves trust. Do you trust me, or don't you? If you don't trust me, you will find that you don't really trust yourself either, and you probably never have. Equally, you can choose not to believe anything I say."

I felt happy with his reply, because it gave me room not to believe him. But I did. It all made so much sense.

"I don't really have a problem with it. I accepted you when you left me on the beach, and my heart *knows* that you are speaking the truth. Of that, I am very certain."

Selph grinned boyishly, then pointed down into the river. Together, sitting cross-legged in a sheer gossamer bubble, we watched a large leopard eel as thick as my arm, as it slid with sinuous ease along the riverbed. Blossom-covered trees lined one side of the waterway, while a profusion of flowering plants grew abundantly on the other side. Sitting suspended over the river induced a strange and haunting sensation, yet in my dream state I was comfortable with it. The clarity of everything around me was sparkling clear, pristine pure.

"This dream seems more real than my everyday reality."

Selph nodded slowly, as though thinking. Even in my dream, he was wearing the dreadful orange T-shirt and the green shorts, but he no longer looked quite as young. Maybe twentyish now, and with a disconcertingly powerful aura of authority.

"Look at me," he said.

As I made eye contact, his power seemed to increase.

"As I said earlier, I've drawn you into this reality so that I can teach you how to reach it for yourself. Here, you can go beyond your pain. Pain is a learned reaction. Reaction has two major expressions: one is a reflex triggered in the moment, the other is a program reenacted from the past. Reflexes are designed to get you out of trouble, but a conditioned reaction will invariably get you into trouble. Pain is a good example; pain is a reaction, love is a response. And I mean love in the context of Love, not lust or sexuality. You can learn to respond in the moment, moving into a place where pain is not a reality. This . . ."

"How do I learn to do that?"

"By keeping your mouth shut and ears open."

"Okay, okay."

"The key to response therefore is . . . what?"

"Er . . . um . . . love?"

"Yes, Adam, LOVE. Loving yourself."

"I'm not very good at that."

"Tell me about it!"

"Okay, I'm sorry I keep butting in."

Smiling good-naturedly, Selph nodded. "Yeah, I know. You probably have a dedication to teaching your teacher all about patience. However, let's get on with it. Understand that this 'dream' as you insist on calling it, is under my control. There are no distractions, thus your concentration will be enhanced. Any last questions?"

"What do you mean . . . last? Am I going to die now, or something?"

Selph sighed heavily. "No, Adam, you are not about to die. I meant can we continue without any more interruptions, like another question."

"Oh. Er . . . no questions."

"Okay. Close your eyes, and relax."

I did so, feeling very relaxed.

"Visualize and imagine a rainbow in front of you. Each color is very clear and defined. Now, stepping into that rainbow, enter the color red. See, feel, and experience red. Feel red flowing through you."

My eyes closed, I had no trouble at all.

"Now step into the color orange, and feel orange flowing through you, merging with you."

A minute pause.

"Next, step into yellow, merging with yellow."

Pause.

"Step into green, experiencing green."

Pause.

"Now blue." Pause. "Purple." Pause. "Violet."

Pause.

"Walk out of the rainbow, and you will see a flight of twenty-one steps. Go down the steps slowly, beginning at twenty-one and counting down to one. As you walk away from the steps, you will find that you are on the bank of this river. Walk along it for a way, noticing the trees, the river, and the birds. Feel the peace. Before you is a large, transparent bubble completely spanning the river. Walk into it, then proceed to the center. Now, sit down cross-legged, and relax."

Pause.

"This is a special place of healing and peace. As you proceed through the steps that will lead you here, you will leave all problems, anxieties, and pain behind. When you are ready, a healing angel will come to you, and by its very presence your healing will accelerate. In this bubble over the river, you simply relax, holding your focus on the river as it flows beneath you. While in this bubble, you may watch the river with your eyes open or closed, whichever feels the most appropriate for you.

"When, after twenty to thirty minutes, you are ready, you will return to the steps, going up them counting from one to twenty-one, and then back through the rainbow in reverse order of colors. When you leave the rainbow you go back into your normal life, while maintaining the calm and peaceful centering that you have achieved. For as long as you can, try to stay in the calmness of your heart, rather than jump straight into the chatter in your head."

Although I had listened to everything, I kept my focus in the bubble. However, I did open my eyes so that I could gaze into the river, and for me, this was a very powerful experience. I found that I could not fix my gaze on the water, for it was flowing briskly under the gossamer sphere, and for a while it confused me. However, as I slowly let go of a need to fix my eyes onto something, I found that in some odd way I was seeing the whole river, rather than only a fixed part.

It seemed that for a timeless while I was suspended within and somehow beyond the river, when gradually, I became aware of Selph and my situation. With a gentle sigh, I looked up at him. "That was wonderful."

"I want you to do this when you are fully conscious in your hospital bed. When the pain is too severe, leave it behind. Respond to the moment by creating a reality of peace and healing. It is far more appropriate, and very possible."

I was silent for a while, listening to the protests that were beginning to stir in my mind. "But the pain is really bad. It grabs my attention, filling the moment with agony. How do I get past this?"

"It certainly isn't easy," Selph said sympathetically, "but it is possible. When you resist pain, you are focusing on it, and the more you focus on it, the more susceptible you are to it. It's a vicious cycle. Pain killers can break the cycle, but they leave you dependent on them."

"Is that wrong?"

"Of course not. It's about choice. Remember what we talked about earlier; you create your own reality. If you continually, or habitually, create a reality of pain, there is a reason and a purpose behind this. By going beyond the pain, you learn about its cause; this allows you to go beyond the pattern of creating it. Let's face it, personal growth sponsored basically by pain and suffering is not exactly the pinnacle of intelligence, is it?"

"No, but that's the way I'm doing it," I said glumly.

"Sure, but there's no reason why you can't turn this purposeful accident into a steep growing curve, and benefit from the experience. On a soul level, that's why you created it. This is your dramatic method of inner growth."

"Gosh! If I only learn how not to repeat it, that will be something in itself. So, what happens now?"

"This is where I leave you for a while."

"Will you come and visit me in the hospital?"

"Of course I will."

"Can I call you if, or when, I need you?"

"Trust me, Adam. I'll be there."

As abruptly as he had appeared, he vanished from the bubble. I missed him immediately. Questions rose in my mind like a flock of squawking, noisy galahs, and for long moments their persistent shrieking almost overwhelmed me.

Closing my eyes, I dived into the peace and profound quiet that had been with me so few minutes ago . . . and I found it. Letting my eyes open, I gazed unseeing into the river, holding on to no defined focus. And again, I floated in some mysterious dimension of peace.

# Five

"Aaaaddaaaaammm. Adam. Aaaddaammm."

The voice was low and musical, with the soft lilting quality that I knew belonged to Amber. I always said that I would know her voice anywhere, and it was true.

Silly as it sounds, I met Amber's voice even before I met her. I was in a restaurant with a girl, Jenny, on a casual date. We were fairly good friends, but this date was not going at all well. She was going on and on about some girlfriend of hers who had gone to a hair salon and had her hair dyed the wrong color. She had asked for strawberry blonde, whatever that is, and, in some mix-up that escaped me, had come out as a redhead.

Jenny had gone into incredible detail over the whole ridiculous affair, and I had drifted away, completely losing all the finer points. Bored, my attention drifted in a dull reverie around the restaurant, as I assessed the merits of the pictures painted by local artists. Hanging on the walls of various restaurants, it was a good way for the artists to make a few initial sales, always hoping that one day they may be recognized as a major talent.

That is when I heard the voice.

Soft, but not faint, the voice caught and held my attention, drawing me easily to its source. More than anything, the musical quality attracted me, each word turning up and then down as though everything were poetry, and needing to be expressed in a like manner. Unfortunately, the woman who owned the voice sat directly behind me, so it was almost impossible to see her without doing an about-face in my chair.

Unashamedly, I sat listening to her conversation. By putting the pieces together, I learned that she was the artist responsible for three of the paintings on the walls, and that she was hopeful of a sale very shortly by one of the restaurant's patrons. I tried deliberately dropping my knife so that I could twist round and see her, but the seats that we sat in conspired to defeat me. This was a choice restaurant, with the plush bench seating very high-backed, thus creating an intimate and private atmosphere. I could just see the top of her head, and it caused me to smile, for although not a real redhead, it was a delightful auburn.

"It's not funny, Adam. Gail is really aggravated. She said that the salon swears that the color is strawberry blonde, but she's convinced it's way-out red."

Sighing wearily, I tried to make conversation. "I couldn't care less what Gail thinks. I mean, what's the problem? It'll either grow out or wash out. So what?"

"Oh! And what's got into you? You haven't been listening to a word I've said. All you care about is yourself and your stupid eco-farming!"

That did it. From that point it was downhill all the way—and fast. Jenny and I parted in a mutual huff, and I have never seen her since. She phoned about a week later, full of apologies for what she had said. I told her she had nothing to apologize for, and that she was probably right, but that was me. She fished for another date, but although I liked her, it ended there.

The next day I was back in the restaurant, looking at the paintings. Carefully, I went through them all, looking for the same name to appear on three of them. One name was on five paintings, several on a couple, and two names on three of them, both female: Sandra Hoskings and Amber Collins. The paintings by Hoskings were excellent still life, while the paintings by Collins were Australian wildlife. Although I was no art connoisseur, I felt that Collins's work lacked the technical brilliance of Hoskings's, but when it came to conveying pure feeling, then Collins excelled.

Following a hunch, I decided that Amber Collins was the artist I wanted to meet. I had nothing to validate that, only my intuition, but as an eco-farming consultant, I had followed my intuition many times, and it had never failed me.

I told the restaurant owner that I was interested in purchasing the painting of a sugar glider, but first, I wanted to meet the artist. Full of enthusiasm, the owner made the arrangements for me to meet Amber.

When, two days later, I went along to the restaurant, I was feeling nervous. It had been arranged that Amber Collins would have lunch with me while we discussed her paintings. A few minutes late, I was surprised that she was at the table, waiting.

Ah, great! She had auburn hair. I had guessed right.

Sitting down, I introduced myself, as nervous as a kid on his first date. Amber was a knockout! I knew she must be married, or have a steady boyfriend, or a dozen of them; no way could she be available. Along with her auburn hair, she had the classic fair skin and wonderful green eyes. I just wanted to swoon in her delightful beauty.

"I hear that you're interested in one of my paintings," she said gravely, after our introductions.

"Er . . . oh, yes please."

She looked amused. "Which one?"

God, she was lovely. "Oh, whichever you like."

"But it's which you like, Mr. Baker."

"Mr. Baker! Please, call me Adam."

"By all means, Adam."

"Er . . . is it Miss or Mrs. Collins?"

She looked demure. "Miss, but call me Amber."

"Oh, I will, I will."

"So, which one caught your attention?"

Beautiful, just so beautiful. "Er, your voice."

Amber looked bewildered, making her even more lovely.

"I beg your pardon, Adam. But are we talking about the same things?"

"Oh! Er . . . the sugar glider."

"What did you mean, my voice?"

Never any good at deceit, I decided to tell her the whole story, starting from the casual date with Jenny and hearing Amber's fascinating voice, to tracking down her name and arranging this luncheon date. But I did genuinely want to buy the sugar glider painting, because the feeling in her work was so strong it reached out and grabbed me. And just incidentally, I felt just the same way about her.

She listened wide-eyed to my tale, her face without any guile as she openly displayed her obvious pleasure.

"Please, how old are you? Do you have a steady boyfriend?" I finished. I held my breath.

She put her head back, chuckling, her hair bouncing in auburn waves. "I'm twenty-four, and I haven't had a boyfriend for the past six months. I did have a steady, and we lived together for a short while, but it just didn't work out. He was a nice-enough guy, but very mixed up. I haven't had time for men in my life just lately. I really want to get serious about my painting."

She was three years younger than me, and available. "If you can find room in your life for me, I'll help you to be as serious about your painting as you wish. Whatever you want, I want it for you." My heart hammered in eager anticipation.

She looked at me in amusement. "You don't beat around the bush, do you?" Her expression became thoughtful, her eyes serious as she studied me. "Okay, I'm open to a date with you, and we will see where it leads us. Is that all right with you?"

"Is that all right? I'll say it's all right! I'll make sure that you never regret it."

But she did. We had married three months later, and I failed her. Without a doubt, she regretted marrying me. She had left me after three years. And that was now a lonely, aching, two years ago.

Sighing at my memories, once again I heard her soft, pleading voice.

"Adam. Aaaadaaaammm. Please, wake up, Adam."

Opening my good eye, I stared at her hungrily. God! How I had missed her. "Did you mean what you said?" I whispered shakily.

Looking bewildered, Amber bought her face closer to mine. "I don't understand. What did I say?"

As clearly as though etched in marble, each word had remained stamped in my mind. "You said, I love you, Adam. Please come back and we'll work it out. You said that you had never stopped loving me." I stopped for a long shaky breath. God, I hurt. "That's why I came back."

Tears trickled unheeded down Amber's cheeks, and I watched them in fascination. I could not quite meet her eyes, afraid I might see nothing more than pity in them, or the lie of her earlier emotional words.

Taking a deep breath, she squared her jaw in the familiar way I loved so much. "Adam, look at me."

Too afraid of what I might see in her expressive eyes, I watched her face, noticing the graceful curves of her strong, but delicate, profile as she glanced momentarily away.

"Adam, please look at me."

My one good eye finally made eye contact.

"Every word that I said, I mean. Adam, I didn't leave you because I didn't love you; I left you because you were impossible to live with. I really want us to try again."

I swallowed, caught between pain and joy. "I said when we met that you wouldn't regret dating me, but I'm sure you did." I closed my eye to shut out

Amber's protest. "Please, hear me out." Looking at her with all the love I felt, I continued. "If you take me back into your life, I give you my most solemn promise that you will never again regret it."

My own emotions were choking me, and I coughed, catching my breath. The blast of pain that blazed through my chest caught me totally by surprise, and as I fought to get my breath through the agony, I slid back into darkness.

❖   ❖   ❖

My eyes opened, and I gently gasped. Both eyes were open, and I could see through my left eye. It felt sticky, and my vision was blurred, but I could see. Sitting in front of me on a stainless-steel chair was one of the biggest men I have ever seen. He was huge.

Closing my eyes hurriedly, I figured that I must be hallucinating. Carefully opening my eyes once more, I peeped out. The giant grinned at me. Wearing a white coat that struggled to meet around his ample waist, an unruly mop of black hair crowned a craggy face that peered from a dense beard. His eyes were dark brown, and very friendly.

"Hi! My name's Pete Morrow. I'm the doctor who has been trying to keep you alive. It's a battle finished. Certainly we have a long way to go, but we're gonna make it."

Despite my pain, I couldn't help but smile. His voice was that of a child, so soft and quiet that it sounded incongruous coming from him. I knew that I liked him.

I nodded slightly. "Yeah, I know, but I can't say that I'm pleased to meet you, like this."

"Can you see out of your left eye?"

"Yes, although it's a bit blurry."

He looked pleased and relieved. "Wonderful." Then he frowned. "Does the eye hurt?"

"It was a ball of fire earlier, but it's okay now."

He nodded. "And the rest of you? The pain's bad?"

"You could say that."

"I get the impression that you are deliberately avoiding painkillers. Why? I can give you pain relief without using heavy drugs."

There was no way that I could explain the whole process to him, but as I searched for a satisfactory answer, I decided to keep it as close to the truth as possible.

"I want to find my own way past the pain."

"Okay, but why?"

Staring at him helplessly, I could think of nothing to add. "It's important to me," I said lamely.

He looked baffled. "Okay. I don't understand, but I'll accept it so long as the pain doesn't continue to be a handicap. Crazy as it sounds, there was a time when the pain was a positive factor, keeping you alive, but as we progress, it has become more negative, sapping your energy. If this continues, you and I will have further words about it, and I'll take a lot of convincing."

"How long have I been here, doctor?"

"The name's Pete. Nearly six weeks."

Six weeks! My God! "Where am I, er, Pete?"

He grinned. "Here is the Whitehills Private Hospital, in the outer Whitehills suburb of Brisbane. And I am the radical, rather alternative doctor that your mother chose to attend you." His teeth were very white as they sparkled through his black beard. "I reckon she has told me more about you than you know of yourself."

I shrugged, then winced in pain. "That's my mother. Please, what's the score?"

Pursing his lips, he gazed down at me. "I hardly know where to start. Quite frankly, just being alive is a bloody miracle. You should have seen yourself when the ambulance brought you in."

"I did." Too late, my unintentional words were out before I could stop them. Perhaps he would ignore them.

Staring at me, he opened his mouth to protest, then closed it. After a few seconds, he nodded. "You know, I reckon you just may have. That's something I'd like to talk to you about, one day."

He was quiet, lost in thought for several minutes.

"So tell me," I pursued.

"To be honest, it's both good and not so good. Your internal organs are coming along fine. In fact, exceptional is not too strong a word, and I expected the most trouble from them. You've had three operations to repair the damage, which, amazingly to us, was far less than expected. The bruising was massive, but you haven't lost any organs or had anything removed." He hesitated, frowning.

"But?"

"But your pain levels are what bother me. Even when you are unconscious, I can monitor the pain to a fair degree by watching the pupils of your eyes. Or right eye, for most of the time. Your left eye is definitely miracle material. Quite amazing." As his enthusiasm rapidly grew, so his voice became deeper. "In fact, it was so mutilated that for a while I seriously considered having it removed. But not only has it healed, it has actually regenerated. Now, having the confirmation that you can see through it, I'm delighted. It really is quite extraordinary."

"Tell me about the not so good."

He hesitated, obviously not sure of what to tell me.

"Well, maybe it's early days to go into all of that; besides, there's quite a list of injuries."

I felt annoyed. This was my body and I had a right to know. "Pete, if you're going to continue as my doctor, you and I had better come to an understanding. When I say I want to know, that's exactly what I mean."

Deciding to shake him up a bit, I thought back to the list of injuries that Selph had reeled off to me. "When I came in here I had multiple fractures of both legs and arms. My pelvis was broken, both shoulders were broken and my left hip was shattered. Eight of my ribs were broken, and my lungs pierced. I had a ruptured spleen and liver, bruised kidneys, and other internal damage. My left eye was laid open, I was nearly scalped, and my left hand was almost severed. Now, nearly six weeks later, it's quite reasonable that I want a progress report."

I did not get it. Maybe I had put too much energy into my words, but a fire started up in and around my lungs, and as I began coughing, fighting to breathe, once again I slid easily down the slippery dip into the darkness of oblivion.

❖   ❖   ❖

When I opened my eyes again, Pete sat in the chair facing me as though only a few seconds had passed.

"You're a very puzzling man," he said mildly.

"Oh, how come?"

"Basically, only your mother and your . . . er, wife have spent much time here with you. After you ended our last conversation rather abruptly, I made a complete fool of myself by phoning both of them and berating them for telling you the full extent of your injuries—information that I considered was not in your best interest at this time." He grinned sheepishly. "I may be big, but those two ladies reduced me to little-boy status in no uncertain terms. So, Adam, how the hell do you know all about your injuries?"

"Er . . . I guessed."

"Yeah, and I believe in fairy stories."

"That's nice, I'm very happy for you. How long is it since I, er, fell asleep?"

"In fact, you did sleep. Deep and peaceful for about half a day. So, pray tell."

"A deal. You give me a proper progress report, and I'll tell you all I know."

Pete sighed melodramatically. "God! How is it that I get lumbered with patients like you? Okay, you have had a hip replacement, and that seems fine, although it needs more exercise. All the various fractures are mending, but very slowly. I'm fairly certain that they are the cause of most of your pain. As I said earlier, instead of losing your eye, it has done the impossible. Your punctured lungs are still giving you a lot of trouble, but . . ."

"Tell me about it," I muttered.

"But your spleen, liver, and kidneys have healed very well. All the lacerations have healed exceptionally well, and your scalp is now very well attached. The almost-severed left hand has responded well to microsurgery, but you need to perform certain voluntary exercises to facilitate proper movement in the thumb and fingers. Your spinal injuries worried me at first, but X-rays indicate that they should heal with no problem, although you are, of course, in a special spinal brace. I say special only because you had so many injuries we had to adapt a brace so as to secure your spine while allowing us access to other parts of your body."

Only now was I realizing just how bandaged, plastered, and immobilized I actually was. My head and upper body were bandaged, and my limbs were in plaster. My left hand was strapped to a pad, both arms strapped to restraints, and both legs held a few inches off the bed by pulleys. All in all, I felt as though I were the loser in a wrestling match with an elephant, and that it was now sitting on me.

On a cheerful note, a huge vase of flowers stood on a bedside table, and amazingly, my favorite bonsai ficus stood on a low table close by. That was definitely an Amber touch.

"So when can I start walking?" I was only half joking!

Pete looked very serious. "That's the problem. The fractures are taking a long time. They are not infected, yet they are not progressing as they should. Quite frankly, I'm baffled. Most of my colleagues suggest that I pump you full of antibiotics, 'just in case,' but that goes against everything I believe in."

"Me too," I said fiercely.

"Right, Adam. I've laid it out for you, now it's your turn. How did you learn so much detail about your injuries?"

Having already decided on my strategy, I gave a slight moan and slumped into what should appear to be oblivion.

Moments later my right eyelid was lifted up, and Pete was staring into it. "Nice try, Adam, nice try, but you underestimate me. I'm still waiting."

"You won't believe me if I tell you."

"Try me, you might get a surprise."

"So might you," I countered.

"I'm still waiting."

Very gently, I sighed. Me and my big mouth! "Okay, you want the truth, I'll give it to you. You probably know that my car was hit by a truck, and that when the car somersaulted off the bridge at Donkey Creek, I was knocked unconscious. The next thing I know, I'm walking down a long tunnel toward a brilliant light at the far end. I couldn't figure out quite how I got there, but it didn't seem very important; all that mattered was reaching the light. As I got nearer to the light, I met an . . . er, angel, who—you're never going to believe this—manifested a cafe, and er, invited me in. The coffee was . . ."

Pete's thick eyebrows were raised arcs of disbelief as he butted in. "Hey, are you having me on?"

"I told you that you wouldn't believe me. Anyway, I had a bottomless mug of the best cappuccino I have ever tasted. No matter how much I drank, the mug stayed full, hot, and frothy. Then the, er, angel, clicked his fingers, and one whole wall became a movie screen. Together, we watched my accident, from being hit by the truck, to being in this hospital."

"I did say I believe in fairy stories, didn't I! So how did you learn about the full extent of your injuries?"

"The, er, angel told me."

"Why?"

"Because I had to make a choice."

"What choice?"

"If I went into the Light, I couldn't return to my body. I would be dead. If I chose to stay physically alive, I had a broken body to mend, and a lot of pain."

Pete shook his head in bewilderment. "I must be going soft, but after a story like that, I believe you. Was death very scary?"

"On the contrary. The Light was filled with love. I knew that death is not the end. It was returning to my body that was the scary choice."

"But . . . if there is no death, why choose the body and all its pain and trauma?"

"When I was looking at the movie screen, I watched Amber telling me she loves me. She said she would give our marriage another go if only I would come back."

"So you did?"

"Yes."

"God's truth? You're not having me on?"

"Truly. It's a condensed version of what happened."

"Whew! I've heard some near-death experiences before, but none as clear and certain as yours."

In that moment I had a powerful insight. "I haven't described a near-death experience; it was a near-life experience. Never in all my years have I been so close to the real essence of life. Coming back into this body feels more like a near-death experience. Pete, I intend to learn from this, and live. And I really mean . . . live!"

Pete looked pensive. "Yeah, I get a feeling for what you mean." He frowned, his forehead furrowing as he lost himself in thought. "I must be mad, but I believe you. What we really know about life and death doesn't exactly add up to much." He grinned. "It's not an easy area to chart. The people who die have nothing to say about it, while the ones who pay a close visit often have very different stories to tell afterward. However, the one thing in common for so many people is that light. Most near-death people see a light of some sort." He sighed. "So you actually chose to come back into the body?"

"Yes."

"No more lights, or other phenomena?"

I hesitated. There was the golden glowing light. And Selph! He was surely a phenomenon! But that was purely my business, and not yet open for discussion.

"No, not really."

"You sound unsure."

"One day there might be some more that we can discuss, but definitely not yet."

My tone conveyed its message, and Pete did not pursue it. We chatted for a while longer about the exercises I must practice, even while trussed up, and he departed.

❖   ❖   ❖

The next day was not a good one for me. I woke up from a terrible dream, where I was being cut apart, one limb at a time. I was reasonably unafraid while first my arms were cut off, then my legs. The terror hit when I was told that to be free, my head must be cut off. I began to struggle, rolling on my torso away from the obscure, unidentifiable figure who wielded the huge ax. As I stopped rolling, the ax flashed down, cutting me in half at the waist. There was neither blood nor pain, but as the raised ax was poised above my neck, terror wrenched a scream from my throat that tore me out of the dream.

I lay in sheets that were wet with sweat, a foul, rancid smell clinging to the bed. Pain crawled around inside my chest, while my limbs and hip felt as though stilettos were being thrust into them at random. Knowing that this was my lunatic choice, I decided to follow the instructions that Selph had taught me.

Nothing worked. Closing my eyes, I focused on the color red. It was an easy color to find, for every stab of pain was echoed by a flash of red behind my eyelids. Moving to orange, then yellow, red was superimposed over both. Red, red, red. I tried for green and blue, more red. The harder I tried to get past red, the more it dominated everything. I tried ignoring the pain, but my thoughts somehow found a pattern within the throbbing, stabbing agony and kept time with it, following the cadence of its cruel rhythm. The harder I tried to focus away from the pain, the more acutely aware I became of my suffering.

A very bad day, it passed slowly. Neither Amber nor my mother came to see me, and other friends had not yet been given permission to visit. I knew that Kate and Bruno had been in several times, but I had been comatose. I tried for a conversation with Pete, but he was busy and, owing to the constant pain, I was in a foul mood.

The one thing that helped was sleep. I regularly fell asleep while trying to get into a meditative state, so I guess that was some compensation, at least. Since I had come out of the coma, I had been reasonably optimistic and bright most of the time, but despair and misery had now caught up with a vengeance.

When, in the evening, my wet, sweat-stained sheets were changed for the third time that day, Pete arrived with the couple of nurses. He did not mince words.

"Right, Adam," he said briskly. "Give me one good reason why I should not sedate you."

"Because it's my body," I growled.

For a moment he was nonplussed. It was a good reason!

"That may be so," he countered, "but your body has been put into my care. You have messed it up badly; I have to put it together. Your stubborn cussedness isn't helping. This continuous pain is wearing you down, and I won't allow it."

Humble pie was definitely in order. "Please, Pete, give me one more day. If I can't get past the pain in the next twenty-four hours, I'll submit to nonchemical pain relief."

Pete groaned. "Christ! Another twenty-four hours of your present pain stress represents a serious setback for you. How about acupuncture treatment? Surely that will be okay."

In my agitation, the pain was so bad that red flashes were dancing over Pete's white coat. "No," I gasped. "Give me one more day. Please."

His face angry, Pete spun around and stamped out. "Let him bloody well suffer then. Jesus Christ! Why don't I become a vet? Why do I suffer bloody minded people? Why do I put up with . . ."

He was still grumbling and muttering as he walked out of the room, while the two nurses followed him quietly. At the last moment, one nurse turned back. "Don't worry, he'll get over it." She gave me a smile of encouragement, scuttling away as a bellowed, "NURSE," echoed down the corridor. When angry, Pete had a very loud voice.

All my smug assurance at being able to beat the pain had been erased. This was one of my first days of being fully conscious all the time, so instead of being able to slide away from the pain into oblivion, I had to deal with it. But I was unable to. Despondent, I wondered what had happened to Selph. Where was he living? Where was he? Even thinking was difficult. Waves of pain battered me, smashing down my reserves of energy, and gradually, for the first time, I found that I no longer had the strength to resist. As a sandcastle on a beach, the incoming waves of pain were tearing down the walls and structure of my being. Somewhere deep inside me, I recognized that fear was howling and screaming around the last turrets of my defense, but gritting my teeth, I fought back, defying the pain with everything I had. Somewhere, within the ongoing fight for my survival, I fell deeply asleep.

I was awakened by a hand on my cheek. The touch was gentle, yet I felt energy surging from the fingers as though each finger carried its own unique current of power. Shocked, I gasped for breath, my eyes jerking open.

It was very dark, and I knew that nobody should be in the room. A glance at the illuminated dial of my bedside travel clock showed that it was two o'clock in the morning.

As I came fully awake, I knew who it was. Only one person made their own rules of life, regardless of everyone else's reality.

"Selph?"

"Hello, Adam. I take it you're not feeling so good."

He was no more than a dark human shape against the black background. "Dumbest choice I ever made, coming back to this. And who ever said that I could control the pain? My God! If pain is a learned reaction, then I've been in the throes of educated stimulus for about six weeks. I'm not sure I can take much more."

"Hmmm. At least your humor is still intact. Maybe you should settle for the pain relief that Doctor Morrow wants you to have."

"It's not humor, I'm delirious. I must be. How the hell can you tell me to get pain relief after that lecture about creating my own reality. I want to learn how not to ever do this again, and if that means learning the lessons involved in this acci-purpose and all the pain I've created, then so be it. That is, assuming you're right."

"Oh, I'm right. I always am."

"Sometimes you're a real pain."

Selph chuckled. "Who is a real pain? It sure ain't me. Seriously, Adam, I came here to help you. You've got a ton of courage, and this is good. Nobody gets to know their own truth without courage and commitment. You've proved that you have both. So, let's get . . ."

"Are you actually here?" I cut in, "or am I dreaming that I think I'm awake?"

"I'm here Adam, and you are physically awake."

"But how did you get in here? Oh, sorry, stupid question. You have your own set of rules."

"Adam, let go of questions. Relax, listen. Do you remember meeting me near the Light? Do you remember how attracted you were by the Light?"

"Yes, very clearly."

"And do you remember that you were not in your physical body? Remember, I referred to you as the essential you?"

"Yes, of course, I remember everything."

"The reason you were so attracted to the Light is because the essential you is a Being of Light. This is a basic human truth. Light attracts Light. Beyond the Light, the essential you continues without a physical body, and your reality is every bit as powerful and real as your present everyday reality. Okay?"

"Yep, fine. I'm with you, but what's your point?"

"Very simply, I'm going to teach you how to reach the essential you, and return to the Sphere of Tranquillity over the river. If you can reach and enter the sphere, you will be able to change from reaction and pain to response and healing. And you can do it."

"But Selph, you taught me that. I've been trying all day, and I couldn't do it. The pain is so unrelenting, it beat me."

"How is it now?"

"It's changed. Instead of knives stabbing into my limbs and chest, blunt hammers are pounding me, grinding me down with throbbing agony. I hurt, Selph. I hurt."

He moved, his vague outline shifting closer to my side. Then, he was still and silent for what seemed a long time.

"What's wrong?" I asked.

He sighed regretfully. "I'm tempted to ease your pain, but I know that it's not in your long-term interest to do so. Would you believe me if I told you that your suffering is also mine? I don't mean this in a physical sense, but your suffering is pure discord for me."

I could think of nothing to say. It did not make sense, but I somehow knew it was true.

"Right, we are going deeper into detail this time, thus we will create a more powerful reality. Before we start there are a few points that I wish to emphasize. First, when I say 'imagine and visualize,' I want you to do this on a level of participation. In other words, imagine and visualize yourself involved and doing; not watching yourself on the screen of your mind as though in a cinema watching a movie. You are the player on the screen, not the onlooker. Do you understand what I mean?"

"I sure do."

"Second point: you will not be playing a game, or involved in a fantasy; you will be creating and expanding your own reality. What you experience will be real. As real as your physical reality of lying in bed injured and suffering. As contrary as it sounds, it's a good thing that you are in pain right now, because, fully conscious and aware, you are going beyond pain into a greater reality, and it will be you who makes it happen. Be very clear about this; I will guide you, but it is you who will expand your reality and make it happen."

"Can anybody do this?"

"Of course! Why?"

"Well, I wondered if it was just for pain relief."

"Good heavens, no. The exercise you are going to be involved in is a path to an altered state of consciousness. Anyone can do this for expanding their consciousness."

"I can't wait."

"First of all, I want you to close your eyes and relax your whole body, especially your head, jaw, and throat. Under normal circumstances I would suggest you sit in a comfortable chair rather than lie down, because the whole idea is to be consciously awake and aware throughout the exercise. But in your case, bed will suffice.

"To begin, focus on your body and on your identity. Feel the pain in your body and be aware of how powerfully your identity connects with it. Now . . ."

"I'm sorry to cut in, but what exactly do you mean by focus? You use the word a lot."

"By focus, I mean drawing together your mind, awareness, and attention into a point of total concentration. If you are thinking about anything, you are not focused. To be focused means that you are absolutely concentrated in the moment. Okay?"

"Yes, thanks. But that's tricky."

"Of course it's tricky, that's why so few people are ever focused. Most people live in a state of confusion that is so integrated into their daily reality that they don't even know it. However, focus is possible. It comes with inner discipline and practice.

"Okay, let's continue. Having held a focus on your physical body and identity, I want you now to focus on the essential you. To do this, imagine and visualize a body of light that contains your physical body. It can be egg shaped, or body shaped; the shape doesn't matter so long as this light-body contains your physical body."

He paused for several minutes, while I visualized a body of light containing my physical body. It was not as difficult as I thought it might be, almost as if I were being drawn into something that was entirely natural.

"Okay, now release your identity/body focus and place your sense of self—the essential you—into the body of light. You are now aware of the essential you as a Being of Light. Focus on this. Visualize it. Build it strong with your imagination."

Again he paused, while I continued to develop the imagery, strengthening and maintaining it.

"Before you a rainbow appears, the colors a shimmering arc of invitation. As a Being of Light, step away from your physical/identity body—it will be perfectly safe—and, walking across to the rainbow, enter it in the color red. As you walk into red, let go of any physical tension that you may have retained. You are a Being of Light, and red sweeps through you without any resistance. Experience the color with taste, touch, sight, smell, and even hearing. Be with red."

He paused for maybe a minute, while I experienced red. I felt as though the red flames of a fire were licking at me, and I could feel the pain. "As you enter orange, let go of any anxiety or fear, allowing orange to wash it away as the color sweeps through you. As before, fully experience orange."

Another silent minute passed, while I relaxed into orange. I found hidden pockets of anxiety, and a fear that red would continue to pursue me, but as I found them, I visualized orange light pouring as a flood of color right through me, until I was saturated in it.

"Walk now into yellow, releasing any thoughts that may be clinging to you, distracting you. Soak your Light Being in the full experience of yellow."

Again, a minute of silence while I moved into yellow. I was still aware of pain, but it no longer felt as though it belonged in my present moment. It had become more of a background pain, no longer dominating me. Occasional flashes of red shot through the yellow, but yellow was undiminished.

"Step now into green, feeling the peace and calm of nature sweeping through you as you surrender to green. Experience green with all your senses ... and more."

Green was easier. Although in a rainbow, I imagined my light-body being in a rich green meadow, and like a child, I rolled in it, over and over.

"Move now into blue, where an ocean of love awaits you. Experience blue with every part of your Being."

Another minute passed while I explored blue. I was swimming in a blue ocean, surrounded by dolphins. I felt mildly shocked as I realized that I had not imagined them being here, yet they were with me. For a moment, I was almost lost in speculation on the "how" of it, then I released it, surrendering to the rapture of blue.

"Next, the spiritual aspirations of purple enfold and encompass you, raising you to a finer state of consciousness as you explore and experience purple."

I spent the minute bathed in a purple light so powerful that I was a purple Light Being being light.

"Step now into the color violet, where you become fine-tuned to the pure harmonic of harmony. Experience violet."

A sense of peace and bliss swept me, followed by waves of an inner strength that I did not know I had. I was again a child, picking violets beneath the greengage trees in my great aunt's orchard. Consternation hit me. I did not have a great aunt who owned an orchard, especially in Europe, yet the memory and imagery remained crystal clear and focused. Again, I surrendered to the images, no longer struggling to understand. And I felt harmony.

"Move now into the color pink, feeling the health and healing of pink as a total experience."

My pink was a soft rose pink, as I stood in a massed bed of perfumed roses. I felt the color washing through my limbs of light, and with a vague realization knew that I was also being physically affected. Well-being engulfed me.

"Step now into pure white Light. Let all the colors be vanquished, becoming the all-color of white. Experience the purity of whiteness."

The rainbow had vanished, and I stood in a ray of white light that poured into, and through me. I felt uplifted, cleansed, vital, pure, and whole.

"As you walk away from the rainbow, you see a flight of white steps leading down to deeper levels of being. You look down the steps into an inviting Light. Slowly, you go down the steps, beginning at twenty-one . . . twenty . . . nineteen . . . eighteen . . . seventeen . . . sixteen . . . fifteen . . . fourteen . . . thirteen . . . twelve . . . eleven . . . ten . . . nine . . . eight . . . seven . . . six . . . five . . . four . . . three . . . two . . . one. As you leave the last step, you find that you are on the bank of a river. Take time to see the river and all the life that abounds along it. Take your time. Experience it."

My flight of steps was very wide, and made of white marble. I was in no rush as I slowly stepped down them, although I had a longing to be with the river again. When I reached the last step, I looked for the river, but I was surrounded by a dense white mist. As I stepped off the last step, the mist evaporated, and the river was there again, a river out of Disney. Why it had the superabundance of a cartoon I did not know, but the overwhelming exuberance of flowers, birds, and river was very welcome. I felt safe and nurtured.

Walking along the riverbank, I looked for the Sphere of Tranquillity, but there was no sign of it. Ruefully, I knew that I was trying to go ahead of myself, so I brought all my attention back to the river. As I watched the water flowing over the shallows, I observed that it was no longer cartoonish. The river itself was real, the water clear and sparkling as on any sunny day. Around the river, squirrels nimbly played in the supergreen, superabundant trees, while rabbits and hedgehogs visibly scuttled through the luxurious vegetation. One thing was certain: this was no Australian river, yet I felt as though I had known it forever.

For a while I sat on the bank, my feet dangling in the deliciously cool water. What a beautiful idyllic place. The songs of many different birds blended into a single harmonic broad-spectrum note of pure sound that had never known a physical expression. This place was more real than everyday life, more complete, more whole. It combined newness with the familiar, creating a totally different experience. Nothing here conformed to a normal reality. There were either new rules or no rules, but this place was not bound by the laws of physicality. For a while longer, I simply followed the river, involved in the abundance of life around me.

I was so involved with the river that unnoticed, I almost bumped into the sphere. A huge bubble spanning the river, it had the same aura of pristine purity as before. This time, I carefully and gently walked into it, feeling its tactile, flexible strength, as I was willingly admitted into its interior.

For the first time I focused on the physical me. I was aware of being awake in the hospital bed, and aware of a distant murmur of pain in my physical body; pain that no longer held me imprisoned.

With a sense of exhilaration, I walked to the center of the river, and sitting down cross-legged a bubble thickness above the water, I stared into the depths, not attempting to focus on anything. How much time was involved, if any, I do not know, but very gradually the water lost all definition, expanding . . . and expanding . . . becoming . . . nothing . . . and . . . everything.

Somewhere, in the deep seat of my consciousness, I felt an energy of healing that vibrated right through my light-body, tingling into every atom and molecule of my physical body. From a vast distance, I felt pain reaching a crescendo of violence as though opposing all healing, and I felt it submit . . . overwhelmed, crushed, and destroyed. In that deep seat of my soul, I knew that an addiction to suffering that had survived for eons had been vanquished. And I knew, in the great paradox of truth, that it had been defeated by my inner surrender.

# Six

As I came back to my awareness, Selph was sitting in the Sphere of Tranquillity beside me. He beamed his approval.

"Very good. You dived deep."

Nodding slowly, I closed my eyes. I felt as though I had been at one with a vast ocean, and that I was now trying to adjust to once again being a single drop. Logically, I should be feeling diminished, but instead, I felt expanded.

Opening my eyes, I stared at Selph, his intense blue gaze staring back at me. He waved his arms around him in a sweeping gesture to indicate the sphere. "You can stay here for as long as you are comfortably able to, but when you leave, be sure to always exit the sphere with love and appreciation for the gift you have received. Return up the steps from one to twenty-one, and through the rainbow in reverse order. As a Being of Light, walk back to your physical body, and refocus the essential you that is now in your light-body, back into your identity and physicality. Don't short-circuit this by taking your awareness directly back into your physical body from this sphere. You will gradually disempower the process."

My stare still fixed on him; I attempted to grapple with the mystery he posed. How could he be in this sphere with me? Was this a two-person reality? And how did he get from physical to nonphysical realities so easily? Questions I had, in plenty, but I was short on answers.

"Selph, if we each create our own reality, how can you and I both be in the sphere together? I didn't invite you, or bring you into my reality. Don't misunderstand," I added hastily, "it's great to have you here, but how do you do it?"

"I'll reply with a metaphor that is intended to explain, not offend. The butterfly knows the caterpillar and its capabilities, but the caterpillar knows nothing of the butterfly or its ability. In nature, the caterpillar is biologically programmed to become a butterfly; that is its destiny. Although humans are destined to *consciously* become Beings of Light, there is no preset biological program; only free will, choice, and focus. This exercise you are involved in is an expression of all of these."

His smile was friendly, even cheeky, his garish T-shirt as awful as ever. "I'm going to leave you now, but one last thing to remember. This is a potent exercise, and it will reestablish a process. Each time you return to the sphere it will continue. However, its effects are designed to also act on your everyday life. To empower this, focus on your feelings of calmness, of peace, of being centered and serene as you leave this exercise. Become aware of those feelings and retain them for as long as you are able. Recapture those feelings and live them in your daily life. This won't be easy, but it will continue to expand your reality."

"Yes, I'll do that. It makes sense. I'm puzzled though, is the Sphere of Tranquillity available to anybody?"

"Of course! Why? Do you want exclusive rights?"

"No! It's not that. I just thought that it could get awfully crowded in here if lots of people all try it at the same time."

Selph's giggling laughter seemed as loud and real in the sphere as in a physical reality. For a while he spluttered and choked over his own private amusement, starting a fresh bout of giggling just when he seemed to have it under control. Just like a kid!

"I'm dammed if I can see the joke!"

This started him off again, so I said no more.

"Adam," he finally chuckled, "if a million people all came with you at the same time, you would be the only person here, and it would be as pristine pure as it is now. This is not a physical realm, and it doesn't conform to physical law."

"I don't get it."

"No, you don't. You're only touching on the edges of a greater reality. Reality is multidimensional. However, this is irrelevant for now. I'm going."

"But when will I see you again?" I asked hastily.

"When it's appropriate. Bye."

And he vanished, just like that. He didn't fade out, or walk away, he simply ceased to be with me.

I stayed for a while longer, letting go of the questions he always invoked, refocusing on the feeling of serenity that infused me. My love and appreciation arose easily, and I shared this with the sphere and the river. Very clearly, I felt its acceptance, as though this were a perfectly natural and reciprocal exchange of energy. With this established, I got up and, walking to the translucent outer skin of the sphere on the riverbank, I stepped through it.

I had only walked along the riverbank for a short way, when the flight of white marble steps rose up before me. I went up them slowly, one at a time. The rainbow was a radiant arc, but without the white ray, or the pink band I had earlier walked through. I went through each color at a pace that felt most natural to me, neither hurrying nor overly lingering. When I left the rainbow, I walked over to my physical body lying in the hospital bed; my identity was awake, and aware of all that was happening. In my light-body I enveloped and embraced my physical body, moving my focus back to my identity.

Laying awake, I stared into the semidarkness of the private room. On one level I felt that I had been gone for an eternity, but a glance at the clock revealed that forty-five minutes of normal time had passed. Tentatively, I focused on my body, but apart from a dull, insistent, low-pain throbbing, all was well.

Closing my eyes, I fell into a deep, peaceful sleep.

The next morning began my first good day. As I awoke, I had an instant recall of my meditative journey in the night, and I reached into my psyche for the feelings of peace and serenity. To my surprise, I quickly found them, and for about ten minutes I held a focus on these qualities. The early flutterings of serious pain gradually receded, not by forcing them away, or by effort, but by simply relaxing into a different place of my Being.

"Well, well, well. I don't know what you've been doing, but keep up the good work. You look like a different person, and a much brighter one." So saying, man-mountain Doctor Pete was leaning across me, peering into my eyes as he beamed a shaft of light into them from his little pocket torch.

He straightened after a few minutes of low muttering, peering at me with an expression of amused amazement. "I just don't know what to think about you. Yesterday you were suffering intense pain, today it appears to be at its lowest ebb yet. Why? Did you do something very clever, or did this just happen? Is this an example of you going beyond your pain, in the way you wanted?"

I nodded, feeling flippant. "In a way, yes. My angel visited me in the night and taught me how to do it." I stopped, shock racing through me as I heard my own frivolous words for the first time. My God! Selph . . . an angel! Of course, why not? It fitted perfectly. Then I hesitated. No, that feels wrong. Somehow I know he isn't. I don't know how, or why, but that's not the answer. What or who Selph is baffles me, but I'm somehow sure that he is not an angel. In a way, I wish he were. It would all make sense, and be explained, but I have a gut feeling that there's a much deeper mystery here, and I'm not even close to solving it.

My face must have registered some of my passing thoughts and accompanying emotions, for I was suddenly aware of Pete's voice going deep as he rumbled his concern.

"Are you all right, Adam?"

Grinning at him, I replied, "The best by far since my CED. I'm definitely on the mend."

"CED?"

"Close encounter with death."

"Is there any point in my asking what you did, and how you did it?"

"Yes, sure, I'll tell you." And I did, although it was a brief, rather condensed version.

"I'm very impressed. Could you teach other people how to make that journey?"

"I don't see why not. But they would have to *really* want to learn. First and foremost, the exercise is about life; pain relief is a side effect."

"And it would also work for stress relief?"

"Sure, pain is stress, but mental or emotional stress would be alleviated also. Remember what I said, however; it is really about expanding your consciousness."

Pete spent nearly another hour running a series of tests on me. He questioned—or should I say interrogated—me about the pain in my many injuries, and each reply I gave was checked and tested on my body. His examination was thorough and exhaustive. Much of that time he was whistling under his breath, a soft tuneless refrain that droned on and on.

Finally, he stood back regarding me, his hands on his wide, well-padded hips. "Absolutely bloody incredible. You have made more progress in the past twelve hours than in the previous two weeks." He shook his head in bafflement. "We have psychologists here who teach meditation techniques to patients where it's considered it would be helpful, and with very good results, so I'm not new to that, but I have never seen such a rapid and remarkable improvement as yours. I'm convinced that there is more to your case than meditation."

"I agree. Try timing and commitment."

Pete frowned, looking like a huge, unhappy St. Bernard.

"I simply don't understand. There's a lot I want to discuss with you, but right now I don't have time. So, let's get down to the immediate basics. We are going to remove the pulleys, disconnect all tubes, and give you an opportunity to gently—and I mean, gently—wriggle and stretch as much as possible." He paused, thinking. "Oh, yes, and about a ton of those bandages can come off now, beginning with the one on your head." He beamed, a very pleased wide smile. "How does all that sound?"

"Like hoo-bloody-ray," I grinned.

"I'm sorry to say that the back brace will have to stay put for a considerable while longer yet."

"Oh. Ah well."

"Do you think you could handle visitors?"

"Could I ever! Family and friends are just what I need right now."

"Well, we won't overdo it, but your mother and Amber both phoned yesterday, wanting to see you. I refused permission then, but I just might let them know you are ready and able again. At last!"

Smiling broadly, he turned to go. "Doctor," I called out. "I just want you to know that I really appreciate all that you are doing for me. I couldn't be in better hands."

Looking acutely embarrassed, but rather pleased, Pete mumbled a few words about just doing his job, and departed.

Within fifteen minutes, a couple of nurses were busy removing all the medical apparatus, following this with a much needed and appreciated bed bath. For the first time, I truly noticed the nurses who were looking after me, inhaled their perfume, and was able to relate to them. It was just great! "I'll try not to sweat so much," I smiled.

They grinned, carrying on the humor. "You've wet the bed more times than a baby. And smelly too."

Oh, the joy of being disconnected from tubes and medical paraphernalia, of being unrestrained by bands and bonds, of being able to wriggle and squirm, unfettered. Plaster casts and the brace still created their own definite limitations, but I was no longer secured into one confined position. I had a few bad moments when I overdid my wriggling, pain plunging a needle shard of warning into my spinal column. Instead of fighting it, I relaxed, reaching for the calmness and peace, feeling again the tranquillity and the healing. My relaxation went so deep that I was startled when I suddenly heard my mother's voice.

"Oh, Adam, at long last."

I glanced at the bedside clock. My God! I had relaxed away nearly one and a half hours. "Mum," I exclaimed, "how did you get here so fast? And . . . Dad!"

For the first time that I can remember, my father awkwardly put his arms around me, and silently cried. I didn't know what to do, or say, but it felt wonderful. I could not hug him, the plaster casts would not allow it, but as he straightened up, I huskily called him back. "Dad, come down here a moment," indicating that he should lower his head for a conspiratorial whisper.

As he did so, I kissed him. Another first in memory!

Dad blushed crimson, and maybe I did, but we both looked mighty pleased, even if slightly bemused.

Mum was crying just to see what happened, and to cover her confusion, she started off talking at her usual rate.

"Oh, Adam, you're finally recovering. You've had us all so worried. Poor Amber has been beside herself with worry. We all have. And your poor dad hasn't been able to work or concentrate on his farming for weeks on end. Look at him, he's even thinner than before. We're all gaunt with worry."

"But how did you get here so quickly?" I persisted.

"We drove up yesterday, and stayed at a motel. We plan to stay for a few days."

"How's the weather?" It seemed a trite question, but to people who live on the land, the weather practically rules their lives.

"Not a drop of rain. It's terrible, not a single drop. Oh dear, I don't know what we'll do if it continues much longer. Lots of the farmers are having to walk off their farms, just abandon them. It's terrible!"

Switching my attention to Dad, I asked him. "How is it on the farm, Dad? Can you last out?"

He sighed. "We're into the third year now, and no rain. The thought of another year is heartbreaking, but I've got a feeling it's a fair way from finished yet." Although the subject was depressing, Dad was on familiar ground, and he quickly perked up from his earlier emotional episode. But he had more to say. "I . . . I . . . don't rightly know how to say this, but I need to try." He paused, and swallowed, his obvious embarrassment mingled with a look of determination.

"I, er . . . I was more affected by your accident than I dreamed possible. The thought of you dead, or dying, haunted me. I know I've been a difficult, grumpy old sod, and I probably won't change much, but I need to tell you that I've missed you. Ever since you and I split, I've missed you. I don't know why I could never tell you, but I could never find the words. It all just went wrong." He sniffed heavily, his eyes watering, and he slowly blew his nose, as though he were summoning his last shreds of courage. Staring at me, his mouth silently opened and closed a few times, until at last, "I want you to, er, know . . . I love you, son."

I was crying, Mum was crying, and Dad was crying, when Amber walked quietly into the room. As we realized she was there, she was already turning around to creep back out, her soft lilting words apologetic. "I'll wait outside."

"No! Don't go," I called out. "Please, I want you."

I swallowed an emotional lump, but I too had something I needed to say. Something that I knew was part of my healing. And I had to say it now. Looking Dad in the eyes, I told him, "Dad, I love you. I know we've had our differences over the years, but you were always my Dad, and I've never ceased to be mighty proud of that."

I knew instantly that I had found the right words. Dad did not need to be gushed over, or too many emotionally charged words; he needed to know that he was wanted, that he had never been rejected, that I was proud of him.

Looking as though he had been kicked by a donkey—and loving it—Dad stepped back out of the limelight. He had displayed more emotions and feelings in the last few minutes than in many, many years. He needed to recover!

My attention riveted on Amber, I beckoned her over to me. As she came close, her face and lips coming down to mine, it all proved too much. I burst into tears, crying just like your average baby.

And like a loving mother, Amber soothed me. "Theeere, theeere, you cry, my darling. It's all going to be all right. Theeere now, I love you." Her hands gently stroked my face, cool on my hot brow. Her sweet, fresh breath mingling with mine, less sweet, her lips brushing my face as she softly kissed my mouth, my nose, my eyes and cheeks.

Dad was standing up against the wall, but watching our reunion started fresh tears of happiness trickling down his seamed cheeks. To have Amber back in his life was something he had longed for. Mum reacted with an expression of sheer, unadulterated joy, her hanky darting in an eccentric pattern from dabbing her nose to wiping her eyes.

Straightening up, Amber whirled around and grabbing Mum, hugged her, just as her own tears started. After a long tearful hug, she went over to Dad, embracing him, beckoning Mum to join them in a big, shared hug. Tears were flowing freely all round as Pete ambled in, pushing a small, well-loaded surgical trolley before him.

"My God! There's more water flowing in here than down in the washrooms. "I've brought you all a mug of coffee, I figured you might need it. As you might know, I'm very proud of Adam. He has now established himself on the road to what, I hope, is going to be a smooth and rapid recovery."

Passing everyone but me a mug of coffee, Pete grinned broadly as the sniffles gradually dried up. Raising his mug high, he called out, "Here's to Adam, and his return to good health. May he progress smoothly."

Goggle-eyed, I was staring at Pete's mug. In every detail of color, design, and shape, it was identical to my earlier bottomless coffee mug. But there was, of course, one difference. Pete quickly emptied his! Had Selph known of this moment when he created the coffeehouse? Had he deliberately chosen this not-at-all-common design to place on the bottomless mugs? My God! The implications were beyond imagining. I looked at my family, the people I love, wondering if, or when, I could tell them about Selph. Without meaning to belittle him, I knew Dad would never understand. Mum might just, possibly, but Amber would have no problem at all. Yes, when it felt right I would tell her.

Pete did not stay long, but I was grateful for his very timely intervention. Although our emotional purging had been long overdue, we needed now to laugh and talk, lifting our spirits on the wings of a new joy. How strange! If I had not had the acci-purpose, Dad and I would still be locked in the strained, self-defeating roles that had held us both captive for so long. I thought again about Selph's words; we each create our own reality, continuously, every moment. To be aware of creating our reality, and create that which most uplifts ourselves and those we love; surely this must be the ultimate purpose and achievement for everyone.

Three hours sped past rapidly as Amber held my hand, while Mum and Dad each sat at my bedside. We talked of many things, all part of a family healing, but gradually, to my consternation, I could feel the ragged edges of pain slowly accumulating, while an ever-increasing fatigue dragged at me.

Pete's timing was impeccable. Just as Amber was voicing her concern for my growing discomfort, Pete loomed into the open door. Glancing at me briefly, he called out. "Time, ladies and gentleman, please. The patient is exhausted."

Dad squeezed my good hand with open affection, while Mum and Amber kissed me good-bye. "No more visiting until tomorrow, folks," Pete boomed, quickly ushering them out.

He was back in a few minutes, his voice soft and childlike with concern. "How do you feel?"

I smiled feebly, amazed at the depth of my fatigue. "Like I just ran a hundred miles." I smiled at him. "Talking about that, there's a journey I need to make. I would be grateful if you could ensure it remains quiet for the next hour, or so."

Pete nodded, understanding. "Guaranteed, Adam. Just you do whatever it is you do to continue the healing."

The door swung closed behind him, and I closed my eyes. I wanted to sleep first, then make my journey while awake and aware, but despite my tiredness, it seemed the pain might be enough to keep me awake.

Relaxing, I began the process of refocusing the essential me into my light-body. I went easily through the colors, but although I seemed to experience them quite strongly, a gnawing, persistent, unwanted pain insisted on accompanying me. It almost drew me out of the exercise, but I continued doggedly on, relaxing ever deeper. When I entered pink, I felt that I wanted to stay forever. For some reason, pink reached deeply into me, soothing and easing the pain more than all the other colors combined. I stayed there for quite a while, before eventually going down the steps, along the riverbank, and into the Sphere of Tranquillity.

Once again, I sat cross-legged on the gossamer skin of the bubble over the center of the river. And again, I allowed my focus to lose itself in the water, attaching to nothing . . . and expanding . . . expanding. Briefly, for a long micromoment before I lost all focus, I was aware of some presence close by. I could feel an energy of healing pulsing through my body of light and into my physical body in bed . . . then everything was lost in . . . nothingness.

Some time later, I extended my love and gratitude to the river, sphere, and presence, before carefully returning in the way that Selph had taught me, omitting no detail. As my awareness became centered in my physical body, I only had time to note that the pain was no more than a soft murmur, before falling into a deeply satisfying sleep.

❖ ❖ ❖

A week passed, and although occasional pains and deep-seated aches remained numerous, the serious stuff was a thing of the past. I made the inner journey every day—Pete made sure of that—for I had now reached the stage where the medics from physiotherapy were continually hounding me.

Fingers were lifted, wiggled, and rotated, arms and shoulders gently exercised, and my legs put through a vigorous daily workout in readiness for the day I would attempt to walk. I say vigorous, but that is a comparative statement. To me, it was vigorous, but any healthy six-year-old would have probably slept through it all. I, however, sweated and groaned as my weak, out-of-condition limbs made their protests known. My hip replacement created its own problems, slowing things down a bit, but it was no more painful than the fractures. My nose had repaired, the massive swelling subsided, and I could again breathe through it. The hand that had required microsurgery to repair and save was basically healed, and it was this hand that received the most vigorous and thorough workout.

According to Pete, my internal organs and all inner and outer bruising and bleeding had long healed. Even my punctured lungs were rapidly healing, along with the many bone fractures. My back was also healing now, as though a time-delay switch had been deactivated; I was sure it had!

That was something I needed to discuss with Selph. If I created my own reality, had I, in fact, caused my own delay in healing? Had it been because I needed to overcome the pain consciously, rather than complete my healing in a sedated or comatose condition? With the questions clearly stated, I just as clearly knew the answers. Yes, on both counts. For me to have healed in a coma or under sedation would have rendered the whole incident meaningless and purposeless.

A very relieved Mum and Dad had gone home, with Dad at last able to concentrate on the problems of drought on his farm. Kate and Bruno had been in to see me several times, and Bruno told me that his relationship with Dad had also recently gone through a remarkable improvement. Without doubt, my brush with death had precipitated some major changes for the better in Dad.

Much as I loved my family, it was Amber that I longed to see. When she came through the doorway, my room lit up. Even the physio' boys gave up on me when Amber came to visit.

"Keep him at the exercises, Mrs. Baker," they would grin with knowing and suggestive smirks, then leave us to become immersed in each other. Mind you, it's not all that easy to become immersed while you are still encased in a brace and plaster. But, by God, I tried!

The days seem to pass quickly, and I often wondered if Selph would come to see me in the capacity of a normal visitor, but he did not. I had not seen him since the illicit early morning visit when he had taught me how to make the journey, and had then shown up in the sphere. I often sent him silent mental messages suggesting he visit, but I guess he did not find it "appropriate." As soon as I had first become conscious and aware, I had asked Amber to make sure that my house plants and bonsai were watered and cared for. In hindsight, this was probably ridiculous, because they would all have died in the preceding weeks of neglect, yet this was not the case. Amber had gone to my home soon after the accident to make sure that everything was in order, and had found that the house and my plants were obviously being cared for. Despite several chance visits to find or meet whoever was responsible, she found no evidence of anyone. She had then questioned my neighbors, Mum, and Kate, puzzled that it was none of them. At this stage she had decided to put the issue on hold until I was better.

Now, with me rapidly healing and out of danger, she decided that the time had arrived to resurrect the mystery of who was responsible. Perplexed, she gave me a detailed account of all that had previously happened.

"Without exception, every time I went to water your plants, they had only recently been watered. Finally, I stopped bothering. I mean, what was the point? I take it you don't have someone else in your life?" she asked, her eyebrows raised in a hesitant, uncertain, mock seriousness.

My own hesitation proved to be my undoing.

"You do?" Her eyes flashed wrath, quickly recoiling into hurt, her whole face reflecting her dismay. "But why didn't you tell me?" Even her voice was bruised.

Sighing deeply, I knew that explanation time had arrived, although I had hoped to delay it until I got home.

"First, Amber, my darling, there is no other woman in my life. You have always been the 'one and only.' However, there is another person, if . . . that's what he is!"

So saying, I launched into a fairly detailed account of meeting Selph and the events that followed, concluding with the most recent status of our relationship. Wide-eyed, she listened without interruption, occasionally shaking her head in silent amazement, or amusement.

When I finished, I looked at her expectantly.

Her lips puckered, Amber regarded me from squinted eyes. "Do you really expect me to believe such a story?"

I knew she did. "Of course."

"I think that you must be very special to bring someone like that into your life," she said seriously.

"I don't agree. I'm not any more special than anyone else. This is really about an inner longing that goes back for as far as I can remember. I have always known that some vast and essential knowledge, or insight, has hovered in and around humanity, but so few people have ever connected with it. Much of my problem with you was based in the immense, and scary, dissatisfaction that I found in life, but I neither understood it nor knew how to resolve it. So I became moody and resentful, blaming other people for what, deep down, I knew to be my own failures and inadequacies."

Taking Amber's hands, I sighed. "In you, I found an innocence that almost freaked me out. You seemed so close to that 'essential insight' that I felt reduced. Not that this was your fault," I added hastily. "I realize now that I reacted to you, trying through blame and attack to reduce you to my own miserable status. In some warped way, this was supposed to make me feel better about myself. Of course, the very opposite happened, I felt even more reduced, becoming increasingly more threatened and unhappy." I smiled sadly.

Kissing me on the lips, Amber gently mussed my hair.

"Having heard all that, I don't have a shred of doubt that you and I are going to live happily ever after. If Selph is responsible for such insight and understanding, and facing it without the guilt, then I want to meet him. I'm ready for a teacher like that."

"Er, although I like the idea, Selph may not agree. He chose me, just as much as me choosing him, and the timing is absolutely critical. He said it then, and only now do I see how true it is; the timing was perfect. I was ready, even though I didn't know it!"

"What do you mean exactly, timing?"

I gazed at her thoughtfully, trying to find the right words. "Well, the longing was already there, but it had to align with a total commitment to create the timing. Obviously, it all came together. As I just told you, Selph knew that I was going to have the acci-purpose, and that I would have to choose between life with my battered body, or life that would no longer be physical; there is no death choice. And he knew that you were part of that equation. When I saw you next to my bed, and you told me that you loved me and that we had a chance together, I knew that I wanted to be with you. But—and I have to confess to this—as much as I truly love you, if choosing you had meant that Selph would no longer be my teacher, then I would have chosen to relinquish the body. As awful as it sounds, I would have forgone both you and my physical life, if that is what it took to continue with Selph. Even I was shocked to find this in me, but it was there, so I guess it revealed the extent of my commitment to experiencing who I am. I hope I haven't offended you," I said anxiously, "but I have to be honest about this. I should add that to offset my fear of returning to a body wracked by pain, the choice was made easier because only by doing so would you and Selph continue to be in my life. That was a blessing."

Amber smiled broadly, her eyelids lowered. "It's okay. I'm not at all offended, although I have to admit to being staggered. You are definitely not the same Adam that I married and lived with for three years."

"You wouldn't want me to be," I added wryly.

My comment ended our flow of conversation, but having missed two years of kissing, we had plenty to make up for!

❖   ❖   ❖

The day that I was both dreading and longing for had finally arrived. It was "up-and-at-'em" day! The staff in physiotherapy had told me that from this day on, I visited them; they would no longer come to me. Quite a challenge!

In preparation, I had had my plaster casts removed a couple of days earlier, and replaced with more comfortable, much thinner, lightweight supports. Even my back brace had been changed, offering support with some extra flexibility.

Pete was whistling his usual tuneless monotone as he pushed my wheelchair toward the fitness center.

"Gee, what a maze of corridors," I said.

"Yeah, well, you had better learn your way, and fast. I've got better things to do than push you around."

"Nonsense! The only reason you're here is so you can laugh when I fall flat on my face."

"Hmmm. That's a nice positive statement."

"You're right. I'll try not to fall."

"Yeah, I suggest you try very hard. I'm not sure that we could put Humpty Dumpty together again."

Our trivial conversation was an attempt to cover the tension we were both feeling. I knew that Pete was almost as anxious about the outcome as me. In truth, I was frightened. The thought of falling was enough to set my nerves on edge, as I subconsciously anticipated the pain. Everybody had been so encouraging, and I had awaited this day for weeks, but right now I was excited, and scared.

The double doors were wide open as we entered a very large, high-ceilinged room filled with a bewildering assortment of body-building and muscle-toning equipment. Many of the accoutrements were familiar, but there was plenty of apparatus I had never seen before, and whose functions I could only guess at.

A couple of staff came over to meet us. Maybe in their mid-thirties, both the man and woman looked superfit. Both blonde, with similar friendly features and with a loose, athletic build, they could have passed as twins. They each wore identical white singlets and pale-blue-and-white-striped shorts. They smiled at me encouragingly.

"Hi, Adam. My name's Jim, and this is my twin sister Mandy. We're going to be working with you, getting you onto your feet and back into action. Having studied your case history in great detail, we have planned a series of exercises aimed at carefully rebuilding both your strength and flexibility."

I nodded and smiled at each of them. "I hope I'm going to be okay. I honestly have no idea what I'm capable of, or even if I'm ready to walk."

Mandy smiled, her teeth whiter than white. "Don't worry, our first step is to put you through a series of tests to assess your capabilities. We proceed from there. Tell, me, how do you feel in yourself?"

"You mean mentally?"

"Yes."

I gave it some serious thought. "Generally speaking, I feel optimistic about my future, although I have my bad days. I basically accept what happened to me, and now I just want to get strong and mobile."

"This will certainly be the most painful and difficult part of your recovery process. Are you prepared for that?"

"Yes, of course."

And so it began.

# Seven

How little I knew. I only thought I was prepared; the reality proved to be quite different. It was so painful that there were times when I plunged into deep despair. I soon learned that the building was not a fitness center, as I had earlier supposed; it was a torture chamber, and I was expected to be a willing participant in my own torture.

In over three weeks I had managed no more than a few shaky steps as I clung to the parallel bars. Mandy told me over and over that I expected too much, but I was bitterly disappointed by my dismal performance. My weakness shocked me. From being a strong, physically powerful man, I was reduced to a trembling, shambling, feebleness that left me weepy and humiliated.

I sweated so copiously that Pete began to worry over my loss of condition. My limbs were expected to bend and flex in all the normal places, but with a will of their own, they were shaky, rigid, and unyielding. I learned far more about the extent of the damage to my body in those three weeks than I had during all of my time lying in bed. Selph's recital of my injuries was one thing, but trying to flex and bend and become mobile revealed just what it all added up to; I was a physical mess, a shattered human wreck.

However, to my credit, I persevered. Daily, from one device to another, I went through a grinding regime that left me exhausted and trembling. Through it all, Jim and Mandy seemed devoid of pity, continuously devising ever more energy-sapping routines. I was certain that their smiles were permanent fixtures, carved into their features at birth. For a while I nursed a secret belief that even if they were to cry, they would still be smiling. I was wrong.

How it happened, I'm not sure, but I had been struggling to walk, shuffling one reluctant leg after the other for maybe twenty minutes at the parallel bars, when I turned away, reaching out for the nearby safety frame where I could relax. Normally, this is a very stable unit—it needs to be—but I was trembling so violently from combined pain and exhaustion, that I clumsily stumbled, impossibly pitching headlong over the whole darned contraption.

As though a bug smashed flat between two gigantic bricks, an explosion of pain ripped through my spine and body in a rising crescendo of red agony. I have no recollection of crashing to the floor. It seemed that for a while I floated high, held in a seizure on an unbelievable spasm of suffering. In some odd, nonphysical way, I could see Mandy below me, squatting on the floor next to my crumpled body. Cradling my head, tears were streaming down her cheeks. Epitomizing care and compassion, she held me in a gentle rocking movement, crooning softly. Once again I could see the large, hazy, golden glow of some strange celestial presence that I had encountered before, and once again it was hovering close by my body. More powerfully than ever I felt an urge not just to claim it, or recognize it, but to unite with it, becoming . . . ?

For a long, timeless moment I seemed to be locked in slow motion, then, with steadily increasing speed, everything began to spin around and around, forming a long dark, spiraling funnel . . . and I was falling into it.

Rather than falling into the revolving spiral, it felt as though, with an awful deliberation, I was sucked into it. Like a sky diver on his first jump, I slowly spun over and over as I fell through space, unable to right myself or gain any control over my body. I wanted to scream, but I was unable to produce any sound from my mouth, even though it opened and closed in the manner of a stranded fish. At first I fell at what seemed a tremendous speed, but gradually I slowed, falling ever slower and slower, until eventually I felt my feet touch onto solid earth.

❖   ❖   ❖

Landing with a soft easy bounce of flexed knees, I grinned at my fiancée.

"See? I'm as fit as anyone could possibly be. I'll climb down and get it and be back before you know."

Elizabeth shook her head vigorously, her voice rising to a pitch of desperation. "NO! It's far too dangerous. The stupid purse does not matter. If you climb down there I shall be furious." She scowled, her black eyebrows almost meeting in her concern and anger. "You really ought to have better sense, James."

Laughing, I peered over the edge of the cliff. There, no more than fifty feet below me, lay Elizabeth's purse, wedged in a small crevice of rock. She and I had been gazing out to sea, watching the gulls as they followed a school of tiny fish. Clutching her purse, Elizabeth had suddenly pointed to a large sea eagle as it plunged like an arrow through the swooping gulls, to dive deeply into the school of fish. With a sharp cry, she had lunged ineffectually to catch the purse as it slipped from her fingers, to bounce over the edge of the cliff. She looked at me in exasperation. "Drat! I've got five pounds in there. Ah well, that's the end of it. I hope Father will not be too angry."

Taking a deep breath, I exhaled slowly. Great Saints! Wherever did she get so much money? I knew she came from a wealthy family, but five pounds in her purse! Five pounds was one hell of a lot of money. I had to work hard for about five months to earn five pounds. There was no way I could depart and leave that much money a mere fifty feet away.

I peered anxiously down the face of the cliff, noting that its ruggedness offered a wealth of hand and foot holds. That was a plus. On the minus side, the cliff face was vertical, dropping away below me for about a hundred feet before it met the golden sand of the beach. Wrenched from the face of the cliff by the powerful fingers of frost and ice, a number of rocks lay scattered where they had fallen onto the sand.

Unbuttoning my thick corduroy jacket, I slipped it off, ignoring the protests of Elizabeth. My breeches were reasonably loose around my hips and buttocks, but quite tight in the leg. Buttoned just below the knee, they would allow me a clear field of vision to see where I placed my feet. My boots were ideal, made of strong but supple leather, and buttoned halfway up my calves, they offered me excellent support. Because it was warm, I also stripped off my thick, rather tight top-shirt, retaining only my warm, more flexible undershirt. I was fit, strong, well prepared, and ready.

Elizabeth was pleading now, genuinely frightened for me.

"Please, James, please my dear, reconsider this folly. The money does not matter. Father will throw a few impolite words around for a few minutes, then forget it." Her eyes went wide as an idea occurred to her. "We can even come back with some men from the estate and a long rope to retrieve it. Oh, James! Admit it, this is the sensible thing to do."

I knew she was right, but when you are twenty-two, and offered a chance to demonstrate your physical ability and prowess, one does not always act with caution, or even consider the wisest way of doing things. Standing side by side on that lonely cliff, the breeze tangy with salt stolen from the vast ocean, I felt a closeness and love for Elizabeth that made me want to prove myself to her; something that I knew she could never understand.

Her family was considerably more wealthy than mine, and although neither her parents nor siblings had ever indicated that this was not to their liking, nevertheless, it irked me. I wanted, nay, needed, to prove myself, and this wayward purse offered a perfect opportunity.

Without any more ado, I was over the side of the cliff, and carefully feeling my way down. To my surprise, it was almost ridiculously easy at first, and I breathed a sigh of relief as holds came easily to hands and feet. Within moments, I was halfway to the purse, and grinning in eager anticipation of Elizabeth's greeting me on my return. She is a lusty girl, with a healthy appetite for sex. Her gratitude would quickly lead us into a very delightful situation on this lonely clifftop.

Progress was smooth and easy for a while longer, when suddenly, it was much more difficult. I was now only about fifteen feet from the purse, but hand and foot holds had become scarce. For the next ten minutes I sweated as I managed to descend another ten feet, but an added problem was the stress on my fingers and feet. I was unused to my fingers taking my whole weight, or just the toes of one foot as I reached to full stretch for the next hand hold.

Only five more feet and I would have it. Elizabeth's voice floated down from above, filled with anxiety and concern for my safety. "Oh, James. Do please take care."

Reaching the purse, I had it in my hand, and was in the process of tucking it into a pocket of my breeches, when the world fell out from under me. The chunk of rock that had held my weight for the past minute, simply fell away, and with a shocked cry, I plummeted the remaining fifty feet to the sand, to fall flat on my back.

Lying slightly stunned in the loose, yielding sand, I could scarcely believe my luck. I was all right. Sure, I had dull pain in my lower spine, but I was alive. From the top of the cliff, directly above, Elizabeth peered down at me, a scream frozen on her pale face.

Struggling, I tried to get to my feet. My arms moved with no problem, and I could twist and wriggle my shoulders without pain, but I was unable to get any movement out of my hips or legs. They were paralyzed!

Lying back in the sand, I groaned. Holy Saints! I was crippled. I tried wriggling my right hand under my back, but it encountered a piece of rock no bigger than my boot. Screwing my eyes tight shut, I was unable to stifle the scream of despair that tore at my throat. "Oh, dear God, no. Please, God, not crippled." Staring up, I saw Elizabeth staring down, her face a pale mask of shock and pity before it abruptly disappeared. I almost went berserk then, thrashing around in the sand as I struggled to sit up, but the dull pain in my spine steadily increased, and with a moan of hopelessness I was compelled to stop.

Never, in my short life, had I felt so helpless. I had always taken my strength and physical ability for granted, now I could not even get to my feet. Badly frightened and despairing, I lay sobbing for perhaps ten minutes, when I heard the soft susurration of countless tumbling grains of sand, a sound that sent a chill of fear rushing through me. The tide was coming in.

Twisting my head, I tried to see how close it was. Oh God! My slight elevation at the back of the beach revealed that the waves were within ten feet of me, and remorseless in their intent. I knew, without needing to look, that the tide came right up to the cliff face, and at high tide it would be several feet deep.

It seemed that my fate was sealed. Without doubt, Elizabeth had gone for help, but, short of a miracle, that help would be hours away. At a guess, I had between thirty and forty-five minutes! I lost all reason then, and in a blind panic I thrashed around in the sand like a beached fish, getting nowhere, until finally, sanity returned. On my back, I knew that I had no chance. If I were to move any distance in the soft sand, I had to somehow roll over. I had no idea that such a normally simple maneuver could be so difficult. For the next several minutes I tried in vain to force my body over, twisting my shoulders this way and that, but to no avail. It felt as though an unrelenting weight lay on my lower body, pinning me uncaringly to the sand.

The waves were getting nearer, and I no longer needed to listen to them to gauge their closeness. Gradually and surely, their swishing rush up the beach brought them ever closer, while the sand was now becoming wet all around me. I had to do something. As I lay there, I noticed that a large rock was quite close to my right hand, and the idea of leverage came to me. Wriggling with a controlled intensity, I was able to get several inches closer and, after another burst of effort, I secured a good hold on a section of the rock. Finally, with the rock as an anchor and using all the strength of my arm, I managed to pull and strain until my body was now turned over.

I wanted to rest my tortured body, for pain was now dancing in spasms along my spine, but I had no time. The first tiny forerunners of the waves were reaching me, gently licking at me, carrying an awful threat.

Forcing both arms under my chest, I began a painful crawl on my forearms to the cliff. I had already made an assessment of the vertical rockface where it joined the beach, and one shelving rock offered some modicum of hope.

Apart from a dull ache accompanied by spasms of pain in my spine, I was able to crawl with no damage to my arms as I valiantly raced the waves to the cliff. We arrived together, and the water actually assisted by initially lifting me onto the sloping rock. I could only pray that the highest part of the rock would remain above the high tide mark.

With grim perseverance, I inched my way up the rock, a trail of blood marking my progress. Barnacles were thickly clustered all over the lower rocks of the cliff's face, and as I dragged myself over them, they cut into my flesh as easily as a razor. On and on I dragged myself, until, on reaching the highest part of the rock, the pain and torment finally overwhelmed me, and with a heavy sigh, I fainted.

Considerably later, I learned that Elizabeth, her father, and a number of his men had had to wait for the tide to go out, before searching for my body. That I had drowned they had no doubt, for Elizabeth had waited long enough to ascertain that I was crippled by the fall before rushing for help. They had been both amazed and delighted to find me wet, bedraggled, unconscious, but alive, high on the only sloping rock. I had been carried to their nearby horse and cart, and on Elizabeth's insistence, taken to her home.

There, I had been stripped, washed, and their doctor had attended me. Both of my forearms had been badly shredded and were now bandaged, along with my stomach, thighs, and legs, all cut by the indifferent barnacles. To me, however, this was a trifling matter, for I had also been told that it was unlikely I would ever be able to walk again. The real irony of my situation was something I overheard, for it was not intended that I ever know.

Initially, although my back had been severely damaged, there had been an outside chance that it may, in time, have healed. By crawling away from the waves to save my life, I had inadvertently made the damage to my back irreparable. Truly, I was "damned if I did, and damned if I didn't."

The next year was terrible. I was taken back to my family home, where my older sister, Anne, devoted practically all her time and attention to me. Despite months of increasingly frantic efforts to move my lower limbs, it proved impossible, and I deteriorated into a deep melancholy that threatened to consume me. My beloved Elizabeth left me, driven away by my despair and rejection, for I knew that I could never be a husband to her. How ironic, that it was she who so clearly revealed this to me. She had been on one of her many visits, trying to get me out of my gloom by talking and sharing the events in her life. I was in a wheelchair, and she had pushed me out into the gardens, where we were sheltered and private.

To my delight, she kissed my lips and face with a high passion, her mouth creeping over my chest and down to my stomach as she opened up my robe. When I felt her hand take hold of me, I almost gasped for breath. Taking my poor shriveled thing in her hands, she had tried to make it stand erect and proud, kissing it, even running her tongue around it and nipping it with her teeth, but although I nearly swooned with desire, my thing remained flaccid and impotent. The injury that had paralyzed my legs had also robbed me of ever again being a man.

Humiliated and mortified beyond endurance, I had pushed her away, swearing that I never wanted to see her again. Maybe it was a noble act, for with her passionate nature, we clearly had no future, but my rage, despair, and rejection were no act at all.

From that day forth, it was downhill all the way. Most of the time I lay in my bed, being fed and cleaned by Anne. As my loathing for myself grew, I tried to make Anne hate me, but she ignored all my insults, my tantrums, my ranting and raving, my outbursts of temper, continuing to care for me. By now, even my parents avoided coming to see me, for I took my rage out on anyone who could walk.

Week after week, I lay in bed growing ever weaker and more pale as I cursed one day into the next. A thousand, nay, a million times I went over the details of that fateful day, cursing myself for a fool, an idiot, a maniac. Day in and day out, I dwelt on my broken spine, hating it with a loathing that left me gasping for breath. A thousand times a day I cursed myself that I had escaped the waves, that I had avoided being drowned. Hour after hour, day after day, and on into weeks and long, dreary, hating, months, my focus of pity and hatred ate its way into me, until my loathing of myself was absolute. I truly despised myself, reaching the point when I knew that I was lost. I no longer wanted to live.

Many times I had begged Anne to bring me my dagger, but she refused. For weeks and months I argued with her to no avail, until, defeated, I let the matter drop. Then, exactly one day less than a year since I had had my accident, I had an idea. Without any cursing, I politely asked Anne if she would let me have the pony and trap so I could go out for a ride on the morrow.

She was delighted. As far as she was concerned, this was a breakthrough. I even asked to be nicely dressed for the occasion. Anne happily arranged for a man from the village to assist me into the trap, and all was prepared. Next day, she had me dressed and ready by the time the man arrived. As strong as an ox, he scooped me up and carrying me out, gently placed me in the driver's seat of the trap.

Hovering alongside, Anne chatted happily. "Oh, Jamie, I only pray that you have turned the corner, for you can still live a good life, you know. This ride will be so good for you. Please, Jamie, let me accompany you."

We had been through all that on the previous day, and she had only relented when I insisted that if I were not alone, then I would not go out at all. Shaking the reins, I clicked my tongue at the pony, and away we went.

I took it slowly, just trotting the pony as we went down the lane, up and over the small hill and, skirting around the village, headed to the cliffs some six miles away, where I had had my accident. It was exactly one year to the day.

It was so pleasant in the trap that for a while my resolve wavered. The sun was shining, and life abounded. A covey of partridges flew in a noisy burst of wings from the hedgerow alongside us, while skylarks sang from above as they hovered over their mates on the high sweet songs of love. I reflected on the kindness of Anne, of her unfailing attention to me, with never a single complaint at my shabby treatment of her. I hoped she would not be too hurt by my actions of this day. I had written a short note to her, of apology and sincere thanks, that I would leave in the trap. Somehow, I was sure that, deep within her, she would eventually accept it as inevitable, and even understand.

Without hurrying, it took the pony and me about one and a half hours to reach the cliffs; leaving the dirt road, we slowly picked our way across the meadow to the very place where Elizabeth and I had stood just one year ago. For a long while we stood quietly, the pony stamping occasionally, or vigorously twitching an ear, while I stared unseeing, lost in my reverie. For the first time in the long and dreadful year since I had fallen to my doom, I was calm, even though I was eaten up with bitterness and resentment. In this, my final act, I would not fail.

With great care and difficulty, I slowly backed the well-trained pony, ever backward, until the rear of the trap hung over the edge of the cliff. The wheels were still on firm ground when I called out "Whoa" in a loud, firm voice, and the obedient pony stood her ground.

Using my arms as crutches, I dragged myself to the rear of the cart, ignoring the pain flaring up my spine. The tide was on its way in, lapping the final strip of beach along the base of the cliff. Below me lay several large fallen rocks. Just what I had hoped for. With just a tad of luck, the tide would take my body away with it, hiding my shame forever.

Balanced precariously on the very rear end of the trap as it hung over the cliff, I called out in a loud, determined voice. "Gidup." With a nervous jump, the pony jerked strongly forward, pitching me headfirst over the cliff onto the waiting rocks.

I was aware of a long moment's falling, a soft soundless thud, then once again, I was falling . . . falling. . . .

❖   ❖   ❖

I lay where I had fallen for several despairing moments before staggering to my feet. I was standing in a tiny stone room, almost choking in the acrid stink of fresh vomit. Around me, the walls were damp, coated in a thick layer of slime and mildew, while rotting human excrement lay scattered in small piles of putrid stench.

Wiping my mouth with the back of my hand, I realized with horror that the vomit was my own, and that the "room" was a tiny cell. I was a prisoner! My clothes were filthy, a shapeless array of hessian draped and sown to roughly fit my emaciated body. I ached. I hurt. I was dizzy and ill. But way, way, beyond that, I was terrified.

"Torture!" That single word hummed and throbbed through my mind, shouting and screaming its obscene message until I crouched whimpering on the filthy floor. In the near dark, huge cockroaches openly crawled from one pile of shit to another, unafraid of their degraded human benefactors.

I cringed anew as a piercing shriek rose on the wings of a terrible inflicted pain, reaching an impossible high before it cut off with ominous abruptness. The low sobbing moan that slowly replaced it carried its own message of utter and complete hopelessness; a hopelessness that peered into the ultimate depths of despair and misery, knowing that only a slow, cruel, deliberately drawn-out death awaited.

Too weak and ill to stand, I slumped to the cold stone floor, sitting in a drawn-up fetal position, while inside, I slowly died. I knew that death would be delayed long enough for me to go to the rack; just that thought carried a chill of the utmost dread. Slowly, in a numb daze, my thoughts moved into the recent past. Had I been alone, starving, I would never have attempted to steal the rich man's purse; but my mother's plight was more than I could bear. A brief anger seized me. The rich in their posh London homes had no idea of the poverty in the hovels. Their lack of concern went far beyond indifference; it met and merged with arrogant cruelty, displaying a pious inhumanity that surely bordered on a contempt for God. I had managed to get the purse, all right, but had been too weak and incapable to escape the whistle-blowing Peelers who had chased me. The big mistake I made was in snatching the purse of a clergyman. I swear that they were glad I had got rid of the purse, for it enabled them to question me, and there was no doubt that they enjoyed it. Mercifully, I fell into a disturbed slumber, not really sleeping—I had not truly slept in years—but no longer conscious or aware of the atrocious horror that awaited me.

Even the scraping, crashing thud of the cell door being abruptly thrown open was part of their brutalizing treatment, and I awoke with sudden rush of dread.

"Ye're next, offal."

Somehow, somewhere, in the deepest recess of my psyche, I found my last scrapings of courage, and instead of the two debased guards grabbing me and tossing me bodily out of the cell, as was their wont, I stumbled painfully ahead of them.

Each footstep was a torment as I made my way from the dark gloom of the underground cells, up to the ground-floor level where the torture took place. The guards had a mock name for it, "The Confessional," for ironic as it seems, the persecution took place in the name of God.

The hard, uncaring brutality in the eyes of the priest as he questioned me told me that my fate was already sealed, only awaiting its announcement and delivery.

In stark contrast to the cruel truth in his eyes, his voice was a soft, melodious caress.

"Did you steal the purse, my son?"

"I took it so I could feed my sick mother."

"That is a confession, my son."

"No. Considering that I knew what my punishment would be if I got caught, I'm describing an act of love."

He was unruffled. "It is our love for you, in the name of God, that will reach out to teach you better ways. We, of the Church, will care for the soul of your mother."

"Maybe, but you don't give a damn for her body."

"We care for all of God's flock."

"In a pig's eye!"

"Believe me, my son, you will soon learn the error of your ways."

Clinging to the fading shreds of my courage, I had had enough of this farcical exchange. With a large, carefully nurtured gob of phlegm, I spat straight into his face.

His voice a hiss of pure venom, the priest uttered a single word. "Rack."

Stripped to a cringing nakedness, I was hauled into a large room filled with the instruments of torture. In an ever-increasing daze, I lost all awareness of what or who was around me as I was quickly and efficiently strapped onto the rack. Almost immediately, I could feel my limbs being stretched to the limit, while pain danced in every joint of my body. But as bad as that was, it was overwhelmed by the rippling pain in my spine. A flowing river of agony, my spine was slowly breaking apart. I felt my bowels burst, hot stinking fluids gushing out of every orifice of my body, while I choked on screams, curses, and vomit.

Suddenly, within all the pain, it seemed that there was a hush, a pause, and the priest was looking down at me, his voice smooth and silken once more.

"Do you now see the error of your ways, my son?"

My last reserves of defiance and contempt rose to the surface, and I stared into his eyes. "I see only a fart stuck in the arse of God," I gasped loudly.

He recoiled, his voice rising to a scream as he spun around. Grabbing at a knife, he slashed the blade down onto my eyes, and in a burst of white-hot fire, my left eye split wide open. My face a mask of blood, I dimly heard his triumphant hiss. "Then I shall cast out your eyes that you may see anew."

The next moment every joint in my body was stretching far beyond limits, s-t-r-e-t-c-h-i-n-g, until, in a last flare of unendurable agony, my spine snapped. Shocked, I was hurtled out into space, spinning over and over, free to curl into a fetal position as I fell through space, sobbing in fear and bewilderment as both my pain and physical reality ebbed away.

And I fell.

An eternity . . . falling . . . slowing . . .

❖   ❖   ❖

When, moments later, my feet touched land, I was standing in the garden of a large manor house.

"THOMAS." The nearby voice was a deep bellow, and I gaped in confusion at the man who came striding toward me. Thickset and muscular, he looked as though he could juggle stone-bricks indefinitely, his arms bulging with corded muscle.

"Thomas! Don't ye stand there gaping, son, come along wi' me."

The authority and order was unmistakable, but where the hell was Thomas? Why look at me?

His hand fastened on my arm with the grip of a blunt-toothed bulldog, and completely indifferent to anything I might want, he tugged me in the direction of a copse of trees some few hundred yards away.

"I have ye're gun with me, and I'll want to see ye use it afore I'm satisfied. And it's no use ye arguing wi' me. When the pheasant are flushed, I expect to see ye bag a brace in the manner I taught ye."

Aghast, I stared at him, my feet skidding along the turf as he bodily hauled me along. "Wha . . . What . . . er . . . who?"

"Don't ye babble, Thomas. Ye Gods, man, I have trouble enough accepting that it was me tha' sired ye. Ye're just like ye're mother, soft and stupid. Don't ye see, son, I have to do this for ye, if ye are to ere be a man."

Man! What the hell did he think I was? Christ! What was this? Where the hell am I? WHAT IS GOING ON? Is this muscle-bound cretin my father?

My thoughts were rudely interrupted as, reaching the copse of trees, the brute swung me around to face him. "Now, Thomas, don't ye disappoint me, or ye know what'll happen."

And suddenly, I did know. I knew that he and I would put on a pair of boxing gloves, and that under the rules laid down by the Marquis of Queensbury for the noble art of boxing, he would once again have the perfect excuse to beat me senseless, while feeling completely vindicated. In that moment of clarity, I knew also that my mother had died many years ago, traumatized and brutalized by this stern, unyielding man as he tried to cast those around him into his own implacable mold.

As he so aptly said, I was my mother's son: frail and sensitive, a poet and dreamer. And I knew, with a dreadful certainty, that I would not survive this encounter.

The gun he thrust into my hands was huge, the barrel long, heavy, and overbalanced, the stock thick and chunky. Wet with sweat, my hands had difficulty handling the gun—it, too, being slick with a smear of thin oil.

"Father, please don't make me do this."

His eyes were bright with contempt, and, I swear, hatred. "Ye miserable little sod. Ye will shoot a fine brace, or face me wi' the gloves." He shook his head grimly, anger a heavy cloud around him. "Seven sons, I have, all like me. Seven of which I am proud. But ye! 'Tis certain, I am, tha' I never sired ye! And, by God, ye will suffer for tha' insult ye carry to flay me wi'."

My own anger had risen, and I glared back at him with a hatred of my own. "If there be one thing I pray to God for," I hissed, "it is tha' you are not my father. Tha' is a shame tha' would haunt me to the grave."

He hit me then, an openhanded clout across my face that swept me off my feet. I fell back, my arms flailing wildly, almost deafened by the blast of the flintlock as my finger inadvertently clutched at the trigger.

In slow motion, I watched his shock as the charge of heavy shot blew away his leg just above the right knee. I watched as he lay on the bloodsplattered dirt and grass, and, with careful deliberation, seized his own gun that leaned within easy reach against a tree. With the same careful deliberation, he aimed the gun at my body, his face a strange and terrible mixture of revulsion, hate, and pain.

Desperately rolling over in an attempt to get away from him, I did not hear the gun detonate. Instead, a vast weight crashed into my spine, knocking me spinning into a spiral of eternal darkness . . . falling . . . falling . . . into oblivion.

# Eight

When I opened my eyes again, I was in my familiar private hospital room, lying flat on my back in bed. I knew also that I was Adam. A glance at the clock revealed that it was now late evening; around nine hours had passed. I lay in disturbed astonishment, my memory clear as I browsed back over the incredible experiences I had undergone during that time of nonphysical reality.

In the name of God, what did it all mean? A hundred questions clamored for attention, but at that moment the door swung open and Doctor Pete strolled in.

"How are you feeling?"

It was a good question. How was I feeling? My lower back throbbed with a deep-seated pain, but it was a long way from the agony of the experiences I had just encountered. Apart from that, I felt very shaken up, but passable.

"I've definitely felt better," I replied.

"I don't doubt it. Are you in much pain?"

"Nothing I can't handle."

"We X-rayed you after your fall, but nothing was refractured or dislocated. Kerrr-hrist! How did you manage it? Nobody, but nobody, has ever managed to fall over the safety frame before. I wasn't there at the time, but they reckon you not only went right over the top of it, but you cleared about three meters before you landed. Just what in the hell are you trying to do? Don't you want to get better? My God! You are nothing but bloody awkwardness and trouble."

"Feeling better?" I asked mildly.

Pete grinned sheepishly. "Yeah, well . . . I guess I've had my say for the time being."

"I never dreamed that learning to walk after being smashed up could be so difficult. I'll get the hang of it, eventually. But I would like a day or so to recover."

"You're scheduled for another session of X-rays in three days, to make absolutely certain nothing escaped our detection. When you get the all clear, it's back to the fitness center."

"Back to the torture chamber, you mean," I grinned. But even as I spoke the words, memory of a true torture chamber flashed strongly to mind. I shuddered.

"Oh, come on. It's not that bad."

"No. You're right," I said. "It isn't. You can't even begin to imagine just how bad real torture is."

My whole attitude to the fitness center had just this moment undergone a dramatic change. Although I had thought that I was keen for the rehabilitation of my body to take place, somewhere, deep in my subconscious, I had strongly resisted the whole process. Why? Was it anything to do with the shocking experiences I had just revisited? That they were real, I had no doubt. In my past lay a trail of pain and horror, and I had the uncomfortable feeling that I had not yet fully plumbed the depths of it. However, despite the past, I still had to resolve the present trauma and work willingly with the people who were struggling to put me together. What irony! While unconscious, I had briefly relived some of my past, where certain people were trying their damnedest to take me apart. Memories of James flashed into my mind, and I knew that I also had been, and maybe still was, one of those people bound to my own destruction. I had to change that. I now knew that this fitness center was a place of hope, of people who truly care, of rehabilitation, of new opportunities to rebuild my future. Suddenly, I just couldn't wait to start again.

Pete had been watching me as the thoughts and images flashed through my mind, and he had noticed the change in my demeanor as the resolution for new beginnings had been made.

"You think too much," he said gruffly.

I met his dark eyes with mine. He was so big, almost menacing in his hugeness, yet his eyes were alight with compassion. I realized again just how lucky I was to have this man caring for me. "Pete, we know so little about life, it's a miracle we manage from day to day. I've just learned that our past is with us always, like a shadow we can't see, yet it's superimposed over our lives and affects our every moment. And nobody seems to know. How is this possible? Why is life a vast, unfathomable mystery? Are we meant to solve the mystery, or flounder through it for a lifetime, forever locked into ever-increasing despair?"

"Bloody hell! Don't get morbid on me, Adam."

Chuckling quietly, I smiled at him. "I'm not getting morbid, truly. I'm just beginning to see that life is not the consensus reality that we so readily accept. Daily I'm learning that reality is multidimensional and timeless, and that to live fully, we have to take this greater reality into our everyday lives."

"How do we do that?"

"I don't know, Pete, but I suspect that for every single person there is a different answer."

"Okay, how will you do it?"

I gave that some thought. How indeed? I had no format of success. But, I did have Selph. "I think that step one for me is to be much more open to life. To be more open in each moment."

"Open how?"

"More open to people asking me damn fool questions when I've got no answers to give. I don't know how! I just know that if I am more open . . . there will be more happening."

"Don't you think that you've had enough happening?"

I groaned in exasperation. "Are you being deliberately provocative, or what? The more open I become, the more there will be to be open to."

Pete looked pensive. "Like, the more you see, the more there is to see. Hmmm."

"Yes, something like that. But it's all held in the moment. I don't understand how, but I know that the moment is the key to everything. The moment transcends time, that I know, but I don't understand it."

"Great! That explains a lot."

For a moment I was tempted to tell him about the extraordinary experiences I had just been through, but I knew that it was not appropriate to do so. If this conversation was proving anything, it was that I needed to know what I was talking about before I started talking!

I gave Pete a weak smile. "It's not easy to explain things that insist on remaining inexplicable. I can't even explain it to myself."

Pete's smile was oblique. "I *was* being provocative, and you've told me a lot more than you probably realize. I did get an education, you know, before I became a doctor." He paused for a while, his eyes losing focus as he scratched into his memory. I could see the moment in his face when he found what he was looking for. "Ah yes, one last question. Early in this conversation you said, and I quote, 'You can't begin to imagine how bad real torture is.' What provoked that odd statement?"

Glancing up at the ceiling, I sighed. "That's part of the inexplicable. One day perhaps."

Pete's mouth opened and closed, his words unspoken, and I could see regret in his eyes before his massive shoulders shrugged in dismissal. He surged to his feet, the steel chair squeaking as his weight left it, and powered toward the door. "Ah well, can't sit chewing the cud with you all day, there's work to be done and people to mend. Bye."

The next three days were rather pleasant, because Amber, alarmed by my fall, had decided to sit with me. I think that she may have been talking to Doctor Pete, because at first she tried to probe me for my memories of what might have happened while I was "out" after my fall, but I refused to be drawn on the subject. The memories of the horror were like a raw wound that could not yet bear probing. She knew me well enough to know that I was hiding something, but accepted my explanation that I would tell her when the timing was right.

As she kissed me, her soft lips both giving and demanding, one thing became quickly apparent, I was getting better. I felt as randy as hell.

"God, what a waste," I murmured in her ear. "I've got a king-sized erection for the first time since the smash, and I can't do a thing about it."

I felt faintly shocked as her hand crept under the bedclothes, down across my belly, and firmly took hold of me.

"Let me take Sir Knight in hand," she whispered huskily. "There may be nothing you can do about it, but I can."

And she did!

❖  ❖  ❖

Only a couple more X-rays were taken, both of my spine. Luckily, despite the intense pain during my flip and fall, I had come out of it undamaged. The brace had undoubtedly saved me. Once again I was scheduled to begin working out in the fitness center.

Amber was with me as I guided my battery-propelled wheelchair through the maze of corridors to the center. As we went through the open double doors, I looked around in surprise. Was this the same place? Obviously it was, but I was coming from such an improved attitude, such a changed perspective, that I scarcely recognized it. Whereas before I had quickly related to all the apparatus as devices of pain, I was now very clear that the equipment was for the regeneration of my body. No, it was not the fitness center that had changed, it was me.

I looked at Amber, and smiled. Mind you, it is easy to smile at Amber. She was wearing a mid-green dress that not only showed off her long tanned legs, but it also suited her. Some clothes are designed to flatter the female body, but no matter how well they fit, or even tease, they never rise above a contrived art. In every way possible, Amber and the dress were made for each other. She has a highly developed sense of dress and style, and uses it. In that green dress her natural elegance was enhanced and, oh so tastefully, flaunted.

She could see the hunger in my eyes as I looked at her.

"Adam! Down boy! Keep your mind and your energy for more important things," she teased.

"*More* important?"

She gave me a mock frown. "Well, they are today."

The arrival of Mandy cut off the banter between us.

"Hi, Adam. Hello, Amber." She smiled at me. "Welcome back. I only hope you're not going to repeat your last performance. That was quite something."

"Mandy, you won't even know that I'm the same person."

She had the same impersonal attitude as before, but this time I had a memory of her cradling my head in her lap, crying over me as I lay unconscious. I now realized just how much she cared about the people she worked with—it was part of the job—but she could not afford to get emotionally involved with her patients. She would be wiped out. Her impersonal approach was her emotional defense.

"Okay. Here's what we are going to do. We are going to put you through another series of tests for stamina, strength, and flexibility; you know the drill. Then we'll take it from there."

I had the impression that there was some conspiracy between Amber and Mandy, but I was nevertheless surprised when, during my tests, I saw Amber in pale-blue gym gear. While I was doing my best in one device after another, Amber was working up a sweat on a large complicated rowing machine.

Then something odd happened. As I lay back, face up, on a padded board, and my ankles were being strapped down, I had a brief and shocking flashback to the rack in the torture chamber. Instantly, every muscle in my body went into a spontaneous convulsion, and I cried out in shocked pain.

"Oh shit! What's wrong?" Mandy stared at me, her eyes wide with alarm.

Soaked in sweat, I fought my shuddering way back from the image of the past to the present reality.

"Shit! I wish you wouldn't do things like that. You scared hell out of me. What happened?"

By the time I had myself under control, Amber was at my side, and I knew that I had to offer some explanation. I decided it was time for some of the truth.

While Amber wiped the sweat off my face and limbs with a damp sponge, I gave them a scaled-down version of my visit to the torture chamber of my past, and how it was somehow all interwoven with what was happening to me now. I explained that, although there was much I did not understand, one thing was certain: traumatic pain was the connection between the events in time.

Mandy looked at me in utter confusion. "But, but are you saying that all this took place in a past life?"

"Yes."

"But . . . reincarnation is a myth, a joke. We couldn't possibly live one life after another. That's rubbish. When we die we go to heaven. Everyone knows that."

"Some people believe that, Mandy," Amber said quietly, "but I'm not one of them. I definitely believe that I have lived in other lives. And I would have to say that there is a vast amount of evidence to support this belief."

Clearly shocked, Mandy could only gasp. "But that's utter rubbish. The whole church, my religion, it all denies this. The Pope couldn't possibly be wrong."

"What about all the religions that teach reincarnation as a spiritual truth?" Amber asked softly.

"They are wrong. Undeniably and absolutely wrong," Mandy said vehemently.

Happily, the conversation had rapidly brought me back to my present reality, and it was obvious that Mandy was extremely threatened by any reference to past lives. Hmmm, interesting, I thought; I wonder what's locked up in her psyche. "Mandy," I said, "I'm simply telling you what happened. You can interpret it in any way you like, but I am the one who has to deal with it. Now that I'm prepared for this to happen—if it ever does again—maybe I won't react in the same shocked manner. So, strap me onto the board and let's continue with the tests."

With Amber standing anxiously close by, the tests were resumed. I lay on the board, my ankles were strapped down, and all went well. There was no recurrence of the flashback. Finally, after three hours, and just as I was about pooped, the tests were finished. I was pleased to learn that my performance was better than expected.

Accompanied by Amber, we returned to my room, but much as I wanted to spend time with her, I drifted into an exhausted slumber while a nurse was sponging me down. I have no recollection of the remainder of that day.

Daily now, I spent hours in the fitness center, and I gave it my all. However, there is only so much you can do if strapped and braced, even when it is a lightweight polycarbonate material. I saw Amber quite regularly, but I was encouraging her to get into the series of paintings that she so wanted to do, and that consumed much of her time. All in all, we had a lot to share with each other. She waxed enthusiastic about her art, while I raved on about the improvement in my physical rehabilitation. There came a day that was not so good. Perhaps an old pattern from the past superimposed itself over me, or maybe I was feeling negative, but I had a day of difficulty and pain. There were no more flashbacks in the gym, nothing like that, but it was a day where I had to struggle and strain my way through the exercises. By the end of the day, I was not only physically exhausted, but also psychically depleted.

Maybe that was the trigger for Selph to reappear.

Doctor Pete stood in the doorway to my private room looking vaguely puzzled. He had the look of a man who is doing something that he really did not intend to do.

"Er, Adam. I don't know what to make of this, but, er, there's a young man to see you. He says he's a personal friend, name of Seth. He wants to see you."

"That's okay, wheel him in."

"But . . . you're exhausted. You need rest."

"Thanks Pete, but I'd like to see Selph."

Frowning, as though I had said the wrong thing, Pete beckoned Selph into my room. "Er, don't be too long, you hear. Not too long."

As Pete hesitatingly walked away, Selph strolled in giggling, his round cherubic face a study in innocence. "He's a nice guy, Adam, a really good man."

"Yeah, he is," I said laconically, "so what did you do to him? It's rare to see Pete looking confused."

"Why, Adam! What would I do to a nice doctor?"

"Yeah, what indeed? There is no way he would have let you in here if you had not put a whammy on him. He looks after me like a mother hen."

"I simply asked if I could visit you, and he refused. He said you were exhausted and needed rest. So I told him that was exactly why I was here. He glared at me, and point-blank refused again."

"And then what?"

"Well, I gave him a big smile, and asked him if he would change his mind."

"And?"

"He did."

"Just like that?"

"Yep! Just like that. It truly is amazing what a nice smile can accomplish."

I chuckled at the images Selph offered. "He will be okay, won't he? He is far too good a man to tamper with."

Selph managed to look both innocent and offended at the same time. He looked like a typical fifteen-year-old caught in a fib. "Believe me, your doctor is unimpaired."

"But you did do something, didn't you?" I pursued.

Giving an exasperated and exaggerated sigh, Selph held up his hands in mock surrender. "Okay, I confess. I did smudge his intent just a shade, so that he lost focus on just what he did and did not want me to do. A perfectly simple process that, happily, very few people can do."

I watched him carefully. "Have you, or would you, do that to me?"

He looked at me seriously, the playful boy gone. "No. I have not, nor would I do that to you. I am your teacher, and to do that to you would entirely defeat both your purpose and mine. Each decision you make is your own."

"Could you teach me how to do it?" I grinned.

He did not respond to my humor. "We have more important things to discuss," he said seriously, "and your good doctor is going to realize his real intent before too long. Not unexpectedly, he's going to be annoyed."

"Ah well, you can always vanish."

"Oh yes, and how will you explain that to him?"

I grinned in triumph. "It's your problem, not mine."

Sitting carefully on my bed, his direct and startling eyes met mine. For long moments he looked into me, reading me, and I was unable to glance away. He looked thoughtful.

"You appear to have had some interesting revelations. How do you feel about your experiences?"

"I'm still shocked . . . both by the process and by what it all revealed to me about myself."

"Such as?"

"As you once suggested, I seem to be addicted to pain and suffering, plus I seem to have a back injury fixation."

"Very well put. You definitely show all the symptoms of a serious case of RTS."

"RTS! What the hell is that?"

"What the hell indeed. It has all the makings of a living hell. You have, no doubt, heard of RIS, otherwise known as repetitive injury syndrome?"

I nodded.

"Well you have given this a refreshingly new twist, and made it into RTS. Repetitive trauma syndrome."

"How did I do that?" I asked in bewilderment.

"Before I answer that, give me a brief summary of what happened in your experiences."

I gave him a fairly detailed account about each unhappy incident. "Why is this happening?" I asked him, "and what perpetuates it?"

"It's all rather obvious, really. In every incident, you injure your back and experience intense pain. This is no accident. Remember what I told you about accidents? An accident is the outworking of purpose. Somewhere in your murky past, you have badly injured your back and lived on. Unless I am very much mistaken—and I never am—you spent the rest of that life hating and loathing yourself. You invested most of your time in self-pity, and in this way, you became traumatized. Now, get this! It was *you* who created the trauma, not the injury. The injury was only the catalyst. You reacted negatively, whereas you could have responded positively. So, if you can accept that you are responsible, then you will see that it is you who has to end the whole traumatic and repetitive chain of events."

"How do I do that?" I asked glumly.

"The first step is to uncover the root cause. You most probably need to get in touch with what happened in that very first incident."

I squirmed uncomfortably. "Isn't there any other way?"

Selph looked thoughtful. "Yes, sure. Just 'fall in love with who you are' and it's finished. The past is healed."

I gazed at him blankly. "How do I do that?"

"There is no 'how,' Adam, it's a leap in consciousness. There are no techniques to true Love. It's all about total—and I mean, total—self-acceptance. Do this, and you will not need to reexperience your original trauma."

"I can't," I said gloomily.

"That's a nice positive statement. But I agree, even though I disagree. It is possible, but it's also unlikely. I don't doubt you are going to do this the hard way; it's a most unfortunate human habit."

"That's the problem. *I'm* an unfortunate human habit."

"Oh dear, back into self-pity?"

"Not really," I said with a wan smile. "I'm tired."

"Okay, Adam, I'll let you sleep. But in your dreams, remember this: anything of the past that is unresolved is unresolved now. And it is in the *now* that resolution can be reached. I'll see you later."

"Wait! Was there anything in particular you wanted to see me about?"

"No. It's mostly been said. I'll keep in touch. You realize, of course, that eventually I will get to meet your family. How will you explain me?"

I grinned sleepily. "Can't you smudge 'em all?"

"No, but I can smudge you." So saying, he reached one hand slowly toward my eyes and as I watched it approach, the lights gradually faded out

❖    ❖    ❖

The next month passed in a blur of activity. Except for the spinal brace, all the other supports were removed from my body and limbs, and it felt wonderful. I was a bit hesitant at first, inwardly cringing at expected pain, but remembering what Selph had said about pain being a learned reaction, I focused my mind on sparkling rivers and spheres of light. The hip replacement felt vaguely odd, but the more I used it and exercised it, the more flexible it became. Or, to be accurate, my muscles became stronger and more flexible!

I had expected more exercises dealing in strength, but the program was definitely focused in stretching muscles. I learned that damaged muscles invariably shrink and retract, leading to all the attendant problems associated with that. Age alone can do it, but a beaten-up body certainly speeds things along. To my great delight, I could now walk, albeit with the aid of a stick. Thanks to weeks of effort on the bars, I had progressed from armpit crutches to elbow-type crutches, and now I was using only a single stick to assist with the plastic hip. I did not see a lot of Jim, but Mandy was clearly delighted by my progress. Once Amber was convinced that I no longer intended to do somersaults over the safety frame, she got back into her painting, so I saw less of her in the fitness center. Without question, I was definitely getting fitter.

There were other, unexpected, compensations.

One evening, when Amber came to visit, she closed the door behind her and, producing a key, she locked it.

"Why have you locked it?" I asked in bewilderment.

"So that we can be undisturbed, my darling."

"But . . . but what if Pete comes to see us?"

"He won't."

I was completely perplexed. "How do you know that?"

Looking at me as though I were some wayward and delinquent child, she slowly peeled off her sweater and casually dropped her skirt. I gaped at her. Just as casually, she deftly unhooked her bra, her full breasts almost springing free. Even if my mind was slow in catching on, my body had no doubts about what it all meant. Within seconds of gazing at Amber's breasts, I had a full and quivering erection. I gulped as she slowly teased her briefs down over her hips, sliding them in a silken sigh to the floor.

Walking to my bedside, she took hold of the few bedclothes and, in one surge, threw them onto the floor. Wearing only a pajama top, my readiness was apparent!

"Oh," she breathed huskily, "Sir Knight is primed, and ready for a tournament."

Reaching out, she undid my pajama buttons, then gently following a thin scar-line, she ran her hands around my brow, slowly down onto my jaw, down my neck and over my shoulders. Feather-light, her fingers softly caressing, she traced the scars over my shoulders and across my ribs, then onto the heavy scarring on my chest. Her hands continued very slowly down across my belly, following some of the scars from my abdominal surgery, finally reaching and gliding around Sir Knight, who by now was frantically bobbing up and down, screaming 'Here here,' and on down my thighs to my calves and feet. Her fingers had actually reached all the way to my thighs before I realized that I was holding my breath. I released it shakily.

In one easy, supple move, she was onto the bed and astride my body, with all the interesting parts very, very close to where they should be.

I reached my head forward just as her nipples came toward my face, and gently, I rolled my tongue around them.

Amber groaned softly, and with a mild shock, I realized that she was as hungry for me as I was for her.

Her voice was husky, low, and musical. "Adam. It's important that you lay flat on your back and let me do all the work. Your hip and back are still vulnerable, and I'll be more careful than you."

Nibbling on a nipple, I whispered, "Who says so?"

"Your good doctor and I decided it together."

To say that I was shocked was putting it mildly. I was so startled that I let go of her nipple. "What! You and Pete arranged this . . . and how we should do it! My God, that's downright . . . indecent."

As a smiling, mocking, and fully aroused Amber sat up with a wriggle, that most moist and accommodating part of her lower anatomy somehow drew the most vigorous and thrusting part of my lower anatomy fully into her.

"Oh . . . Adam. You mean we shouldn't do this?"

The waves of pleasure engulfing me denied any reply. Pulling her closer, I thrust deeper, yet I was careful to stimulate her own pleasure zone. I had long ago learned that plunging in and out with mindless energy might well have the desired effect for a man, yet leave a woman unsatisfied and frustrated. Making love is an art, and the canvas needs time spent on it.

Soon, close to the bursting point, I whispered for Amber to slow down as she moved up and down on me. It was not long, however, before the delicious groan and shudder that came from her told me that it was time for an energetic finale. She tantalized me for a moment, then I too felt the incandescent wave of shuddering release sweep up through my body, and I moaned my pleasure into her hair.

"My God! I had no idea how much I needed that," I whispered."Making love to you is a tonic."

"It's the same for me, Adam. I love you so much."

We lay entwined for a long time, her luscious body moving and breathing against mine, and gradually I became aroused again. "How about another longer, slower session of physical therapy?" I asked.

She said nothing, but her reply came in action as she gently moved up and down on me. We lay close, moving little, touching and feeling each other as we reacquainted ourselves with each other's body. Her lips were on mine, her tongue in my mouth, when the slow groan of her orgasm came. I smiled. I always do. I can't help smiling when she has an orgasm. It makes me so happy. Suddenly, Amber was sitting upright on me, moving up and down on me with ever-increasing speed, and for a while I lay lost in the sheer physical delight and pleasure of it. Suddenly, once again I felt the sharp and sudden thrust of my own release.

For long, soaring, ecstatic moments, we lay together, wrapped in each other's arms, murmuring our love.

"Ooohhhh, wow! I'm better. You've just healed me."

"There's no doubt, I'm quite a doctor, aren't I?"

"My darling, you can heal me anytime you like. By the way, did you and Pete really discuss this, or were you having me on?"

Amber turned to me and kissed me. "Truly, we discussed it. In all honesty, it was Pete's idea, although once I got over my surprise I needed no encouragement."

"So what happened?"

"Well, Pete asked me if you and I were back together now. I told him we most definitely were. With some embarrassment, he asked me if we had had sex while alone in your room. I told him that was hardly likely, with him popping in and out, not to mention nurses and other people. Looking acutely embarrassed, he suggested that careful lovemaking might be very good for you now. How did I feel about that? I told him that if he would ensure our privacy, I would be more than happy to oblige. At that stage, he gave me the key to the door, went as red as a beetroot, and fled."

"Wow! What a doctor," I marveled.

Amber was now all brisk business. "Come on, we smell sweaty! We definitely need a shower. I'll help you."

Only now did I notice that instead of one, two white bathrobes hung from the usual peg. We put them on and walked the short distance down the corridor to a shower.

"Hang on a minute. This is a men's shower. You can't come in here."

"Oh, perhaps you would rather come into the ladies'."

So saying, she opened the door to the men's bathroom, and entered a large cubicle. While I gaped at her, she calmly took off her robe, and faced me, naked and waiting.

"Are you coming in, or am I on show?"

Hurrying into the shower, I closed the cubicle door; turning on the shower, we stood under it, soaping each other and giggling like a couple of naughty kids.

Amber stayed the whole night, and we slept side by side, very close and a bit uncomfortable in the single bed. But it was the best night of my entire life.

She left early, and I was alone when Pete came in on his usual rounds.

"Hi, Adam, did you sleep well?" he asked ambiguously.

"Pete, when they made you a doctor they threw the mold away. You're the best ever . . . and thanks a million."

Pete grinned. "If it helps the well-being of my patient, then it assists the healing process. You are very welcome. Er . . . was it good?"

"Fantastic, Pete. Ab-so-lute-ly fantastic."

# Nine

Deeply involved in the process of rehabilitation, time seemed to rush along, and my progress was sure and steady. Eventually, I knew that I was ready to go home. The only support I wore now was for my spine, and even that was light and reasonably comfortable. I would be in that for several more months. The spinal damage had healed well, although the earlier problem still persisted to a degree. Despite the fact that my left leg was a touch uncooperative, the overall treatment had been beneficial to that early injury.

The weeks and days had been full and busy. Daily I had worked out, stretching and strengthening my body, and late each evening I had made that inner journey to the river and sphere. The pain had long since ceased to be a problem, and although it persisted on a low, niggling level, I was easily able to ignore it. As Pete said, "You don't beat your body near to death and walk away without some sort of permanent reminder."

Mum and Dad had visited me a few more times, and although a touch of Dad's reserve had returned, I had expected it. At least now our relationship was blossoming, with a shared respect and love between us. Kate and Bruno had come in for several evenings, and my previous rather remote friendship with Bruno had deepened. I looked forward to when Amber and I could entertain them in our home.

Amber had moved back into our house, and just the thought of spending my days with her thrilled me in the way it had when we were first married. We had seriously considered having a second marriage, but mutually, we knew that our first lovemaking since our separation had sealed something deep within us. We had learned that a wedding does not a marriage make; that true marriage is not a ceremony, but a soul-level commitment. We knew that now, finally and irrevocably, we were married.

"Doctor, I want to go home," I said formally.

Pete and I were sitting in the canteen discussing my progress, while sipping coffee.

"Just as we get to be good friends, you want to walk out on me." His dark eyes twinkled. "It so happens that I plan to release you in exactly five days' time. I've talked this over with Amber, and she agrees with my suggestion." He held up a massive hand to cut off my protest. "First, another series of tests. Then, if you pass, you may leave my exalted company."

It was useless trying to argue with Pete, so I accepted the five days gracefully. After all, what was five more days after all the weeks I had been hospitalized?

I soon found out! The tests began the next day. Pete had given me no idea of how thorough he intended to be, and hours passed while I was hooked up to various gadgets and equipment that gave him digital information about my blood pressure, heart, lungs, et cetera. I was performance and endurance tested, and tested while relaxed. My bone strength over the fractures was measured, my innards scanned, my hip and spine x-rayed and tested, on and on. Pete told me exactly what was going on for a while, but the figures became more and more meaningless to me as we continued from one test to another. I was taken into places in that hospital that I had not known existed, and met a whole new spectrum of doctors.

It seemed they found me an interesting specimen, for word had got around about my refusing all pain medication. It was also believed that I had found "mental" ways of controlling the pain, so apart from the sly jokes at my expense, there was also a genuine inquiry about just how I had managed such obviously high levels of pain.

For me, there were altogether too many people asking too many questions, so I repeated one stock answer over and over. I told them that I had simply imagined it away. While this was not a lie, containing part of the truth, it was obviously not all of the truth, and they knew it. However, I resisted their attempts to probe the information out of me. There is a timing to truth, and their overall skepticism indicated that this most definitely was not their moment. Because of his openness, I figured that the timing would arrive for Doctor Pete Morrow before any of the other doctors in that hospital. Highly respected, I learned that Pete was considered as brilliant, but he was also known as an oddball doctor, a renegade in the field of medicine. Thank God they exist!

To my astonishment, the tests took the best part of three days, even to the extent of checking my mental faculties. I thought that was a bit much, but apparently my refusing pain relief was highly suspect within itself. I learned that I first had to undergo Pete's tests, and then there were the hospital's tests. Pete and the hospital did not always see eye to eye.

"My dream is to have my own private hospital," Pete confided, after the last of the tests was concluded. "Then I will be able to do everything my way."

"You should let Frank Sinatra know," I said with a straight face.

Pete looked completely baffled. "Eh . . . why him?"

"Because . . . I did it mmmyyyy way," I sang, off-key.

He scowled at me. "Idiot. I was being serious."

I could hear his voice as he continued our conversation, but my attention wandered. We were sitting in my room by the open window. Outside, a large jacaranda tree had just finished putting on its new foliage, and it was verdant with nature's green energy. Dropping low in the sky as evening gathered, the sun illuminated the lacy dancing leaves as a soft breeze stole silently among them, while one small, shaded branch near my window had come into flower over a month after the rest of the tree.

Staring at the late sprays of lavender-blue flowers, I watched the last of the honeybees before they returned to their hive. Crawling in and out of the flowers, a few native bees could be seen, tiny and black, with no sting. I realized how much I had missed nature, stuck in a hospital all this time. And now I could go home.

"Are you listening to me?" Pete asked in a much louder and rather pained voice.

I smiled at him fondly. I really liked this gentle man-mountain who had put me back together. "I'm sorry, Pete, I was with that tree out there. Look at it. Doesn't it just grab you? Doesn't it take your breath away?"

He gave it no more than a cursory glance. "Yes, very pretty, I'm sure. So what's that got to do with anything?"

"Pretty! Pretty isn't the word, Pete. Try 'awesome.'"

He frowned at me, his huge body trying to find comfort in the inadequate chair. Squinting his eyes in a deliberate gesture, he sighed heavily and stared out of the window.

"Just look at the flowers, Pete. When did you last take time to see them, or better yet, to smell the flowers?"

He held his gaze on that small branch for several minutes; as I watched him, I could see the tension flowing out of him. His massive shoulders relaxed, letting go of their load, and his breathing became easier.

Almost imperceptibly, he nodded. "Amazing," he breathed in his soft, low voice. "I see the usual flowers, a branch, just another tree, yet I feel . . . so very much more." He looked at me, quiet now, and pensive. "So what happened?"

"You went beyond your eyes, Pete. You stepped briefly into the zone of feeling, not with your emotions, but more deeply, with who you are. For a few moments there, you connected with a tree. So tell me, isn't that awesome?"

He looked at me respectfully. "Is this how you operate as an eco-farming consultant, on a feeling level?"

"I use science as well. The soil is tested and analyzed, and I interpret all the figures and convert the results to natural organic fertilizers, instead of chemical stimulants. But, yes, as I walk on the various farmers' land, I attune with it, learn from it, deeply empathize with it."

"How do you know you are not daydreaming, or playing games with your imagination?"

I looked at him thoughtfully. "That's a good question. In all truth, you don't know, but with practice you learn to trust yourself. If you apply what you learn from your attunement and you get positive results, it gets easier to trust yourself. If you get negative results, you look for a job more befitting your own nature."

"Hmmmm. What's attunement all about?"

"I guess it means 'at one in the moment.' To attune with a tree, or the land, you have to tune in to the moment."

"Why is the moment so important?"

"Because I am learning in my own life that the moment is where all the action is. Life is in the moment. I'm getting a bit out of my depth here, but I strongly suspect that we humans are seldom ever in the moment. We live in our heads."

Pete stood up, stretched, yawned, shook his whole body vigorously for a moment, and sat down again. "Bloody arse-numbing chairs," he grumbled. "So, having been revived and educated by a tree, how does this get back to my dream of a private hospital?"

I looked at him blankly. "Huh! I didn't know it did!" I chuckled. "You never forget where you start a conversation, do you? No matter how much we diverge, you always find your way back. You know, you and I are similar. I'm out on a limb as an eco-farming consultant, and you as a qualified doctor who specializes in natural healing."

We gazed at each other in a speculative and companionable silence for quite a while, each happy with our own thoughts.

"Two bloody mavericks," Pete finally grunted. "Each looking to make the world a better place in our own way."

I was startled. "You are, aren't you? You really are trying to make the world a better place. I never even thought of that. I do what I do because that is me being me. I wonder if there's a real difference between us."

Pete nodded. "I've got a feeling there is a difference. I reckon trying to change the world is like pushing string uphill. You, on the other hand, are just being yourself. That's pulling string uphill. A bloody sight easier, that's for sure. Ever tried pushing string uphill?"

Again, there was a long silence as we followed our lines of thought. "You know, Pete, maybe, just maybe, the jacaranda tree does hold the answer to how you get your own hospital," I said.

"Really! Some bloody tree! I'll turn it into a shrine."

"Seriously. When the seed of that tree started its growth, it followed the blueprint of its truth. It didn't have to worry about being a pine, or get caught up in being a eucalyptus, any other tree. Its seed held both its life pattern and its purpose. Sure, it could get killed, or chopped down, but that's something else again. Suppose we each have a blueprint within us that contains our life pattern and our purpose—a blueprint we don't know about."

Screwing up his eyes, Pete rubbed a large hand over his face. "As if I don't have enough to worry about already. So what is this overwhelming point you're trying to make."

"You just said it. The jacaranda tree simply grows, using all its energy for growth, and it becomes what it should be, effortlessly. It never worries at all. Maybe we should do just that. Use all our energy to do what we do, be who we are, and allow our flowering to unfold naturally. I'm pretty sure that worry takes an enormous amount of energy, and it probably aborts or obliterates the blueprint of our individual expression in the process."

Pete looked at me in surprise. "That's not half as daft as it sounds. I had no idea you could be so profound. In my own way of thinking, I've followed similar speculation before, and I'm inclined to agree with you. The only problem is, I've never put any of it into action. I still worry, and grumble and groan, and try hard, and all that other strange human rubbish. Maybe I'll wise up one day."

I sighed. "It does have to be lived, there's no doubt about that. A truth is not our truth if we don't live it."

"See, you're doing it again, going all profound about truth. You really are a seeker of truth, aren't you?"

Feeling caught out, I was defensive. "I suppose I am. So what? There's enough confusion and misery in the world. Besides, I have more than enough of my own. If there is an enlightened way of living, and some way of getting there, it's definitely for me."

"Now, now, now. Don't get all defensive, I'm not attacking you. I admire your seeking. I'm a closet seeker myself. I'm also looking for sanity in an insane world, and every day I learn more clearly that if I don't find it within myself, I'm not ever going to find it at all."

I put a hand on his shoulder. "You don't surprise me. It takes one oddball to recognize another. Seriously, Pete, when I leave here, I don't want to just walk out of your life. I have too much respect for you." I was feeling a bit embarrassed. "I like you. I want you to know that you have an open invitation to visit Amber and me just whenever you want." A thought suddenly struck me. "My God! I've never even asked. Are you married?"

He looked rueful. "I was . . . a fair while ago. I married the cutest little blonde you ever did see. Amy. She had a sweet nature, a lovely person, a delight to be with. Cultured, well-educated, and intelligent, she was my dream come true." He looked sad. "The only problem was, one man was not enough for her, neither were two, nor three. I had to bale out, but it took me a long time to recover. We're still good friends, and it still hurts. I think I probably still love her. She never did marry again. Not much point really. She has a string of wealthy married men all after what she is so brilliantly able to provide. Poor Amy, she has a problem she refuses to even consider. When it comes to sexual expertise, she's a genius! Imagine that, a genius in bed, or out of it, come to that."

"So you never remarried?"

"No. To be honest, I got scared off. I married my profession instead and, like a true mistress, it takes all the energy I've got to spare, and more."

I squeezed his shoulder again. "I don't know what to say. That's a sad story. Anyway, I repeat, you are always welcome at our place."

He smiled. "Thanks, Adam. I appreciate it, and I'll certainly take you up on it, often."

"There's one other thing I want to say before I leave here, and that is to thank you for saving my life and putting me back together again. I know what . . ."

"No thanks are necessary," Pete cut in. "It's what I get paid to do." He smiled. "It's my line of work."

"As I was saying when I was so rudely interrupted, I know what a borderline case I was when I was admitted to this hospital. I was watching, remember? I know how many long hours you worked on me. I know that you sat at my bedside when you should have been sleeping, and I know that you gave everything it's possible to give of yourself to keep me alive. And I want you to know that from the bottom of my heart, and from Amber's, how much we appreciate it. Words can never express my gratitude, so I have set myself a goal. I am going to do my best to help you get your own private hospital. To me, you are not only a physical giant, you are also king-sized love in action. Nothing less than the realization of your dream can adequately express my thanks."

He stared at me, his mouth opening and closing. Tears sprang to his eyes, and he blinked rapidly. "Christ! Do you get a kick out of making people cry?"

Simultaneously getting to our feet, we hugged. As gentle as he was, it was like being hugged by a gorilla.

"You really mean that about the hospital, don't you?"

"I sure do. I don't know how, and I don't know when, but I know that with jacaranda power, it's possible."

"Jacaranda power! Oh, looney tunes," Pete chortled, as sniffing loudly, and fruitlessly patting his pockets, he ambled out the room. I could here his voice fading as he walked away. "Bloody hell! Jacaranda power, oh what . . ."

❖   ❖   ❖

With all the tests passed, the big day had arrived. Pete had arranged for me to go to a physiotherapist in our nearby town of Nambour three days a week.

"His name is John Relish, and he is one of the best. I can't really understand why he chose to live in a little country town, but he reckons the quality of life is what it's all about. He will be expecting you. Amber has a list of the things for you to do and not do, so take notice of her."

"Obviously John relishes the country," I chortled.

Pete clapped a hand to his forehead in a vastly exaggerated gesture. "Oh God, spare me your puns. It's about time you went home," he said dramatically.

All the hospital staff whom I knew had come in to say their good-byes, and with some surprise I realized that they genuinely liked me. I found that odd, because for so long I had been unable to like myself. Jim and Mandy both came, but when Jim walked away, Mandy lingered.

"I have to confess, I'm still disturbed that you believe in reincarnation," she said hesitantly. "I would hate to think of you ending up in hell with the devil."

I knew that I had to take her seriously. "That's really nice of you, Mandy, but I honestly believe that hell is a human concept. I don't believe in the devil, or hell, other than the one we make for ourselves in our own daily life. But, thanks all the same."

She looked increasingly agitated. "You shouldn't say things like that. It's blasphemy. Hell is a real place, and if God turns you down, then the devil will take you."

"Do you believe that God is a loving God?" I asked her.

"Of course. Everyone knows that."

"Well, how could a loving God give you to the devil? Where is the love in such an action? It's a denial of love."

"You don't question things like that," she hissed in agitation. "You simply live as the Scriptures dictate."

I reverted to my usual blunt self. "Mandy, as a therapist you're compassionate and skillful. You're truly wonderful, and I would recommend you to anyone. But the way you see your religion is pathetic. Be your own person."

Her face red with anger, Mandy spun on her shapely heel and stalked off. "Good-bye, Adam."

I sat in my room for a while thinking about our conversation. Whereas religion did not affect her ability as a professional, it sure stuffed up her personal life. Maybe I'm judging, I mused, but what an incredible limitation to place on yourself. Mandy's personal life would eventually become a series of "Thou shalt not . . ."

By prior arrangement, Amber came to pick me up in her car at midday. I was caught out by her arrival, for having woken up early that morning and maintained a state of almost perpetual excitement, I was snoozing on the bed when she burst into my room.

Her two reactions chased each other. "I don't believe it, you were asleep," she said, followed immediately by "Oh, Adam, my darling! Are you all right?"

"I like the second one best," I replied.

She stared at me as though I had lost my senses. "Adam, whatever are you talking about?"

So I told her. "I am all right, really. Fancy, I've waited over four months for this moment, then I doze off. I suppose . . "

My words were cut off by her lips on mine, so I gave serious concentration to kissing her.

"I told you, my dear, he thinks too much," Pete said as he followed her into the room. "You never know what he'll come out with next."

I ignored him, continuing the long kiss.

"That's lip power, Adam. Beats hell out of jacaranda power," he chortled.

Amber broke away. "Adam, what's he talking about?"

"Beats me," I replied. "I reckon he's been confined in this hospital too long. He's gone mad. Probably why I like him so much. I think too much, he talks too much."

Laughing, Amber spun around and, hugging Pete, kissed him with fierce passion. "Thank you so much for mending my man," she said softly. "I love you."

"And I love you, little lady," Pete replied gruffly. "You can be sure that I'll be around to see you both soon. Adam, don't forget that I want you back here for regular checkups, starting one week from today."

"Yes sir, Mister Boss Man. As you say, sir!"

"And one other thing, Adam. You'll have good days and bad days, so be prepared. Don't let the bad days get you down. They are part of the healing cycle."

I would have liked to run out the hospital, but I had to settle for a sedate and careful walk with my stick. I did not like the hospital stick, and I intended to change it for my bush-walking stick as soon as I got home.

There was only one mild cloud on my personal horizon as I got into Amber's car. I was surprised that Mum and Dad were not here, or Kate and Bruno. For me, this was a great day, and I would have liked to share it with them.

Automatically, I had gone around to the driver's seat, but Amber headed me off. "No, Adam. For a while, at least, you are under my orders. Doctor Pete said so. You relax. I'm driving."

I allowed her to help me into the passenger's seat, and I was rather surprised to find that I needed help.

Pete stuck his huge, hairy, smiling face in my open window. "You do as the little lady tells you, Adam. Doctor's orders, remember. Besides, as pretty as she is, she just has to be a whole lot smarter than you. Bye, see you soon."

"I just love that man," Amber purred as we drove away.

The feelings that ran through my mind were very strange as Amber drove north, heading sedately toward the Sunshine Coast and our mountain home.

Everything I looked at seemed more intense, more alive than I had ever noticed before. I wondered at the pure marvel of life, my life, all life. Not long ago I had been smashed to pieces, physically broken, and I had been repaired. But something far beyond that had happened. I had found aspects of myself that belonged in past lives, and those aspects had been broken so badly that they had never been repaired. I knew that in this life I had to find some way to repair my past, all those lives of pain in which I had lived and failed. I not only had to heal this present body, but I had to heal those other aspects also. I knew, too, that this was my path to self-awareness. To find my truth, I had to reengage the whole me, bringing all those other damaged personas into one whole relationship. Thinking about the car smash, I realized that this destructive way of smashing myself into oblivion had, in its own unique fashion, propelled me to dimensions of reality I would never have found in a less shattering manner.

"You're very quiet. Are you okay?"

I smiled at Amber absently. Sure, I thought, I'm okay. But I'm also shocked by the vastness and the depth of life. I've learned that life is not a frivolous adventure on the skin of an ocean; it is the totality of every drop and the incredible depths that makes the ocean a whole. It's all so very overwhelming.

"Adam! Please, tell me what you're thinking."

So I told her.

She listened attentively. "Where did this new you come from, Adam? I mean, where was this person of depth and insight in the first years of our marriage? Did you think along these avenues then? Why didn't you share such thoughts? These are the things I think about, the things that concern me."

Closing my eyes, I leaned my head back onto the headrest. "I carried so much self-loathing and self-contempt that I could seldom get away from the negativity of it all. The inquiry was there, and I guess the depth was also, but it was a deep, dark pit that kept sucking me in. I was so very destructive in my thinking." I sighed deeply. "Instead of encouraging you to help me out, I tried to drag you in. You had no choice but to leave me, your survival as a person demanded it. But, oh God, I'm so glad that you've come back."

The car came to a stop, and switching off the engine, Amber gently took my face in both of her hands. She kissed me; a kiss so tender and loving that I began to cry. Tears ran down my cheeks, and I sniffed loudly.

"What's the matter, my darling?"

"I don't know. My emotions are all muddled up. I'm feeling such incredible joy at being out of the hospital and just being with you, yet it's all mixed in with an ocean of grief. I feel I'm crying for my past, yet I'm so very happy with this moment. One thing I am clear about, I love you so very, very much."

"There's a lot that's happened to you since that accident that you haven't told me about, isn't there?" she said with keen insight as she stared into my eyes.

"More than you can imagine. But I will."

We kissed, and she started the car again, continuing along the road toward home. The kilometers slipped away rapidly as we headed into sugarcane country. Ideally suited to commercially grow pineapples, avocados, macadamia nuts, litchi, and cherimoya, our climate grows a huge range of tropical fruits. I could hardly wait to eat them again.

The one-hour drive passed rapidly, and soon we turned into the driveway to our house. *Our* house! It felt so good. Amber stopped the car in the large carport, and turned to me as I fumbled with my door.

"Wait, Adam. Just for a few weeks you must get used to letting me help you. I'll open your door."

I sat patiently, unsure of how I was going to deal with being waited on. I shrugged. I would soon be fit and strong, then I could help Amber. That's what I would do! I would return tenfold all her care and kindness.

Ducking my head while bending over as I got in and out of the car seemed to find muscular aches and pains that all the best equipment in the fitness center had been unable to find. I was glad of Amber's help as I slowly straightened up. I stretched. "God, it feels so good to be home."

Together, we walked to the front door, and Amber opened it. I gazed indoors with surprise. Just inside, hanging from a ceiling beam so that it hid all the room, was a large bedsheet with four very big words painted on it: WELCOME HOME ADAM DEAR.

Grinning like a kid at a surprise party, I kissed Amber.

"Thank you. That's a nice touch."

Amber walked over to the sheet, and gathering up one side of it, she snatched it from the beam.

"SURPRISE! WELCOME HOME ADAM!"

They were all here. Standing in the room waiting for us were Mum and Dad; Kate and Bruno; Amber's parents, Max and Noreen Collins; even Joe and Joyce Steadman and some of our neighbors were here. But standing in front of them all, his face a picture of youthful innocence, was the real shock—Selph! I did not know whether to laugh or cry, and for a few embarrassed moments I had to struggle with it. Amazingly enough, it was my usually reserved dad who stepped forward and hesitantly hugged me. "Welcome home, son."

I clung to him like a kid and silently cried, while he gently patted my back. "It's all right, son. You're home now. You're home again. You're back with us, and back with Amber. It's okay, son. It's all okay now."

For the second time in a few weeks, I was crying in my dad's arms, but I had the feeling that for both of us, it was where I belonged. We did not hurry it. Dad made no attempt to pull away, and I clung to him until my emotions had stabilized. "Thanks, Dad. I needed that. I love you."

Patting me, he smiled, and turned to Mum. She was across the room like a shot, and as he let me go, she was in my arms. "Oh, Adam. Oh, Adam. Oh it's so good to have you home again. Are you sure you can manage? You and Amber can come and stay with us for a while if you want. We would love to have you both."

I kissed and hugged her. "Thanks Mum, but I think we'll manage. If we can't, you'll be the first person we turn to. You can't believe how good it is to be home. I've waited for this moment for what seemed a long, long time."

"Oh, Adam, why didn't you tell us before? What a splendid idea you came up with."

With a puzzled frown, I held her at arm's length. "Tell you what, Mum? What are you talking about?"

She beckoned to Selph, who approached like your average shy adolescent. "This fine young man has told us that he is your new assistant. He is going to learn about eco-farming from you. That's such a clever idea. He will be able to do all the hard legwork for you. You really should have told us, you know." She put an arm around Selph's waist and pulled him closer to us. "And he is such a nice, well-mannered young man. I find him quite charming."

Selph's face was turning more cherubic by the moment, but as he gave me an expansive smile, his smile and his eyes held different messages. His smile said, "Aren't I just the most adorable," while his eyes said, "Don't you reckon it's a nice twist to the truth?"

"Ah, er, yes. Well, er . . . it was a very recent decision," I stammered, quickly recovering. "Wouldn't you agree, Selph?"

"Why do you call him Selph?" Mum asked with a frown. "His name is Ian. Ian Selph."

"Ian! Really?" I began to laugh. "Ah, well, you see, Mum, he didn't tell me that." I looked at Selph. "So, young man. Why didn't you tell me your full

Michael J. Roads

name?" I gave a few "Tut tut tuts," giving him no chance to reply. I was enjoying this. "So . . . it's Ian Selph, hmmm. And where does your family live, Ian? What sort of work does your Dad do?" I grinned at him jauntily. Get out of that one, I thought.

His reply was lightning fast. "But don't you remember, Adam? I told you that I'm far from home. That's why you invited me to live with you and Amber."

"I did what? Oh. Yes, so I did. Fancy that! I'd completely forgotten about our prior arrangement. It must have been the accident," I said, turning to Mum. "All that suffering made me forget the minor details of life."

"Oh you poor darling. Of course it would."

Selph's grin was one of admiration before he, too, turned to Mum. "We must let him go, Mrs. Baker. There are other people wanting to welcome him home."

Mum flashed me a quick smile. "He's a nice boy, isn't he, Adam? And so considerate."

I had completely forgotten to mention to Amber about Selph living with me, and I wondered what she would say. She was the other side of the room with her parents when I caught her eye. She joined me within moments.

"Er, did I say anything to you about Selph living here?" I began, a bit lamely.

She smiled brightly. "That's all been taken care of. He's been here, off and on, for the last week or so."

"You didn't tell me," I said in surprise.

"Ah, yes. Well, I have quite a lot to tell you also."

She kissed me on the end of my nose, took my hand, and led me across the room. "Come and say hello to Mum and Dad."

"How do they feel about me?"

"Oh, it'll be okay. When we separated I simply told them that we were incompatible. That's all they really know about it, and actually, that was the truth."

"Adam, I'm so happy to see you better again. But even more than that, I want you to know how pleased I am that you and Amber have resolved your differences." Noreen gave me a careful hug and a quick kiss. She too, had auburn hair, with a trim figure, mostly overdressed, and a sharpish, businesswoman approach to life. She owned a number of very successful hair salons, enjoying a wealthy lifestyle. Max, on the other hand, was almost her opposite. He was a dark-haired, plump, florid-faced man, a casual dresser, and seldom serious about anything. How they managed to live as a couple confounded even Amber, but oddly, they were happy together and entirely compatible. Max played the stock market with a vague, uncaring approach, yet he always seemed to come out on top. I suspected that he was a whole lot smarter than he liked people to think. Not unnaturally, he and I had always got along famously together.

"Adam, my boy. Good to see you again. What a dreadful time you've had to be sure. The news of your accident really shook me. And you can't imagine how pleased I am that you and my daughter are back together. I've never seen her happier. You always were my favorite son-in-law." He chuckled at his own joke, knowing that with Amber as their only child, I was their only son-in-law.

As he firmly shook my hand in both of his, I realized with a mild shock just how much he meant it. I did not know either of them well, but I had always found Noreen rather preoccupied with her business. I realized, now, that although Max and I got on well together, I had never really bothered to get to know him. I determined that I would. They lived a fair way down the coast in New South Wales, and the distance between us had held us more than physically apart.

Amber and the ladies were serving food and drinks as I looked around for Joe Steadman. "Gawd! But it's good to see you again," he said, nearly shaking my arm off. He noticed me briefly wince, and dropped my hand as though it were suddenly red hot. "Gawd! I'm sorry, Adam. I'm too clumsy by half."

I patted his shoulder. "I'm okay, Joe. It's great to see you and Joyce. I've missed you. How's the farm?"

Joe was a biggish man, balding, with a battered, but friendly, face. He shook his head sadly. "It's a bugger, this drought. We're suffering, everybody's suffering. But I would have to say that our cattle are still hanging on better than most. I get the feeling you're going to be a busy man when this drought breaks. There's many a farmer has asked us what it is that we're doing different to them." He shook his head sadly. "It's a heartbreaker, Adam, it's a bloody heartbreaker."

"Don't you go bothering poor Adam with your problems right now, Joe Steadman, he's got quite enough of his own."

So saying, Joyce stepped between us, and gave me a hug and kiss. "Oh, Adam, you frightened us half to death. First thing we heard you was dead. Then we heard you were still alive, but dying. Then we heard you were dead, then you were alive. I hardly knew whether to bawl my eyes out, or laugh with relief." She kissed me again, her ample body firm with the muscle of hard work. "Welcome home, Adam."

I smiled at her, loving her genuine kindness. "Thanks Joyce, you can't believe how good it is to see you again. How are the kids?"

"They're fine," she beamed. "Mattie's looking after the boys, and she said to say hi."

The boys were an energetic handful, but I knew that Mattie could deal with them. Tall and pretty, patient, and self-reliant beyond her years, Mattie was a very capable and dependable girl.

Joyce stood back to allow space for Kate and Bruno.

"Hi, Adam. We thought we would let some of the folks who haven't seen you get at you first. Welcome home, brother dear." Kate and I shared a long hug.

"Isn't it stupid how you have to nearly die to realize the incredible value of a sister, and of relatives and friends. You have to nearly lose all those you most love, to really understand the value and meaning of love. I love you, Kate." I kissed her.

"We were close before your accident, Adam, and I think I knew you well, but it feels to me as though an Adam did die, and that a new Adam has emerged. I love you." Kissing me, she patted her tummy where the five-and-a-half-month baby was developing. "Feel here."

Placing my hand on her tummy, she moved it slightly lower. "Can you feel the baby kicking?"

Thrilled, I could detect just a faint quiver of movement. "I can't wait to be an uncle. God! What a privilege." I looked at her sagely. "Who knows, you might have twins."

Bruno had joined us, and he laughed. "I think not, Adam, there are no twins in either family." He hugged me. "Welcome home, Adam. There's a whole new life waiting for you now, with Amber. I'm so very happy for you both."

Soon my neighbors had also added their well wishes, and everyone was occupied with sandwiches, cakes, and their drink. I was about to go outside, when I noticed an old man in a big chair right at the back of the room. Walking over to him, I realized that he was Dad's father, my granddad.

We stared at each other. I had not seen him for perhaps ten years, and although I knew he must be in his early eighties, he looked like Methuselah. Shriveled, shrunken, and dried out like an old prune, he gazed up at me through watery eyes. Granddad lived way up north in the heat, tucked away in a retirement village. His wife had died maybe twenty years ago, and old James had been alone ever since. Most people who knew them said it made little real difference to him, for he had always been old and had always been a loner. He and I had never really got on at all. When you are a kid, grandparents seem really old, but communication can generally bridge that gap. My granddad, however, had hardly ever spoken to me, so the gulf had remained. Even my long-dead grandma was only a hazy memory, what with the distance involved and the few times we ever got away from the demands of the farm. She had been fat, very fat, and I could hardly recollect her ever moving from her kitchen chair.

Bending over, I placed my face close to his. "Hello, Granddad. How are you?" I said loudly.

"Middlin', boy. Fair to middlin'."

I smiled, knowing that this was his unfailing answer. "I haven't seen you in a long time," I said.

His head shook slightly as he peered up at me. "No, you haven't. "His eyes squinted a bit. "Who are you, boy? Do I know you?"

"I'm your grandson, Adam," I said loudly.

"You don't have to shout, boy, I'm not deaf."

"Do you remember me, Granddad?" I asked more quietly.

"Eh, wassat? You'll have to speak up boy. No good muttering at me. Who are you, anyway?"

Knowing when I was beaten, I patted his shoulder, leaned over and kissed his forehead, then turned away. Out of the corner of my eye, I could see him wiping at his forehead as though I had spat on him. I sighed. Is that what aging does, or do we do that to ourselves? I looked back at him as he stared stonily into space. No wonder Dad grew up into the type of person he is. How could a son of this man grow up to be outgoing, or free and easy. Dad was his father's son. And that's how it continues, from one generation to another. Thank God that Dad and I are breaking the pattern. I felt a sudden and vast sympathy for Dad. He had been locked away inside himself as a kid, and had never found the key to his prison. I vowed that not only would I get free, but I would continue to help releasing him as well. We had made a poor start, but we were making good progress now.

Slipping out of the house and into the garden. I drank it in through my eyes and into my heart. I've missed you, garden, I thought. Walking over to my bonsai, I stroked their leaves and admired them. I've missed you too, but you've been well looked after. A light breeze stirred the leaves in the gum trees, setting up a sudden rustling high above my head. Looking up, I saw a magpie watching me, his eye bright as with cocked head he followed my every movement. Do I know you? I asked silently. As a boy I had kept a magpie for a pet, but it had been killed soon after it was a couple of years old. I had mourned that bird. Could this be my pet reborn, and here to visit me again?

All around me it felt as though the garden were welcoming me home. A few of the shrubs were flowering, a splash of yellow here, and a few sprays of pink over there, but the drought was even affecting us on the coast. I walked over to the swimming pool. This is where I intended to do a lot of my exercise, plus plenty of beach walking.

As I gazed into the water, I saw my reflection joined by Amber's as she came to my side. I pointed. "Our reflections came together before you had quite reached me. It wouldn't surprise me if, on a soul level, we never really parted. We had to physically separate for me to grow up, but you were always in my heart. There was never anyone else."

"It was the same for me," Amber said softly. "I didn't go out once with another man. I never stopped loving you, even though it caused me so much anguish."

We kissed. There were no more words. A mutual healing was already in process.

A few more people came, and some left, but there was never a crowd. In all truth I had only a few friends, for I was not one for much socializing, and after Amber had left me, the only people I ever met were to do with my work. And I still liked it that way. I had always preferred a few quality friendships with people I really cared about, rather than a large circle of more casual acquaintances.

By mid-evening only my parents, Amber's parents, and Kate and Bruno were left—and, of course, Selph. I was sitting in the most comfortable armchair with my legs up, relaxed.

Closing my eyes, I sighed in contentment. Amber brought me a drink and sat near my knees. As I looked at her, my heart was bursting with gratitude. "It was worth it, you know," I told her. "If the car smash had done nothing more than bring us back together, it was worth all the pain and suffering I've been through. And more. Sitting here, and watching you moving around the room, talking to people, just being you, I have to pinch myself to make sure it's not a dream. To wake up and find it was all a dream would be worst the nightmare imaginable."

She squeezed my hand. "It's real, Adam. Believe it!"

"We have to go now, Amber love," Mum said, as she and Dad came over to us. "It'll be late when we get home."

"Stay the night, Mum. We've got plenty of room," I protested. "You don't need to make that long drive now."

"But what about Max and Noreen? I thought perhaps that they would be staying."

Noreen shook her head. "No. We're up here for a few days, and we came rather unexpectedly, so I booked us in at a nearby motel. We have a nice room and are very comfortable there." She smiled. "Besides, it's tax refundable. I have some business to see to while I'm here."

Mum looked at Dad. "What do you think, Fred? You're the one with the work schedule."

"Come on Dad, don't go yet. Let's make an evening of it. You'll be fresher for driving in the morning."

Dad "ummed and ahhed" for about ten minutes. He wanted to stay, that was obvious, but his old habit—his pattern—was to leave early and not get too involved. I reached out my hand to him, and he took it. "Dad, I want you to stay."

That clinched it. He grumbled mildly, but my direct appeal had touched him. Both he and I were drawing up a new map for our father/son relationship, and we both had to work at it as we headed into unknown territory.

"How about Granddad?" Mum asked. "Do you have room for him?"

Having completely forgotten him, I grinned, and looked at Amber inquiringly. "Have we?"

"No problem. He can have, er, Ian's bed, and Ian can sleep on the settee."

"Ah, yes . . . Ian's bed," I said grinning at Selph. "I had forgotten about Ian. Good old Ian. Mum, is Granddad staying with you?"

"Yes. He's on holiday. Or at least, he's having a change of environment. I don't think holiday has any meaning to him at all." She shrugged, chuckling. "I chat away to him all day, and he grunts about twice an hour in reply. He always was an old misery, now he's worse."

"Maybe he never learned how not to be lonely. I wonder what his Dad was like," I said.

Mum looked at me thoughtfully. "That's a good point, Adam. From what I can remember, I'm almost certain he had a suppressed childhood, with extremely religious parents."

"That says it all," I said sadly.

Bruno and Kate had prepared supper, so as a family we sat around the supper table and chatted. Selph handled all personal questions put to him with such casual, unguarded ease that I felt sure he must have done all this before.

Family time is precious, and I reveled in just seeing the family around me. After Granddad had sat staring at his plate in silence for about ten minutes, Amber offered to help him. He shook his head violently. "If you think I can't eat," he wheezed, "you're wrong. But I don't eat this strange stuff. What'n the hell is it?"

We all spluttered with suppressed laughter. Cooked by Bruno, with all his culinary expertise, the meal was certainly a touch exotic, but it was done especially for me. After all, I had just endured over four months of hospital food. We were eating bamboo shoots, asparagus and kohlrabi, all covered in a white sauce thick with tiny school prawns. A basically white meal, with a touch of green and pink, it was simply delicious.

Bruno winked at us. "Mister Baker. You are eating a selection of vegetables with prawns."

"Well why'n hell didn't someone tell me?" Granddad grumbled. "A man don't know what he's eat'n today, what with all this fancy cooking an' such."

He tucked in, smacking his lips with relish as the food hung from his gap-toothed mouth.

Grinning at Selph, I murmured, "He can even beat you!"

When my fatigue came, it hit me powerfully. One moment I was engaged in conversation, when suddenly I was half dozing. Amber did not miss it.

Jumping up, she took my arm, helping me to my feet. "Come along, Adam. You're nearly asleep. Doctor Pete would not approve."

She was right. I was so exhausted that I just waved my hand to everyone, gave a tired, "Good night," and let Amber help me to our room. "Just lay down, my darling. I'll do the rest."

I was aware of her tugging at my clothes, but I was asleep before she had even finished.

# $\mathcal{T}en$

By mid-morning, after much hugging and well wishing, Mum, Dad, and Granddad had departed, and the three of us were alone. It was fantastic being home, although I was aware that I had a lot of adjusting to do, not only sharing the house again, but also being rather dependent on Amber.

We sat at the poolside, sipping on the coffee that Selph had brewed for us.

"Thanks, Ian," I said with heavy humor. "Very nice."

"Actually," he replied, "I didn't tell your mother that my name is Ian. That's what she heard, and I didn't correct her. What I said was, Iam, spelt with an 'm,' not an 'n.'"

"Iam!" I echoed. "That's an odd name."

"Think about it, Adam. Use your brain," Selph grinned.

Amber chuckled. "I get it. Iam. I am. I am Selph!"

"Gosh, you crafty so and so," I rebuked him. "You said it that way deliberately, didn't you?"

Selph shrugged. "I didn't come here to confront your parents, I came as your teacher. I let them hear what was comfortable for them. If you give people a reasonably close approximation, they see or hear what they expect. It's called living in yesterday's world. In England, where you might live on a busy street, you can buy a sticker for your front gate that says: POLITE NOTICE, NO PARKING. What people read however is: POLICE NOTICE, so they go elsewhere."

I smiled. "There's a small local shop named FISH AND CHIRPS. They sell tropical fish and cage birds. The owner told me that even after six years he still gets people going in to buy fish and chips. I have to confess, it was a year before I read it correctly myself. I used to think what a poor location it was for a fish and chip shop."

Selph shrugged. "I rest my case."

Looking at Amber and Selph, I had to ask the obvious question. "Happily, you two have become friends. Is it possible that you can teach both of us, Selph? Or has that already been decided?"

"It's already been decided," Amber said regretfully. "Selph has told me that he is not my teacher." She smiled brightly. "But that's okay, my turn will come."

"You don't really need a teacher," Selph said seriously. "Adam does. At another time, in another place, I made a promise. My role with Adam is the result."

"Really?" I said in surprise, "Can you tell us about it? I think it's appropriate."

Selph nodded thoughtfully. "I agree. The timing's right. I'll tell you a little story that you may not understand, but I won't explain. Listen carefully. I was in a busy street crowded with people. However, I was walking about a foot above the heads of the crowd, and no one saw me. There were maybe five other people in that crowded street who walked on the same level as me. One of them, a woman, hurried toward me. As she came closer, she suddenly dropped down into the crowd, and was momentarily out of my sight. I hastened to her, and found that she was giving birth to a child. I knelt near her knees to assist her. Even though no one fell over us, and we had plenty of space, nobody else could see us. It was a difficult birth, and when the baby came into my hands, the woman spoke to me. "Promise me that you will take my baby home," she asked me. "It's time."

I assured her that I would. With the baby in my arms, I stood up, again above the crowds of people, and walked away."

Amber and I looked at him expectantly, waiting for more.

He gestured with his hands, "That's it."

"Oh come on," I said. "No explanation to a story like that is ridiculous. Tell me one thing, who was the woman?"

He met my eye. "You."

"Huh! Then who was the baby?"

"You."

Baffled, I looked to Amber for consolation. "I must be thick. Do you get it?"

She looked thoughtful. "It sounds to me like a metaphor. I get the feeling that you have given a cosmic scream for help that was so loud it has reverberated through many dimensions and realities. And your cry was answered."

Selph nodded his head in admiration. "Amber, you really are quite special. Take it from me, you don't need a teacher. You're right. I am the response to his scream. Adam was seriously stuck. He still has to get himself out of it. I can't do that for him, nobody can."

"What happened to the woman?" I asked.

"She is waiting to be reunited with her child."

I groaned. "This is all too much for me. I'm a simple guy. I like to be told things in simple, straightforward terms that I can easily understand."

"Don't take it so literally, Adam," Amber suggested. "It feels as though the woman and the child are aspects of you, and they have become separated. To be whole, they need to come together . . . and I get the feeling that they've been apart a long time. Too long."

"I might as well go home, I reckon," Selph said. "Amber could continue from here."

"Don't you dare," Amber laughed, "your mission is not yet complete."

"Did I get stuck as Adam, or when I was some other identity."

"Ah ha," Selph nodded approvingly, "now we're back in business. You didn't get stuck as Adam, but you remain stuck in this present reality."

"Have I met the identity yet?"

"No. I'm afraid that's the tricky part. This is all about pain, suffering, and avoidance."

"Don't you mean being traumatized and terrified?"

He nodded. "Yep. That too."

"What's this all about?" Amber asked, the concern apparent in her green eyes.

I told her. I told her of all the past lives I had experienced after my fall in the fitness center, of the horror, terror, and pain of a broken back. And when I finished that, I told her about the experience with Selph in the tunnel of light, and of my subsequent decision to continue with a physical life. All in all, it took me nearly two hours to carefully detail the whole story. I figured that because Amber and I were now together again, I owed her a full explanation of all that had happened.

"My God," she breathed finally, "I had no idea. You poor darling, no wonder you screamed for help."

A sudden wave of fatigue caught up with me, and even though I smothered my yawn, Amber insisted that I go to bed for a nap. I felt too tired to argue.

❖   ❖   ❖

Around mid-afternoon, I woke up. The sun was shining, and our summer warmth was already apparent. I stared out the window, thinking about the passing of time and how relative it is to our daily existence. It had been around the middle of May when I had set out on my almost fatal drive home from visiting Mum and Dad. Now it was officially spring, although spring is really early summer in our subtropical climate. I had been in the hospital all winter struggling to live and walk. This was a good time to be out and about. It is the season of growth; maybe I could grow and flourish with the season.

With a quiet gentleness that was so much part of Amber, she entered the bedroom and sat next to me. I took her hand.

"Have I told you that I love you?" I asked.

"Yes," she said seriously, "and I hope you never stop."

"So what happens now?"

"Nothing much until you are fully recovered."

"I feel impatient to do things."

"There are things you can do. Taking your time, you can do the seasonal mulching. I'm fairly sure that the plants all need it. And there are other jobs in the garden."

I nodded. "You're right. I'll enjoy that. What about Selph, will he be any bother to you, or would you have preferred us to be alone?"

"Being alone was generally your preoccupation, Adam. I'm happy for him to be here, especially in the capacity of your teacher. Besides, he's an interesting enigma. He's not at all your usual, regular-type, of guest."

"You can say that again," I said feelingly. "Have you noticed that he doesn't cast a shadow? That's really bizarre. And he can come and go pretty much instantly. Nothing about him adds up to normality except that bloody awful orange T-shirt and those oversize green shorts. Even that's strange. They always look new, yet he never seems to change them. That's a neat trick if you can do it."

Amber lay down on the bed next to me. "He has a power about him. It's both subtle and blatant simultaneously. Very odd, but I really like him. He's nice."

"He's a bit blunt and forceful. Dealing with him is rather like dealing with a human jackhammer at times."

Amber chuckled. "Ah ha, you've met your match."

"Oh come on," I said indignantly, "I was never like that. A bit forthright, maybe, but no more."

"How old is he?"

"When I asked him, he said, 'How old do you think?' I said, 'About fifteen.' He said, 'That's it then.' But I think he's ageless. Fifteen is a joke. His body may look fifteen, sometimes, but his eyes!"

"Like I said, he's an enigma."

"An enigma teaching me to let go of dogma," I joked.

She smiled. "At least some things never change."

Rolling onto my back, I sighed. "I didn't expect to get tired so quickly. I was pooped. Why? I haven't done much."

Amber shifted onto her side, propping herself on an elbow so she could see my eyes. She always was an eye contact person. If you did not look at her when she spoke, she would simply stop talking.

"It's because you are now fully involved in life. In the hospital you were always in either a closed, or a controlled, environment. You were shielded and sheltered, and your pace was determined for you. That adds up to more protection than you realize. Now you are home, and you have to determine your own pace, and measure your own energy. Be patient."

"How come you know all that?"

"Pete told me. He prepared me for this."

"He's a good man," I said fondly.

"Yes, he is. And talking of Pete, don't forget that you have an appointment with John Relish, the physio guy in town tomorrow."

"Hmmm, I'd forgotten."

Amber bit me playfully on an ear. "That's why you have me with you. I'm the brains of the outfit."

I rolled toward her and slid a hand up her inner thigh. "Is that what you are? And I thought that *you* were the physical therapist."

We snuggled together for a while, kissing, then she rolled away from me. "I'll make some tea, and see where Selph is."

When I joined her in the living room a few minutes later, she was alone. "Where's Selph?"

She shook her head. "I have no idea. He just comes and goes, and he doesn't need a car to go."

"Yeah, I noticed that."

"And while we've been sharing the house for the past few weeks, his bed hasn't been slept in once."

"Yep," I grinned, "he sure is a light sleeper. Just think, my love, we can make as much noise at night as we like. Sure beats hell out of being quiet."

She mock scowled at me. "That's just what I need, a permanently randy patient to have to deal with."

"I'm glad about that," I said mildly, "'cos that's what you've got. And it takes no more than just thinking about being in bed with you. So, do I have a problem?"

"Nothing I can't deal with," she smiled sensuously.

After searching in a few cupboards, I found my favorite bush-walking stick, and tried it out. It fitted my hand perfectly, offering me a more comfortable support. I had cut the stick myself from a clump of kurrajong, and it was both superlight and strong. I was told that the aboriginals used to dry and harden them on fires to be used as spears.

I spent the next hour wandering around the garden, doing nothing at all other than looking at and being with it. The garden was a bit neglected, and that pleased me, for now I could do something I really enjoyed to keep me occupied.

At one end of the house we had a flat area on which I had once planned to build a workshop, but it had never eventuated. Now, however, to my surprise it housed a cozy building made of wood. Curiously, I opened the door and entered. Amber was there, standing before her easel, a frown of concentration on her face.

"Gosh! I didn't know about this. Why didn't you tell me? Your own art studio, it's great."

She stared at me, open-mouthed. "Didn't I? Honestly, Adam, I thought I had."

"And you're the brains of this outfit?" I laughed. "It's just fantastic. Who did you get to build it?"

I expected her to name one of the local kit home suppliers and builders, but she surprised me. "Selph did it, with some help from me."

At that precise moment, as though he had waited for his cue, Selph made a grand entrance. "A whole lot of help from you, actually. It was a joint venture, and my contribution toward your hospitality to me."

"Selph," she said in exasperation, "you don't require any looking after. You don't sleep here, you cook as much as I do, and considerably better, and you're involved in everything. You contribute to the house all the time."

He smiled, looking genuinely pleased. "I'm glad you see it that way. So let's call this a love offering."

She hugged him. "That's fine, because I love it. The vibes in here are just great. The studio combines both nature and inspiration all rolled into one great feeling."

I agreed with her. What amazed me, however, was Selph's abilities. He did not look old enough to have learned to build with such skill, or even to cook with such expertise. What else could he do? This studio was quite something! Amber's description summed it up well; there was an unusually powerful energy in the room, and a very pleasant one.

Her easel and canvas stood in the center, while on the floor before them lay a large, thick rug with a deep pile. Amber liked to be barefoot when she was painting, so the rug was warm and soft. Standing on the rug, she could see out of three large windows, all of which served to pour natural light onto the canvas. Several of her finished paintings were leaning against the walls.

I walked over to see what she was painting, but with an agile leap, Amber stood before it, her arms outspread.

"Please don't look, it's a surprise."

I felt inordinately pleased, and turned away. "Really? That's wonderful. Thank you."

"If you like it, you can thank me when its finished," she said, leading me outside. "Now toddle off and don't get into mischief."

"Yes, Mummy, all right, Mummy," I cooed in a childish voice as I wandered away. "Coming, Selph?" I called back.

Joining me, we wandered over to the goldfish pond I had dug out and built when Amber and I first moved in. As soon as they could see me, the goldfish immediately came to the surface, their mouths opening and closing blindly in the hope, or expectation, of food.

"I enjoy keeping fish. These streamlined beauties are veil-tailed comets," I said.

He nodded absently. "You have a lot to be thankful for with a wife like Amber."

It was my turn to nod, vigorously. "Don't I know it. They say you get what you deserve. Somewhere or somewhen I must have done something right to deserve her."

"So you don't regret choosing to stay with your physical body?" Selph asked.

I sighed. I could feel a low niggling pain in my lower back, another in my new hip, and my surgically repaired left hand ached badly. My left leg still dragged a bit, while my body, generally, was physically uncomfortable, but it was no more than I was prepared for. Pete had lectured me long and carefully about my injuries, and I knew that it could take years for my body to fully recover, if it ever did. I often thought longingly of my body of light, but I was not yet ready for a permanent trade.

"No. No regrets at all. Living with Amber again makes it all worthwhile."

"As wonderful as she is, you will have to find the value of life within you, not just in sharing life with Amber. If she got killed, what would you do? Wither away and die?"

I clutched his arm, my stomach sick with dread. "Oh God, no! You can't mean it."

"ADAM!" His voice was loud and sharp, cutting through my fear. "I used a metaphor. She's okay. I merely want you to see that we live life for ourselves, as well as for other people. If you live only for another person, or for other people, then you miss an essential truth in life. It is *your* life you live, not another person's."

I relaxed with a sigh of relief. "If I lost Amber now, Selph, I would will myself to die. But when I'm fully recovered and less vulnerable, I probably wouldn't." I shuddered at the thought. "I don't want to think about it."

We watched the fish in companionable silence for a while, and I fed them, their ceaseless mouthing finally rewarded. "People are a bit like these goldfish, eyes wide open, yet blindly reaching into life for something, anything, and so often disappointed at the end of the day," I said.

Selph nodded. "That's consensus reality. People do it because people do it. And are so often unrewarded. Ironically, even if they are rewarded, it simply imprints the mindless habit into an even deeper behavior pattern."

"That's terrible," I said feelingly. "How do people get out of such an ingrained rut?"

"By going back to that most rejected of all words: responsibility. Consensus reality prefers the government to be responsible, yet the government is also part of a consensus reality. Result: deadlock, confusion, conflict."

"It's a human problem, the need to blame rather than take responsibility. I wonder why."

"Blame is an expression of reaction. Reaction comes from the past, part of an old survival mechanism. Fear reacts, love responds. Response is based in the moment, and is a choice; reaction is the abdication of choice. Reaction has a place in a life-threatening situation, but in daily life it is no longer appropriate behavior."

"You can understand why it persists, though. Take my acci-purpose, for example. I blamed the truck driver, it seemed so obviously his fault. It would be normal for me to sue him for everything I could get."

Selph nodded. "True. Incidentally, what happened about that?"

"I refused to press charges. The police were quite upset with me. They thought that I was mentally affected. I had to get Pete to stop them pestering me. He didn't agree with me either, but he accepted it. It's strange how life works. It turned out that the owner of the truck had a fleet of them, and he was a religious man. He was so affected by my not suing him, and so grateful, that he sent me a large check as his personal compensation. I guess he accepted responsibility for his driver's error."

"What excuse did the driver make?"

"He didn't have many to offer. He said that in all the many times he had crossed the bridge, the light had never once been red, and he had never before seen any other traffic on it. So this time he assumed it would be clear."

"A bit weak, and very foolish."

"Yeah. But he was only playing his part in my drama."

"I presume that you refused to press charges because of our talk. You decided to accept responsibility for yourself."

"Of course. What you said was true, my heart knew that. My life is my responsibility, as is each person's, even if they don't know, or even don't agree. So I had to act on it. Knowing what I know, I had no choice! If I didn't, I would be living a denial and perpetuating my role as a victim. And that's a habit I need to break!"

Raising his eyebrows, Selph nodded. "Very good, Adam. I'm impressed. You may hold yourself back sometimes, but you have undoubted courage, and the ability to live your truth. Just those two ingredients can set you free. Never forget: Truth lived, can set you free."

I felt as pleased with his praise as I used to as a kid when my Dad praised me, and that was not too often! The police business had seemed a bit like a dream at the time, not quite real in a world of endless pain. Memories of their annoyance and frustration were all a little hazy. But I do remember clinging to my truth, and my determination to act on it. I learned, then, that living your truth is nonconformity in a world that accepts blame and guilt as normal.

"Is it okay if I teach Amber how to enter the Sphere of Tranquillity?"

"Of course. It's only natural that you would want to share such an experience with her. And you may get a surprise."

"Oh, such as?"

Selph laughed. "If I tell you it won't be a surprise."

He jumped to his feet. "I must go. I'm cooking tonight, so I have to get prepared."

I grabbed his arm. "Who *are* you, Selph? Why the guise of a boy? Where, or when, do you come from?"

He looked at me seriously, and for long moments it seemed that his body subtly altered into that of a very old sage, then the moment passed. "Never be fooled by bodies or identities, Adam; they are transient, illusions. Look into the eyes of a child and what do you see? Is it a child, or is it ageless life? Look into your own eyes. Do you see who you truly are, or do you see Adam, the identity? And who looks? Is there truly a where or when in eternity? As you ponder my words, use your heart/feeling center, rather than your brain/intellect. This is where Amber excels; she *feels* truth."

Even though I was still holding tightly onto his arm, he walked away, and I was clutching nothing. Goose bumps ran over my shoulders and into my scalp. "I wish you wouldn't do things like that," I shouted after him.

He waved, leapt up and down with his hands held above his head in a victory dance, and continued to the house.

I stared down at my hand, still clenched as though holding his arm. There was no explanation! Like the osprey, it was a mystery that defied normality. Suddenly I saw a parallel: Truth defies normality. The daily reality of society is considered normal, yet it is a denial of the principles that Selph is teaching me. He lives at an altogether higher level than most other people. I could find no explanations for Selph and his teachings in normality, nor could I expect to remain normal if I accepted him and his teachings. And I had accepted them! So why try and remain normal? That was conflict material. I felt mildly shocked. It occurred to me that an explanation of his abilities was possible, so long as I threw away all conventional ideas and limitations.

I sat comfortably watching the goldfish for a long time as they swam near the surface of the pond. Each time they saw me move, they would mouth the water surface again, waiting for some offering from beyond, then, forgetting me, they resumed their continuous swimming. Occasionally I waved my hand over the water, and the mouthing would instantly start again, only to fade out as they received nothing. This is religion, I thought. If I offer them manna from above, they congregate for the offering. No miracle, and they lose interest, so I have to catch their attention again. And what's in it for me? I thought about that, trying to avoid the obvious: power and control. I am not a cynic, nor do I attempt to be, but the parallel between these goldfish and mindless worship had one thing in common: expectation. The fish and the congregation both awaited some divine intervention to feed them. For the fish it was directly as food, for the congregation it was the nourishment of hope and salvation.

My earlier comfort had eroded, and I needed to move my body. The various aches and pains were teaching me that a whole new set of rules now applied to my physical body, and I could not disregard their messages. I shambled away from the log I had been sitting on like an old man, stooped and slow as I groaned my way upright. However, by the time I reached the house, my body and limbs were moving nicely. It made me acutely aware of my need for continued exercise, rather than prolonged pondering on the imponderable!

We ate our dinner quietly, with little conversation. I was too busy comparing myself with a goldfish to have much to say. Selph was fully involved in his food, both serving it and eating, and I suspected by the faraway look in Amber's eyes, that she was still involved in her art.

"I won't be in tonight," Selph announced.

I smiled at him pleasantly. "You mean you ever are?"

Looking at me directly, his eyes were challenging. "When you go to bed, I go elsewhere. Do you have a problem with that?"

My smile bland, I shook my head. "None at all. I am, however, curious about 'elsewhere.' You can't get much more ambiguous than that noncommittal statement."

He nodded thoughtfully. "Fair enough. I'll try to be brief. You and the vast mass of twentieth-century people live in a frame of reality that you call the present time. When I leave here, I enter another frame of reality where those people also believe it is their present time, yet it is a totally different time than here. It isn't, of course; it only appears that way, because all time occupies the same space. Okay?"

I gaped at him, totally perplexed. "I'm sorry I asked," I said in a small hurt voice.

Amber spluttered for a few moments, swallowed, and then burst out laughing. "You should see your face, Adam," she chortled. "You're a study in pained confusion."

Despite myself, I grinned. "Is it possible that one day I'll know exactly what you mean?"

"You certainly will. You and I, all people, live in a vastly greater reality than you perceive; thus, your perceptions limit your experience. As you begin to live Truth, your perceptions and experience of life will expand. Eventually, you will learn that reality is timeless and measureless."

"Is 'elsewhere' your home?"

"No."

I was surprised. "So why do you go there?"

"It's all about a promise to help."

"But . . . you're helping me."

"Adam's the child, right?" Amber said shrewdly. "Do you go to help the mother?"

Selph bowed to her with genuine respect. "Absolutely right on both counts."

Confused beyond comprehension, I held my head in both hands. "I give up. Be Amber's teacher. Why waste your time and energy on a blockhead like me?"

"By referring to yourself in that way, you diminish both yourself and your reality. Your universe shrinks, your potential is denied, and your problems increase. And you do it to you. Nobody else can, but you. If I were to call you that, I diminish myself and my reality, not yours."

"Suppose I agreed with you?"

"Then we diminish our lives together."

"Adam, my darling, why did you insult yourself? Don't you know that you are intelligent, courageous, and . . ."

"A blockhead," I intervened, laughing. "However, I do see what you mean, so I withdraw my remark to myself about me. Listen me, you/I are/am intelligent, courageous, and ab-so-lutely lovable."

I smiled at them both. "Is that better?"

Selph brought his hands together sharply, making a strange, high-pitched, clapping sound. My ears popped, and I felt what seemed like a ripple run though the house, floor, garden, me, everything! Briefly, that earlier surreal quality was back, as though a dream were being remembered, and everything was just a shade out of synch. But even more odd, I swear that the light of day brightened in the moment of that clapping sound, and that everything was suddenly more clear, more sharply defined, even more real.

I looked at Amber at the same moment that she looked at me. There was awe in her eyes.

Selph's voice was powerful and stern. "Never, ever, diminish yourself again. Turn the light of your life up, higher and brighter, never dimmer or duller. You are the Light Keeper, learn how to use it."

Turning, Selph walked though the doorway leading from the living room to the kitchen. I followed almost on his heels, a couple of questions coming nicely to the boil.

The room was empty!

"Wait," I shouted into the empty room, "come back. You haven't done the dishwashing yet."

Walking back to the dining table, I shook my head.

"That's a neat trick. First you see him, then you don't. My God! Did you feel what I felt when he clapped his hands? Gosh! If he weren't my teacher, he'd be scary."

"Adam, you shouldn't have shouted to him about washing dishes," Amber admonished me. "It's not nice."

"Aw, come on! If he doesn't know by now that I've got a highly developed sense of humor, he . . . he never will," I finished lamely. "And just to prove I like him, I'll wash the dishes. Never mind about my poor battered body and my tired aching limbs. I'll struggle through it."

"This is one of those times when it would be nice to have a dishwasher," Amber laughed, as together, we gathered up the dishes.

We have to catch our rainwater and store in large ten-thousand-gallon tanks, so dishwashers and their extravagant use of water were out. Not that we cared. A few minutes at the sink, and we walked into the lounge.

"Anything worth watching on the TV?" Amber asked.

"Is there ever?" I replied.

"So we can have a lovely, quiet, cozy read instead."

I nodded. "Yep, much better than the goggle box."

After an hour, or so, my body felt increasingly uncomfortable, so I had to change chairs. "Let's talk."

"Okay, my darling. What would you like to talk about?"

"That queer happening when Selph clapped his hands. What did you experience? Can you describe it for me?"

She could, and did. And it was virtually the same as my experience. "What do you think happened?" I asked.

"I've thought about it, and felt into it. My intuition says that he affected both your and my reality in some way. My logic says that's not possible, but I trust my intuition."

"Yeah," I reflected thoughtfully, "I trust it too." I chuckled. "It's hard to speculate on someone like him, or what he does. It all leads nowhere. You have to accept both him and the mystery of him."

Amber got up, and, pulling me to my feet, kissed me lightly on the lips. "I think he's one hell of a teacher, and I have no trouble accepting him at all. Now, my darling, you go to bed, and I will bring us a drink."

"It's a bit early," I protested, glancing at the clock.

"Early! Did I hear you say that it's too early to go to bed with your wife?" Amber said in mock incredulity. "Oh, glory be! Have you had enough sex already?"

I clapped my hands to my head in mock surprise. "Ah! You're right. You are the brains of the outfit!"

We sat in bed chatting for a while as we sipped our way through the hot chocolate, and I had definite lust and lechery in my mind as we finally lay down together. Just briefly, I closed my eyes, but when I opened them again, I was alone, the morning sun streaming though our window.

# Eleven

It seemed strange not to have to jump out of bed ready for a busy day. Hospital had broken my pattern of getting up early; but at home, it seemed the thing to do. I was flexing my limbs, trying to ease out the stiffness and twinges prior to getting up, when Amber walked in with breakfast on a tray.

Selph followed her, pushing a lightweight bed-table on casters. The table was adjustable, and reached right across the bed, making it easy to sit up and eat. I was not sure whether to be pleased with this innovation, or grumpy.

"I know you don't like breakfast in bed," Amber said smoothly, "but we think it would be a good idea for a week or so. The way you flaked out last night suggests that you are trying to do too much too soon. So, Adam Baker, please don't argue about it."

Checkmate! I sighed. I had a history of spilled coffee, and marmalade on the sheets. "Okay, thanks. The table's good. It should certainly make it easier."

Amber kissed me affectionately, and gently mussed my hair. I looked at Selph. "Are you going to kiss me too?"

"I'll pass."

He was wearing the perennial orange T-shirt and the oversize green shorts. "Do you have to wear those bloody awful clothes all the time? Is there nothing else you can wear? I'll happily buy you some clothes."

He shrugged. "This is my cosmic gear. It's the in thing for cosmic teachers. I take it you don't approve."

"Looks more like comic gear to me."

Amber frowned at me. "Adam, don't be rude."

I sighed. "So what's on the agenda today?"

"First you drink your coffee and eat your toast and marmalade without getting any on the sheets, then you shower and dress. Soon after that, I'll be taking you into Nambour to meet John Relish, your new physiotherapist. Then, time permitting, we'll have some lunch and I'll bring you home. How's that?"

"Sounds good to me." I grinned at Selph. "How about you? Got any other worlds to visit, or are you coming with us? You're very welcome." I frowned thoughtfully as I chewed. "By the way, how the hell do you vanish so damn quick. It's very disconcerting, you know."

Selph's smile was wide and innocent, his usual "butter wouldn't melt'" expression. "Particularly if the dishes are left unwashed!"

"Gosh! You heard me?"

"I heard."

"But, you weren't there."

"You know that for a fact, do you?"

"Er, you vanished, so . . ."

"So you assumed the rest," he interjected.

"Well, yes. It's a fairly natural assumption in a normal world. If I can't see a person in a room, and they aren't hiding, then there's no one in it. That's been a belief that has served me very adequately, until now."

Selph shook his head sadly. "You have just outlined the limits of consensus reality. Far more is happening in a greater reality than you can see with your physical eyes. There is also an invisible, intangible world that occupies the same space as your familiar physical one. In that reality, the room may have non-physical people or even other Beings in it, so please don't deny its existence. Denial propagates limitation."

"So you could become invisible and walk around the house spying on us?"

"Adam! I'm ashamed of you," Amber burst out.

"I said he could. I didn't say he would," I said defensively. "I apologize, Selph; that demeans me."

He nodded, grinning. "I accept. I'm here to challenge you, breaking down your attachment to normality, so your reaction is not entirely unexpected."

"You're so kind," I muttered.

"What was that, Adam?" Amber said in a vexed tone. "Were you saying how grateful you are that Selph should care so much about you?"

Feeling annoyed, I looked at them both squarely. "Look, let's get one thing clear. Selph pushes my buttons, and I react. Maybe one day I won't, but right now I still react. I'm the student, right? That means this is a learning process." I met Amber's eyes. "Selph is quite capable of putting me straight without you doing it as well. I feel as though I'm being ganged-up on. It hurts, and even though that's my reality, and probably quite pathetic, I'm the one who has to live with it."

Amber took a deep breath, letting it out slowly. She nodded. "Yes, I can see that, Adam. Okay, this is a new situation for me. Fair enough. I won't interfere in any heated exchange between you and Selph, even if the heat is all coming from you."

"No matter how wrong you think I am, or how stupid, you won't butt in to reprimand me?" I pressed.

"No, but I might tell you about it afterward."

"Fine. I welcome that. I love you, and I have nothing but respect for you, so that's not a problem."

Selph smiled, spreading his arms wide in an embracing gesture. "I love you guys," he said.

"One of us ain't a guy," I retorted with a grin, "but thanks. I think I speak for both of us when I say, we love you."

Amber kissed me, then walked over and kissed Selph.

"Do I get a kiss each time Adam reacts?"

Hands on her hips, Amber looked at him with a perplexed smile. "There's an imp in you. You know, I'm just beginning to realize that a teacher can also be a scallywag."

I gave an exaggerated cry of pleasure. "Hallelujah! At long last my wife has seen the Light."

Leaving me to the remains of my breakfast, they both left the bedroom. Finishing the coffee, I pushed the table out of my way and lay back with a contented sigh. I thought about the Sphere of Tranquillity. With a whole new routine to get used to, I had not been there since leaving the hospital. Obviously, leaving it until bedtime was not a good idea. As I thought about the river and the sphere, I knew that I wanted to go there, and I wanted to take Amber with me. Maybe this afternoon might be the time.

I got out of bed slowly and carefully, and went into the bathroom. As I waited for the shower water to get hot, I reflected on having to do everything slowly and carefully. I was not used to that. I had always been an active man, not overly fast perhaps, but certainly not slow. I sighed. Right now, I had little choice. My body felt uncomfortable, with many constant twinges of pain, and sudden movement, or haste, invariably increased the discomfort.

Stepping under the hot water, I relaxed. This was good. I could feel the aches and tiny hurts easing away as the heat invaded my body. I stayed longer than I should, but it felt so good that I broke my own rules about wasting water.

Amber was waiting with a towel as I stepped out of the shower. "Does that feel better?" she asked, as she gently dried my back.

"Does it ever. I always liked a shower in the morning, but now I truly need it. It's rather like lubricating a squeaking hinge, and I'm the squeaky bit."

Smiling mischievously, Amber guided the towel around my crotch. "I thought this was the squeaky bit."

"If you keep on doing that it'll do a lot more than squeak," I warned. "I'm not that decrepit."

Having dried my body, I sat in a chair while she dried my feet. "It's embarrassing. I can't get at my back or my feet. I just haven't got the stretch to reach them." I sighed heavily. "I hope John Relish is good at his job."

"Relax. Pete said that he's the best in the area."

❖   ❖   ❖

Exactly an hour and a half later, Amber and I met John at his Nambour clinic. He was older than I expected, going bald, a bit stout, not as tall as me, but gifted with an exuberant abundance of enthusiasm.

"Come in, come in." He shook hands with both of us and greeted us warmly, then turned to me. "Doctor Morrow has told me all about you. I've been going through your records, Adam. My my, you did have a terrible prang. You're lucky to be alive."

My mind flashed back to being in the tunnel and making my choice about life and its continuity, and about how little luck had to do with it. The Truth that Selph revealed did not always fit with our everyday language. I was not sure how to respond. I hated the idea of speaking something that was no longer my truth.

"I'm very fortunate," I replied. "Most of that fortune, however, is based in the people who have cared for me, and supported me." I squeezed Amber's hand. "Like this lovely lady, for one."

John gave me a shrewd look. "Right, let's get down to business."

And that's exactly what he did.

Three hours later, I had been through a series of his tests while he assessed my condition, making continual notes on a large pad. He clucked, ummed and aaahed almost without a pause, peering at various dials through thick spectacles. He was brisk, courteous, and very thorough.

By the time we left, I had an appointment with a local fitness center that worked with his patients, a list of exercises that he had taught me to help alleviate the various aches and pains, and a small soft ball to squeeze in my left hand while I was reading.

And I ached. "How about that. I get prodded and probed, stretched and squeezed, and three hours of questions. Now I ache all over."

"You poor dear. Never mind, I'll make you better when we get home."

We were sitting in Holly's Coffee House, eating prawn crepes and drinking Earl Gray tea, while I bemoaned my fate.

"Do you mean what I think you mean?" I asked hopefully.

She smiled at me bewitchingly. "No, I don't. I mean something else entirely, but you'll looovvve it."

I raised my eyebrows. "Hmmm. I can't wait."

We went into the local supermarket, where I insisted on helping with some shopping. I ended up both pushing the shopping trolley, and hanging on to it for support. By the time we got home, I was again tired.

My legs walked into the bedroom on pure reflex, and I collapsed onto the bed. Amber followed me, and to my surprise began to help me off with my clothes.

"I thought you said no sex?"

"Why does it mean sex if I help you take your clothes off? Is there nothing else on the horizons of your unclothed reality? Or do you have a sex fixation?"

I felt baffled. "Apart from having come through a very severe two-year sexual drought, I plead innocent."

She kissed me. "Just wait and see."

Crossing to one of the large built-in wardrobes, she fiddled around before emerging with what appeared to be a huge ironing board. She set it up in the middle of the room.

The penny dropped. "I get it. That's a massage table. But who's going to give the massage?"

She looked at me in amusement. "I am. Mandy taught me the basics, and I practiced on some of the people at the fitness center. She reckoned I'm a natural. I wanted to be able to help you when you got home, and Pete thought that this would be the perfect way. And I wanted to surprise you."

What a wonderful gift. My eyes went all blurry on a surge of emotion. "I'm surprised, all right. You're such a very special person," I choked. "All I do is grouch, but you never stop giving. I love you so much."

"After what you've been through, you're entitled to a bit of receiving, so enjoy. Anyway, I do it because I love you."

She helped me onto the massage table, and placing my face over the padded hole, I felt her hands spreading oil over my back. I groaned in sheer pleasure.

For the next hour Amber gave me a strong, deep-tissue massage that did absolute wonders for me. I had expected to drift off to sleep, but the strength in her fingers would not allow it. I was soon groaning in pain as she kneaded the tight knots out of muscles, the heel of her hand firm on the tender pressure points. She was sensitive and careful over my injuries, but the overall massage was a very powerful experience: a natural tonic.

When she finished, she insisted on helping me to the bed, where I limply collapsed. Pulling the sheet over me, she gently kissed my lips, and walked quietly out. I could hear the shower running, and I tried to think of some things that needed thinking about, but I was so relaxed that I just floated away into a deep, restful sleep.

Well over an hour later, I awoke refreshed and energized. I dressed, and went to look for Amber. She was not in the house, so I walked to her art studio.

She must have seen me approaching. "Please don't come in, Adam, I'm working on your surprise painting," she called out.

"Okay. When you're ready I want to talk to you."

"I'll be with you in about twenty minutes. Will you make me a mug of coffee, please?" she called back.

"Your slightest wish is my instant command, madam," I shouted flippantly, before wandering over to the fish pond. I spent more time with the fish pond than anywhere else in the garden. I love water. The energy of water seems to contain a vast volume of serenity, and being near it allows me to soak in its tranquillity. Personally, I prefer my water to be in small rivers and streams, or ponds and lakes. Huge wide rivers seem to lose it, and although the ocean has it in abundance, for me, it seems more remote, less available. Give me a pond with water lilies and some fish, or a waterfall or two, and I will happily sit by it, lost in its serene beauty.

It seemed I was only by the pond for minutes, but when I finally hurried to the house, Amber was at the poolside, sipping her mug of coffee. She gave me a mocking smile as I arrived. "My slightest wish is your instant command, huh!"

"I'm sorry. My intentions were honorable."

She smiled. "I'm only teasing. I saw you standing by the pond. You were in another world. You really love that old pond of yours, don't you? Did you feed the fish?"

"Yes, I do, and yes, I did. But speaking of another world reminds me of what I want to talk about."

Amber's eyebrows lifted. "Sounds mysterious." Her hair caught the evening sunlight, and for a moment it seemed to catch fire. Her eyes, green and direct, were focused on me. She was so beautiful my heart almost missed a beat.

"When I was in really bad pain, only the memory of your words of love at my bedside kept me alive. I hung onto them, and when it all got too bad, they were my focus to live. Despite that, however, I needed . . ."

"Oh, Adam, I knew that my love helped you, but I didn't realize it was to that extent," Amber interjected.

I nodded. "It was, believe me. However, as I was saying, I needed more. Because I refused medication for pain relief, I needed to be able to control it myself, but I couldn't. Then one day, or it may have been night, I guess it doesn't matter, all I know is that the pain was pretty grim, I had an incredible dream. When I was in it, I learned that Selph had taken me into a reality that is beyond our normal physical world, yet it was also my dream. He and I met in a transparent sphere over a river."

"A transparent sphere?" Amber echoed.

"Yes, rather like a huge bubble that floats over a river. He called it the Sphere of Tranquillity. Anyway, the purpose behind all this was to teach me a way of going beyond my pain. He said that a focus on pain maintains it, while a powerful focus away from pain breaks its grip on you. The first thing he taught me was how to enter an altered state of consciousness. The sphere is then accessible."

"Can anybody do this, or is it only for pain relief?"

"Anybody can go there for any reason at all, or even for no reason other than peace and tranquillity."

"Even for consciousness expansion?"

"Yes, that in particular. That's what I am getting at. I want to teach you how to reach the sphere. I think it's possible that we could even go together. How about it? Right now?"

"Oh, Adam! I'd love to."

We went into the house, and I called out to Selph, but there was no reply.

"He's out, so we'll be undisturbed. It's best to sit, rather than lay down, but I can't sit comfortably for long. How about we take a comfortable chair into the bedroom for you, and I'll lay on the bed?"

Amber grabbed a light chair. "That's fine by me," she said, carrying it into the bedroom.

I lay on the bed, and Amber was seated. I had explained what the exercise was about and what it involved. We were relaxed, our eyes closed. "I'll speak the induction process at a fairly slow pace, until we reach the riverbank. Then I'll be silent. Whether we are on our own, or together from that point will just unfold naturally."

Speaking slowly and clearly, I took us into our light-bodies, through the rainbow, down the twenty-one steps, and onto the bank of the river. Then I stopped speaking.

I was alone. Where Amber was, I had no idea, but as I walked along the riverbank, there was no one to be seen. The river was the same extravagant, Disneylike overabundance as before. Each sparkle of light on the river gleamed and flashed with an individual brilliance, while the fish that I could see were impossibly clear, colorful, and defined. I liked it. I thoroughly enjoyed a reality where the flowers on a tree smothered it in pink blossoms, while each leaf was an almost emerald green. This was so much a total opposite to my everyday drought reality that I reveled in it. I was not bothered that small European animals mixed and mingled with Australian marsupials, or that the birds I could see and hear belonged to no single country. I had lost all need for a rational and logical reality; this was an expression of resplendence, of a nature that was unconfined, unlimited by earthly rules and regulations.

I wandered slowly along the riverbank just drinking in the sight and sound. The animals and birds were clearly aware of me, but it was I who had to walk around them. They showed no fear at all, and only the mildest curiosity. When, eventually, I reached the beautiful Sphere of Tranquillity, I was surprised, having almost forgotten about it. As before, it was a large, transparent bubble spanning the entire width of the river, with rainbows of light flickering over its surface.

Stepping close to its resilient skin, I walked into it, clearly feeling that moment when the skin yielded to my pressure. It opened without an opening, simply allowing me access to the interior of its mystery. I stepped in, and the bubble was once again intact. Within the sphere it was silent. My usually overactive thoughts became quieter, more subdued, yet my awareness grew keener, my inner knowing more clear and sure. As I walked further in, my steps took me out over the water, and, as before, I walked on a gossamer film of bubble to the center of the river. In my thoughts, I called to Amber and Selph, but neither of them were to be seen or heard. With nothing to see in the sphere, I sat down, suspended over the river.

For a while I watched the water, just gazing into it as it raced over the riverbed, glimpsing the occasional flash and gleam of a fish. Very gradually, I developed the feeling that a presence was with me. Standing up, I looked around. At first, I saw nothing, but with an ever-growing awareness, I knew that the presence was of Love. Then, as though I had overlooked it, I saw a large volume of golden glowing light quite close to me.

Very clearly, into my mind came the knowing that if I merged with this golden light, something incredible would happen. I grappled with my thoughts, trying to understand how this was possible, and what it might mean, but as I did so, the golden glow swiftly faded away. As it vanished, I felt an overpowering loss.

Sitting down, I reflected on what had happened. I had failed, of that I was certain. What or how I had failed eluded me. As I sat quietly trying to grasp the meaning of it, a memory surfaced in my mind: I had encountered this mystical golden light before. I strained to recall the memory of that elusive event, but that too, eluded me. For moments longer, I struggled, then I gave up.

Once again I gazed down into the river and, surrendering my thoughts, I watched the movement of the water. Time has no meaning in a timeless reality, but when I looked up again, it seemed that I had been there a long time.

Suddenly the memory I had struggled to reach was clear: I had encountered the golden glow when I had fallen in the fitness center. As the terrible pain had blasted through me, I had lost association with my physical body. Floating in a disembodied state I had seen Mandy cradling my head, and I had seen the golden glowing light hovering close by. What did it mean?

The question did not bother me, nor did it feel important. All that felt meaningful was the peace that I was feeling; that had value. Thanking the sphere, I shared my appreciation with it, then I turned to leave. Walking through the skin of the sphere, I continued back along the riverbank. As always after my visit to the sphere, I felt more connected with life and myself, more whole, lighter. Yet, strangely, as always on my return, the river and all nature was far more real than when I entered. It baffled me, but it was nothing that concerned me.

Soon, reaching the steps, I went back up them, through the rainbow, and back to the physical reality of my body.

I opened my eyes and without moving, looked at Amber. She was watching me. "Hi. Welcome back," she said.

I took a long, deep breath, releasing it slowly. "We got separated," I said, smiling.

She nodded. "Yes, you weren't with me, but it was a wonderful experience."

"Would you like to tell me about it? You don't have to if you feel you'd rather not. I understand."

"I'd really like to share it. How about you? Will you go first?"

"Happily."

She jumped up, got us each a tumbler of water, and sat on the bed next to me. I drank my water, then lay back and told her everything as best I could. "It's not easy to bring some of the experiences and events into words," I ended. "It happened in a reality that is far more subtle than our normal reality. The spoken word is inclined to make it more defined than it was, or paint in colors that simply weren't there, or fail completely with colors that were. Words can be very cumbersome and incapable."

Amber nodded gravely, her face serious. "How do you know that it wasn't pure fantasy, all created by your own imagination? That's what most people would believe."

I nodded, frowning. "Yes, you're right. I've talked with Selph about this. Let me give you a question to consider. Let's say that you are walking across a city park, following the footpath. There are dozens of other people all around you, some walking, some skating, and people sitting on park benches. As you walk along, you see that there are lights swirling and flowing over a bed of flowers, so you walk over to them. The flowers are roses, and quite a number of other people are also admiring them. As you get close, you see that the lights are tiny fairies, and you stare at them in awe. You turn to the woman near you, and excitedly point to the fairies. "Can you see them?" you ask.

"See what? You mean the roses? Of course I can. Do you think I'm blind, or something?" she replies.

A bit agitated, you point to the fairies that are now right in front of her. "Can you see the, er . . . fairies?"

She stares at you. "Fairies! Are you all right, luv? A touch of the sun, perhaps." She walks away laughing, shaking her head, and you see her talking to her friend about you as they stare at you, pityingly. You look again at the roses, and very clearly you see the fairies."

I looked at Amber. "My question is: would you be able to accept the fairies as real if you knew that you were the only person in the park who could see them? Or in other words, could you accept your own reality when it had no validity from any other person? And even more than that, could you accept your reality if all the other people said you were wrong, or you were seeing things, or, that you were imagining it?"

Amber was quiet for several minutes. "Hmmm, I see your point. In truth, I can't answer that. I'd like to think that I could accept my reality, but I know that it would be very challenging. My God! What a need we have for approval, and to ... to ..."

"To share a consensus reality?" I suggested.

She looked pensive. "Yes. Wow! It really hits home when you put it like that. It shows how frightened we are of standing alone with a belief, or an experience. It shows just how afraid we are if our experience strays from the accepted normality. One step over the boundary and we are straight into denial."

"And that, of course, is self-denial."

"Which puts us right back into consensus reality," she finished.

Leaning toward her, I gently kissed her lips. "So we are back where we started. I've shared my experience with you, and I can tell you, with all honesty, that I accept my experience as real. Even more, I'm convinced from the quality and clarity of each happening that it's possibly more real and more true than this physical reality we are now sharing." I kissed her again. "And I find this very real."

"Did you find it as easy to accept your very first nonphysical experience?"

"No. For quite a while I was convinced it was a dream state that Selph had created. But as I learned to go there for myself, and I was able to go beyond pain into a rich experience of incredible peace and healing, I reached the inner knowing that it is real." I put my arm around her. "When I had that major fall in the fitness center, and experienced those past-life dramas, I knew as it happened and afterward, that it was real and true. Of that, I have no shred of doubt."

Amber nodded, a wry smile on her lips. "So it's up to each one of us. The question is not whether we imagined a fantasy or not. The question is: can we accept our own reality when it's no longer either validated, or physical."

"That about sums it up. I've learned that most people not only distrust their imagination, they don't believe in its validity, and even hold it in contempt."

"That's terrible. People are imagining all the time."

"Yes, we are, and mostly we imagine the worst."

"And get it," she said sadly.

Rolling onto my side, I flipped back Amber's skirt and kissed the soft inside of her thigh. "Let's not get morbid," I said, kissing my way higher and higher.

It started off as play, but one thing led to another, and thirty breathless minutes later, we both lay naked on the bed, clasped in each other's arms.

"I love spontaneous lovemaking," Amber murmured, her hand caressing, then gripping, the exhausted Sir Knight.

"And I like your definition of lovemaking as opposed to sex. It suggests that women make love while men have sex. Would you agree with that?"

"There's no doubt about it. Making love is romantic, and women love romance. Having sex is physical, and is often devoid of romance. Having sex is a male attitude."

"Be fair," I protested. "We just made love because of my sexual overture. I mean, it's sex that kicks it off, and generally male sex."

"Maybe, but if more men made love to their partner, instead of merely having sex, I bet there would be a lot fewer divorces. Let's face it, rape is having sex violently without consent. Even without violence, and with consent, just the act of having sex as opposed to making love is a form of abuse. The woman may well have an orgasm, but the spiritual factor is missing. And that spiritual element is love."

"Perhaps you're overlooking the obvious," I said. "You have to be in love to make love. I suspect that there are many more women in love than there are men. Having sex is a primal driving urge, mostly male, while making love is an intimate human expression of tenderness, commitment, care, and closeness to your loved one."

Amber wriggled around, and kissed me.

"Adam, that's a beautiful way to put it. Now, tell me honestly, were you making love to me or having sex?"

"Can't you tell the difference?" I asked, abashed.

"I think so. In all honesty, I think you were having sex for about the first five minutes, and then you began to make love. Am I right?"

I felt ashamed. "Absolutely right," I said in a subdued voice. "But how did you know?"

"Oh Adam, do you think a woman can't tell? The change in energy is so obvious, so apparent. Don't feel bad about it. As you said, your sex kicked it off, but you then began to make love to me. And it was wonderful."

Her grip on my exhausted part tightened. "Arise, Sir Knight, that I may thank thee."

And like a miracle, the exhausted part arose. "What power I have," Amber chuckled. "I can exhaust Sir Knight in a major tournament, and then so easily replenish his energy."

"Yeah, I'm bewitched by a witch."

Laughing, Amber let go. "Sir Knight, I will let thee rest for now, but I thank thee for thy services."

We showered together, although Amber was gone before I was hardly wet. "Take your time. If you can't dry yourself, call me. Meanwhile, I'm going to get us some supper."

It took me a while to get dry, but I managed it. Drying my feet was the tricky part; they were so difficult to reach. When I could again dry them easily, I would know that I was much more flexible. Putting on a dressing gown, I wandered into the kitchen. Outside it was dark, and I was surprised that it was late evening. "Time sure goes fast when you're having fun," I commented.

"You haven't told me about your inner experience yet," I reminded Amber as we munched on toast and Tasmanian brie.

She nodded. "I know. You and Sir Knight diverted my attention, if you remember. Let's eat, wash the few dishes, and go to bed. I'll tell you then."

Twenty minutes later we lay in bed. "So what happened?" I asked. "Did you find the Sphere of Tranquillity?" I blinked drowsily, my eyelids feeling heavy.

"I'll tell you as I go," Amber replied. "I went into my light-body, through the rainbow—I particularly liked that—and down the steps. However, this is where it all became very different from your experience. As I left the last step, I was standing on a wide, long beach. I walked along it for a little way, when I heard splashing nearby. Turning around, I saw a dolphin watching me. It . . . Adam? "

Her voice had become a fading, distant echo.

"Good night, darling," I faintly heard.

# Twelve

For a few minutes I lay blinking at the bright early morning sun, then I rolled over and kissed Amber. "Have I told you that I love you?"

She turned sleepily toward me. "Never enough," she muttered. "What did you say?"

"I said I love you."

"Ah, yes, tell me more."

"I love you 'cos you're gorgeous, sensitive, wonderful, caring, and 'cos you're kind to Sir Knight."

"All the essentials, eh?" She smiled, and kissed me.

"It's very strange," I said as I lay back. "I've been trying to remember what you told me about your experience with the Sphere of Tranquillity last night, and I can't remember a damn thing. I must be losing my memory."

Leaping out of bed, Amber leaned over me and gave me a hard smacking kiss on the lips. "You silly goose, you fell asleep while I was telling you. What a way to treat a lady!"

I grinned. "Is that what happened? Hmmm, it must be because I treated the lady so well a short time earlier."

Half an hour later we were having breakfast. I smiled at Amber as I chewed on toast and marmalade. "Ma deah, ahh jest luvv maarrrmaalade," I drawled, Texas-style.

She shuddered. "What a phony accent. If that's an attempt at cowboy language, you need a lot more cow."

"Right, enough frivolity," I said briskly, "tell me about your altered-state experience."

She nodded. "Okay, how much did you hear?"

"Ah, um . . . going down the steps," I muttered.

At that precise moment, Selph walked in. "Good morning, folks. I hope I'm not intruding," he said, smiling at us.

"Of course not. You're always welcome. This is your home while you are, er . . ." Amber faltered.

"On our planet," I finished.

Selph poured himself a coffee, and sat down, chuckling. He was wearing the usual, spotlessly clean, but ghastly orange T-shirt and long baggy green shorts. I shuddered.

"Allow me to clarify something for you. I don't zip on and off the planet, as you infer. I simply move in and out of frames of reality."

"Oh, is that all," I said with exaggerated humor. "Well Amber, my love, I'm just so happy to have that clarified."

Amber put her hand on Selph's. "Selph, dear. That doesn't make it clear. Mere mortals like Adam and me have no idea what frames of reality are."

Selph chuckled. "I know that. You don't want me to make it too easy for you, surely."

Amber frowned. "Selph, there are two categories: 'too easy,' and 'what the hell are you talking about.' We are now well into the second category."

I gazed at her approvingly. "Well said, darling. Sock it to 'im."

"And you shut up," she said severely.

I grinned, Selph grinned, Amber grinned, then we all burst out laughing.

Selph held his hands up in surrender. "Okay, I was playing. But in all honesty, this is not the moment to talk about frames of reality. Really, believe me. There's a timing to this, and right now doesn't fit. Let me just reiterate something I told Adam earlier: all time occupies the same space. Frames of reality are rather like time."

"That's it?" I said. "No more?"

"For now," Selph replied.

Amber looked concerned. "Is it because I'm here, and you don't want to teach me?"

Selph took her hand and gently kissed it. "Amber, I honor you and your spiritual insights. I would be proud to be your teacher, but I'm not. Your teacher left you in your past life, for she was no longer needed. I'm here for Adam because his timing has arrived, that's the simple truth. I will never avoid what must be said, whether you are with us or not. Also, anything that Adam shares with you, or passes on from my teaching, is fine by me."

"Oh, Selph, I'm sorry for what I said." Amber threw her arms around him and kissed him.

For long moments he looked like a rather shy schoolboy. Then he grinned at me, and the illusion vanished. "I like it when we make up," he said chuckling.

"Selph, I said it before, and I'll say it again. You really are a scallywag," Amber said, grinning.

"Amber and I did the altered consciousness exercise last night. Amber was just going to tell me about her experience when you walked in, Selph. That's the third interruption we have had, so now I want her to finish it."

"What were the other two interruptions?" Selph asked.

"Never you mind that," I said hastily, then I grinned at him. "Besides, the timing's wrong!"

"One thing I've definitely learned," Amber said. "It takes a scallywag to teach a scallywag. Now, pipe down you two, and let a lady think." She looked mildly embarrassed. "I'm not sure if Selph wants to hear about this."

Selph jumped smoothly to his feet and gave a deep and courteous bow. "Madam, I would be honored if you would allow me to remain in the room so that I may hear all about your spiritual adventure."

I stared at him. A modern man would find bowing rather strange, and would look pompous, or awkward. Selph turned bowing into pure, flowing grace, as though he had bowed many thousands of times. I could not decide whether it was something he had done before, or if he had a natural ability to do everything perfectly. By the time I had thought it through, I decided that the latter was probably true.

Standing up, I stretched cautiously and carefully. "I want to get to the beach today for a walk. Let's sit by the pool while Amber tells her story."

Not all of our chairs were comfortable for me since my car-smash, but the poolside seats were. We sat down.

"As I was saying before I was so rudely and consistently interrupted . . ." Amber started.

"Be nice," I interjected.

She gave me a sweet smile, and began. "As I left the last step I was standing on a long, wide beach. The sand was golden, and the sea very blue. I walked over to the sea, and followed the shore for a little way. There was the sound of splashing behind me, and I turned around to see a beautiful dolphin. We made eye contact, and instantly I could hear the dolphin speaking into my mind.

"'Welcome,'" it said.

"I didn't know what to say, so I went over to it and held out my hands. 'May I touch you?' I asked.

"It nodded its head vigorously, and I placed my hands flat on its skin. It felt strange, as though I touched a cool breeze, and the next thing I knew we were flying through the air together. I felt concerned for the dolphin.

"'Can you breathe all right?'

"'I live in the Light,' it replied, 'breathing is not important. Although you too live in the Light, you perceive it as more dense, so you must breathe it to maintain your physical body.'

"'Are you a regular dolphin out of the sea?'

"'No, I am here for you. Together we are going to reveal a great truth to you: a truth that will enable you to unfold and flower.'

"'What is this truth?'

"'Be patient, little one. You will see.'

"I realized then that the dolphin was really very big, far, far bigger than a normal dolphin, and that it was taking me ever higher into the sky. The odd thing is that the flight felt just as I would expect if I were physically flying high into the air. I could feel the air rushing past my face and forcing my hair back, yet in no way did it seem to cause us any resistance. The dolphin held me close to its body with a flipper, and I had the feeling that it was female energy that held me. As we went higher, I wondered if I would be able to breathe, and then I realized that breathing was not necessary. I was in the Light.

"There came a time when I no longer felt the air rushing past my face, and there was an absolute physical silence, yet on an inner level all space was filled with sound. It felt so odd, such a paradox. I could hear dolphins and whales so clearly. They were calling to each other, and, crazy as it sounds, I knew they were talking to other dolphins and whales that belong in a different time than the one we presently live in. I knew this beyond any doubt."

"Do you have any doubt now?" I asked her quietly.

Amber looked at me with a faraway gaze. "No, none at all. The whales and dolphins were communicating across time zones, and it was perfectly natural. I listened for the inner voices of humans, but there were none. I felt sad about this. 'Are we so ignorant?'" I asked the dolphin.

"We were still ascending at an incredible speed, although it felt as though we were now unmoving. 'Humanity believes in separation,' the dolphin said, 'so they create isolation and aloneness. Dolphins and whales know only of oneness, knowing nothing of separation and isolation, so we experience the connectedness of all life. We do not accept that time separates, and thus it does not.'

"'But we do, and thus it does,' I finished.

"As we continued ever higher, I could see our planet Earth getting ever smaller, until it appeared no larger than a perfectly round house far beneath us. It was beautiful, but as we went higher, for the first time I heard a few human voices in the absolute silence. 'I can hear people,' I said.

"I could feel the dolphin smiling. 'Of course. There are many people who, through the ages, have discovered the oneness of all life. It is, after all, the most paramount of truths. The voices of these people fill all of space and all of time, whispering those truths that others might hear, and know. Listen, child, and learn.'

"And I heard some words. I heard a voice deep within me whispering as though a distant echo: 'You are the creation of love; you are born of love; you are an expression of love. This is your Truth. Live this truth, and you will awaken to love. Love will consume you; you will fall in love with love; and in love, you will be free forevermore.'

"The moment these words were imprinted into me, I knew that I would never forget them. With the words came an inner knowing of their truth, an acceptance and a commitment. And in that moment there was an almighty splash, and the dolphin and I were cavorting in the sea.

"'Did that really happen, or did you do something to me?' I asked the dolphin.

"'Your experience was true, little one,' the dolphin replied. 'I enjoyed your company, again. I love you.'

"At that point, the dolphin leapt out of the ocean and dived deep, and I saw no more of it. I left the sea, crossed the beach, walked back up the steps, through the rainbow, and back to my physical reality."

There was a long silence. "Oh, wow!" I exclaimed. "Don't ever tell me that you haven't got a teacher."

Selph shushed at me. "Give me a summary of what you have learned from the experience," he asked Amber.

She was quiet and thoughtful for several minutes. "I spent an hour or so in bed last night going over it. My big question was why we went so high into the sky. When I lay thinking about it with my eyes closed, I seemed to get the same perspective again. I got the feeling that we went above our everyday spite, above all our anger and hate, above our never-ending gloom and negativity, in fact, far above all the clutter of human thoughts. We went into a place that was unsullied, pristine pure, somehow never-endingly new. And there I learned that life is absolute continuity. The whales and dolphins know it, and, thank God, some people know it. By continuity I mean you and I and everyone is continuity. Time is meaningless, no more than frames in the continuity of all life. I . . . ! Frames! Yes, that's it! Life appears to be held apart by frames of reality, but it isn't. Apartness is not separation. I learned that it is Love that connects the all to the all. If each one of us lives the most pure expression of Love that is possible for us, then we each consciously connect with All That Is." She looked at us breathlessly. "That's basically what I learned. Thank you so much for asking me, Selph, because I didn't know I knew all that."

Selph took her hand, and looked at her seriously. "Now do you see why I'm not your teacher? Your teacher is with you, and doing a remarkably good job of teaching." He swept the fingers of his other hand through the air close by her face. "It's that close, Amber. It's that close."

"What is?" I asked.

They both ignored me.

"Amber, any time you so choose, you can make the quantum leap. I guarantee that it will be in perfect timing."

"Of course it will." She smiled. "Everything is."

I felt as though we had all gone for a walk together, yet somehow, try as I might, I had been left far behind.

"Why can't I take a quantum leap?" I asked peevishly.

Selph laughed, and turned to me. "Because you are still on an obstacle course."

"Really. What obstacle?"

"There is only one. You!"

"Oh boy, you're a real tonic for my self-esteem. I know I've got problems; what I don't know is how to fix them. That's where I need help, Teacher," I said sarcastically.

"Don't you approve of my methods, Adam? Don't you trust my ability? Would you like me to leave?"

"Okay, Adam," I said aloud, "you've done it again. You got yourself into this mess, so now you have to get yourself out of it. Just cut a big slice of humble pie, Adam. Tell the nice teacher that you felt left behind and, let's be honest, threatened, by Amber's ability, and because he's a nice teacher, he'll let you off the hook."

Selph chuckled. "You may well be on an obstacle course, Adam, but you badly underestimate yourself. That was Amber's inner experience that she shared with us. It was her insight, and her moment of inner knowing. Hers, Adam, hers, just as you also have yours."

"I know," I said glumly. "I'm sorry. It was just so profound and wonderful that I, I, well, like I said, I felt threatened. I suppose I felt inadequate. Perhaps that's one of my obstacles. However, apart from that, I want to know about the frames of reality that first you, and now Amber, have referred too. Methinks the timing has arrived."

"I agree, Selph. Tell us what they are," Amber said.

Selph nodded. "Fair enough, the moment's here. Amber put it beautifully when she said, 'Life appears to be held apart by frames of reality, but it isn't.' Imagine a deck of cards, only this is a cosmic pack with an infinite number of cards. To give license, you could say that all the cards basically occupy the same space. Each card is a frame of reality. I am able to move from one frame to another, as I will. Obviously, this is not a regular ability for people in this particular frame of reality. And no, this frame of yours is not my home frame."

"Can people in other frames move around at will, like you do?" Amber asked.

"Definitely not. There are frames where people live in such a degenerate state that you would be seriously shocked just to see it. There are others where all the people are enlightened, and they can change frames at will. Then there are all the shades of difference between the two extremes, and other frames that are so utterly different that they are totally inexplicable."

"Could we change frames?" I asked.

"Not just by wanting to. But a true quantum leap may take a person from one frame to another."

"Do you mean in their current life?"

"Almost always those people live out the rest of that incarnation in their current frame. It is not unusual, however, that their physical life comes to an abrupt end. And then again, there are a few who purposefully continue in the same incarnation in the same frame for an extraordinarily long time afterward."

I stared at Selph in blank astonishment. "Why doesn't everyone know all about this? Why is such knowledge hidden?" Then I laughed as it hit me. "Of course, silly me! While Truth remains as Truth, it is not a person's Truth if it's out of their timing. Right, Selph?"

He nodded gravely. "Exactly right, Adam. And each person decides their own timing."

I got up from my chair, stretched, and turned to Amber just as she, too, got up. Putting my arms around her, I hugged her. "I'm very proud of you," I said quietly as I held her. "That was a truly wonderful experience. But tell me, do you believe in your reality, and trust it, or was it just your imagination and fantasy?"

She nodded, smiling. "Good one, Adam. I put myself through that laying in bed last night."

"And what did you decide?"

"I decided that it was as real, and maybe more so, than any physical event in my life. I decided to honor it."

"Great! I love you."

"And I love you, my darling." She kissed me with a mixture of passion and tenderness, her eyes screwed up as she faced into the sun. "It would seem that the Sphere of Tranquillity is not my destination at the moment. After your car smash, tranquillity would be both a necessity and a healing for you."

I grinned at Selph. "It makes a change from drama!"

❖   ❖   ❖

Following our leisurely breakfast, we had a busy day. Selph took off on business unknown, while Amber and I went to the fitness center to get me started on my course of new exercises. It went very well. Mac, the guy who had devised my program, was a fitness enthusiast, and under his tutelage I spent an hour on a few familiar machines, and a couple that were new to me. It became obvious that Mac would be a hard taskmaster. "Streeeetch, Adam, get into it, man. You've gotta streeeetch. Moooove that body, moooove it, man."

I streetched and moooooved, while Amber stood by with a little grin of sympathy. But she got caught out. "How about you, Missus Baker?" Mac called out. "You look as though you could do with a workout. Why don't you join your husband and get fit?"

A frown of annoyance crossed Amber's face. "I happen to think I am fit, thank you."

Mac took it as a challenge. "Oh, we'll see." He stared across the huge room to some people on the far side. "OI," he bellowed. "SALLY, come over 'ere, luv."

Without doubt, Amber is lean and fit, but the Sally that came loping across to us was a female bodybuilder. She looked to be the typical stereotyped blonde bimbo, with muscles. Within minutes of conversation with her, I had learned not to make hasty judgments, for she was friendly, articulate, and very bright. I liked her instantly.

"Okay, er, missus . . ."

Amber's voice was resigned. "Call me Amber."

"Right, Amber, let's see how you shape up next to our Sally."

"Come on," I protested, "that's hardly fair."

Mac was unflustered. "I didn't say beat her, or even equal Sally. I said, let's see how she shapes up."

It turned out that Amber shaped up very well, and Mac was vocal in his praise. "I'll be dammed! Bloody good, Amber, if you'll pardon my French. You've got a job here any time you want one. A month or so and you'd be superfit."

Amber nodded, looking breathless and pleased. "Maybe, but I'll get Sally to design a program for me. I'm puffed."

"Welcome to the sweat club," I grinned.

When we left the fitness center, we went round to Holly's Coffee House for a well-earned cappuccino. I noticed that, because I walked fairly slowly with a stick, a lot of people looked at me, assessing my problem. I tried scowling at a few who really stared, but it gave me no real or lasting satisfaction.

"Adam, don't scowl. It won't stop people staring."

"I know, but scowling at them is appropriate."

"Appropriate?"

"Yes. I haven't had a good scowl in ages. Everyone's been so nice and kind. Mind you, Selph gets me scowling."

"Are you serious?"

"About scowling? Yes. I'm only just learning to like people. It's a whole new experience for me."

"You know why that is, don't you?"

"Is this is a trick question?"

"It's because you are only now learning to accept and even like yourself."

I shrugged. "Yes, I suppose. I hadn't thought about it quite like that. I have to remember that I'm a nice guy now."

Amber put her face close to mine. "You always were, you goose. But if you couldn't accept it, you couldn't be it."

"You know something, you really are clever. But just think about this. If I'm married to a clever, beautiful, and caring woman, you have to admit that on some level, I've been very good to myself."

"That's true, my darling, but don't forget that I left the old Adam, and renewed my marriage to the new one."

I sighed. "That about wraps it up. You win. I am a freshly and newly wonderful man, married to a perennially perfect and wonderful woman."

She hugged my arm as we walked to the car. "You see. I knew you would understand if you just worked your way through it. Men are very slow, but they usually get there."

❖   ❖   ❖

I had been looking forward to my time on the beach, but it turned out to be a disaster. I had to abandon any further thoughts about beach walking. Luckily Amber was with me, otherwise I may well have ended up stranded, and in serious trouble. Altogether, it was a strange and exhausting event.

We started out in fine form, with firm to hard sand, a gentle breeze, warm sunshine, the works. Just perfect. I felt energized by my earlier workout, and for me, we walked fairly briskly. Several times Amber suggested that we turn back, that we had walked far enough, but I argued that I wanted a good long walk to test myself. I got the test, right enough, but not in the way I had expected.

We had been walking for about forty minutes when I decided it was time to turn back. We were at a familiar part of the beach, where it was sheltered by tall cliffs. As I sat on a rock to get a breather, I glanced idly at the cliff face and various fallen rocks at its base. My blood ran cold as goose flesh crept over my shoulders.

I recognized it. This was the place where I had fallen all those lifetimes ago. Getting to my feet, I walked closer, staring up at the cliffs as though they were haunted.

"Adam! Are you all right? You've gone as white as a sheet. What's the matter?"

My mouth opened and closed, but no words came out. As though peering through a mist, I saw James climbing down the face of the cliff, getting ever closer to the purse. I saw the easy part end, and the torturous care he used as he got closer. His hand reached out, and grabbing the purse, he tucked it into the top of his breeches. Knowing what was about to happen, I ran forward with a cry, "NOOOOOOOO!"

I was too late. With a thin wail, James plummeted from the cliff face, landing with a sickening thud on the sand. At the instant he hit the sand, a sharp pain exploded in my lower spine, and with a soundless cry, I collapsed.

Everything was spinning about me as I tried to focus on a voice. I knew that I should know who was calling me, but I was having trouble finding them. The voice was suddenly closer, more clear. "Adam! Adam! Oh God! Adam, what's happened? What's the matter? Speak to me. ADAM!"

That last shout did it, and I saw Amber. Staring at her, I tried to understand how she could be here. I was lying on my back at the base of the cliff, staring up at its rocky face. It was the same rock face I had seen so many times, crumbling sandstone, unstable and unsafe. I gaped up at it in confusion. This was not where James had fallen? It was quite different. I could feel Amber's arm under my shoulders as she held my head off the sand, and I felt a tear fall on my face. Gradually, I realized what had happened.

"Oh Adam, please talk to me. What's the matter?" Amber sobbed. "Please, please talk to me."

I tried to sit up, but pain flared in my lower spine.

"I'm sorry, Amber," I gasped, "but the weirdest thing just happened. Do you remember me telling you about those past-life incidents where I injured my back?"

She held me carefully, aware that I was in some pain. "Of course I do. Why?"

"Well, I just had a stunningly vivid recall. I saw this cliff as the one that James climbed down, and I saw him fall. In the instant he hit the sand, my back gave way. It hurts."

"Oh my God! I'll have to run and get help. The tide comes right in here, and over those rocks."

"I know. It's incredible, that's exactly what happened to James. In trying to avoid drowning, he ruined any chance of healing his back."

Amber stared at me, her face ashen. She was wearing dark blue shorts and a white T-shirt, so she was well prepared for a run. She jumped up. "I'm going, now."

"NO!" I shouted sharp and loud. "I think I can get up. I can't have injured myself, I didn't do anything. I'm sure that this is some sort of memory pain; a pain from the past, as it were. The source has got to be in my psyche, or my emotions. It can't be in my back."

Amber was looking frantic. "Adam, I calculate that we may have about two hours before the tide is in. We're going to need all that time to get help, and get away again. I just daren't take the risk of waiting."

I rolled onto my stomach and forearms, and very slowly, I brought one leg up at a time, until both of my knees were under me. "Okay, give me a hand now, please."

Amber is a strong woman, so with her assistance I came easily upright and onto my knees. It took a bit more grunt and effort, and some nasty stabs of spinal pain, but with her help I got to my feet.

"See," I grinned. "Nothing to it."

She was not amused. "Oh sure. We go out for a simple walk, and end up involved in past-life therapy. You just about frightened the living daylights out of me."

Suddenly she was all business. "Okay, let me check your back brace, and then we'll see if you can walk."

She undid the top of my trousers, and fiddled around under my T-shirt. "Not now, my dear, Sir Knight just isn't up to it," I said with a smirk.

For a moment she looked so angry I thought she might smack my face, then she visibly relaxed and laughed. "You really are the giddy limit. This is serious. We've got to get you off this damn beach, and you make jokes."

I took a determined step forward, leaning heavily onto my stick, and, staggering to keep my balance, I nearly fell flat on my face. With the tide coming in, the sand had suddenly turned soft, and the stick had buried itself for nearly half its length.

"OH! AH! AH!" I shrieked as pain stabbed anew.

"Oh my God! What now?" But even as she shouted at me, she saw the problem. Holding my shoulders as I slowly straightened up, Amber's mood changed. It was only then that I realized just how badly frightened she had been.

"All right, my darling. We can do this together. I won't leave you to get help. You're strong, and so am I."

"Bloody useless stupid stick," I groaned as I savagely threw it away.

With weary resignation, Amber retrieved it. "Idiot. You'll want this another day. And don't think I'm about to play fetch, okay?"

We looked at each other, and chuckled. Then, with one arm over her shoulders, I began a slow, limping walk back along the beach. But our problems had not yet ended. With fickle ingenuity, the weather changed. The sun disappeared behind black storm clouds, the breeze became a strong cold wind, and large waves came tearing up the beach. And as though that were not enough, the sand had gone soggily soft. Each step was now a laborious effort as we sank nearly to our ankles in the loose, yielding sand.

"Was it you or Selph who told me you're into drama?" Amber asked in a conversational tone. "I have to admit, this is a pretty good effort."

I scowled at her.

Ten minutes later, it began to rain, and within moments we were drenched in a torrential downpour. I laughed in delight. "The drought! The drought's ended. Yahoo!"

It lasted precisely fifteen minutes. The sky rapidly cleared, the sun shone weakly, as though ashamed, while the wind made our wet clothes feel like melting ice.

Amber looked at me with vexed admiration. "You're amazing. You've messed up your back, we're up to our bums in gritty sand, you've turned the weather bad, made it rain so we're soaked, stopped it, and now we're nearly freezing to death. Anything else? How about some hail, or snow?"

I scowled some more.

We were both almighty glad to reach the car, and I slumped in the seat, almost wiped out. I was cold, wet, I hurt, and I felt wretched. As Amber drove us home, I sat and dreamed of a long hot bath.

She started giggling about three-quarters of the way home, and it was not long before I caught it. Soon we were laughing uproariously, regardless of whether I was truly damaged, or not. "I'll run a hot bath for you. You'll soon recover. You poor darling, that was quite nasty."

When we pulled up at the house, Selph was outside waiting. "The bath is filled, and I've put half a packet of relaxing salts into it. Let's get you into it."

I could hear myself asking him how the hell he knew what had happened, and if he did, then why in the blue blazes did he let it happen, but nobody was listening. They were moving me around like I was a stuffed dummy, stripping off my wet clothes, and helping me into a bath of hot, steaming, oh, so deliciously relaxing water.

I lay back, rested my head on a bath pad, closed my eyes, and just as Amber stepped under a hot shower, I went trotting off through the colors of a rainbow.

❖   ❖   ❖

A couple of weeks passed, and I quickly recovered from the shock of the past-life recall and its painful physical repercussions. The long hot bath and my inner relaxation had forestalled any major problems. It caused me to miss a couple of sessions at the fitness center, and it appeared that my first assessment was correct. Selph told us that the memory of the cliff-face fall was deeply imprinted into my consciousness, along with all the other incidents. Until the trauma was resolved, it could continue to replay the appropriate incident, assuming that the reaction impulse was inadvertently triggered. The nasty part was something he had already told me. The key incident—the one that had installed the trauma, beginning the series of incidents—was still in my consciousness, festering like an old sore. This incident was so bad that, even subconsciously, I avoided it.

Selph repeated something he had told me earlier: Anything of the past that is unresolved, is unresolved now. He told us that, until recently, I could not have accessed that particular event even if I had wanted to. However, when I had been in serious pain in the hospital, he had visited me in the middle of the night. At the time I had wondered if I were awake, or dreaming. He had then taught me how to go into an altered state of consciousness. When I had entered the sphere over the river, I had gone even further into an altered state, reaching a deep inner place of healing. I had then experienced the triumphant vanquishing of my long addiction to pain and suffering.

Selph said that because of this, I was ready to face the causative calamity that had begun all the other incidents. Because my addiction to suffering had been overcome, the cause could now be resolved. He also reiterated that it did not have to be this way. I also had the option of "falling in love" with who I am. Knowing me, that's an unlikely option. I seem to have a habit of doing things the hard way. That is where Amber and I really differed. She treated herself far better than I treat myself. Much as I disliked the idea, I knew that one day I would have to deliberately revisit my unknown crisis in the past. Just the thought gave me the shivers!

Obviously, we wanted to know how it was that Selph knew about the mishap, and I pestered him for an answer.

"In consciousness, Adam and I are very connected. This is the prerequisite of a teacher. I felt the discord the moment the incident happened, and I took license to, er, look in, as it were. The rest you know. I observed that you would manage, so I got things ready this end."

"Look in?" I asked.

Selph shook his head regretfully. "I should have known that you wouldn't let that one pass. Let me put it this way, if I can move from one frame of reality to another, surely it's no surprise that I can peep from one time frame to another. Besides, it's a cosmic teacher's prerogative."

Amber and I looked at each other.

"What do you think?" I asked.

She nodded. "I reckon it'll do."

I grinned at Selph. "Okay, no more questions."

He looked genuinely astonished. "Really!"

❖ ❖ ❖

We were having an early breakfast one morning when Amber made a startling remark.

"Do you know, I woke up with a very powerful, intuitive feeling. It was both a feeling and an inner knowing, and I think I'm going to trust it."

"Oh. What was this profound knowing?" I asked idly.

"I think I'm pregnant."

"You what!?"

"I said I'm pregnant. I even know when it happened."

"You do!"

She glanced shyly at Selph. "It was that first night together, in the hospital room."

"I . . . I . . . I don't know what to say."

And then it hit me with a wave of joy. "My God! You're pregnant! That's wonderful." I hurried to my feet and went to hug and kiss her. "That's the most wonderful thing I've ever heard. A baby! Our very own baby."

And then came doubt. "But, you don't really know, do you? It hasn't been confirmed? I mean, isn't it too early for missed periods and all that sort of thing?"

"No, it's not confirmed. I just 'feel' it."

Selph's voice was quiet, almost hesitant. "I can confirm it for you. I've known since the morning following that particular night."

Amber gave a squeal of delight. "You can! Oh, that's just fantastic. I *am* pregnant."

I stared at Selph in shock. "How could you possibly know since then? It's medically impossible."

He shrugged. "Quite likely, but I don't operate through medical possibilities. I saw that the conception had taken place in Amber's consciousness. It's easy enough when you see a greater truth."

"That's a neat trick," I said admiringly. "But what does her consciousness look like?"

"You know what your light-body looks like?"

I nodded.

"Well, pretty much like that. You can read all there is to know about a person in their light-body. That is, of course, if you can see the light-body."

"Is that the same as the aura?" Amber asked.

"No. The aura is aligned with your physical self, while the light-body that I refer to is more aligned to your soul self. The aura will reflect conception, but it would take an exceptionally skilled person to detect it this early."

Amber and I sat grinning at each other like silly kids, tightly holding each other's hands.

"I couldn't be happier than I am right now," I said.

"Nor me. Do you want a boy or a girl?"

"Yes please, I most certainly do. Whichever."

Selph grinned. "As long as we're talking babies, would you like another surprise?"

"My God! What now?" I asked.

"Kate and Bruno are going to have twins."

Amber gave another squeal of happiness. "That's just wonderful. Do they know?"

"No. It's not my business to tell them. Bruno is a doctor, he could find out if they wanted to know."

"I joked about them having twins," I said. "Bruno said it was impossible because there were none in the families."

Amber chuckled. "So much for impossible."

Suddenly, she was all brisk business. "Right, guys, we have things to do. Adam, you go and get ready. Selph are you coming with us?"

We were going to Brisbane. I had an appointment with Pete Morrow, and I was looking forward to seeing him. Selph, as usual, had other things to occupy him, but what, or where, I had no idea. Amber and I had given up questioning him about where he went, or even how he got there.

Within fifteen minutes we were away, with Amber driving as we whizzed along the coast road. Whizzed carefully, that is; the traffic police were forever out to raise revenue. We were quiet for a while, each lost in our own thoughts and idly listening to a political talk-back debate on the radio.

"It never ceases to amaze me that people will argue over politics and political issues," I said, as the debate on the radio got more and more heated. "Do people really believe that any political party is ever going to resolve the issues or problems of a country?"

"If people didn't believe it, there would be no politics to argue over. The idea is that politicians represent the people of a state, and nation. That's why we vote for them. Whether they're any good or not is another story," Amber replied with a smile. "Anyway, you hate politics."

I switched off the radio. "Seriously, the whole basic principle of how politics operates is self-defeating. It can never rise above mediocrity."

"Okay, my darling," Amber said laughingly. "Let's hear your words of profound insight and wisdom on the political system."

"Mock me you may, but consider this: If you and I, or any family, live together in conflict and contempt, the result will be confusion, discord, and distress. Right?"

Amber nodded. "Without any doubt."

"Equally, if two political parties, composed of men and women, oppose each other, each seeking to undermine and defeat the other party by using slander, anger, false accusation, bribery, lies, and every form of deceit and corruption available, then there is only one inevitable outcome: discord and conflict."

Amber glanced at me, her eyebrows raised. "I can't fault anything you've said, so far."

"If, at the highest level, the basis of a government is discord and conflict, then discord and conflict will ripple through every level of every governmental department. Right?"

"It's inevitable."

"How then, can any government that is based in conflict, corruption, and discord expect peace and harmony to flow into the country as a whole? There will obviously be even more conflict, more discord, more corruption, and ever-increasing problems throughout the whole community."

Amber looked at me respectfully. "I take back my mockery. That's definitely food for thought."

"The sacrifices of modern politics are truth, honor, and integrity. And those sacrifices cripple whole nations. The people become the victims, and this is where the paradox is revealed. The people are the victims of the people, for the government is no more, or less, than a representation of the people as a whole. We are our own downfall, our own corruption, our own discord, our own problem." I sighed. "That's it, madam, I rest my case."

"So is there an answer to all this?"

"Of course. If every person found real honor within his or her own life, the governments and their systems would have to reflect it. Each and every human being is the answer: the way we think, speak, and act. That's all!"

"So the grim reality is more of the same."

I shrugged. "I guess so. Maybe this frame of reality is exactly the way it should be for the lessons we need to learn while we're here. Maybe we leave this frame when we've developed those very attributes we need to erase the problems that cause us our growth in this frame. Maybe this frame is so perfect that it's impossible for us to see perfection through the limited framework of human understanding. And therefore, maybe this frame will always have its so-called problems because they are the catalysts for our growth and expansion. Maybe our problems are really our blessings in disguise."

"Mmm! Some maybe's. Adam, don't you ever dismiss yourself again the way you sometimes do. What you've just suggested is really deep."

I decided to change the subject. "Are you going to tell Pete that you're pregnant?"

"Of course. I want to tell the whole world."

I smiled at her fondly. "I'm not sure that the whole world is interested, or even cares. But I do. It sounds daft to say this, but thank you. Thank you for getting pregnant and beginning our family for us."

She glanced at me mischievously. "No problem, my love. You did do your bit in the proceedings, you know. And, of course, the gallant Sir Knight." She chuckled.

We were now well into the suburban traffic, so I said nothing more. I did not want to distract Amber. Quite soon we were pulling up outside the Whitehills Hospital.

As we entered the hospital, Amber held open the heavy swinging door for me with a little grin. "How do you like it when I reverse the roles of gallantry?"

"How do you like equality?" I countered.

She gave a deep, exaggerated sigh. "My darling, I long for the day that men will become equal to women, but I do so despair that I'll ever see it.

I laughed. "Touché."

We heard Pete before we saw him. When he shouted he was very loud, quite the opposite of his normal speaking voice.

"NURSE, LET ME KNOW WHEN THE BAKERS ARRIVE."

I could not resist. "THEY ARE HERE, NOW," I bellowed.

We both heard a startled "Whassat!" and moments later Pete came ambling rapidly toward us.

"Amber, my dear, how nice to see you." He stood like a big kid while she kissed him. Amber seemed to have that effect on men. "And, Adam! Just what in the hell have you been up to. I can't trust you out of my sight."

"Very nice to see you, too," I grinned.

He enveloped me in a gigantic hug, and once again I realized just how big Pete really was. "It's good to see you both," he said enthusiastically. "How are you?"

Amber smiled at him brightly. "I'm pregnant."

I smiled brightly. "I'm responsible."

Pete stared, eyes like saucers, then chuckled. Then he sat on a stainless steel chair and shook with laughter.

"By Christ! You're a pair," he chortled. "We obviously saved the essential part of Adam." And he guffawed again, laughing uproariously at his own wit.

I frowned at Amber warningly. I did not want any of her "Sir Knight" jokes in front of Pete. That was our personal and private humor. She got the message, grinned, but said nothing. I sighed in relief.

"Well, well, well. Congratulations, little lovebirds, I couldn't be happier for you." Suddenly, he was all business.

"Okay, Adam. What in the hell have you been up to recently? Can't you even go for a walk on the beach without getting in trouble?"

I frowned at him. "How did you know about that?" I asked, but a glance at Amber's red face told me everything.

I scowled. "You could have told me."

"She did exactly what I asked her to do," Pete said. "I asked her when you went home to give me a regular report on how you were shaping up. That includes primal therapy on the beach," he said with heavy sarcasm.

He heaved himself up with a small groan. "Bloody primitive chairs," he muttered. "Okay, folks, let's see if the goods are damaged. Follow me, please."

Pete insisted on a detailed account of the incident on the beach. Then, after asking me a number of surprisingly astute questions, we spent the next two and a half hours in the prod, stretch, test, and question routine, as he gave me a thorough examination. Not only was he surprised and pleased with my progress, he was impressed.

"Very good, very good indeed. Your muscle tone has improved enormously, and you're definitely becoming more flexible. The scar tissue is interesting. Although men are seldom concerned with it, you did have some very bad scarring on your chest. In a few more months, it'll hardly be visible."

"The one benefit of a hairy chest," I suggested.

He nodded. "Maybe, but you had major ridges of tissue where the steering column punched through, and that won't grow hair. It's unusual for it to recede so rapidly."

"Good clean living," I quipped.

"More likely the vitamins he takes. Along with garlic and various herbal medicines. That's where the tissue healing is coming from," Amber said firmly.

Pete gazed away pensively. "Strange, isn't it? I'm considered an alternative in medicine because I believe that given the chance, the body can heal itself. So I avoid, or use very reduced amounts of antibiotics and modern drug therapy. Despite that, I'm challenged when you talk about herbal medicines and vitamins."

I looked at him seriously. "Maybe that's where the word doctor comes from: indoctor-inated!"

He frowned at me. "Very droll. So which one of you is into vitamins and herbal whatsit?"

Smiling demurely, Amber replied. "Actually, Adam introduced me to a range of healthcare products when we first got married. I've stayed with them ever since. When something is doing you good, stick with it."

"It never ceases to amaze me that people who have the intelligence to apply themselves to five or six years of intensive study can be so totally one-eyed," I said to Pete. "Most doctors avoid anything that is natural and organic, to concentrate on intrusion and control. Thank God for the few renegades like you."

"You may criticize us," Pete said huffily, "but we damn well saved your life."

I sighed. "Look, I'm hungry, but I can't let that one pass. Can we go to the canteen and continue this?"

Pete looked at his wrist watch, frowned, and nodded. "Yeah, it's my lunch break too. Come on," he said, striding away with a heavy tread.

"Adam! Don't you dare upset him," Amber whispered fiercely as we followed him. "I know what you're like when you get going."

We all tucked into a few sandwiches and coffee before I continued the discussion.

"First of all, Pete, I'm not attacking you or your profession. I've got far too much respect for you to do that. There is, however, two viewpoints to saving lives. Take my life as an example. I remember telling you how I was standing in a bright silver tunnel, and I had to make a choice about living and continuing physically, or dying to my physical body. If I had chosen to relinquish my physical body, neither you, nor any team of medical experts, could have prevented my death. My point is this. How many other people, consciously or unconsciously, have to make the same choice? It's even possible that everybody does, despite having no memory of it. Think about that."

I sipped my coffee. "The idea is obviously far too outrageous to consider, but just embracing it as a concept would engender a whole lot more openness and humility than is presently apparent in the medical profession."

Pete grunted. "Nobody that I know would even listen to such a crank viewpoint."

"So much for openness."

"You live in an idealistic dream, Adam, and you expect the rest of the world to join in. It won't happen, my friend. Personally, I like what you say. Sure, I stand with one leg in the orthodox and one in the alternative so far as medicine is concerned, but that's the way it has to be. If I step fully into the alternative arena, I'm automatically ejected from the field of orthodox medicine. I happen to think I'm doing more good just the way I am."

"I agree." Amber said fiercely. "As far as I'm concerned, you were a vital factor in Adam's recovery, and in his subsequent health." The look she directed at me was pure challenge.

"I agree one hundred percent," I said. "But one day, in the not too distant future, you're going to have to make a choice. When you make that choice, and the commitment that accompanies it, your ability as a healer will increase quite dramatically."

"Assuming, I suppose, that I make the choice of natural medicines," Pete said caustically.

I nodded. "Yeah, how about that? I accuse doctors of being arrogant, then I display all my own prejudices and arrogance. I'm sorry, Pete. I've got no right to talk like that to a man of your caliber and dedication. Despite what I said about the choice of living or dying, I honestly believe that doctors like you have an incredibly positive effect on the people making those choices."

"So you really believe that death is a choice?"

"Inasmuch as death is no more than physical, yes. I'm convinced that our life as an intelligent Being continues, with or without the body."

Pete looked at Amber. "How about you, little lady? What do you think?"

Amber was thoughtful. "I'm not as convinced as Adam is about the choice, because I've never had the experience of having to choose, but I'm quite certain that all life is continuity, forever."

"You sound very definite about it."

"Yes, I am. Adam taught me how to get into that altered state that he uses for healing. I tried it and had a major experience. I learned that life is a very BIIIIIG project, without end."

"World without end, amen," I said smugly.

Surprisingly, Pete looked impressed. "It's a thought," he said. "We say all that stuff, but do we ever once hear what we say? And do any of us believe it?" He kept his attention on Amber. "What was your major experience? Do you mind telling me about it?"

Amber gave Pete a bewitching grin. "I don't mind at all, but it is a bit far out."

"At least I'm an open skeptic," Pete smiled.

As I listened to Amber telling Pete about her inner journey, I watched both her face, and his. Amber was quickly back into the energy of that mystic event, and I could almost feel her connection with the giant dolphin as her words weaved a spell of intrigue. Pete tried to maintain a casual attitude, but his concentration became more and more focused on Amber as she took him high into the sky. When she released him, he sank back with a heavy sigh.

"By Christ!" he exclaimed. "That was something else."

He looked at me speculatively. "How do you do this altered-state whatsit? I need to do it."

"Oh! What's your motive?"

"Just the peace alone would be worthwhile, and maybe I could learn a few things also."

"That's a pretty good reason," I nodded. "Okay, lunch at our place next Sunday, and I'll teach you how."

Pete sighed, and reached for his appointments dairy. "I bet you don't have to check the bloody date every time you want to go somewhere. I'm a slave to time. It gets so bad sometimes I have to check to see if I've got time to pee."

I chuckled. "An altered state would give you time to get out of time. That is, of course, if you have time!"

Pete ignored my wit while he frowned heavily at his book of appointments. "Right." He looked up in triumph. "My little red book says that I've got Sunday clear from ten in the morning until six in the afternoon. Okay, lunch it is. And, thank you. Now I must hurry away."

Jumping up, he kissed and embraced Amber. "Thanks for sharing that, little lady. In all honesty, I envy you such an experience." Giving me another of his bear hugs, he ambled away, huge, shaggy, and very benevolent. He was almost out of sight, when he turned around. "DON'T FORGET TO MAKE AN-OTHER APPOINTMENT FOR TWO WEEKS' TIME," he bellowed.

With a brief wave, he was gone.

Amber and I looked at each other smiling. She rubbed her ears. "Do you get the impression we should make another appointment?" she asked grinning. "Gosh, he's a dear."

"Bear, possibly. Deer, not a chance."

"Come on, smarty-pants. You've got a clean bill of health, and I'm very pleased with you. Let's go home."

# Thirteen

I was having one of those irrational days where little things seemed to aggravate the hell out of me. It even annoyed me that Amber was so accepting of my mood.

It all began with Selph. It always does! Amber and I were out at the pool, and I had swum a few smooth lengths feeling pretty pleased with the speed and endurance I was achieving. Then Selph came ambling onto the scene. The sun was shining, and as he stood at the poolside grinning down at us, once again I noticed that he had no shadow.

Determined to check on the sun and its angle, I got out of the water and stood alongside Selph. My shadow stretched out behind me. Standing right next to me, Selph had no sign of a shadow. Just thinking about it aggravated me. Such a blatant denial of physical law is very off-putting.

"How do you do that?" I asked, pointing behind him.

He knew exactly what I meant, but I guess he decided to be even more aggravating. "Do what?"

"You don't have a shadow," I said in exasperation. "It goes against all natural law. How do you do it?"

"What do you know about natural law?"

I sighed. This was not going to be easy. "I know that because sunlight cannot pass through a physical object, the object casts a shadow. That's elementary physics."

Selph stepped close and smacked his chest with a loud whack. "Put your hand on my chest," he invited.

I did, and it was solid physical flesh.

"Satisfied?"

"Okay, you're physical. I knew that, but it doesn't explain how come you've got no shadow. It's spooky."

"And you need it explained, do you?"

I could feel a trap looming. "Er . . . yes."

"So you can understand?"

Ah ha, I knew this trap. "No. I don't really need to understand. It's more along the lines of curiosity."

He smirked at me. "Oh, good. As long as you don't need to understand, I won't bother to explain." He winked. "Race you to the other end."

I did not intend to go back into the pool for a while, let alone race him, but as though in a dream I could not control, I found myself standing poised next to him at the edge of the pool.

"Go," he shouted.

We dived together, but as I quickly surfaced, he reached the far end. Feeling decidedly sorry for myself, I climbed out up the steps, and watched as Selph swam a few incredible laps. He swam at seal speed, and I knew that he was doing it just to aggravate me. The annoying thing was that it did! I couldn't decide whether he made me feel less capable, or whether his excellence at whatever he did was offensive. His blonde hair plastered wet to his face, barely covering his slick, innocent smile, and a body that looked plump and ineffectual, all somehow combined to aggravate me. Or, at least, it did today.

The weakness that had accompanied my smash-up had taken a long time to overcome. In the early days of my attempted rehabilitation, I had been so weak that my limbs had trembled uncontrollably. Weakness had even caused me to cry at the silliest thing, or the smallest challenge. Now, as I was gaining both strength and endurance, it somehow rankled to see Selph doing things that should not be physically possible in a body like his. I scowled at him.

"Adam, you don't need to practice that any more."

Amber had appeared at my side with a tray of sandwiches. She smiled at my look of puzzlement at her remark. "You were scowling again. Really, you'll get permanent wrinkles if you keep scowling at people."

"I wasn't scowling at people. I was scowling at Selph."

"Oh, I see. So Selph isn't people?"

"Of course not. He's a bloody aggravating enigma who is showing off in the pool, swimming at impossible speeds in a body that can't possibly swim that fast."

"Ah." She looked pleased. "I'm glad you've explained that. I confess, it was beyond me."

I'm convinced that Selph knew my thoughts. As I scowled, he came up and out of the water at the far end of the pool in a single effortless movement.

Smiling at me, he waved, then dived in. The dive was higher than is possible, cleaner, and with less splash than is possible. As though that were not enough, the same instant his body disappeared underwater at the far end, he came smoothly up and out of the water with seal-like ease and dexterity onto the edge next to where I was sitting. It was all totally and utterly impossible.

His wide blue eyes caught and held mine, and to my consternation, I could not look away. If Amber was aware of anything odd happening, she gave no indication.

Try as I might to rip my gaze from his, I could not. Gradually, I felt myself drawn closer to him, as though he were pulling me toward him through his eyes. When a voice spoke into my mind, I knew it was him. "Struggle will avail you nothing. You seek mastery, yet you are threatened by its presence. Only when you give recognition and acknowledgement to your own impossibilities will you find the limitless qualities that are your birthright."

My own inner voice was silent. "I find impossibilities very confronting. I react negatively."

"Don't personalize life. You live and experience so much through your identity. Release the Adam, and become one with life. Let go of categorizing, of defining what you can and cannot do, or be. All categorizing comes from the past, from your experience, from the known, but we cannot liberate the past in any way if we cannot liberate the now."

"I don't understand."

"Good. Don't even try. Touch your heart with truth. Feel. Surrender. Enter this moment, naked."

"I'll try."

"No. I just said don't try. You can only do it. Trying is an expression of the identity. Simply, do it."

"Cucumber sandwich, Selph?" Amber asked, as she offered him a tray. Her expression indicated that everything was perfectly normal, that nothing strange had happened.

As Selph took a sandwich with a smile and thanks, I knew instantly that no time had passed. Our silent conversation had somehow taken place outside of time. As I realized this, I accepted it. Why not? Death takes the people who die outside of time. Why shouldn't life do the same? In fact, the simple impossibilities that Selph hands out so casually all take place out of time. I was certain of this, but as far as understanding it!

All my earlier anger and resentment had evaporated. Even better, I did not feel ashamed or guilty about those feelings. That was a welcome improvement.

Munching on my sandwich, I smiled at Amber. "Did you see that last dive? Quite remarkable. He's great."

Amber frowned at me suspiciously, then gradually realizing that I genuinely meant it, her face relaxed into a smile. "I have trouble keeping up with you."

"How's that?" I asked blithely.

"Oh, nothing," she said airily. "It's not a problem."

A lot of things had been puzzling me lately about Selph, and his role as my ageless teacher. "Can you answer a few questions, Selph? Questions that I often think about, but seem unanswerable."

"Sure, but I have one for you, first."

I shrugged. "Go ahead."

"Have you noticed how easily I control you?"

I did not like the observation. "Er, yes."

"Did you ever wonder why?"

"Probably because you're my teacher."

"Is that the best you've managed to come up with? That's pathetic. I call it avoidance."

He was right. I did avoid the question. I knew that I would not like the answer. "Okay, you tell me."

"As soon as you lose control of yourself, I take control of you. Anybody can. That's the secret of personal power; you cause other people to lose control, then you simply reach out and take it."

"But I thought that you didn't approve of personal power. I thought you called that ego games."

"Investing in personal power *is* an ego game, but strange as it may seem, so also is losing your power. It's the reverse thrust of ego, but ego nevertheless. It helps create self-pity. However, the point I am making is about losing control. You lost it this morning, so I deliberately took it and controlled you. Did you like the feeling?"

"No. But I'm not sure how I lost it."

"Like just about everybody else, you lost your greater control a long, long time ago. When I said anybody can control you, those persons would, of course, have to be in control of themselves, even if only on an ego level."

"So how do I control myself?"

"Why would you want to do that?"

Aggravation flared, and I scowled at Selph. "So people like you can't bloody well control me."

"Look at me," he said. "Eye to eye."

And I did, despite not wanting to.

"See, you lost control of yourself again, and I can now command you as easily as that. Now I'll ask you once more. Why do you want control of yourself?"

I thought about it carefully. Obviously not wanting other people to control me was the wrong answer. So what was there left? Obviously I wanted to be in control of my life, go where I wanted to go, do what I wanted to do. Who did not? Perhaps it was that simple. "Er, if I was driving a car, I would want to be in control of the steering and determine my own destiny."

"Why?"

I stared at Selph in angry frustration. "WHAT THE HELL ARE YOU ON ABOUT?" I shouted. "EVERYTHING I SAY IS WRONG."

I glanced apprehensively at Amber. How did she like the performance of her beloved? Apart from a frown, and a touch of asperity on her face, she was calmly listening. I knew that she was determined not to interfere.

"Whoever said that you're wrong? Did I say that?"

I groaned in despair. "I give up."

"No more reactions? Good. Okay, let's take the car analogy. Sure, as the driver you need to be in control. But what of? The car or yourself? First, if you are the driver, you need to be in control of the immediate you. If you are not in control of you, then despite appearances, the car is not under your control. Let's name the car, circumstances. The car is not going to control the circumstances, it simply is them, going from one to another. If you are in control of the immediate you, then you are in control of any unforeseen circumstances. And if you are in control of circumstances, believe me, other people are not in control of you."

He smiled, reached out, and clasped my shoulder. "If you want, or need to be in control, you will always be in conflict with circumstances. If, on the other hand, you are able to relax, fully happy with who you are, right now, then, because of your relationship with yourself and life, circumstances will be accommodating and, without seeking or trying, you will be in control."

"What about your destination? You forgot that."

"Our car analogy was about life, right? Do you know your destination in life? Do you know what to strive and struggle for? Do you know how to reach your soul purpose?"

"Of course I don't," I said glumly.

"Then relax, and enjoy the ride of life. So many people spend their whole life in a state of anxiety about not having enough money for old age; the end of the ride, their supposed destination. They forgot to enjoy the ride. Live life now. Life is in this moment. Follow your heart, and enjoy. In this way you make the journey and the destination meaningful. And not only that, you are in control."

"But, governments are in control, and police."

"Adam, you don't really believe that. They control your relationship with society and the law, but they cannot control you. To take an extreme; you could be imprisoned, and forced to do manual labor, but even then they only control your body. This is the paradox: You, the essential you, is absolutely in your control, but the only way to realize that control is to totally relinquish it."

"I don't get it."

"Don't despair, you will. Let your heart feel Truth, don't intellectualize it, for yet another paradox lurks in all this. When you relinquish the need to be in control, you surrender to life. Your inner surrender allows the essential you to guide and direct the identity you. This inner directive is expressed as 'direct knowing.' The intellect conceptualizes, the essential you 'knows.' Very different."

I shook my head in dismay. "Wow! That's a lot to take in. How do I release control? If I did, wouldn't I be out of control?"

"Out of other people's control, yes. And the how is very simple. Trust. Trust yourself. Trust your own inner knowing. Trust that you are adequate. If you trust yourself, you honor yourself. If you honor yourself, you honor life. And if you honor life, life will honor you. The circumstances in life will honor you, and people will honor you. That's it! It isn't easy, but it is simple!"

"I'll need to digest all that. And you said you only had one question for me! Now it's my turn, okay?"

Selph grinned. "Trot 'em out, and we'll see."

"Well, it's like this. I could spend the rest of my life seeking my own Truth, and that's okay. But how about you, and your life? With a whole lot of stretching, I can just about grasp that you can move in and out of time, so I accept that you can go back to your place and no time has gone by. But as I grow older, you've got to grow older with me, or people will wonder just what the hell is going on."

"And that's a problem?"

"I think it is. Don't you?"

"Watch." Selph stood up, bowed to Amber and me, and in a theatrical tone said, "Please, don't get hysterical."

As we watched, he began to age. In quick succession, he went from a teenager into the twenties, thirties, forties, fifties, sixties, seventies, eighties, nineties, and then, to our horror, he briefly became a living skeleton, before shriveling away into death. Then a baby stood giggling at us, to become a boy, and finally he was once again the teenage Selph, his smile as innocent as ever. All this took place in about a minute. A minute of total shock!

No conversation was ever ended so abruptly. Amber jumped up with her hand over her mouth, and ran away gagging up her lunch, while I sat and stared at him, aghast. Never, in all my wildest dreams had I seen anything so utterly and totally bizarre and distressing.

"Congratulations," I croaked. "You've just shocked two people nearly out of their wits."

He was entirely unrepentant. "But Adam, you're into drama, and I simple showed you the dramatic process of aging. Be honest. Did you relate to that bodily change as me?"

I had to admit that I did not. It was altogether too weird to relate it to a person, even though we had just watched Selph doing it. "No. I have to confess that even though I just saw you aging, somehow it wasn't you."

"Exactly. Your body sitting there is not you. Age alters you so slowly that you can easily accommodate the change, thus adhering to the belief of being a body." He grinned evilly. "I just destroyed that belief."

"You also destroyed our lunch!"

He waved his arms dramatically. "Pah! So what? What's lunch when a teacher is teaching?"

"Just part of the substance that helps keep our bodies in the great scheme of life," I said sarcastically. "Anyway, you answered my question very graphically. I think I'll go and see how Amber's feeling."

Even as I walked into the house, I had inner visions of the nightmare that we had just witnessed. My God, what a teacher! Despite the shock of it, his words of me being into drama struck home, and I struggled to suppress a giggle.

Amber was just coming out of the bathroom, her face pale and angry. She stalked past me without a word, and by her walk I knew that she was very, very angry. I followed, quite happy with how things were shaping up. Even so, I was stunned when Amber strode right up to Selph, and, her face a mask of fury, gave him a resounding smack on his face.

I flinched as I heard it. My God! I'd make good and sure I never got her that mad.

"Don't you ever do anything like that in front of me again. Adam's teacher you may be, but nothing gives you the right to shock me like that. I'm pregnant, and I want to give birth to a normal baby, not one that's shocked stupid while still in the womb."

Hands on her hips, she glared at Selph. God! She looked beautiful. "Do I make myself clear?"

In all honesty, I don't think Selph was surprised by the onslaught, but he looked very contrite. Dropping to one knee, he gently took the hand that had hit him and pressed it to his lips. "Amber, you have my unreserved apology."

Despite the blaze of red on the side of his face where Amber had hit him, and his apology, I knew that he had never lost control of the situation. I was almost certain that he had engineered it, right down to getting hit. I had an inner knowing that I had just been taught a lesson by a real-life teacher. No matter what the circumstances, you can still be in control of you. Selph had not tried to control Amber, or avoid being hit, yet he was in control of his moment.

I walked over to both of them. As Selph stood up, I put my arms around him and hugged him. "Thank you, my teacher. I honor both your ability to teach me, and your commitment."

He grinned sheepishly. "You just love drama, don't you? However, I'm glad you got the message, I thought it might elude you. I glad I didn't get hit for nothing."

Like the air out of a pricked balloon, the fury drained from Amber. "You mean . . . you mean this was a set-up? You did all that just to teach Adam a lesson about control? My God! That's dedication." Her look became belligerent. "But don't you dare ever shock me like that again."

"Amber, you have my word," Selph replied.

I tried hard to suppress my laughter, but as gurgling noises forced their way out of my mouth, she glared at me.

"Don't you dare laugh."

I tried, but when I glanced at Selph and watched him trying to control his features, it became too much. "You should see your face," I managed to splutter to Amber as I howled with laughter. "I've never seen you so furious in all my life. And look at Selph's face, you've branded him." And joined by Selph, I gave in to gut-wrenching laughter.

Amber looked vexed. "You . . . you . . . nincompoops you." Then the changed mood caught her, and although she tried to resist, chuckling at first, she started to laugh.

For the next ten minutes we laughed until we ached. First one would try to stop, then another, only to be pulled back in by the power of infectious laughter. Finally, we all went back into the swimming pool to cool off.

❖   ❖   ❖

We each did our own thing during the afternoon. Amber in her art studio; Selph, God only knows where; and me in the garden. One hundred bales of sugarcane tops had just recently been delivered, and I intended to mulch most of the garden. Our soil was very low in humus, but by putting a thick layer of organic matter on all the garden soil each year, it was steadily improving. I had expected that I would be able to do the mulching fairly quickly, but the reality proved otherwise. The bales were solid and heavy, and I badly overestimated my strength and ability.

Full of confidence, I got the wheelbarrow from the garden shed and, trundling it across to the bales, placed it alongside them. Grabbing a bale, I tried to swing it onto the barrow, as normal. However, instead of the bale swinging onto the barrow, my own force caused me to sprawl over the bale. Very carefully, I wrapped my arms around the bale in another attempt to get it onto the barrow. Lifting it up, I staggered around in concentric circles, unable to even see the confounded barrow, before I dropped it. Exhausted, I sat on the bale to reconsider the problem. God! I had a hundred of the brutes to move, and I had not yet managed one!

Eventually, after a long struggle, I got the first bale onto the barrow and into position, then began the struggle with the next bale. I sweated, groaned, twinged and hurt, but finally got the second bale onto the barrow and secure.

Deciding that two would be enough, I took the barrow handles, and lifted. At first nothing happened, so I checked to make sure it was not accidentally anchored to the ground. Everything was in order, so, prepared for a mighty effort, I tried again. Up it came, wobbled . . . and tipped over sideways, spilling the bales out of the barrow.

For long moments I did not know whether to laugh, cry, or lose myself in despair. Instead, I simply sat on the bales and reminisced about the time when I had my regular strength and ability. Normally I would easily stack three bales onto a wheelbarrow, wheel them where I wanted them, and quickly spread the mulch. Two days, and the whole job would be done. This was no longer possible, and I had to struggle with the mental adjustment to my changed situation. Finally, I had to cut the bale strings, and put just half a bale into the barrow. I even struggled pushing that. It was a combination of me pushing the barrow, and being supported by it. And half a bale instead of three! For a while I alternated between depression at my loss of ability, and elation at doing a job I so enjoyed. At least I knew what I would be doing with all my spare time for the next month.

At the end of an hour, I had collected and spread just three bales, and I was tired.

Leaving the wheelbarrow with the bales, I walked over to the shrubs, where I had done the mulching, and stood back to admire my work. It felt good. I always had the feeling that the plants approved of being mulched. A dog would physically frisk around in approval, and a cat display affection, yet even though the shrubs could do none of that, I got a strong feeling that on a more subtle level they "embraced" me with flower energy.

Depending on my bush stick a bit more than usual, I made my weary way back to the house. It surprised me how much I had sweated during my labor, so I stripped off, and stepped under the steaming shower.

"Are you all right?"

The question made me jump. "Gee! You startled me. I thought you were in your studio."

Amber opened the shower door and gave me an affectionate smile. "I was, for a while, then I went to find you. I must confess, I stood and watched your antics with the heavy bales for quite some time."

A feeling of shame swept over me. "Oh. Really?"

"Yes. You made me very proud."

I was perplexed. "How?"

"I know how you used to tear along with three bales on that big old wheelbarrow of yours. As I watched you struggle to lift just two bales on, I didn't know whether to laugh or cry. Then, when you got them on, you could hardly lift the barrow handles. And it tipped over. I watched the conflict of emotions on your face, and I wanted to help you with the bales and to comfort you, but I felt that it was your struggle, that I would be an intruder."

"You could never be an intruder in my life."

Her eyes misty, she smiled at me. "I watched you rest, and think it out, and I watched you continue to work taking just half a bale at a time. I knew how hurt your pride was, and how devastated you were by the reality of it. But you carried on regardless. Then I left. I went to my studio; and sat and cried for you; yet the truth of it is, you won."

I grinned at her, and reaching out, I pulled her fully clothed under the shower with me. "I didn't feel like a winner. But the garden needs the mulch."

Amber clung to me like a wet T-shirt. "I could do it."

"I know you could, but that's not the point. It's something I have to do. It's my job; besides, I love doing it. Believe me, difficult or not, it's therapy."

She pulled my head to hers, and kissed me on my lips. Together, we pulled off her wet clothes, but we did not make love. And yet we did. We made love by just holding each other tight with no sexual arousal at all, just being with each other in full bodily contact and sharing our love. In some ways it was one of the most intimate moments I had ever experienced with her. Rather than a predominantly physical closeness, this was a soul connection, making love on inner levels of our Beings.

With the hot water streaming over us, we stood in that embrace for maybe twenty minutes, before the water began to run cold. Such was the almost mystical intensity of our togetherness, it felt more like twenty seconds. Amber looked up at me with wonder in her eyes. "I've never made love like that before."

"I felt it too. We made soul-love."

We dried each other slowly and thoughtfully, aware that something spontaneous, rare, and rather profound had taken place. We had no words to describe it, nor were they necessary. Amber was dressed before me. "Take your time, my love, then come and sit in the lounge while I prepare some dinner."

There was a cup of Earl Gray tea waiting for me, when, with a sigh of pure contentment, I sat back in my easy chair. Physically, I had accomplished little today, but on other, nonphysical levels, I had taken giant strides.

Selph joined us for dinner, and we chatted casually for a while. Then I decided to be very forthright with him.

"Selph, although you look like a teenager, I don't believe it. I want to be frank. Amber and I discovered this afternoon that you can make the most deep, and . . . words fail me, profound love without intercourse. For us, this was an incredible discovery. There was no orgasmic moment, but on a more subtle level there was something even more wonderful. Assuming that you come from an enlightened frame of reality, do you know if this phenomenon is truly real?"

"Would it matter?"

I smiled. Here we go again. "Actually, no," I said with absolute certainty. "I trust our experience and its truth. We both felt it. Something inexplicable."

"Wonderful. Do you remember what I told you about trust? This is it. You are now trusting yourself, and your experience. Great. And that inexplicable something is the more pure, inner-expressive human love. To be honest, if that potential weren't possible between you, I wouldn't be here. Oh, and incidentally, thanks for having the courage to share that with me. I'm aware that these sort of things are seldom discussed or shared in your society."

Amber smiled. "Sex is."

Selph nodded sagely. "Indeed, sex is."

"Would it be a fair guess that sex, as such, is less prevalent in your society, with a greater emphasis on inner-expressive love?" Amber asked.

Selph nodded. "It's a natural progression. We also have the ability to impregnate a loved one's symbol for them to keep. If they are far apart, and want to reach out to each other, they focus on the symbol and feel the inner-expressive love of their loved one."

Amber twitched her nose. "What's the symbol?"

"That's each couple's choice, but generally it's a precious stone in a ring, or necklace. The stone is primed, and becomes the receptacle."

"How do you do that?" I asked.

Chuckling, Selph waved his hands in dismissal. "I can't possibly answer that. It involves techniques that are not yet appropriate to your times. Besides, I'm not allowed."

"So there are certain limits and restraints for you in our frame of reality?"

"Most certainly. Mind you, I have plenty of freedom with you, but far less with other people."

I was surprised. This was a line of thought that I had never even considered. "Really, how intriguing. Obviously Amber is included with me."

"To a very large degree, yes."

"That little stunt you just got clobbered for was too much of a large degree," Amber said, chuckling.

"On an outer, physical level, I would probably hide nothing from Amber, but on an inner, nonphysical level, I'm much more restrained."

"So what would be off-limits to other people?" I asked.

Selph grinned mischievously. "The swimming lesson I gave you is a good example. No way would I allow other people to see that exhibition of physical impossibilities."

"So what was the real purpose with me?"

"To confront you. To aggravate you. To confound you. To challenge you. To get a reaction, or a response from you. To shake up your complacency. To teach you. To . . ."

"Okay, okay, I get the picture. I reckon it did all that to me, and more. I certainly reacted. Negatively."

"Don't feel badly about it. Oddly enough, most people would. If a person does something that is perceived as impossible, it not only threatens other people personally, it also threatens their reality. The barriers are no longer safe, so people react negatively."

"Yeah," I said excitedly, "you just put your finger on what happened to me. It was as though the structure of all normality were under threat, and all your beliefs begin to collapse. Oddly enough, it was scary. My conditioned need to understand was no longer appropriate, and the result was confusion and conflict within me."

Selph smiled, nodding. "That says it nicely."

"Is this how you intend to teach me?" I asked. "Are confrontation and impossibilities the tools of growth?"

He shook his head. "Of course not. There is no format. No do this, or that. Of course, like I've said before, you can just 'fall in love with who you are' and the thing is done. But even that can't happen out of timing." He sighed. "No, Adam, I simply use the moment and what it offers. I take whatever is appropriate in the moment and turn it into a potential lesson." He grinned. "Usually a dramatic lesson!"

For the next couple of days, I struggled with the heavy bales of sugarcane tops, spending as long as possible with them. Generally in one-and-a half to two hours I was tired out, and I would stagger over to a poolside recliner and rest. I knew that Amber kept an anxious eye on me, but she did it very unobtrusively. Selph had offered his assistance, but I declined it, and he did not press the issue. The mulching was something that I did for me and the garden; it was something personal, and Selph recognized this.

I was completely happy struggling away, and I had come to terms with my loss of strength. I think that we all realized that this was probably the best therapy and exercise possible for me. The regular, twice-a-week workout in the fitness center bored me, but laboring and sweating over the mulch bales was both satisfying and interesting.

Sunday arrived, and Amber and Selph had collaborated to prepare a superb lunch in honor of Doctor Pete. He arrived just before noon, so we found him a comfortable recliner in the shade near the swimming pool, and I poured him a cold drink of grapefruit juice.

He looked me up and down in my bathers critically, and then smiled at me pleasantly. "Hmmmm, apart from the scars, you're looking increasingly fit. Damn it, I only saw you earlier in the week, but you look . . . somehow different." He frowned. "Can't quite put my finger on it."

"He's been working hard," Amber called out. "He's getting lean and mean, a cane-bale machine."

Waving to her, Pete gave me an inquiring frown.

"Take no notice of her," I said, loud enough for Amber to overhear. "She's so deliriously happy to be with me that she has moments of hallucination."

An outburst of deliberately exaggerated, feminine fake spluttering and coughing came through the nearby open glass sliding doors that led in to the kitchen. Then Selph came walking out, a grin on his face.

Pete stared at him. "Don't I know you?" he said uncertainly. "Didn't we meet at the hospital?" He offered his huge hand.

Selph took the proffered hand, and shook it. "Yes, sir. You very kindly allowed me to visit Adam one evening."

Pete was lost in a puzzled frown as he stared at Selph. "Yes, that's right, I vaguely recall that." Then he smiled warmly. "And the name's Pete, not sir." He looked around and waved an all embracing hand. "So where do you fit in all this, er, Selph? An unusual name, that."

Selph's smile of innocence was radiant. "I'm helping Adam in every way I can. He will be teaching me about his eco-farming consultancy as soon as he is able, so until then I just make myself useful in various little ways."

I smiled slyly at Selph. "Believe me, Pete. The things that Selph does for me are too numerous to mention, and he's an excellent cook. Selph's one of those rare people who does everything perfectly. I can say in all honesty he truly is amazing. I don't know what I'd do without him."

Subdued and muffled chuckling echoed from the kitchen.

Pete looked from me to Selph and the kitchen with an air of suspicion. "I can feel a conspiracy going on here, but I guess it's none of my business. I just hope that I'm not the butt of a joke."

I glanced an inquiry at Selph, and his eyes gave me a definite "do not tell him" signal. "There is no joke at your expense, Pete. It's more of a private joke among the three of us. I apologize for stringing it along."

Amber's voice came floating from the kitchen. "Selph, I need you. Come and help, please."

Selph jumped up and took off, and only a few minutes later we were called in to lunch.

The dining room was cool and light, and the food on its dishes in the middle of the table drew a murmur of contented appreciation from Pete.

"My, my, that's excellent. I love to see food presented on the table, rather than just served on plates."

It was a cold seafood lunch. Spread out before us were two dishes of assorted entrées, two dishes of halved Morton Bay Bugs; a huge wooden bowl of tossed prawns, tomato, basil, and lettuce salad; a bowl of oysters; a bowl of potato salad; and a huge dish of sliced rock melon. It did look good.

As we sat down, Pete continued. "It's my upbringing, I suppose, but in our family it was traditional to have a large table with all the food served up on dishes. Like this." He indicated our table. "Nowadays, it seems that in most homes, and certainly in many restaurants, your food is served directly onto a plate." He gave a vast sigh. "Takes all the fun out of eating. For me it's nearly as much visual as it is eating." He paused. "But I do enjoy eating!"

I smiled brightly. "I guess I had never really thought about it, but I agree, I like to see my food on a dish. It's Amber who should take the credit, because she was the one who started this when we first got married. When I think about it, Mum served hot food directly onto plates, while cold food was all put onto the table to select as we wanted."

I grinned mischievously at Selph. "How about you, young man? How do your mum and dad serve up their food?" Despite having fun at Selph's expense, I was genuinely interested.

He handled it as suavely as always. "Where I come from we don't eat meat. We have a huge selection of fruits and vegetables placed on the table, or, depending on the meal, we have a selection of grains to choose from."

"God! That doesn't sound very exciting," Pete said.

Selph nodded. "I can understand that. Our family are not big eaters. Quality of food is the vital factor, not quantity. Our selection is also very extensive," he said modestly.

I knew that he was holding back a lot, and I had no intention of pushing the issue, but I was intrigued. "I know you come from an exotic place, but do you have a much bigger selection than we do in Australia?"

Selph eyed me warningly. "You cannot imagine how much greater. Particularly fruit."

Luckily, Pete dismissed the innuendos. "I must say that I'm a meat man, myself. Vegetables without meat is like fur without a cat; bloody unfinished," he guffawed.

I steered the topic away from food and into medicine.

"Pete, do you mind if I challenge you, or rather, your profession? I'd like your comment on a statistic I read the other day. It disturbed me."

"Oh dear," Amber murmured. "You're not going to chew that bone all over again, are you?"

"Only a nibble, my love. Just a quick nibble."

"Go ahead, old boy. I'm in a very good mood with all this wonderful food. I'll indulge you." He dived his fork into his second avocado-and-prawn entrée with a sigh of contentment. "Fire away. Let's hear your gripe."

"You're right, Pete. It is a gripe. As an eco-farming consultant I've had to go up against the accepted agriculture system for several years. I've been subjected to constant pressure to conform to a system of abusive and arrogant techniques that leave the soil structure ruined and degraded. I was labeled a crank, and I've had a lot of opposition to my organic principles. The attitude of the establishment is to attack and ridicule if they perceive any threat to the 'status quo.' I won't go on and on about it, because in all fairness there is a change taking place, even if it's slow. It would be to the advantage of everyone if the different attitudes and approaches could be blended together."

"So how does this tale of woe concern me?" Pete rumbled.

"Because you have exactly the same pigheaded approach and attitude in the hospitals and right through the whole medical profession," I said, heatedly.

"Now, now, keep it cool," Pete said placatingly.

"I just read that well over fourteen thousand people die in Australian hospitals each year through preventable mistakes. Mistakes ranging from wrong operations to misdiagnosis to being given the wrong drugs. That's appalling, yet nothing will be done about it. In our society, that's acceptable.

But, and this is what gets to me, if there was a single mistake made in a natural health clinic, the people involved would be persecuted by the media, raided by the police, and closed down. Even worse, they are persecuted, harassed, and put out of business simply if they prescribe a harmless herbal cure—most especially, if it does cure.

"Let me correlate this with agriculture. In most of the Western world, farmers are not given a real choice in how they farm their land. They are conditioned and pressured to use chemical warfare on nature. Rip a profit from the land today, and pity the farmers of tomorrow.

"It's the same in medicine. The man and woman on the street is forbidden a choice of medical treatment. It is illegal to choose natural treatment. To cure cancer with herbs or any natural therapy is a crime. It's okay to die in the approved medical system, but it's a punishable offense to live through natural treatment. This makes me angry."

I glared at Pete, and the others. "Okay, I've got all steamed up, and I apologize. Now you know why Mum chose you, Pete. She's heard me vent these feelings many times."

Taking a deep breath, I released it slowly. "Right, I've had my say. I won't pursue it any further."

There was a long uncomfortable silence. Pete shrugged, and looked at me helplessly. "What do you want from me, Adam? I agree with you. I share your anger. It just so happens that I'm in the established system trying to bring about change from within. I don't believe that attack or debate outside the system will achieve anything. I, and others like me, are making our impact within the beast. So, please, don't attack me."

"I'm sorry if it seemed that I was attacking you, but honestly, I meant nothing personal," I said contritely.

"Yeah. I can understand you getting all hot under the collar about the hospital deaths, but there's more to this fourteen-thousand-dying figure than meets the eye. Point one: from memory, that represents less than three percent of the people who have been treated in a hospital in any year. Point two: from sheer necessity, I, and many doctors like me, sometimes work double shifts, and up to thirty hours without a break. We, too, are human and fallible, especially when overtired and exhausted. And point three: you told me recently that if you had chosen to die, I could not have saved you, and presumably, because you chose to live, you did. So to use your own theory, that suggests that those fourteen thousand people chose to die, and that the flaws in the established system simply facilitated it."

I gaped at him in astonishment.

Pete grinned amiably. "You can't have it both ways, Adam. Nothing can or should excuse a system that allows any percentage to die from error, but what you told me of your own death experience indicates there may be no error. You didn't blame the truck driver for your own accident, so why blame the doctors for the many accidents involving many more people?"

Amber cut in. "And you could also focus on the ninety-seven percent who recovered and got well while in the hospital. Focus on the positive rather than the negative."

My anger had deflated. "Yeah, well . . ." I shook my head. "What can I say? You're right, Pete. I can't have it both ways. I don't believe that my experience of choosing to physically live or die was just for me. I'm certain that everyone chooses, even though the choice is not an intellectual one. And I agree with Amber. I am inclined to focus on the negative." I looked at Selph. "What do you think?"

Selph smiled lazily. "I'm probably too young to know about things like this, but I reckon that on the deepest level of life, there is no such thing as an accident. Far beyond human fears, separation, and the mental struggle to understand, everything and everybody works out their lives in a network of infallible order. That's what I think."

Pete stared at him, frowning. "That's pretty deep stuff coming from a young man. Have you studied philosophy?"

Selph shrugged. "No. Just observations, and a bit of deep thought and cogitation."

I smiled warmly at my three companions. "Pete, thanks for puncturing my anger and my arrogance. Amber, thank you for being so invariably positive; and Selph, thank you for your ageless wisdom."

Watching Pete as he finished his third entrée, I felt it was time to change the subject. "You do like the prawn-and-avocado entrées, don't you?" I smiled at him.

He chuckled. "You noticed. I consider prawn and avocado as one of life's perfect partnerships." He pulled a dish of Morton Bay Bugs closer, and took several. "It just so happens I like these little fellows too. In fact, this whole meal is tailor-made for my palate."

Pete probably ate as much as the rest of us put together. We sat and yarned for half an hour after our first course, then Selph served up a huge fruit salad desert.

Fruit salad is probably one of my favorite foods, so I had saved room for it. Pete did not need to save space, he seemed to have an endless appetite.

"I'm not trying to be ingratiating," Pete said, smacking his lips with relish, "but this is an uncommonly good fruit salad. I mean, fruit salad is commonplace, and generally, one tastes much the same as another, but not this time. It's excellent. Who made it?"

"Selph did," Amber replied.

Selph gave a modest smile. "I know a bit about fruit. Basically they fall into three categories; acid, subacid, and sweet. Most people don't know this and mix them any which way, so the flavors conflict with each other. You can mix subacid fruit with acid fruit, or subacid with sweet, but never acid with sweet. And never any of the melon family with any other fruit. However, what you're eating is sweet fruit only, and no more than three compatible flavors. In this way they compliment and enrich each other. I would generally recommend no more than three fruits together to avoid the mish-mash of flavors."

Pete's eyebrows lifted. "God! I'm impressed. First he's a philosopher, now he's a fruit connoisseur. I didn't know any of that, and I like food. It's a bit like surgery; you gotta get it right. Eh, Selph? So just which are the acid, er, subacid, and sweet fruits. I intend to try this for myself. It sounds simple enough."

Selph nodded. "There's nothing to it. The basic acid fruits are pineapples, strawberries, passionfruit, kiwi, and all the many citrus fruits. The subacid basics are the berries, like mulberries, raspberries, blueberries, blackberries and all their hybrids, grapes, pears, apples, cherries, apricots, peaches, plums, nectarines, and papayas."

Pete cut in. "You do surprise me. I would have thought they were all sweet fruit."

"The sweet fruit are fewer. Basically there are bananas, cherimoyas, mangoes, figs, litchis, and all the usual dried fruit. To be honest, some of the subacid could fit in the sweet fruit bracket. Apricots and apples, for instance, although it would depend on the variety of apple. Peaches could too. You are eating a mixture of bananas, mangoes, and litchis."

Patting his belly, Pete smacked his lips with relish.

"Would you be good enough to write that out for me? I'm suitably impressed."

"My pleasure."

We all adjourned onto the poolside recliners, and Pete went to his car to get his bathers. Returning, he went into the bathroom to change. When he came back I stared at him in awe. In his bathers, he seemed even bigger. "Christ! Just how tall are you?" I asked.

"I'm six feet seven inches in my bare feet, and those feet need a size fifteen shoe to accommodate them. Believe me, being this big can be a bloody nuisance."

"Oh. Why?"

"Have you ever tried to buy shoes, size fifteen? Have you ever tried to fit a body as big as mine comfortably into a bus seat, or an airplane seat, or a bloody hospital seat? Can you imagine the hassle of buying clothes to fit me?"

I nodded emphatically. "Point taken."

We swam, and I smiled as Pete powered along in the water beating Selph. Little did he know! But to be fair, like many large people, Pete was one hell of a swimmer. Over a short distance he could have beaten me at my best, even if he was short-winded.

We drank French vanilla filter coffee, and alternately swam, lazed, and conversed. All too soon it was time for Pete to return to duty at the hospital.

He bear-hugged me, grabbed Selph and gave him the same treatment, then gently enfolded Amber into his arms.

"Thank you all so much. I've loved it. I'll be back for more." He kissed Amber fondly. "Little lady, if you ever decide to leave old Groucho, come and see me. I'll marry you the very next day."

We watched and waved as he drove off in his huge, ten-year-old, V-8, Ford Fairlane.

"I just love that man," Amber said with a cheeky smile.

# Fourteen

Struggling out of a dream, I could hear someone softly singing.

"Happy birthday to you, happy birthday to you, happy birthday dear Adam, happy birthday to youuuuuu."

I was still fuzzy from sleep, but the nibble on my ear was definitely waking me. I stared at Amber groggily as she cuddled up to me, hugging me.

"Adam, wake up. It's your birthday."

I was genuinely astonished. Of course it was. God! How could I forget my own birthday? I was thirty-three today. But I had forgotten, and no one had mentioned it.

Amber's hand wandered down my belly. "Oh dear, Sir Knight is still asleep. What a shame. I had a special birthday present just for him."

She took hold of me.

"Well, well," Amber whispered as she wriggled onto me, her hair falling over my face, tickling. "Verily, I do believe Sir Knight hath arisen."

"When did you start all this Sir Knight, business," I muttered. "It can be a bit off-putting."

She kissed the tip of my nose. "You mean that Sir Knight is not up to tournament standard today?" She wriggled, then gasped slightly.

"That's very strange," she murmured, "I get the feeling he's already jousting!"

Thirty very vigorous minutes of jousting later, Sir Knight was once again asleep!

I looked at myself in the mirror as I shaved. Apart from the silly grin that jousting seems to cause, I was beginning to look less of the physical mess, and more of my old self. Where once they had been a livid pink, my scars were definitely fading, and although I had them for life, they did not concern me.

Not long ago I had been a thin bag of flesh; now my developing muscles were again making their presence known. All in all, I was shaping up well, and I felt pleased with my progress.

"Adaaaaam. Breakfast." Amber called.

"Coming," I shouted back, then dived under the shower.

Five minutes later I joined her and Selph. They had set out breakfast on the poolside table in the morning sun.

As I sat down, I suddenly remembered something. "Oh gosh! We invited Pete here yesterday so that we could teach him how to reach an altered state. I totally forgot."

Amber laughed. "We all did. Don't worry, there will be plenty of other times, and he really did enjoy himself."

I relaxed, nodding. "Yeah, that's the main thing."

"So, Adam. Happy birthday," Selph said. "And very good timing."

I smiled at him. "Thank you, and what's that supposed to mean?"

He chuckled. "I knew it would provoke you."

"Consider me provoked," I nodded. "What timing?"

Selph sipped his coffee slowly, put the mug down, then sat back and cradled his hands behind his head. "Life is always a probability factor. The only absolute is LOVE. The probability was that you would have the car crash." He grinned at Amber. "I've told him all this before."

Bringing his attention back to me, he continued. "I chose to enter your life before the car crash, to sow the seeds of change. As a result of that catalytic event—the crash—those seeds have germinated, and are growing nicely. You are no longer the man that I met on the beach, even though you cling to some of his old attitudes and habits."

Amber nodded. "I agree. I'm happy to say that the father of my child is not the man that I married."

We all laughed. "Be careful not to say it that way in public," I pleaded.

"Because of that germination and subsequent growth," Selph continued, "the timing of another probability has arrived. You both know that Adam has an addiction to pain and suffering. His back has usually been the target area, simply because this is where it all began. At some time in what you perceive as the past, Adam sustained what was quite probably a horrific injury to his back. As I have said before, it was not the injury that set up the pattern of discord, but his reaction to what happened. A physical injury may cripple you for a lifetime, but if it is accepted, the handicap ends with physical death. However, if the incapacitation is angrily resisted, then the injury is no longer only physical. It becomes psychical, imprinting its discord into the person's consciousness, and the repercussions will keep running through one incarnation after another until it is resolved."

He looked at me. "Do you follow?"

Apprehensive, I nodded.

"A person's birthday is far more significant than they realize. It's a powerful time. No matter what the cause, the big majority of people die around their birthday. It's a catalytic time of new probabilities, of new and greater potential. Unfortunately, because this is seldom recognized, the potential is mostly left on hold."

"Okay. What's my potential?" I asked.

"The probability is that you are now ready to deal with the causative factor of your lifetimes of trauma. I believe that you are."

I took a deep breath. "We're talking major drama, like really big pain?"

Selph nodded. "There's no doubt about that."

"Is this something I have to do today?"

"No. You don't *have* to do this at all. However, in your choice to know your Truth, the probability is that this is the path you will take. In truth there is no path, but having said that, this is the path you are on."

"How do I connect with the cause? When I touched all those other lives, I was basically propelled by pain. Surely I don't have to do it like that."

"Of course not. I can teach you how to approach it without pain, but you have to enter the experience of that life and bring about change."

"That's crazy! You can't change the past."

"You can. It's all to do with reality. Reality is not the event; it's your memory of it. You create your own reality, and linear time has nothing to do with it. However, I'm not going to discuss this intellectually again. You have a choice; when you feel ready to face that causative event, I will show you how to reach it. The rest is up to you."

"I'd rather not do it today."

"Good. I'd rather you didn't. By the way, my birthday present to you is on the dining table."

I stared at him, a silly grin on my face. "Really? I didn't expect anything from you."

"Go and open it, darling," Amber urged.

I got up, and walked into the dining room, the others on my heels. There, standing in the center of the table, was a large object with a tablecloth draped over it. Puzzled, I crossed the room and, taking the cloth, I lifted it carefully to reveal a large, dwarfed ficus. I gazed at it, ecstatic.

Possibly thirty years old, the tree had been kept dwarfed by regular trimming, but not as a true bonsai. Especially grown in a short, wide, plastic bag, the work of pruning and shaping to create a miniature tree remained to be done. I could hardly take my eyes off it.

I spun around and hugged Selph. "That's wonderful. I'm absolutely delighted with it. Gosh! What a surprise."

He grinned at my obvious pleasure. "Yeah, well, I know how you love your bonsai, so I figured you could handle another one. I'm glad you like it."

We went back to the table, and I finished my toast.

"I suppose you are expecting something from me," Amber said coquettishly.

With a grin, I thought of Sir Knight and his recent tournament. "All donations are gratefully received," I smiled at her, "but I won't joust with you over it."

We shared a conspiratorial grin.

"I've been working on my painting to have it ready for today, and it is. So if you would like to come with me to the studio, it's all ready for you. You can come as well, Selph. It's not a private viewing."

We all trooped over to the studio and went in. The picture was on the easel in the center of the room, a cloth thrown over it.

Amber waved her hands toward it. "It's all yours, my darling."

I felt oddly nervous as I went over to the easel and took hold over the cloth.

"And yet another unveiling," I joked.

As I took the cloth off the painting, I had my eyes shut. I felt nervous about looking at it. Suppose I didn't like it? I'm not good at hiding my feelings. Amber would know immediately, and be devastated.

Opening my eyes, I stepped back two paces and gazed at the framed picture. I gasped. It was incredible. On a large canvas nearly two meters square, Amber had captured an image of me kneeling by my pond feeding the goldfish. She had captured the rapt expression on my face, as I lost myself in a world of water and mystery. The main focus was the pond, along with its goldfish, and the flowering shrubs and plants that grow around it. I was over to one side, in the place that I sit, or kneel, and it was all in perfect scale.

I looked at Amber in admiration. "It's beautiful. I love it. Wow! You've excelled yourself." Stepping closer to her, I wrapped my arms round her, kissing her on the lips with fierce passion. "It's just great. I insist that it has the prime position in the house."

"You were worried that you might not like it, weren't you?" she chided me playfully.

I confessed I had been.

"I know how fussy you are about art, so I chose my subject very carefully. I knew you'd like it."

"Like it doesn't get close. I just love it."

Taking the painting there and then, Selph and I carried it with great care over to the house. We all decided that the main wall in the living room was the perfect place for it, so Selph went to get the tools and a picture hook. While I sat back and watched, Selph hung my beautiful picture. What with the dwarfed ficus and the painting, this was just about my best birthday ever.

At precisely midday, the doorbell rang.

"Adam, just see who that is, will you, please," Amber called out. "I'm busy with lunch."

Opening the door, I stared in surprise. "Happy birthday, Adam dear," Mum said, as she stepped into my arms. Dad stood behind her, holding a huge bunch of roses. "I thought you might like these, Amber dear." Mum took the roses and with a flourish, presented them to Amber, who had followed me to the door.

"Oh!" she squealed. "They're absolutely beautiful."

Dad looked at me with a touch of hesitation, not sure whether to hug me, or what. Open affection was a whole new field of exploration for him. I solved it for him by hugging him. "Great to see you, Dad."

He nodded, smiling happily. "Great to see you, son. And a very happy birthday."

"Gosh! What a surprise. I had no idea that you were coming over today. I take it that Amber organized this for my birthday. Thanks so much for coming."

"Do you think we wouldn't come and see our little baby on his birthday," Mum said humorously. "I'm happy to see that you're looking a lot fitter."

Dad nodded. "First thing I noticed. And when I hugged him, I felt muscles in his body. Let's have a look at you, son."

I laughed. "You mean like this?" And so saying, I stripped off my blue T-shirt.

Neither Mum nor Dad had seen my actual body since the accident, and they both sucked their breath in sharply when they saw the scars. There were plenty to see.

"My God, Adam." Mum looked shocked. "I had no idea that you were so badly cut about. I thought it was more internal. Oh, you poor dear."

"You should have seen him a month ago," Amber said chuckling. "Those scars were angry red and purple ridges of flesh. They'll never disappear, but they are receding."

I slipped my T-shirt back on. "That's it folks, shows over. The incredible illustrated man is off-duty."

Mum walked over to the basket she had carried in. "Oh, Adam. I've got a small birthday gift for you."

That it was a book was obvious. A prolific reader, I love my books. I opened the parcel, and grinned in pleasure at the thick hardback.

"Thanks, Mum. That's the one I wanted next. You must have been talking to Amber."

"Well, considering that you've read all Wilbur Smith's other books, and you were reading *River God* in the hospital, it was obvious you would want the sequel. I only checked with Amber to make sure you didn't already have it."

Amber laughed. "I answered the phone, and Mum said, 'Has Adam got *The Seventh Scroll?*' I had to think for a moment to know what she was talking about."

I smiled ruefully. "I'll tell you something odd. I bought *River God* and kept it for about eighteen months without reading it. I had the feeling that I was saving it for if I had the flu, or got laid up for a few days. I wonder if that was a premonition, or just me being me."

"That was you being you," Amber chuckled. "You've always done things like that. 'Savoring the moment,' and, 'enjoying the anticipation,' are ways you describe it."

We were all sitting poolside by now, when Dad got up and, walking over to Mum's basket, fiddled around in it. He came back and handed me a small wrapped object. "Something from me, son. Hope you like it."

I gulped back a surge of emotion. In all my life, Dad had never given me anything independent of Mum. What she gave me was always from them. I glanced up at her, and she read my look of inquiry.

"Even I don't know what it is," she said.

I opened it carefully, knowing that this was more than just a birthday gift. It also represented his reaching out to me. In the package was a small case, and I opened it, the others all crowding around. I gasped. A gold pocketwatch, complete with gold chain and fob, lay in the lined case. For a moment it blurred before my eyes as I just stared at it. Reverently, I picked it up and held it. Elaborately engraved with English pheasants, I saw immediately that the watch was old and valuable. But when I turned it over, the inscription was very new: "To Adam F S Baker. Loved son of Fred S Baker." I stared at it, speechless, reading and rereading those incredible words. Far more than a birthday present, it was a gift of reconciliation.

Everyone was quiet, watching, as I struggled with my emotions. "I just don't know what to say, Dad," I almost whispered. "It's the most wonderful gift any father could give a son. From the bottom of my heart, thank you." I held him, and hugged him, more aware than ever of just how far he and I had shifted in our relationship.

He cleared his throat, and furtively wiped an eye. "When I heard that you was dead, I was shattered. It was like my life had ended. To be honest, I was shocked at just how devastated I was." He smiled at Mum. "Your mum and I talked for hours about the relationship between you and me, and I explored feelings that I didn't even know I had. I cried like a baby for all my misplaced words and unspoken love."

He paused, and I felt fairly certain that he had rehearsed this little speech to get it right.

"Then we heard you were still alive, then dead, then alive again. My God! That was a rough patch, believe me. Then, when we knew that you would recover, I realized that I'd got a second chance. I went to the city and bought this watch when we came to visit you in the hospital. I never even told your mum. It was something I had to do. It's about one hundred and twenty years old, and in perfect condition. I had to get this one, nothing less was good enough. I wanted it inscribed with both our names, and I struggled with that."

He grinned. "For an obtuse old sod, like me, it all came together pretty well."

We hugged each other fiercely. "Don't you ever speak about yourself like that again, Dad. You're my father, and I'm very proud that you are. I love you."

Selph came onto the scene with perfect timing. Handing out glasses of red wine all around, he held his high. "A toast. To Adam, on his birthday, and the love of a family."

Everyone cheered, and drank.

"He is a nice boy," Mum said, as she watched the winning ways of Selph in action. "Where did you say he came from?"

"I didn't, Mum. Actually, I'm not sure. You should ask him."

"Ian, can I talk to you a moment?" Mum called out, and leaving me, she approached Selph.

I grinned to myself. Let him get out of that one. And of course he would, easily.

It had been arranged that Mum and Dad would be staying the night, so we had a light lunch, with the main emphasis on our evening meal.

During the afternoon, I showed them Amber's painting and Selph's dwarfed ficus. Both were admired, although the painting drew by far the most comments. Another surprise awaited me, when, at about four o'clock in the afternoon, Kate and Bruno arrived.

"Happy birthday, Adam," Kate said as she hugged me.

"Many happy returns of the day," Bruno said formally, giving me a hug. "We have a gift for you."

They handed me a package, and stood grinning while I shook it, felt it, and finally, gave up guessing. Unwrapping it, I revealed a slim box.

"A pen set," I guessed, then dismissed it. "No, too big and heavy."

I opened the box, and for a moment did not recognize what I saw, then I knew. "Wow! A bonsai pruning set. Gee, that's brilliant. Mine are rubbish compared to these. Thank you so much, they're great."

"The very latest design from Europe," Bruno said. "We sent away for them. Solid stainless steel."

"That's incredible. Er, Ian gave me a dwarfed ficus all ready to bonsai, and I had already decided that I would get some new, sharp pruners before I tackled it." I frowned at their smiling faces. "Aw, come on. You collaborated."

They all laughed. "Guilty," Selph chuckled.

I felt so pleased with my birthday. The presents were great, but the love and caring was something else again. I reflected on how much my life had changed since the car smash. The pain had been dreadful, but without a doubt it had been a catalyst for change and growth that would never have been experienced otherwise. Hopefully, I would soon be able to find ways of inner growth and change that did not require so much devastating pain and drama.

With a prickle of apprehension, I thought about the light-body journey that awaited me. Without doubt, it would be an excursion into pain and terror. I shivered. At least I would not physically experience the pain, although my previous past life experiences had been grim enough.

For dinner we had roast leg of lamb with mint sauce, and fresh, organically grown, in-season vegetables. It was a time of chatter and talk, interspersed with a story from whoever had something interesting to tell. Dad told us about the drought, and how it was now well into its third crippling year. Kate talked about her pregnancy, but obviously had no idea that she was expecting twins. She was, however, very large indeed.

"You mark my words, sister of mine," I said in a high-pitched and quavering voice. "The oracle has spoken. I see twins kicking in that rotund belly of yours. Mark ye well my words."

They all laughed. "Not a chance," Bruno said. "Just one mighty big baby."

Amber's eyes met mine, and we smiled our shared secret knowledge of the twins at each other.

"Oh yes," Amber said suddenly, as though the idea were new to her. "Did I tell any of you that I'm pregnant?"

The family all stared at her in mute astonishment.

"You what?" Mum gasped.

"Adam and I are going to have a baby." She spoke very slowly and clearly. "Which means, I'm pregnant."

The rush of squeals, congratulations, and wonderful's, was almost overwhelming. It surprised me that nobody knew. But how could they? We had not told them. With a small degree of modest blushing, Amber shared that it had happened in the hospital, so there was indeed, time to know she was in the very early stages of her pregnancy.

"Has it been confirmed?" Bruno asked, ever the doctor.

"Not officially. But I know," Amber said emphatically. "A woman who is in touch with her body knows these things."

Bruno frowned his disapproval. "You can't be sure yet."

"Oh, Bruno. Don't be such a male fuddy-duddy," Kate cut in. "Women know these things. If Amber says she's pregnant, then I don't doubt it."

He raised his eyebrows at me, then grinned, and offered his hand.

"Well, I'll consider myself outvoted. But anyway, congratulations." We shook hands.

Dad said the least, but I have seldom seen him look so totally pleased with anything. He looked like a cat with an unexpected, double ration of thick, full cream. Mum made up for his lack of words, chattering and advising at top speed.

Selph looked at me, and winked. His words were silent, but I heard them with crystal clarity. "Congratulations, Adam. The next step awaits."

"I'm ready," I acknowledged, and realized, suddenly, that I was. If I had to meet the past, then so be it. I was ready.

Although I was involved, I found myself watching the family as though a spectator. It struck me again, even more forcibly, how strange it was that I had to hurt myself so badly before I could realize the value of a family. What did the pain do to precipitate such an awareness? Was it being faced with the loss of everything? Was it because when you are close to losing the people you love, you then realize that our greatest gifts and blessings are each other? Is, perhaps, despair the birthplace of hope? Does choosing physical life offer some hidden insight about life that ignites the soul? Or is it that when you sink to the deepest, darkest, lowest depths of the well, you find the purest, most fresh water? Just maybe, that by drinking the waters of newness, we discover that nothing is ever separated from LOVE. Nothing at all.

Kate and Bruno left quite late in the evening, and I was beginning to fade a bit by then. I sat sleepily in my large comfortable chair, listening to the conversation between Mum and whoever she picked on. Mum did not like silence. If she was with people, she wanted to talk and share on every subject that they could converse on. She gave Selph quite a going over, but with impeccable manners and exquisite skill, he steered her any which way he wanted the talk to go. She would often look puzzled, having started asking him about home and his parents to find herself talking about her hybrid tea roses, but she gushed on, nevertheless.

A hand was gently shaking my shoulder. "Come along, birthday boy. Time for bed, sleepyhead." Amber chuckled.

"I didn't realize that I'd fallen asleep."

"You've been gently snoring for the last hour-and-a half. It's one o'clock in the morning. We didn't hurry you, because you were so obviously comfortable. Oh, and wonder of wonders, Selph is actually sound asleep on the large recliner on the verandah. I've covered him over with a blanket. I reckon he'll sleep the night through."

Together, we went to bed.

# Fifteen

Although I had considered myself ready for the altered-state exploration into that causative past life, a month slid by and I had made no serious move toward it.

Plenty of other things had been happening. Amber had had her pregnancy confirmed, and was under the care and attention of a gynecologist named Jane Sedgewick. They had hit it off immediately, and already Jane had come to visit us a couple of times. Jane was tall, with long, very dark hair, and a serious face; yet her twinkling eyes spoke of a great sense of humor. And it was there. She could pull my leg so seriously that I had some difficulty with her at first. She did not really like men, so it took time for us to warm to each other. Amber was our nexus of mutual affection. She was so obviously fond of Amber that I even wondered if she were gay, but Amber assured me that Jane definitely had no sexual feelings for her.

As I got to know her, our friendship grew ever closer. Like me, Jane was a person who wore her heart on her sleeve, so I understood why she kept her sleeves rolled up! Her care and concern over Amber was touching. I learned that not every patient got quite this share of attention. As Amber put it to me, when she and Jane met it was like each of them finding a long-lost sister. They quickly decided that they *had* been sisters in a past life. Amazingly, when Amber asked Selph if this was possible, he confirmed that they definitely had been sisters, and it was in their most recent life. It was little wonder that their affection for each other had surfaced so quickly and powerfully.

Having finished lugging my bales of heavy sugarcane mulch around, I missed the work. My sessions at the fitness center continued, and I had made tremendous physical progress. I could now walk without the bush stick, and my old stamina was undoubtedly returning. The only real concession I made to my injuries was the back brace I wore in the form of a wide, specially designed belt.

I still needed this, for my earlier back pain was by no means resolved. Sharp twinges and stabbing pains were still commonplace, and if I got too tired, or overexerted myself, my whole body throbbed with a deep-seated ache. Basically, I had now learned to pace myself, stretching my endurance, but staying within certain physical parameters.

I had made a couple more visits to the hospital, and Pete was very pleased with the way I was shaping up. He asked Amber how the pregnancy was developing, and she told him about Jane Sedgewick. Pete told us that as long as it was his suggestion for us to make love in the hospital bed that had led to this, his brilliance should automatically make him an honorary uncle. Smiling, we agreed. Uncle Pete he would be. That was when it first occurred to me that he should meet Aunty Jane!

I mentioned it to Amber on the way home. "I get the feeling that they are just about perfect for each other. Jane needs a man as strong as Pete, and she sure as hell has got the strength to deal with him. The fact that both of them are avoiding relationships will be the mutual attraction between them. And you, my love, are the glue that will hold them together while they unwittingly cement a friendship that will lead to them falling in love." I chuckled. "Is that brilliant, or is it pure genius?"

Amber looked at me with a happy frown, her eyes gleaming as she thought it over. "Adam, I don't know whether it's genius, or what, but I like the idea, very much. I'll organize a dinner party and invite them."

"It's genius, of course," I said modestly.

Everything in my life was running smoothly, except for the journey into an altered state. I visited the Sphere of Tranquillity regularly, and the healing that this instigated was undoubtedly the prime factor in my rapid recovery.

Several times I asked Selph about the impending journey, but his reply was always the same: When the moment in timing arrives, it will happen. Until then, just relax and be in the moment.

❖  ❖  ❖

Two weeks later, that moment arrived. It was no big deal, no fanfare of trumpets, but after breakfast one morning I took Selph aside.

"I want you to teach me how to make that journey, and I want to know right now." I was very firm. He looked me straight in the eyes with his disconcerting, steely blue, stare. After a few moments, he nodded.

"Right. And about time."

"What do you mean?" I asked indignantly. "I've been waiting for you for the last month."

"No, Adam. You and I have both been waiting for you. And that's fine. Now, you're ready."

In that moment I knew he was right. Intellectually, I had been ready for quite a while, but this was not a journey of the intellect. I had needed to be ready on a deeper, more emotional level, a place where fears and resistance resided. And I knew that right now, I *was* finally ready. The fears were there, and my doubts were still in place, but they were no longer forming a subconscious blockade.

In the way of fate, Amber would be out shopping until late afternoon, so we had the house to ourselves. When I kissed her good-bye, she sensed that something was amiss.

"I hope you're not planning anything you shouldn't. I get a feeling of inner tension from you."

Gosh, she was sharp. I would never lie to her, so I was unsure what to say. "I'm fine. You have a lovely day, and don't worry about a thing. Just enjoy yourself. I love you." I kissed her with passion and emotion, aware of how much I loved her.

She smiled and waved as she drove away. "Be good boys," she called out. "See you soon."

"I guess it was best not to tell her," Selph said as we walked back into the house. "She would have worried all day, rather than enjoy the shops."

I gave him a satisfied smirk. "Yeah, she's going to check out the maternity gear, and baby items."

Selph grinned. "You're not the first man to impregnate his wife. It's been done before."

"Maybe not," I smirked, "but it's the first for this man, and I like the feeling. Daddy, Adam. Sounds good!"

A few gray clouds were floating across the sky, and although they held no promise of rain, we decided to sit indoors. I seated myself comfortably in my large armchair, and Selph explained the procedure.

"I have to give you fair warning that this could be very disturbing. Just as you feel the intensity of peace and tranquillity in the Sphere, you will feel the effects of pain, suffering, and perhaps utter despair, with the same degree of intensity. Are you prepared for this?"

"Intellectually, yes, but I can only hope that I'm emotionally up to it. I can't prepare any more than I am now. And in some ways, perhaps I'm more prepared than I realize. I'm not sure that anything could be as bad as the car smash, and its subsequent pain."

Selph nodded gravely. "Right, so you're ready?"

I nodded. "As much as I'll ever be, although I do have one more question. Will you be in this? Can I call to you for help? Are you able to influence my experience?"

"Adam, you need to realize that you will become the persona in distress. You won't know that I exist, much less call to me for help, and I won't be in the experience. What I will do is precipitate the very beginning, or in other words, I'll throw you in and kick it off. You have to get yourself out. Remember, you cannot change the event, you can only change how you deal with it—attitudes, and the like. In this way you will be changing your relationship with the past. This, in turn, will change your relationship with now. Are you clear about this?"

"Yes. We've talked about it enough times. Now I have to translate the theory into a reality."

"Well put. Right, in this procedure, you begin in exactly the same way as your regular journeys. Start by releasing your identity focus, and taking on your light-body focus. You go through the rainbow—in your own familiar way—but when you go down the twenty-one steps, you will notice that they are leading you down to an underground railway station. When you leave the last step, you will go into the station, and turn to the first platform on your left. You will wait there until a train stops for you. Some trains may not stop, and that's okay. You get on the first train that stops. Are you with me?"

"Will I need a ticket?" I asked flippantly. In truth, I was trying to hide my anxiety. It all sounded very strange.

Selph was aware of how I felt, and treated me seriously.

"No, you won't need a ticket. However, you may see some other people. Once you are on the train, you might as well relax until it stops. The first stop is where you get off. At this point, you are on your own, and you must do whatever seems appropriate to you, moment by moment."

I looked to him for reassurance. "But no matter what, physically, I'll be sitting here, safe and comfortable."

"Yes, that's true, but be clear about this. It's the identity-you who will be here, while the essential-you will be involved in another happening. If you didn't believe that you were fully involved, and experience it as such, then nothing creative could come from it."

"In other words, it'll be like those other past-life experiences. Bloody horrible, but I will come back here and leave it behind. Right?"

He nodded.

"You're not going to watch me, are you? I would feel very embarrassed, and that could complicate things."

He smiled. "Okay, I'll stroll off for now, but I will keep an eye on things this end. I won't say good luck. Luck is where preparation and opportunity meet. You're well prepared, and now is the moment."

Having said that, he gave my shoulder a squeeze, smiled encouragingly, then turned, and walked out. Rather than sit and think myself into a nervous wreck, I decided to get on with it. Taking a number of deep breaths, I wriggled myself comfortable, and relaxed.

My eyes closed, I focused on my physical body, my identity. Feeling comfortable with this, I visualized and imagined a body of light containing my physical body. As this became established, I placed my sense of "being me" into the light-body. Soon, in a body of light, I walked across to the beautiful rainbow, and slowly went through the colors.

As always, red was very strong, and basic, then on into orange, where I let any feelings of distress wash away in the color. I continued on, where my thoughts were swept away by the properties of yellow, then on into a wild green meadow that always awaited me. I stayed in the meadow quite some time, lying in the grass, even rolling in it, before moving on into a blue ocean, where I swam and frolicked in an energy of love. Continuing, I entered the uplifting color of purple, staying lazily purple until I moved on into the color violet, where I lay among the beautiful flowering violets.

As I left the rainbow, a sphere of white light hovered before me, scarcely touching the ground. Although this was new to me, I walked into the sphere, entering its brilliant inner illumination, and slowly walked through it, emerging on the other side. I felt refreshed and vital.

Directly before me, a flight of wide concrete steps led down to a thick mist, and although I could vaguely see into a building, it was shrouded in fog.

I went down the steps, beginning at twenty-one, twenty, nineteen, eighteen, seventeen, sixteen, fifteen, fourteen, thirteen, twelve, eleven, ten, nine, eight—and I could now see that I was going underground—seven, six, five, four, three, two, one. I left the last step, and walked into the open entrance of an underground railway station.

The station was dirty, old, and abandoned, and I wondered if the exercise was to be one in futility. Oh hell! Had it all gone wrong? I turned to my left, and walked only a little way before I was on a platform. Everywhere appeared neglected, yet I did see one or two people in the distance. They seemed to be fellow travelers, with not a guard or station master in sight. The roofing was very high, and as I looked around, I got increasingly confused. I was supposed to be underground, yet this station was an above-ground small town station in its last stages of neglect and disrepair. How the hell could I be underground in an above-ground station?

A few pigeons flew down from overhead beams, nodding at me hopefully, and looking for crumbs as they strutted around my feet. A woman walked onto the same platform as me, and was standing at the far end, so I moved closer to her for some modicum of support. I soon wished I had not. She was old, so old that I swear it was not possible to be alive. Her face was shriveled into a tight death mask, her eyes deep, dark, hollows. Her hair clung to her skull in only a few patches, and she reeked of decay.

I hurried hastily back to the other end of the platform, wanting to run out and quit. It was perversity more than courage that kept me from running, but I did want to see this thing through. A few other people arrived, until there were five of us on the platform. Each in his or her own way were odd. A little girl seemed incapable of seeing me, despite my wave of greeting; and her mother wore a period dress of some bygone century, and constantly talked to herself. A man paced up and down, wearing a modern, dark gray business jacket, complete with waistcoat and bowler hat, yet he wore a full-length evening skirt, with stiletto high heels. Looking totally absurd, he was completely unconcerned, as were the few other people on the platform. In fact, as I observed them, I finally realized that I was the only one aware of any other people. Even worse, I got the feeling that they were not even aware of themselves! Knowing that I was dressed in a human-shaped body of light, I guessed it was just as well that they could not see me.

Like a silent phantom, a train came rocketing into the station and straight on through without the faintest sound. I caught the briefest glimpse of a blur of white faces peering through the glass windows of the carriages, and it was gone.

Shocked, I gazed after it, but there was nothing to see, nothing to even indicate that a train had just rushed through the station at an impossible speed.

I looked at the other people to see how they reacted, but it was obvious they had seen and heard nothing. I tried walking among them, trying to catch their attention, but that too, was impossible. I knelt in front of the little girl, even ran my hand gently over her hair, but she totally ignored me. For her, I did not exist.

Finally, I just stood and waited.

When the train came, it was an old steam engine, yet I heard nothing until it entered the station. It slowed, and with an incredible screeching of brakes, and mighty blasts of hissing steam, the train came to a shuddering halt. Then I blundered. As the engine passed me, I looked to see the engine drivers. I wished I had not done that. I had the impression that there was nobody in the two suits of battered clothing that performed the necessary tasks to keep the train moving. And I mean, no bodies. Just what in the hell had I got myself into? Hell?

The train stopped with a carriage door directly in front of me, cutting through my hesitation. I had come this far; I might as well go the full ride. I looked at my companions on the platform. Not a single one of them showed the slightest awareness of the train. Without any doubt, they could neither see it, nor hear it. Unbelievable! Steam was gushing out with a minor shriek, the platform swirling with it; yet I was the only one who knew.

Opening the carriage door, I stepped into an empty compartment. I breathed a sigh of relief. Having seen the available company, I did not want any. Sitting in a fusty, dusty, seat, I leaned back comfortably. So far, so good. In an old-fashioned, long-discarded style, the compartment had seating for six, but it was a far more luxurious and richly upholstered seating than today's modern rail transport. This would have to be first class!

I looked out of the window to check if the other people were still on the platform, and gaped in shock. The green countryside was racing past at a stupendous speed, a blur to my confused and frightened eyes. Unlike the old railway that I had ridden as a boy, there was no clickety-clack, clickety-clack as the wheels passed over the rail joints in a regular rhythm. It was deadly quiet and smooth. Supernatural!

I lost all track of time as the train rushed at an appalling speed through unrelenting countryside. I went from frightened shock to terrified, then to a numb acceptance of my fate. It was out of my hands. I had no idea what I had started, but with every passing moment my ability to quit was fading. There came a moment where I knew that I was irrevocably committed. I had no way back, or any ability to reverse this terrible journey and go back. Then the thought struck me. Back where? Where had I come from? I? Who am I? Where am I going? And why?

I sat blankly gazing out the window at the blur of greenery. We were going so fast that I could not tell if it were crops, meadows, or trees that we were hurtling past. I only knew that it went on and on, forever.

I felt some distress at my loss of identity, but there was nothing I could do about it. My body had seemed oddly light at one stage, but now I was comfortably solid, my tight brown leggings gripping sturdy legs, a thick jacket, and high, leather boots of very good quality. It must be that I had had an accident, and bumped my head. I had heard of people losing their thoughts. Maybe I was suffering memory loss, and somebody would be waiting for me at journey's end.

As though on cue, with a harsh screeching of brakes, the train came to a grinding stop, and I looked out the door onto practically nothing. The station was no more than a single platform. An elderly man was waving to me, calling out a name. Opening the door, I stepped out the carriage and onto the high platform. Immediately, as though triggered, the train let forth a tremendous blast of steam, and moved smoothly away, vanishing as though it had never existed.

"Master Jacob. Over here. Come on, we got to hurry. We got a long way to go."

The man beckoned to me as he called, and I knew that I must be Jacob. I shook my head in bewilderment. Where had I been? Where had I come from? With no other real choice, I walked over to the old man. My gosh, he was old. He coughed and wheezed for breath, muttering constantly.

"I got me the fever, Master Jacob," he whined, "an' I got to get me back to bed. Come on, the carriage is waiting. I'll take yer home to yer father and yer aunt. They will be right pleased to see yer."

"Er, why didn't Father come and collect me himself?"

The old man stared at me in surprise. "Ah, come on, Master Jacob, don' be pulling an ole man's leg. Your father be busy, as he allus is. You know that."

I could see the carriage, and dimly recognized it. This was one of father's fast combinations. A pair of powerful, sleek horses were harnessed to a moderately small and light carriage. It was all about speed, and father loved speed. His speed had killed my mother. She had sat with him on this very same carriage as he whipped the horses along, and it was said that she was as besotted by the thrill of it as he was. One of the wheels had hit a rock as they crazily careered around a tight bend, and mother had flipped into the air, to land on her dainty neck. She had been killed instantly.

Father had mourned for two years, then remarried. I lived with my father, and my stepmother. Although I had been only seven when she died, I had never been able to call my stepmother, mother. She was Aunt Maud. A strong, rather dominant woman, she was strikingly pretty, with soft blonde hair and very fair features. She was also good-natured and patient. It took her several years, but she won over my affection to the point I grew to love her. She and father always called me Jake, but staff were not allowed to.

As I watched old Lyle climb shakily up onto the driver's seat, I wondered just when his age would force him to retire. But what really bothered me most was: how did I get to this small country village so far from home? We had a journey of about fifty miles ahead of us, and I had no recollection of having come here by horse and carriage, and there was no other form of transport that is available. Ships for the sea, or horses for the land, that was the only way we could travel in the year of our Lord, fifteen hundred and seventy five. Of course, we could use Shank's Pony—walk—the most common form of transport, but it was obvious that I had not walked here. Why had I come here, and how? It was a mystery.

"Lyle, did you see how I arrived in this village? You were waiting for me, were you not?"

He gave me a puzzled look. "Come on, Master Jacob, don' play games with me. You bin waiting two days fer me."

Baffled, I shook my head at the mystery and gave up on it. Climbing nimbly into the carriage, I settled back for a long ride as Lyle whipped up the horses. We bounced and swayed our way along for mile after mile, meeting the occasional carriage, and passed on a few occasions, by a fast horse and rider.

We made good time that day, and spent an uneventful night in a wayside tavern. Next morning we were up early, collecting the horses from the hostelry and getting them in harness. Old Lyle looked really sick, and I suggested that we change places. I would drive him. His pride was hurt, and he flatly refused to relinquish his job. "It's what I git paid fer, Master Jacob. Iffen ye take over, it'll be the end of ole Lyle."

I could not very well force him, so with some misgivings I again climbed into the carriage. We had been traveling for about an hour, when I noticed that we were going far, far too fast. The carriage was now bouncing about and swaying from side to side in an alarming manner, and I knew that something was very seriously wrong.

Sticking my head and shoulders out of the carriage, I yelled up to Lyle, "Slow down, you'll get us killed."

At that moment a violent jolt threw me back into the carriage with a thud, smashing my head against the wooden side, and I knew that my worst fears had come to pass. Lyle had collapsed, fallen off, or just plain died on the carriage. It was time to get out. Dizzily clambering to my feet, I had my hand on the handle of the carriage door, when, with a sickening lurch, the bottom fell out of my world.

Down, down, and down we fell, a tangle of screaming horses, the carriage twisting over and over, and me being slammed from one side to the other. Despite my terrible battering, it all seemed to happen with nightmare slowness, but there was nothing I could do to help myself.

When we slammed into the earth, it was with appalling force, and I felt my body shatter under the impact. Smashed beyond recognition, the carriage was a twisted mass of broken and splintered wood. A horse was screaming in a long and frightful cry of stark terror and agony, and I could hear one of its hooves kicking repeatedly into the side of the carriage. I tried to move, but I was pinned to the carriage by debris. Opening my mouth to shout, I gazed stupefied as instead of words, a gush of blood shot out. Only then did I see the long, thick sliver of wood that had entered my chest, to emerge alongside my shoulder blade. I blinked at the blood trickling from my scalp, shocked by injuries that seemed to carry no pain. Throughout it all, I did not faint.

The wreckage seemed to quiver and shake, then the whole tangled mass began to slide sideways. For a long horrible moment everything was falling, then we made a soft, swishing impact. As I tried to gather my wits, I heard the splash and gurgle of water, and the single living horse went berserk. It lashed out with its hooves, and in our new position, a hoof slammed into me. I felt the impact jarring my whole body, then one kick came after the other, like sledgehammers smashing into me, gradually shattering and pulping my leg. I tried to understand why I could feel nothing, no pain at all, but I was too confused. The desperate dying struggle of the horse must have caused him to move, for when the hoof slammed into my hip, then my ribs, the blinding, shattering agony came screaming from my distorted mouth. And through it all, I was unable to mercifully faint.

Gradually, the kicking slowed, to finally stop as the horse drowned in a gurgling frenzy. I was broken and twisted so badly that I could not have moved even if I laid on a soft bed. Pinned in the wreckage of the carriage, I was helpless. Blood seeped in a steady trickle from my scalp, neither leg would move, and the pain in my lower spine that accompanied a terrible broken, grating feeling held the awful suggestion that I was back-broken. As if that were not enough to bear, one eye was hanging from its socket. Everything that should move seemed to be broken, and I floated in a cauldron of seething pain. Yet despite it all, I was unable to faint away from it.

Something was wrong with my lungs, for breathing was only just possible, bubbling and burbling as one breath remorsefully followed another. I wanted to live, but what was the price that I would have to pay? Another scream tried to tear its way from my throat, but all that came out was a gush of blood and vomit. Fighting for breath, while breathless from agony, I waited for help, and still I could not faint.

Time seemed to stand still, when a movement caught my good eye. The child's face was like a vision of an angel. She stared at me, said something, then she was gone. It seemed a long time before I heard voices. The next face I saw belonged to a man, and he stared at me in shock. After long astounded moments, he pulled back.

"Holy Mother of God! She be right. There's a man in 'ere still alive. Mind you, 'e ull soon be with 'is Maker."

Two more different male faces peered at me, and I could see the pity in their eyes. "What'n we do?" I heard.

"We can do no more than carefully remove 'im. If 'e survives that, we ull fetch the apothecary."

"Fat lot of good that ull do."

"Mebbe, but we can't just leave 'im."

Despite the unbearable agony, I was unable to faint. The pain had now reached an unbelievable pinnacle, and there I hovered, held in a realm of undiluted agony while the men slowly tried to free me from the wreckage. Every slight movement of my body was torturous, yet it had to be done. I was soaked in blood, with vomit and piss adding their stench to the horror I had become. When they had my body finally cleared of the wreckage, the three of them gathered around to lift me out. They looked at each other apprehensively.

"This is goin' to 'urt, young master."

Hurt! Holy Christ! Could anything possibly hurt more than the flaming agony I was in already? I was unable to communicate with them, for my mouth was so full of blood and vomit that I dare not open it lest I choke.

Even when they lifted me clear of the wrecked carriage, I was unable to faint, while shards of red-hot pain hammered and stabbed at my body with remorseless fury.

Time seemed suspended. They had laid me slightly on one side, so that the huge sliver of wood that pierced right through my upper body should not be in contact with the ground. This suited me well, for it allowed the blood and gore to run out of my mouth. Then, amazed that I still lived, they sent for the help of an apothecary.

He seemed to arrive fairly quickly, although time and agony make strange companions. I stared up at him through my one good eye. He was an elderly man, and he gazed at me in shock. The concern in his eyes suggested that he was a good man, but he looked baffled.

"If we pull the splinter out, mayhaps it ull kill 'im?"

"What'n choice is there?"

"Iffen we leave it, 'e ull die anyway."

"The pain and bleedin' ull kill 'im."

"Well 'e couldn't be in more pain than 'e is now, and 'e ull most likely die, no matter what."

"Why don' 'e swoon?"

"Ain't natural, 'is'n not swooning."

"Mayhap's the devil be punishing 'im?"

As I watched and listened, two of the men crossed themselves. I tried to shake my head, but new stabs of pain made it impossible. A sudden cough shot a gush of blood out of my mouth, splashing the apothecary.

I watched him jump back, and he appeared to make his decision. Clenching his jaw in determination, he reached into his bag, and sprinkling some liquid onto a piece of cloth, he squatted next to me.

"I ull do my best. You 'ave my word on it."

He placed the cloth over my mouth and nose, and although my lungs fought for breath as the most terrible suffocation imaginable engulfed me, pain searing and stabbing me at my every move, at long, long, last, I plunged into merciful darkness.

# Sixteen

I opened my good eye to a small, rather squalid room. For several moments I lay in a daze of hammering pain, thinking that I must be in the middle of some terrible and repellent nightmare, then the memory of the wrecked carriage came crashing back.

I had been washed, and cleaned up, and the huge splinter had been pulled out of my chest. A stench hung around, and I wondered what was going rotten. Rude and clumsy strips of cloth had been wrapped tightly around my body, with more crude wrappings around both arms. I could feel wood splints holding each arm out stiff, with the wrapping over it.

Below my waist, I could feel nothing. My lower body was ominously dead. I was paralyzed! Covered over, I was unable to see my legs.

Sweat burst out all over my body as the awful truth hit me with a shattering impact. Oh Christ! I was paralyzed! The pain in my hip and back was appalling, and my chest . . . ? It was impossible to separate one pain from another in the flood of agony that washed over me. I groaned in utter despair. Why had I lived? How? It should not have been possible. My sheer inability to move drove home the dreaded reality that I was back-broken.

I tried to take a deep breath to call out, but I was unable to do so. Fluid hissed and bubbled in my lungs as I wheezed and fought for every breath of precious air. With a sudden jolt of unwanted memory, I remembered that back-broken victims are unable to control their bladder or bowels, and the full horror of my injuries overwhelmed me. I shuddered as I thought about my future. I knew, then, that I had no future. There was nothing left to live for.

Unable to call out for help, I pondered my fate. Had my father been notified? Did anyone even know who I was? And what about old Lyle? Was he alive? Obviously I would be a cripple for the rest of my life. Suddenly, and clearly, I knew that I did not want to live. Maybe I would be damned to hell for wanting to die, but nothing could be worse than this. This *was* hell; a living hell.

I tried to get comfortable in the rough bed, but I knew in that moment that for as long as I lived, I would never, nay, could never, be comfortable again. Tears ran hot from my good eye, and I could feel it leaking from the other empty socket, down onto my cheek. That I had lost my eye was never in question. I could feel hot coals burning like an unholy fire in that empty place, a pain that filled my whole head with throbbing misery. Oh God.

When a floorboard creaked, I looked to the doorway. The girl that appeared was the earlier angel that I had seen. She was older than I had thought, maybe fifteen or more, her hair fair, her face soft and vulnerable. As she stared at me, I had the impression that she looked a touch vacant, but mayhaps I was in error.

The girl called out in a low voice, and an older woman, worn, and tired looking, quickly appeared. I knew then that I was in the cottage of a bonded man and his wife, for the life of hard physical labor was deeply etched into her features. But there was also kindness, and care.

"Who be you, young master?"

I tried my hardest to speak, but only a scratchy gargle issued from my lips. I looked at her in despair, and she read my plight and misery.

"Ush, now. Another day, mayhaps." She sniffed the air around me, and pulled the coarse hessian covering off my body. "I'll need to clean yer."

There was nothing I could say. I wanted to scream my pain from stretched lips as she handled me, pulling away the stinking sacking to replace with more, but only gurgles of bubbling liquid issued forth. The stench was not abated, and the woman leaned closer, sniffing my chest wrappings.

She backed away hurriedly, crossing herself.

"'Oly Mother, 'e got the rots."

She called out, and a tall, weather-beaten man appeared. He too, had the appearance of a man overworked, and I knew that the squire that owned the village and all its people, was a hard, unyielding man. Unfortunately, it was all too common. The gentry often considered their serfs as no more than inferior servants. My father had never done that, nor did those in his circle of friends. His serfs were loyal to him, and our family, all too aware of how things could be.

"Whassup?" he asked.

She indicated my chest. "Ee got the rots."

235

The man came over to me, his eyes averted, then pulled the chest wrappings aside. He stepped back abruptly as the stench, now released, filled the room. "Bugger me!"

"Ee's bin 'ere three days," the woman said, "an' 'e ain't dead yit. Git the apothecary agin."

"Yus, an who pays?"

She looked at me grimly. "The young master is gentry. When we fin' who 'e is, they ull pay, an be 'appy to. You go git the apothecary, while I gie 'im some broth."

The empty rumbling in my gut and my terrible weakness indicated that I needed food, but I was not sure that I could eat. When the woman returned a few minutes later with a bowl of steaming broth, she stared down at me in concern. Rather than try to get me upright, she stuffed some sacking under my head, and began to spoon the hot liquid into my mouth.

I choked and spluttered, trying my best to swallow, but the woman had little patience, spooning more in before I was ready. Watching in agitation, the girl suddenly stepped forward and, taking the bowl from her mother, slowly and with care, began to feed me. Mayhaps half the bowl was coughed from my mouth, but the amount that I swallowed helped me.

The woman had left, seemingly repelled by the stench. The smell was so bad I was having trouble trying not to vomit up my meager food. The girl cleaned my face, then gazed at me, and I watched her watching me.

Obviously not bothered by the awful smell, she smiled at me.

"An there summat more I kin do fer yer?"

Once again, I tried to speak, but this time in a thin, slow, slurred, whisper. And I succeeded. "Thanks for finding me," I managed.

She frowned, trying to understand what I had said, then her eyes cleared. "That's orlright. Be yer dying?"

"I hope so," I whispered painfully.

Her eyes filled with tears. "Dun do that, young master."

There was nothing more that I could say, and as I looked at her, and all her health, I knew that half-wit, or not, she was the fortunate one. I tried to think about father and Aunt Maud, but the hurt was rising in such massive waves of terrible pain, I was exhausted.

I must have fallen asleep. Opening my eye, I noticed that the girl had gone, and I could hear heavy footsteps approaching my room. When the apothecary came in, I was wide awake, waves of agony engulfing me.

He swore at the smell, and pulling a pocket cloth from his clothing, tied it over his mouth and nose.

He was the same man I had seen earlier. He looked down at me, pity in his eyes.

"Beats me 'ow 'e's alive," he muttered.

Only then did I see that the woman had followed him into the room, with the girl close behind.

"I'll need 'ot water, an' cloth," the apothecary said.

The girl scuttled away, while the other two just stared at me.

"Lookit, the pus en fair bubblin' et 'is chest," the woman said. "Ee be got the rots."

"I never see a man so badly 'urt," the man sighed. "An' God only knows how he's still alive."

I was feeling sick, frightened, and I hurt like the fires of hell, and listening to them was no help, but I had little choice in the matter. When the girl came in with a wooden bucket half filled with hot water and some old rags, I was more than ready.

The girl looked at the apothecary. "The man dun spoke to me, sur. Yer need ter git close."

His eyes gleamed, and he looked at me thoughtfully. "Did 'e now. Mayhaps 'e can speak to me." His eyes met mine.

"Can you tell me your father's name, young master?"

Holding the kerchief tight to his nose, he brought his ear close to my lips.

"Randolph Gifford, from Berwick," I whispered.

He jumped back. "Excellent, just excellent." He went out the room bellowing. "Giles, send word to find a Master Randolph Gifford, of Berwick. Now we're gitting somewhere."

Waves of relief mixed and mingled with waves of pain. I dreaded what the apothecary must now do.

His mouth shut tight, and the kerchief firmly in place, the apothecary began unwrapping my chest. He tried to be gentle, but it was impossible not to cause me fresh pain. I gasped. I was so weak that trying to move left me shaking and trembling with exhaustion, and I had no choice but to let him and the woman handle me as they would.

We could all see my chest as the wrapping was finally removed. A black-and-purple hole entered the right side of my chest between armpit and nipple. What it was like at the back, I do not know, but the splinter had emerged between my spine and shoulder blade. Thick festering pus was running from the wound, along with clots of blood and a stinking, foul slime. The smell of it left me gagging.

Washing the wound and cleaning the hole out became so unendurable, that my open mouth bubbling and gargling was more than the apothecary could stand.

"It's risky, but this'n too much."

So saying, he got a dark brown bottle from his bag, and pouring some of the contents onto a piece of rag supplied by the girl, held it over my mouth and nose.

Once again the terrible feeling of suffocation swept over me, and I fought for breath. Gradually, with an inner shriek of terror, I was engulfed by darkness.

❖   ❖   ❖

My body was shaking and trembling uncontrollably, and despite not wanting to leave the blessed darkness to return to my pain and misery, my good eye opened.

The girl smiled at me, and I thought that I had never seen anyone so beautiful. I was becoming convinced that she was an angel.

As though water were boiling in the cavity of my chest, my chest was a caldron of pain. I groaned.

"Your'n stump be got the rots too."

Stump? What in the hell was she talking about?

Almost as though she could read my thoughts, the girl leaned close.

"They 'ad to cut orf a leg."

Shocked, I stared at her, numb. A leg, gone! Oh Christ, what next? How much more could I take of this? And then the grimness of the joke hit me. I was back-broken. Paralyzed. I could not use my legs anyway, good, bad, or missing!

I stared at the dirty ceiling in that dingy little room, the pain in my body meeting and merging with the pain of my thoughts. I had no refuge, no place to hide from the agony of my despair, of a life laid to waste. I was now a cripple, a burden to myself and everyone who knew me. Just the thought was unendurable. I lay in wretched silence, not sure how much more I could take of this. And that is when the terrible truth hit me. I would have to take it for as long as it lasted; the rest of my life!

I lay there for quite a long time, the girl patient and undisturbed. She seemed to want nothing more than to be with me. I stared at her, finding it difficult to understand why she was so caring about me. She seemed able to read my expression, for just when I was wanting her to come close, she put her face near mine, her breath heavy with onion.

"What'n?"

"Tell me your name," I whispered around the gurgling fluids that still threatened to drown me.

"I'm Poll. Polly Stringer."

I stared at her. Poll. Polly. How incredible that she should have the girl's name I most favored, Polly. I felt strangely comfortable with her presence. More than that, I felt comforted by her being with me. A bit simple she may be, but she was no half-wit. Her eyes held a guileless compassion, and in my sickness and injuries, I did not feel reduced by her. Seeing other men and women who were healthy and capable made me feel more hopeless and more crippled than ever. It was ridiculous, but that's how it was.

It occurred to me that Polly was only a few years younger than me, for I had only recently had my twenty-third celebration. From being worlds apart, we now had one thing in common—a hopeless future. Hers was one of drudgery, work, and childbearing, with a man who may, or may not, care for her. Mine was . . . ? It did not bear thinking about. Oh Christ! Both arms broken, my hip smashed to pieces, and speared right though my body, I had the rots, and worst of all, was back-broken. I was black and blue with bruising and a mass of cuts, and God only knew what was wrong inside me. For the first time since my mother died, I surrendered to my plight, and wept in utter misery.

"Don' take on." With her words, Polly gently stroked my face and hair, as though I were some favorite dog, yet just her caring touch was a soothing tonic. Although my chest burned as though I had a shaft of fire through me, and my hip pained as though bedded in spikes, along with the throbbing pain of my back and arms, so exhausted was I that, under her soothing touch, I fell asleep.

When I woke up again, I knew that I had been more than asleep. I knew instinctively that I had walked the place between heaven and hell. The room was dim with light, and I was alone, except for something very strange. Close by me, there hovered an apparition, yet it held no fear for me. Two or three times bigger than a man, yet of a vague and obscure shape, I saw a glow of hazy, golden-colored light. I stared at it, not knowing what to do. The thought came to me that this golden light was an angel from heaven, but it simply hovered near me, doing nothing.

At that moment Polly walked very quietly into the room, and the golden glow slowly faded away. It was obvious that Polly had not seen it, and I had a knowing that it was for my eyes only. Mayhaps I was dying. When Polly looked at me, I could see that she had been crying.

As our eyes met, she gave a start of surprise.

"Yer be alive!"

They must have thought that I was dying. What a shame that I still lived. God had not been that merciful.

"Yer father be here, sun."

I smiled at her. God only knew, there was little enough to smile at. A cough tore at my throat, and my lungs burned as I fought to get my next breath. Whatever would father say to me? And what had happened to old Lyle?

As I looked at Polly, she leaned close to hear me. Amazing. It was as though she could read my very thoughts.

"Did anyone find an old man?" I wheezed.

Polly stared at me for a moment frowning, and I realized that my voice was not easy to understand. Then her face cleared, and she nodded.

"They fun' an ole man dead along the road just afore the bridge. Is 'e yer man?"

I gave a tiny nod. My bad eye was giving me trouble now. Molten lead was surely bubbling in the socket. Pain roared through my head, and on a rising wave, it overwhelmed me as I went sliding down, down, into the welcome dark.

❖  ❖  ❖

It was hard to make out what was happening. As if I were not suffering enough already, my body was bouncing up and down, sending hot stabbing pain through me. I groaned in misery, my agony unendurable. I felt a need to vomit, but I knew that if I did, it would kill me. Jostling and bouncing, I lay floating in an ocean of pain, and I came to realize that I was in another carriage. Comprehension was slow, but it finally occurred to me that I was on my way home. Someone spoke quite close to me, and I lay listening to their words. The man's voice was familiar, and the person who answered was my father.

"To be honest, Randolph, I don't know what is keeping him alive. He's in a very bad way."

My father's reply was gruff, his cover-up voice when he tried to hide his feelings. "He's a fighter. He always was a sassy little sod, but . . . God! What chance that he can ever walk, James? What chance to even live?"

"Not good, I'm afraid. He has the rots in three places, his chest wound, the eye, and his leg stump. And as though that were not enough, I think he's back-broken. You'll have to accept that he will be crippled for life. Christ man, did you see the leg that they cut off? It was smashed to pulp. Kicked to pieces by a drowning horse. And then it smashed his hip. Can you believe such foul luck? Luckily the apothecary was fairly competent. He cut the leg cleanly enough, but the rots is into it. As you well know, if we can't stop the rots, it'll soon kill him. It's a miracle he's still alive."

"What a bugger. I should never have let old Lyle go to collect the boy. Now he's dead, and Jake's dying. What the hell happened to Lyle?"

"I had a look at his body, Randolph. Best I can make out he choked to death on gob. His mouth and throat was full of thick yellow gob."

"The bloody fever was in his lungs. That's the other big fear now for Jake, getting the fever in his lungs. Just listening to him breathe makes a man shudder. He's in a very bad way, isn't he?"

"Yes. I've never seen anyone recover from injuries like his, so you must be prepared for the worst, but, he is still alive. Once we get him home . . . who knows?"

For what seemed hours I bounced up and down and swayed from side to side, while the pain seemed to grow ever greater. It struck me as almost funny that, in all the terrible pain, I was hungry. I knew that soon, I would faint again, so I just lay and waited for it.

❖　❖　❖

I was dreaming that I lay on a huge block of wood. The wood was hard, uncomfortable, and studded with large iron spikes. I lay on the spikes, and I could feel them driving into my flesh, piercing me, tearing their way through me. One long spike had driven through my chest, another through my head, and another my hip. Even in my dream, I knew that this was a nightmare of the worst kind. I woke up, sweating . . . and the nightmare became a living reality. The pain was at its worst ever, and sweat ran from me. A quick glance revealed that I was in my own bedroom, a room that I had always liked. It was large by the standards of the time, and even my bed had been specially made. Most beds were rather small, with the head end of the base as solid wood. Mine had the ropes that supported the straw mattress laced from one side to the other—rather like a laced-up boot—going the full length of the bed. I had always considered it to be an exceptionally soft bed, but at this moment, it felt like jagged iron.

That I was feverish was obvious. I alternately sweated and froze, one minute feeling as though I were boiling, then shivering and shaking in icy cold sweat. I hoped I would die. My father had said I was a fighter, and I knew that there was some truth to that. I had been a rugged type, and very stubborn, but right now, I only wanted to die. Could I fight to die, or did it only work one way, to live? I wanted to give up. How did I do that?

Aunt Maud's cool hand was on my brow before I even knew that she was in the room. "My poor, poor, Jake. I'm so very sorry, Jake. Please fight to live."

She thought that I was still in the faints, or dying. If only I could. Trying to control my shivering, I moved my head and looked up at her.

"Aunt Maud ... food." It was the same whispering croak as before, but with no Polly to understand me.

"Jake! Are you awake?"

"Food," I croaked.

"What are you saying, Jake? I can't understand you."

I tried to get her to put her face near mine, but she did just the opposite. She held well back from me. I, too, could smell the rot in my chest and stump, and my eye must be a repelling sight. Yet none of that had bothered Polly. Surely Aunt Maud was not going to add to my problems.

Gradually drawing in a deep breath, I spoke as I exhaled. "I'm hungry."

This time she heard me. "Oh, God! You must be simply starving. I'll go and get you some food."

When she came back, she had Nell, one of our housemaids with her. "Nell is going to see to your needs, Jake, so just you tell her whatever you want." She looked very distressed. "And Nell will keep you changed."

I sighed. Of course, if I drank and ate, then I had to piss and shit. Oh God. No!

Nell was a well-meaning woman, elderly in her forties, but with a brisk, curt manner that spoke volumes. Like so many, she was in service to us because of her working-class necessity. She did not like what she did, and it showed. Now, she looked at me with pity, and distaste.

In an effort to keep the fluid in my lungs from choking me, several pillows had been placed under my shoulders and behind my head. Because of this, I was now able to be fed without being moved.

Nell spooned hot lamb broth into me, but she was both careless and impatient. She did not mean to be unkind, but she increased my humiliation. As I coughed and gagged on the food, swallowing some and coughing out the rest, she kept her eyes averted. Grimly, I persevered.

Aunt Maud had left, and Nell looked at me more boldly than was her wont. "Forgive me fer saying it, Master Jacob, but you shud jest die. It ain't right ter suffer so."

My injured body and limbs were now bound with fine cloth strips, and my privates swaddled in a thick, absorbent material. Nell pulled this away from me with a grimace of distaste, and washed me in grim silence. She replaced it with fresh material, and stalked out the room. As I watched her go, I knew she would have to wash the shit and piss from the material, and I prayed that she would be thorough.

❖   ❖   ❖

During the next month, the housemaids were given turns at looking after me, and without exception, they were a pitiful lot. I had never seen them the way I now did. It was a unique perspective, and one I would willingly have forgone.

My father had come to see me as soon as I was home, and we had shared hesitant greetings, but it had been another two weeks before I had felt capable of talking to him. He had stared at me in helpless anguish.

I had beckoned him close. "If I were a horse, you would put me down."

At least father was not too squeamish to come close. His ear was almost in my mouth during our conversation, and despite my slurred words, he understood me. He had jumped back in dismay. "That's enough of that talk, Jake. We are going to get you better. James is the best apothecary possible to look after you, and our maids will give you the very best of attention."

"James Standish? He's hopeless, and the maids all despise cleaning up my shit."

We both knew that James was a dandy, and as a friend of the family, it had never mattered. Never, that is, until I was on the receiving end of his attention. He was clever with words, appeared competent, but was only passable at ministering to the sick. Mostly, he sold useless potions, and was already spooning some of them into me.

Father had frowned. "You are hardly in a position to criticize him, so I suggest you address your manners." He stared down at me, anguish and torment on his face. "Oh, Jake, what are we to do with you?"

"Cut my throat?" I suggested.

Father had reacted badly. "I know how much pain you are in, but that will recede eventually. You will get better and who knows, you may even walk one day."

I dismissed the talk of me walking, that was just Father avoiding the full reality of what had happened, but as for pain, he had not the faintest idea what pain truly is.

"You don't, Father." His face was close. "Not in your wildest dreams do you have any idea of the pain."

"But it will pass, Jake, and you will get about."

"Liar.

"JAKE!"

He waited for an apology, but I just stared at him. It was he who relented. "Why did you call me that?"

"I'm back-broken."

He took a deep breath, pain flashing into his eyes. "Ah, yes. I'd forgotten that. Never mind, there will be things you can do, and ways to get around."

"Horse shit!"

"If you are going to take this attitude Jake, you are in for a bad time."

"And if I don't?"

He looked defeated. "Yes, well, attitudes help."

He was right, and I knew it, but the hopelessness I felt overrode all my common sense.

"There is one thing I really want," I whispered. "Can you get Polly to look after me?"

He looked mystified. "Who is Polly?"

I was fading. "The girl who found me."

He nodded. "I don't see why not. How old is she?'

"About fifteen. Her father is Giles Stringer."

"I'll see what I can do. They will probably be pleased to have her off their hands. I'll send a man to get her. She can come into service with us, and spend all her time looking after you. Is that what you want?"

"Yes. Thank you, father." Two weeks later, Polly had arrived, and she was every bit the blessing that I had hoped for. Everyone was only too pleased to pass the burden of me onto her, and from then on, Nell and the other maids were all far more pleasant to me on the rare occasions they came near.

From the first day, Polly made it very clear that she wanted nothing more out of life than to care for me. My welfare was her only concern, and she had hardly left my bedside before she was back again. She was happy and content. She did everything for me. Cleaning shit from my arse, or helping to shift me to ease the added burden of bed sores was all done without a word of complaint.

Nothing could ever compensate for my former health, but Polly was the light in my life. In a way, she was also a curse, for she gave me the will to live, when I wanted only to die. Ironically, she made living so much more meaningful. I learned too that I was wrong about her; she was not simple, not a bit. She was compassion and love in human form.

Father and Aunt Maud were delighted with her, and they treated her exceptionally well. She was given her own small room, a rare honor, and besides her board and lodgings, they paid her a small wage. She was considered my aide, and was never expected to help with household duties. They both actively liked her, and although I know she relieved their conscience about me, I was pleased that it had all worked out so well. Because they were of similar build, Aunt Maud even gave Polly some of her castoff dresses, something quite unheard of, but it was when I heard Aunt Maud correcting Polly's speech that I realized Polly was becoming a type of adopted daughter for Aunt Maud.

I was stunned at first. Watching Polly and thinking about people was the only way I could deal with my pain, so I did a lot of it. Aunt Maud had never had any children of her own, and just as she had easily taken to me, so now the same was happening with Polly.

It had become obvious to me, and everyone, that I was not going to die. Where the hell my strength came from I do not know, because I wanted to die with an ever-growing intensity. I can only suspect that it was Polly. I was in love with her. For me, she was compassion in a world of pain, love in a world of pity, tenderness in a harsh and unkind world, light in the terrible gloom of my future.

My lungs were congested all the time, and breathing was still difficult. My back was a deep throbbing ache, rather than the stabbing sharp pains in my hip and both arms. But I have to say that the pain was easing. Easing, that is, from unremitting agony to never-ending pain! James had tried a trick to heal me that had nearly cost my life. One day, about two weeks back, he poured undiluted brandy into the hole in my chest, back, and eye. The scream that had been torn from me had turned him pale, and I learned afterward that Polly had attacked him. As for me, after the scream had been ripped from me, I had fainted clean away. Thankfully, it was the last time James ever treated me.

It had been a full day before I opened my eye again, and they had believed me dying. Their thoughts were very close to the truth, for I had again walked the borderland twixt heaven and hell. At one time I had looked down from above at my deathly white body lying in the bed. Strangely, I had again seen the misty glow of golden light hovering close to my body, and oddly, had felt a compulsion to merge with it. In all truth, I tried, but I did not know how. I think that I needed to die for that to happen, but die, I could not.

Although my broken bones were mending, my body wound, stump, and eye socket continued to ooze a foul, thick, yellow pus. Why the poison did not kill me is a mystery.

❖    ❖    ❖

One day, about five weeks after Polly had arrived, she came into my room in a state of great excitement.

"Jacob. I have got yer a healer to come."

With great difficulty, Polly had been persuaded to call me by my name. I hated the "young master" tag, but we could not get her to call me Jake. For her, that was just too much disrespect! Both Father and Aunt Maud were encouraging her to be less formal with us, leaving the servant image behind. And very slowly, it was happening.

"Got 'you' a healer," I corrected her in a wheezy whisper. "What healer? Do I know him?"

"It ain't a him, she be a woman. Some think that she be a witch, but she saves lives. She's a good woman."

"When is she coming?"

"This very day, before the sun sets."

"Does father know?"

"Yes, I dun told him. He said, good."

Father and Aunt Maud would allow anything if there was the remotest chance that it would benefit me. Their concern for my welfare was touching, and their inability to do more for me cost them much in unfounded guilt.

It was late afternoon when Polly came in with a woman who commanded immediate attention. She was middle-aged, with striking black hair, slim, and with sharp, aquiline features. She smiled easily, with a gentle nature that belied her rather fierce countenance. With Polly's help, she uncovered my wounds, unwrapped my limbs, and had me generally stripped. A few months ago I would have been mortified at the idea, but now, my pain and despair had removed such trifles as being embarrassed over nakedness.

Her name was Ellen Fieldwell. Together, she and Polly rolled me onto my good side so she could inspect the leakage from near my shoulder, and she dug her fingers carefully into the bones of my lower back and hip. My eye was examined, my stump, my chest, and the broken arms. She took a long time, and was careful to an extreme. Even so, the pain was so bad I was almost fainting by the time she had finished.

They laid me back in my propped-up position, and I sat watching them, my fate in their hands. Ellen was very honest with me, and I could see that my injuries distressed her.

"Poll tell me that you're sick, but this'n is far worse than I ever imagined. You're a very strong man."

"I'm weak as hell," I wheezed.

"Strong in spirit, is what I mean. When I go 'ome, I shall make a brew of 'erbs fer yer to drink four times a day, and another mixture of 'erbs fer yer wounds. They must be replaced daily. I'll come and see yer daily fer a while."

She left with Polly, and I could hear them talking to each other as they left the room. Were there things I did not know, or should not know?

When Father came to see me that evening, I asked him if he would pay Ellen generously.

"Jake, I'm always generous. You know that. I'll tell you what I'll do. If her mixtures cure the rots, or help you in any positive way, I'll give her enough money to keep her, and I'll invest some for her future. If she can heal you, I will be very grateful." He looked at me, embarrassed. "You are my only offspring, and I had such big plans for you. I do care for you very greatly, you know. Please don't give up on yourself, because I haven't, and I do not intend to."

True to her word, Ellen came next day with the herbal potion to drink, and another thick, gumlike substance to paste over and into the wounds. If I smelled bad, the paste was far worse, and the taste of the potion . . . !

"Either these ull cure you quickly, or . . ." And she shrugged, her stern face softening compassionately.

"Or, I'll die," I wheezed. "What about my breathing?"

Ellen held out a sachet. "Poll ull 'old this at yer nose to inhale. Do it offen. Iffen it works, I'll make yer some more." She smiled at me. "Yer've 'ad a bad go of it, but I can fix yer, just yer see iffen I don'. The potion ull also 'elp 'eal yer lungs."

The next month proved her as good as her words. She had named many of the herbs that I had been drinking, but the few that I remembered seemed as good as their names, Speedwell, Knitbone, Feverfew, and the like. The first week it had seemed that nothing was improving, then suddenly, my terrible sweating came to an end, along with the never-ending wanting to vomit. But even better, the paste had worked miracles on my rots. At first the paste had burned like fire, but Ellen had assured me that this meant it was working.

"Iffen you don' feel it, then it be no good," she said.

She had also given Polly a sleeping draught for me, and that had made a huge difference. Sleeping soundly, I built up strength, and she also had me drinking stout, a barley-and-oats brew of ale. That, at least, was no punishment!

By the end of a month, the rots had been banished, and my flesh became pink, slowly healing. The sachet of strong-smelling herbs had improved my lungs, along with the potion I was still drinking. My broken arms had mended, and they were now unwrapped. I could use the fingers of each hand, and although my arms ached badly, I was exercising them on a regular basis, and beginning to get them working again.

But of all this, the most outrageous suggestion that Ellen had made was for my body to be immersed to the neck in a tub of hot water. She said that if I did it once, I would want to do it daily. I had almost laughed at her.

"Do you mean, have a bath?" I asked, incredulous. "I normally have a bath twice a year, but once a day!" I chuckled at the absurdity of it. "I think not."

Ellen had prevailed, supported by Polly, and father had a special high-sided tub made, in which to place me. Ellen had explained that my body would be lighter in the water, but at this point, I had thought her absurd. The water was heated in the kitchen, and carried up to my room in large buckets by a burly, strong man named Ebb, one of my father's horse grooms. After Polly had stripped me, Ebb had gently lifted me from the bed and into the filled tub.

It had been the most blissful experience I had ever known. As the heat soaked into my hip, my back, my arms, my whole body, I had almost floated into heaven. And, glory be, my body was lighter in the water. Buoyancy it was called, and it floated all the weight off my back and hip. Polly had washed my hair and beard, and then cut them, while I relaxed in the tub. Ellen was right, despite the pain I had to endure from my back and hip through the whole process, the daily tub of hot water, with the healing oils that Ellen provided, was the highlight of my day.

Father and Aunt Maud had been astounded, and giggling, Polly had told me that secretly they had tried the hot bath themselves. She said that if the laughter and other sounds coming from it were anything to go by, they too enjoyed it.

Life settled into a daily routine of exercising my arms, moving my body around to avoid the worst of the bed sores, and terrible, unrelenting, overwhelming, boredom. I had been an active man, and although I had some schooling and could write my letters, and such, I was not a scholarly man.

Polly had become my only purpose in living. She had quickly improved her grammar, and had become very close to Aunt Maud. To see them in my room together, they looked like mother and daughter. Without a doubt, Polly's entry into our family was a blessing. The only pity was that it had to be under such torturous circumstances for me.

❖   ❖   ❖

A year passed, and I was no longer in pain. My lower back and hip held a deep, chronic ache that nothing could abate, but I had learned to live with that. Polly and I had become very close, and she looked after me and my welfare with indefatigable energy. She cut my hair regularly, trimmed my beard, and told me that with my eye-patch in place I looked very handsome and dashing. The only problem was, I could not dash anywhere!

According to the seasons and weather, I was taken outside for the fresh air, and as much as possible, made to feel part of the everyday family. That I would never walk again had now become very apparent to everyone. Father had kept his promise to Ellen, and Polly told me that Ellen was better off now than she had ever been. It was ironic how many other people were benefiting from my calamity.

Apart from being crippled, it would appear that my life was improving, but that was not the case. One other result of my injuries was only now making its presence felt.

Slowly, but unrelentingly, my back and hip were twisting my whole body sideways and downward simultaneously. It was as though a vice were turning, one slow twist at a time, and my poor body was forced to follow the contortion that this dictated. This, even more than the earlier pain, gave birth to the ultimate of despair. By the end of the first year, I had given up all idea of living. Earlier, under Polly's kind influence, I had found the will to live, even to accept my handicap, but this new burden proved too much.

Often it came to me that I should strengthen my resolve to live, that if only I could release the despair, and with an attitude of greater acceptance, continue on, then, just possibly, it would all be bearable, but I could not find that last reserve of inner strength. I was beaten into submission.

❖  ❖  ❖

The second year came and went, and while Polly grew ever more beautiful and became more liberated, I became ever more imprisoned, as, twisted and contorted, my bones forced me into a curved, bowed, mockery of a man. And as I lost my human shape, so I lost my last remnants of self-respect. Self-loathing grew, slowly eating away at the inner me, and while my body had long ago been cured of the rots, a new, and more virulent, rot was eating me from within. I knew it, but I was powerless. Even my relationship with Polly was slowly changing, but I would have to say that the change was all from me.

Polly treated me with the greatest love. She had even told me that she loved me. She told me that she had loved me from the first moment she saw me lying broken in the carriage, and I believed her. She lived it. She lived her love for me in every action, in her words, and in her care. It was for no other reason that I continued living for yet another year, fighting to control my despair, but that despair was now a deep, dark pit in hell, and I was its sole occupant. I was never unkind to Polly, or unpleasant; I could not do that, but I withdrew myself from her. And she knew, but, wise beyond her years, she had patience. She believed that, given time, I would accept myself for the way I am, and find my inner nobility. Would that I could, but there is none left. Alas, I am not the man Polly thinks me to be. I am a shell, a husk sucked dry, waiting to die.

❖  ❖  ❖

The third year came and went, and by now I was truly beaten. My body had continued to relentlessly twist and contort, and by the end of the third year I was solidly locked into a fetal position. I was told by Ellen that babies began their life in this position, and as I looked into her eyes one day, I saw that she knew with utter certainty that I would end mine in the same way.

Father hardly ever came to my room to see me now. It was not because he did not care, but he could not stand the hurt of seeing his only son crippled, slowly misshapen, and so terribly reduced. Aunt Maud came two or three times a week, and she too could hardly look at me for fear that she would burst into tears. They could not be more lost to me than if I were truly dead.

The humiliation and frustration of being not only crippled, but also shockingly twisted and deformed, was beyond my ability to endure, and I began to plot my end. The years of having to continually leak my shit and piss into special pads, to be cleaned several times a day, or lay in the wet misery of it, had all eaten away at me.

At first, I rejected the ideas of how to kill myself, but time had become my enemy. If I waited too long, there could come a time when I was totally immobile. Now, twisted and contorted as I was, and looking like some grotesque caricature, I could haul myself around bodily to some degree by the strength of my arms. And my arms had become very strong. But there was no evidence that the terrible twisting distortion would ever come to an end.

Day after day, week after week, I lay on my bed cursing my fate, and I felt emotions that I had never known existed.

Misery, hate, and rage left me trembling when the faces of healthy people gazed down on me, pity in their eyes. How I hated the way they took their freedom for granted, and as I silently cursed the world, I was battered by self-loathing.

Apathy came silently on winged feet, leaving me lost, and wretched, hoping that a miracle would come, bringing back all that I once knew. Apathy whispered that this would never be, that all was lost, gone, destroyed.

Hopelessness came creeping in, unbidden, whispering that the past was locked away, and that dormant, I will lay and stagnate, helpless, yet hatefully alive.

I also prayed. I cried aloud for God to right this wrong. How dare He strike me to this accursed doom. Oh, gentle God, please remove the inner pain, and make this crazed, distorted body whole again. I beg you, make me whole again. Please, I will pray and love you every day. Please, God. Oh, please.

Memory is the worst by far of what I have to bear. Of remembering when I laughed, of the girls I admired, of rain, sunshine, forests, farms, of everything I loved. Oh, the pain of memory, it wracks me as though upon a cross. The memory of that last moment in the carriage, of the one moment I might have escaped my fate, the dreadful fear . . . and loss.

Loss! Of all that never will be, and all that could have been, all gone. Never, ever, to make love to Polly. My every hope, every desire, every dream, every want, all lie in the graveyard of loss and ruin. No life with Polly, no love, no caring, no affection, no children of my own, not any more of anything, for my life must surely end.

Daily, I plotted my death. There could be no mistakes. It was more difficult than I had thought, and I abandoned one scheme after another. I wanted no more injuries and added pain. It had to be clean and certain.

It was not unusual for me to ask Polly for quill and ink, for I often wrote poetry when the mood took me. Over a number of days, I wrote several letters. I wrote one to father and Aunt Maud. I told them that I loved them, and from my heart, I thanked them for all they had done for me. I told them that really, I had little choice, and I sincerely apologized for letting them down. I asked that they care for Polly, and let her replace me in their hearts and lives. I asked them to accept her as a gift from me. The next letter I wrote was to Polly. I told her that I had been in love with her since the first time I spoke to her, and that I would carry my love for ever and always. I asked her to accept father and Aunt Maud as her new parents, and to please do me the honor of marrying a good, loving man and living a happy life. I told her that by doing this, she would give meaning to me, and to my death. I told her that she, alone, had been my reason for living, and she alone, had been the light in my life. I asked her to forgive my cowardice, but I could no longer face a life where, remorselessly, I was crippled more grossly with each passing year.

The last letter was about my legal affairs, and I left everything that I owned, or would inherit, to Polly.

I carefully hid the letters under my bed, ready for when they would be needed. I felt strangely peaceful, for now, my strategy for death resolved, my letters written, and my decision made, I could calmly wait for the perfect timing. My affairs were in order, and in time, from my death those I most loved could find new happiness. While I lived, not only was I a prisoner of my helplessness, but father and Aunt Maud were imprisoned by their unyielding despair, and Polly, also, was held in the willing prison of my utter dependence on her.

I had to wait three months for the perfect day. Father and Aunt Maud were out to a late-night party, and not expected home before the early hours, if then. Polly was briefly visiting a nearby aunt, and would be away for one night only.

My plans had long been laid, and I felt calm about how I would proceed. Death had long ago lost all fear for me, and even the messy business of dying held no qualms. I had visited hell, and lived there. I was qualified.

I had my regular hot bath far later than usual, and instead of the tub being placed in the center of the room, I had it placed right next to the bed. Retrieving my letters, I put them under a pillow. It was late evening when the kindly Ebb undressed me, lifted me from the bed and placed me gently into the tub.

"You go now, Ebb, thank you. My arms are very strong, and when I'm ready, I can lift myself out the tub and directly onto the bed. As you can see, I can manage very well."

I knew that Ebb would do exactly as he was told. That was his lot in life, and he did it with good will.

For a while I sat and soaked, enjoying the heat, the buoyancy, and the mobility that the water allowed. The tub was the perfect shape. Rather like an elongated barrel, I could hold the sides and lift myself up and down. Whereas I had never lifted myself out before, I knew that I could do it. I sighed. So young. So short a life.

Within me, the moment arrived, and I did not hesitate. Grabbing the sides of the tub, I heaved myself up and out of the water, collapsing onto the bed with stabbing pain to my hip and lower back. For one terrible moment I wondered if I could, indeed, do what I had surmised, or if the pain would now defeat me, then my determination returned.

Wriggling and maneuvering myself into position on the bed next to the tub, I grabbed the tub with my outstretched arms and hands. The heavy weight of the water stabilized the tub, and with huge effort, I heaved myself up, and headfirst into the tub, while it stood as firm as a rock.

There was no way back. Having thrown myself headfirst into the tubful of water, I was stuck, and there to drown. Despite my resolve, I foolishly and fearfully held my breath before it exploded out of me, and I sucked in water. My last awareness was of vomiting as I drowned.

# Seventeen

Doubled over on the carpet in the living room, I gagged and vomited onto the floor.

"ADAM. ADAM. Come out of it. ADAM."

I could hear a voice. Oh God, no. Polly was going to rescue me. No, I couldn't let it happen. I screamed, trying to force myself further into the tub. I must drown. Please. Please don't stop me. Oh God, no.

Two hands suddenly clamped onto my head, and a high voltage charge of the most incredible peace and love held me transfixed. When, minutes later, the hands relaxed their hold, I collapsed in a limp heap.

For long moments I floated in some strange nonphysical space. I could see my body lying on the floor of the living room, with vomit splashed around me. Amber was on her knees next to me, turning me over and wiping my face. My nose was bloody, my lower lip gashed. Selph was close by, looking a touch shaken, when Amber glared up at him, screaming her unbridled anger.

"YOU CAN'T DO THIS TO HIM. IT ISN'T HUMAN. LOOK AT HIM. HE'S NEARLY KILLED HIMSELF. HE'S SOAKED IN SWEAT. YOU, YOU . . . MONSTER."

Abruptly, my whole awareness was of being me, Adam, lying on the living room floor. But I also remembered Jacob, and every single day of his pain and anguish.

I groaned, and opened my eyes. Looking up at Amber and Selph, I grinned a messy grin. "Hi there. I don't think I'm too good at this sort of thing."

And then I cried. Gut-wrenching, heartbroken crying that tore its way from me in a flood of tears and inner hurt. I cried for Jacob, for his courage and his weakness, and I cried for me, because I shared them.

254

Nobody tried to stop me from crying, but through my shuddering sobs I heard Amber apologizing to Selph. "I'm sorry I lost it, but I was nearly frantic with worry."

I even heard Selph reply. "I understand. I too, am shaken by the intensity of his experience. He . . ."

The rest of his words were lost as a fresh outburst of deep inner hurt shook my body, and I cried out in anguish. My lower back hurt, and my new hip, both aching and throbbing as though I had been kicked. I had to cry it out, and we all knew it, not that anybody could have prevented it.

I have no idea how long I cried, only that it was very powerfully cathartic. Jacob was as clear and fresh in my mind as my own present identity, but rather than despise him/me for his weakness, I felt an ever-increasing respect for his strength. The circumstances of his life had no true parallel with today; no opportunity for modern surgery or a new hip, no antibiotics, no clever mechanical aids, nothing. You lived or died, but either way, you suffered.

I guess, finally, Amber decided I had cried enough, for as my wracking grief and inner pain began to subside, I heard her voice, firm and decisive.

"Right, enough is enough. Selph, you take one arm, I'll take the other. I want him on his feet and into the bath."

I felt them lift me, and I needed their help. I was a bit confused about my ability to stand, and to walk. I had just spent over three years of a different time reality as hopelessly crippled!

With their support, they walked me into the bathroom, where the bath was already filled and waiting. Helping me out of my soiled clothes, I clambered shakily into the bath. By this time, I was definitely coming back to my present reality, but I felt a sudden shock as I sniffed the fragrance from the bath water. Lavender, the same oil that Ellen had provided for Jacob's therapeutic hot tubs!

I lay back and soaked with a sigh of content. Shock was still with me, but now it was subdued, combined with a sense of awe and wonder at the greater mysteries of life. Part of my mind struggled to believe that such a past-life experience was possible; while relaxed, I marveled at the sheer incongruity of linear time, and its incredible deceptions.

"Did you know that a herbalist named Ellen Fieldwell invented the therapeutic hot tub in the year 1575?" I asked Amber with a wan smile.

Selph had left us to our privacy, and Amber's face was still a mask of concern and worry.

"I don't care who invented hot tubs. I leave you two crazy people for just one day, and look what happens."

Although I was not yet quite with it, her words got through to me. "You mean I was in that altered state of reality for the whole day?"

"No, I don't mean that. I mean that I went down to the Maroochydore Plaza for a day's happy shopping, and I had to come back. I knew when I left that something was going on. I felt the tension in you. Two hours later I felt so uneasy I just knew that something terrible was happening. So I came home. And what did I find? I found you sitting in the big chair, your face contorting with the pains and emotions you must have been going through. Against my better judgment, Selph persuaded me to wait for you to come out of it in your own way. He begged me not to interfere."

"Thank God, you didn't."

She looked contrite. "Really?"

"Really, believe me. If you had interfered, you would have ruined everything. That's why I decided not to tell you; I didn't think you could handle it. But I won't keep you in the dark again. As it is, I get the feeling that what I thought was a failure may well be a triumph. It was rough, sure, but it was the most worthwhile thing I have ever done. More than that, for me, it was essential."

Amber looked even more abashed. "Poor Selph. When you pitched onto the floor, vomiting, I really lost it. I just screamed at him."

"I know. I heard you."

She looked puzzled. "But you had fainted, or were unconscious. For a terrible moment I thought you were dead."

"I don't really know what was happening, but I was looking down into the room. I saw myself on the floor, you cradling my head and wiping my face. I saw the bloody nose and split lip where I mashed my face into the floor. I could also see a fairly distraught Selph, and I heard you call him a monster. Does that cover it?"

She grinned at the memory. "Yes, gosh! That's amazing. I've got a million questions, and I want to hear the whole story, but Selph has made coffee and is getting some lunch ready. So finish your bath, and then we'll join him. He'll want to hear it all too. Now, sit still while I wash your smelly hair."

She washed my hair very vigorously, keeping a monologue going at the same time. "I've never seen anyone vomit on the floor, then push their face into it. What ever possessed you to do such a thing? What could you have been thinking about? Of all the stupid things to do. You've upset your back, and you said your hip hurts. How do you manage to do such stupid things to yourself? When . . ."

"How long was I in that experience?" I cut in.

"Over three hours."

"My God! I experienced over three years. Every minute of every day, week after agonizing week." I shook my head at the sheer mind-numbing wonder of it.

In much the same way as my incident on the beach, once I had my reality firmly reestablished in the present moment, the pain in my back and hip quickly faded to a deep-seated ache. To someone who was a veteran of undiluted pain, an ache was so minor a thing it was negligible.

Amber left me soaking and relaxing, and after thirty minutes in the hot water, I was able to stand up by myself. Stepping carefully out the bath, I dried myself. Dressed in clean clothes, I felt like a new person. And in many ways, I was! I felt reborn.

Amber and Selph were chatting when I joined them, and we sat outside eating our lunch. The few earlier clouds had dispersed, and it was sunny and warm. The swimming pool and the modern furnishings of today all helped to center me in the present time frame. Even the sun felt new, and welcome, for Jacob had spent very little time in it. Not unexpectedly, I missed Polly, but as I watched Amber caring for me, getting my food, and a drink, and I saw her obvious love in her every little gesture, the way she constantly glanced at me, and in her actions, an incredible realization hit me. Polly was now Amber, just as surely and as certainly as Jacob was now me.

My amazement must have been clearly visible.

"Adam, are you okay?" Amber was looking anxious.

Smiling, I nodded. "Life is just stunning. I've just realized that the one great sacrifice I had to make in releasing the woman I loved, was probably the very act that ensured all our lives together."

Amber looked baffled, and apprehensive. "What woman you loved . . . and who, together? What are you talking about?"

"I'm sorry. I need to tell you both the whole story. It is just incredible. So, settle back, because this is going to take a long time even if I skip over most of it."

It took me the next two hours to tell it, starting from the moment I left the last of the twenty-one steps, and only ending with my last memory of vomiting as I drowned. Apart for one quick refreshment break, I was uninterrupted. When I finished, there was a long silence. I looked at Amber.

"Just as Jacob is now me, Polly is now you," I said.

Amber stared at me in anguish, and then quietly, she began to cry. No shuddering or shaking sobs, but a quiet crying that took nearly twenty minutes before it ended. I felt awkward about it, but I let her cry, knowing only too well the value that such a release can offer. While she wept, Selph and I said little, but we sat with her, offering our love and support just by being there.

Selph slipped away to make some fresh coffee, and just as Amber's grief ended, he appeared with full mugs. For a while we sipped in silence, for there was almost too much to say, and none of us wanted to rush it.

Finally, it was Selph who broke the silence.

"Okay, Adam, you've told us what happened, but tell me how you feel about Jacob now."

I grinned feebly. "That's a big one!" I thought about it for a while. "Let me go about answering this in my own way. When I died as Jacob, I died with my self-loathing intact. I died despising my physical deformity, my life, and myself. I despised my cowardice, my helplessness, and my loss of manhood. And for me, this was all so real that I've carried it ever since. As you have told me so often: anything unresolved in the past, is unresolved now. I hated my broken back, and I blamed it for everything, so I unwittingly established a pattern of discord in my consciousness that is still repeating the same theme. I have broken my back, or injured it, in so many past lives that it has become established as my life-path. A continuity of pain and suffering."

I paused, thinking, and no one hurried me.

"Although I truly changed nothing in Jacob's life by revisiting it, my whole reappraisal of Jacob—me—is now totally different. As I just said, Jacob saw only his lack and his failure, whereas I see his incredible inner fortitude and strength. What he suffered was indescribable. Nothing I've said gets close to it. Yet he persevered for over three terrible years. Unrealized by him, he found his nobility in his love for Polly, and in his death, but it has taken until now for me to recognize it. He knew that his death would, and did, release his parents and Polly from a life of despair, but instead of recognizing his gift to them, and focusing on it, he focused only on his self-loathing."

I shook my head sadly. "From judgment and condemnation I created lifetimes of more pain and suffering, and none of it was necessary. Equally, I could have accepted that death was the only avenue I could take, and I could have honored my capacity to take it, for this was the only way available to me of giving to the people I loved." I leaned into Amber, and kissed her gently. "That's what I meant, earlier. You—Polly—were and are the woman I loved, and love. I get the feeling that my ability to set Polly free resulted in the togetherness we have shared ever since."

I looked thoughtfully at Selph. "Amazingly, I have very few questions. Everything is so clear and real. I know that I've resolved that past-life event, even though I didn't do anything, because paradoxically, of course, I did everything that you and I both hoped for. But I do have one or two questions. The whole beginning was weird, to put it mildly, yet I can even accept that. The station and train, no problem, but the people? Who were they? Then there was the gradual fade-out of Adam, and the slow integration of Jacob into the train. That was a masterpiece. Did you do that?"

Throughout everything, since my vomiting on the floor, until now, Selph had said almost nothing. He looked at me now, his blue eyes intense, and I could see a profound respect in them. Maybe it had always been there, but I had never before seen it.

He got up, and came to sit closer to me, then put both of his hands on my shoulders. "I'm very proud of you. I happen to know that you've been through a minor hell, and you have come back not only unscathed, but healed. You have my admiration and respect."

Releasing my shoulders, he sat back, and in a shimmer of light, both Amber and I saw him become a white-robed sage, ageless, and radiant. Looking at me, he spoke just three words. "I honor you."

His changed appearance lasted for fully half a minute when, in another shimmer of light, the familiar Selph was back, grinning at us with his usual innocent, cheeky grin, and clothed in the awful orange T-shirt and baggy green shorts.

He continued as though nothing had happened. "To get the process under way, I removed your subconscious blocks about going into the past. Those inner blocks, along with your belief systems and your conditioning, hold you bound into a linear reality. In truth, nobody has ever been denied access to a greater, nonlinear reality. But out of timing, it's just as well that those blocks remain. Your mental hospitals have many patients who, through various types of alcohol and drug abuse, have inadvertently plunged themselves into that greater reality, and insanity and instability has claimed them. As always, timing is essential."

He stopped, noticing Amber's tiny puzzled frown.

"A fledgling bird flies from the nest only when its flight feathers are fully developed, otherwise it will crash to the earth. You cannot tear open the petals of a rose bud without ruining the flower. Timing is the essential factor."

Amber nodded, comprehending.

"Adam's timing had arrived. Just as my timing to arrive in Adam's life was shortly before the car crash, so that very experience opened Adam to a far greater awareness of his own potential. Under my guidance, and yours too, Amber, Adam began to rehabilitate not only his broken physical body, but also his crippled past, his attitude, his psyche."

There was another digestive silence.

"What about those odd people on the station, and the rather horrific implications of the place?" I asked.

Selph smiled at me. "Ah yes. Don't take offense, but that was your doing. You obviously must have been feeling or thinking along the lines of hell. Probably when you arrived at the station. You use the word quite often. How many times have I told you that what you think is what you create? Anyway, I removed your subconscious blocks, put the station there, and set you going. You did the rest. The old woman who was clearly from the grave, symbolized your buried fear of resurrecting the past. The child was you, unseeing and innocent, and her mother was you talking nonstop to yourself in your own thoughts. The man with male and female clothing was your confusion, your inability to see things clearly. And, to give you credit, your determination to see this through caused the powerful loss of identity. To be really successful, the identity switch had to happen, but I left that to you. If you could not have fully taken on the persona of Jacob, then you would have been indicating that for the essential you, the timing was faulty. Like I said, Adam, considering the station scare, and then the terrible trauma you had to endure, you were courageous and triumphant. I want you to really acknowledge this."

My smile was wry. "But I still don't know who I am. I haven't reached my Greater Truth."

"Be patient, and allow the timing to unfold. You will only know your Greater Truth when you surrender needing to know it."

"More ambiguity?"

He laughed. "It's easy enough to know what I mean intellectually, but that surrender is not intellectual. You will only *know* your Truth when you no longer need to know. I can't talk you into that Truth, it cannot be explained, and I can't give it to you. You cannot take that Truth, nor seize it, nor in any way find it, or control it. Only when you release your need of Truth totally, will you find it. And you cannot even release that need by trying to release it."

"Wonderful! So what's left?"

"Life, Adam. Live it fully in every moment and let the timing take you unawares. Your intent will do the rest. It's that simple."

"What do you mean, my intent?"

"Every person has an inner intent. It may even be hidden from the persona, but it's there. Your intent is to Awaken. So by living life fully in a way that honors you, your intent will express its purpose. And you Awaken."

"Awakening is enlightenment?" Amber asked.

"Of course."

Amber looked puzzled. "But you make it sound like such a casual thing. Human philosophy and spiritual practices indicate that one has to live a life of dedication, strict discipline, and often, worldly denial. Even then, we mostly assume that enlightenment is only for the very few, more evolved souls."

Selph sighed. "Let me give you a parallel. If you want to be an authority on any subject, you only have to study that subject for five years to be a national authority. Double that time of study and dedication, and you become an international authority. Equally, if you want to be a great body-building champion, or a great athlete, you would need to invest approximately the same amount of time. Considering the adulation, fame, and money this can achieve for you, comparatively, it is only the very few who do it.

"Consider then, how few are going to devote time to an inner search that will go unannounced and unconcerned, will achieve no kudos, possibly some ridicule, and is not income generating. Add to this the beliefs that you have mentioned, austerity and denial, and you have thinned the ranks down even more. Then add the belief that you can't obtain enlightenment because you are 'not good enough' or 'not evolved enough' or some other such rubbish, and you are down to the very few, especially in your Western society. Then, finally, it cannot happen out of timing."

"So are you saying we are all good enough, and evolved enough?" Amber pursued.

"I'm saying that your timing in spiritual evolution has arrived the instant you ask, 'Who am I?' I'm saying that any person who asks that question from their heart and soul—for it is not an intellectual question—is definitely good enough. In relation to humanity, there is no such thing as not good enough;

only, not yet ready. 'Who am I' speaks of their readiness, their inner intent, the search for Truth. The paradox is that for as long as you continue to search you deny, yet without the inner ache of searching, an even greater denial is in place."

"That sounds like a self-defeating loop," I said.

"To a clever person, it probably is. Cleverness will not Awaken you, but inner trust and simplicity will. Remember what a Master said, 'Be again as little children,' trusting and simple. Simple is not simplistic; it is being guileless and vulnerable. Follow your inner truth, live it, express it, relax, and be in love with life. In this way you honor yourself. That's the recipe. Live that wonderful mix, and timing will take care of the rest."

"What will happen?"

"You will discover that you *are* life. That you are the microcosm and the macrocosm; the All That Is; One."

"And on that profound note, I'll leave you both to it," Amber said, as she got up and stretched.

"I think I'm about overloaded with profundities," I said. "It's time for a swim. I can truthfully say that I am well and truly back, as Adam." I frowned at Selph. "And yet I still have all my memories of Jacob intact. I've got two clear sets of memory of my past three years that interrelate, yet belong in different times and different realities. Will it stay this way, or will Jacob's reality fade?"

Selph shrugged. "There are no rules concerning this. I suspect that you'll retain the two memories of the two realities. Your experience as Jacob was so intense, it's unlikely that you'll just forget it. As you know, you had a real experience, not a dream." He grinned. "It'll be fun to hear what pops out of your mouth in conversation with other people."

I laughed. "Maybe it'll teach me to think for a moment before I speak, or even to listen to what I'm saying. But I have to admit, although I would shudder to repeat that life, I cherish the memory of Jacob."

Selph smiled at me approvingly. "I'm glad to hear it."

Amber emerged from the house wearing a pale blue bikini. She gave us a smile, and dived cleanly into the pool. I watched as she lapped the pool a few times in a fast, rather punishing, overarm. She swam until she was puffed. Wet hair clinging to her shoulders, she smiled up at me.

"That's better. I was still tense from all you put me through. A good workout has done the trick."

"I didn't put you through it," I said. "You did that to yourself. You could have trusted Selph, and me, and the process."

"And if the roles had been reversed, you wouldn't have worried about me?"

I nodded. "Good point. I would have been frantic."

She grinned. "You have to admit, throwing yourself onto the floor, vomiting, and pushing your face into it, isn't your usual everyday behavior."

What could I say?

❖   ❖   ❖

I had to be dreaming. I kept telling myself over and over that I must be dreaming, but instead of the dream coming to an end, or changing under my influence, it relentlessly pursued its terrible way. I was lying on a huge block of wood, and a large, menacing, rather shadowy axman was slowly cutting me apart, one limb at a time. I had lost both of my legs, and an arm had just been severed. I could feel the horror gathering in my throat as I tried to scream, but nothing emerged. In some odd way, I knew that I had agreed to this, for it would help me to obtain my freedom, but as my left arm was painlessly cut away, I was terrified. After my right arm, I would be cut in half, then my head would be cut off. Cutting away the limbs and my body was one thing, but to cut off my head! The ax came whistling silently down again, and my right arm fell away, then the huge ax lifted, poised, and flashed down, cutting me in half. As it was lifted again, to hover above me, with a flash of insight, I knew that I should submit and let my head go. But as the ax had risen, so too, had my fear. I stared up at the ax, and all the fear of all my many lifetimes reached a peak. The scream that tore its way from my throat ripped me out of the dream and halfway out of the bed as I screamed aloud in terror.

Poor Amber. One moment she was quietly asleep, the next moment she was sitting up in bed, also screaming. "ADAM! OH MY GOD! WHAT NOW? Oh, God, what's happening?"

I sat holding my head, visibly trembling, while Amber rapidly gathered her scattered wits. Putting her shaky arms around me, she held me, whispering and murmuring. "It's all right, my darling, just a dream. Just a nasty dream. Just relax, you'll be all right."

We both heard the soft tapping on the bedroom door.

"Everything okay in there? I heard a scream."

"Come in, Selph," Amber called out.

Selph walked in, and coming over to us, he put one hand on Amber's shoulder and one on mine, while Amber was holding me tight. The energy of calmness and peace that flowed through us was like an electrical current, so powerful was it. We both felt it not only pour into us from his hands, but also through and into each other from our hug as if it were completing a circuit. Within seconds, I went from being shattered and shaky to calm and clear.

"Holy moly! You sure are charged up," I gasped. "Do you carry that sort of energy all the time?"

Selph smiled. "Questions! He's better." He looked at me inquiringly. "So what happened?"

I stared at his orange T-shirt and baggy green shorts, and scowled. "Don't tell me you sleep in them too?"

"Adam, don't be evasive," Amber said in exasperation.

"Let's go get a hot drink," I suggested, "and I'll tell all. Not that there's much to tell. But it's the second time that I've had this dream, and I don't like it."

Amber quickly made three mugs of hot chocolate, and at two o'clock in the morning, we sat around the kitchen table.

"It wouldn't surprise me if I give birth to a child whose hair is white from shock. This is getting to be a habit," she grumbled.

"Well, if we have a darling daughter, we can name her Snow White," I quipped. Then, getting serious, I told them about the dream, omitting no details.

Amber shuddered. "Horrible. I'd wake up screaming too."

"You never let up, do you?" Selph said. "Drama by day, and drama by night. Man, you do love drama."

"Well, thanks a lot," I said huffily, "but it wasn't my idea. I'm quite ready for a peaceful life. Anyway, what does it mean? What's it telling me?"

"That you like drama," Selph chuckled, "plus a few other details. It suggests that having your limbs cut off is symbolic of rendering yourself helpless. Basically, you are symbolizing surrender. It appears that you can handle this, so well and good. The fear really comes to the boil when your head is about to be cut off." He smiled at me. "Hmmm, very interesting. The head represents your identity. This dream is symbolizing that you should not only surrender to life, but also surrender your identity. Understandably, you are overwhelmingly threatened by this, so you resist, and wake up screaming."

"Why are you so sure that my head is my identity?"

"Well, if you watch the movies at all, or are involved in a real-life experience, you will find that dead bodies are generally identified by their features, the face, head. If you go to a masked ball, it is the head that is disguised, not the feet. The same with robbers; they hide their faces because we identify people this way. Your dream is a message from your superconscious telling you to release your control of life, surrender to the process of inner growth, and to let go of your identity."

"Why? And how?"

"Did you say that this is the second time you have had this same dream?"

"Yes. The first time was soon after I made the decision to physically continue, while I was in the hospital. I thought it was to do with all that pain and suffering."

"Adam, in the dream you are telling yourself to let go of the last bastion of your ego and identity, the face and head. You ask why. Are you Jacob? Are you James? Are you the poor wretch who was tortured? Are you Thomas? Are you Adam? Or are you any number of other identities whom your essential-self has expressed its continuity through? Who you are is none of these and all of these. You will never discover your Truth through your identity. I expect you will have this dream at least once more. When you do, let the axman chop off your head. Trust."

"What will happen?"

Selph laughed. "Sorry, Adam. You'll just have to do it, and find out."

"Gee, thanks a lot. I might wake up and find myself dead. Then you'll have Amber after your scalp."

Amber took me by the hand. "Come on. Finish your drink and come back to bed, oh strange one. Wow! Little did I know what I was in for when I married you."

"Actually, Amber," Selph said, "if you hadn't married Adam, I wouldn't be here now. I told him when we met that you are part of the equation that brought me here. You *were* Polly, of course, and the interaction and love between you two through many lives has been the catalyst for your own, rather exceptional, growth. Adam needs, and has needed you, just as much as he now needs me. I won't explain this, but what we are now doing for Adam is the return of a great gift he gave to us, you and me, in another time frame you call the very distant past. You could say we owe him!"

I stared at him, open-mouthed. "Really?"

He nodded. "Yes, really. Once, Amber and I were on the receiving end, plus a large number of other people."

Why, I don't know, but I felt good about that. It was not an ego thing, but it just felt good. When I went to bed with Amber, I had no questions about that other time; it did not matter, but I was glad that Selph had told me.

We lay together, snuggled in each others arms, Amber's breath tickling among the hair on my chest.

"I'm sorry if I frightened you," I said.

"That's all right, it wasn't deliberate. Good night."

For the remainder of the night I slept peacefully, feeling none the worse for our interrupted sleep. But at breakfast the following morning, a memory came popping into my mind. As I thought about it, I was surprised that I had forgotten, and had never even mentioned it to Selph.

The mornings were very warm now, and porridge had been abandoned for either muesli or toast and marmalade for breakfast. As I chewed thoughtfully on my toast, I turned to the others. "Do you know, there's something I've never mentioned to either of you, but for the life of me, I don't know why. It's odd, because it's like a memory of a memory, yet it's as clear and as lucid as any reality."

"Adam, don't waffle, tell," Amber ordered.

"Oddly enough, the more I think about it, the more it seems to have empowered my recollection. A bit like that awful dream, it began soon after my decision to return to Amber. During my in-and-out moments of consciousness, I remember seeing a large, hazy, glowing golden light. It seemed to be hovering near my physical body. When I say large, I don't mean in a clearly defined way, but it had about three times the volume of a human body. I saw it several times, once or twice when I was actually conscious. I don't know how I forgot all this, but I did. What's really strange is that Jacob also saw it near him."

"How did you feel?" Selph asked.

"I think it . . ."

"How did you *feel? Feel!*" Selph interjected

I paused, while I thought about it.

"You see! You are trying to think about how you felt," Selph said mockingly. "Just share what you felt, coming from your heart, rather than a discourse from the head."

I hesitated, not sure how to share the memory of those undefined raw feelings. "Er, safe and nurtured in its presence. That it was a Being of Light. And, oddly, that I should merge with it. I had the feeling that if I did this, something rare and wonderful would happen."

266

"So why didn't you?" Amber asked.

"Because I didn't know how. Jacob tried, and so did I, but it was impossible. As soon as I tried, or thought about how to do it, the golden glow just faded away." I looked at Selph. "Anyway, what was it? What did it want?"

"You."

I waited for him to continue, but that was it. You! What did that mean? Baffled, I frowned at him. "What do you mean, me? Me what? You mean it wanted me? It wasn't me, so what are you talking about?"

"I've got nothing more to say. You figure it out, but please, don't think about it. Just open your heart. It's all there before you, everything you need, all that you are."

Gazing at him blankly, I turned to Amber. "Can you tell me what I'm missing here? Because it beats me. Perhaps I went to sleep in this conversation and missed something. You both seem to be a league in front of me, so, er... help!"

Amber's eyes met Selph's, but if there was any exchange between them it eluded me. She looked at me, and shrugged.

"I'm sorry my darling, but Selph is your teacher, and it's you he's teaching. I love you, but I can't give you answers to things like that. All I know is that if you look for what you're seeking through questions and answers, then you'll never find it."

I frowned at her. "Well, marvelous, thanks a lot. You just joined the 'far-out' club! You sound just like Selph."

Amber gave me a challenging grin, rather than a nice sympathetic smile, so pulling the shredded remains of my hurt dignity around me, I finished my coffee in a great gulp, and with an "Excuse me," I wandered off into the garden. The pond drew me like a magnet, and sheltered among the shrubs, I sat down at the waterside. To be honest, I did know what Amber was saying. Questions and answers created separation, so obviously, this is not the path to wholeness. Selph had told us both that you cannot formulate a question without knowing the answer, yet we have developed a subconscious habit of separating them. It seems a stupid way to victimize ourselves, but we do it all the time. He told us that it all begins in the way we think. But what a handicap, not only to not ask questions, but to avoid thinking them. I was not sure that I could manage it. When I think things out, it is generally through a question-and-answer dialogue. I could, of course, think about the questions, but I need not chase the answer. Maybe that's it. If I define the question, and then just leave it alone, what I need to know will emerge in right timing. Live within inquiry, but leave it open ended. Yes. I like that.

I chuckled as I realized what I was doing. Gazing into the water, I was sitting by the pond, pondering! I reached to where I kept a tightly sealed jar of fish food under a shrub. By now, the goldfish were getting quite agitated, cruising around with their mouths wide open as they waited for the manna from heaven. That's me, I thought. I cruise around looking for answers, my mouth opening and closing as it spills out useless words. But am I really in touch with the question? So what is my question? I have seen a Being that appears to me as a golden light. Why does it only appear in moments of extreme pain, or stress? Right, that's one question, so now leave it alone. Another question, what did Selph mean—you? Me what? I sighed. Forget it. The questions are asked, now it's up to life.

Giving the fish their food, I watched them for a few minutes, before groaning my way slowly upright. Ugh, I should not sit like that. My hip hurt, and my back ached from sitting on the ground. I sighed deeply. I would have to concede to my injuries, a small pondside chair was now a definite essential.

Limping my way to the house, I walked indoors, around several rooms, then back outside. I wandered around the garden, into Amber's empty studio, back to the fish pond, and then indoors again, where I sat in my large chair with a deep sigh. At least I had walked the aches away, but where was everybody? Another question!

Right on cue, Amber strolled in. Wearing a pale pink minidress, she looked stunning. Her widely spaced eyes swept the room in a glance, then landed on me. Her jaw set in its determined position, I knew that she was about to make a strong declaration. But no. Walking over to me, she hitched her dress one modicum higher, then sat on my lap, one long shapely leg on each side as she faced me.

"You're making a very suggestive statement to Sir Knight," I said, as I ran my hands along sensuous thighs.

"You're bored, aren't you?" she said.

I nodded. "Yeah, I guess I am. I don't know what to do. I've mulched all the garden, and repotted all my bonsai, pruned them, and done everything I can to them. I've done it all. Everything that needs doing, I've done." I ducked my head and kissed a very perky breast. "Mind you, I can think of a short-term solution."

"Adam, would you have sex just because you're bored?"

"It doesn't sound nice when you put it like that."

"How would you put it then?"

"I'd put it in gently, then I'd wriggle it," I chuckled.

Despite trying not to, she grinned. "Adam, you've got a one-track mind."

"Only when I'm bored," I protested.

"Right, so back to my first question. Do you want sex just because you're bored?"

"Ah, well, I can't answer that, because I think it was Amber the Oracle who just a little while ago told me that if I seek the answers to questions, I'm never going to find what I'm looking for. So if you want to know why I feel horny, you'll just have to seek within. Come to think of it, that's what I want too. Why don't we both go into the bedroom and seek the answer together, within."

Amber threw her head back, and laughed. "Oh, you witty one, you. But no. I won't submit to sex from boredom."

"You have my word that I won't be bored."

Chuckling, she kissed me on my forehead.

"Absolutely, not. No. No. No. Do you understand?"

"Er, you're undecided."

Amber laughed, and getting off my lap, she mussed my hair. "I'm sorry if I was sexually provocative. That wasn't fair. I watched you wandering around the house and garden, so I came to see if I could entice you to Maroochydore Plaza to do some shopping. I didn't finish, if you remember! We can have lunch out. How does that sound?"

"No other offers?"

She thought for a moment. "Yes. You can scowl at people as much as you like."

I smiled at her in delight. "Really. You're on!"

# Eighteen

Another month came and went, while I pursued my quest for physical rehabilitation at the fitness center. But I was growing ever more bored. I felt caged, and useless. I had now reached the stage where improvement was slow, not so easily seen and measured. The little pains, aches, and occasional throbs persisted, but I had no problem with that. I was bored. Plain and simply, bored.

Amber was very involved in her painting, encouraged by some good recent sales. She was building a definite reputation as a sensitive wildlife artist, and her work could now be found in many galleries around Queensland. As she became more involved and engrossed in her art, finding fulfillment, I was becoming ever more irked by the monotony of repetitious tedium. The fitter I grew, the more acute the symptoms of boredom.

Each day I made my inner journey, and gradual changes were taking place. The Disneylike character of nature along the riverbank had gone, replaced with a more realistic expression. The sphere remained, and I thoroughly enjoyed my time in there, as my healing continued. But I could not spend all day in inner spaces, and I was fed up with doing nothing. I knew that I had to get back to work. There was no other solution. I had been driving for quite a while now, and I could walk well, albeit with my usual limp. As far as I was concerned, I could see no reason not to get involved in my eco-farming consultancy. But, of course, I had yet to get agreement from my overprotective wife.

I broached the subject that evening. "Look, I don't intend to argue about this, darling, but I want to get back to work . . . now."

"I agree," she said quietly.

"It's no use you . . . ! You what?" I gasped, as I finally heard what she just said.

Michael J. Roads

"I said, I agree," she said demurely.

Still trying to adjust, I chuckled. "I thought you would disagree, then bawl me out," I said lamely.

She looked at me squarely. "To be honest, I don't fully approve, but I've been expecting this for the past month. I admit, I think you would be better occupied than wandering around bored all day, or reading with a long-suffering look of resignation stamped on your face. I've even spoken to Pete about it, and he agrees, with reservations."

"Oh, and what are they?"

"Well, your mother had the perfect solution."

I seemed to spend half my conversations perplexed these days. Mum . . . with a solution? "Amber, what are you talking about? What solution?"

"You can take Selph with you. Remember, he told Mum that he was your new assistant." Amber gave me a sly conspiratorial grin. "You might enjoy ordering him around."

A smile came from deep inside and grew all over my face. "You're a genius. You darling. What an ab-so-lutely brilliant idea."

"Well don't look like that," she murmured.

"Like what?"

"You've got a positively satanic grin on your face."

I continued smiling and nodding. "Just thinking about it is a tonic. Oh, what a splendid idea. Just this once, Selph might regret his words."

We had not seen Selph that day, and it was about eleven o'clock the following morning when he wandered in. I told him our plan with great glee, and of course, he spoiled it completely.

"Fantastic," he said enthusiastically. "I'd really enjoy that. Great idea. When do we start?"

"You're kidding me," I said, surprised.

His open, smiling face was total innocence. The sort of face he has when deep traps are looming close. I thought long and hard from every angle possible, but no way could I spot a trap.

"Why would I kid you, Adam? It's a great idea. Just give me the word, and I'm ready when you are."

Perplexed, I departed. I still had the feeling that Selph was setting me up, but how, I did not know. Could he genuinely want to learn from me? Or did he know already, and I would be the student, as usual? More questions! Leave them alone. Get on with life.

271

I had a large roll-top desk in a corner alcove of the dining room, complete with phone. It was my personal space. I went over to it, and for the first time in a long while, I sat at my desk. Before me was the phone pad, with all my clients' names and numbers. I opened it on S, for Steadman.

I dialed, and waited. Just as I was about to put it down, I heard Joyce. She sounded breathless.

"Hello. Joyce speaking."

"Hello Joyce Speaking, nice to hear your voice."

There was a long pause, then she chuckled. "Oh my goodness! Adam! Is that you?"

"Yeah, it's me. How are you, and the family?"

"Oh, we're all well. You just caught me on the run. Busy as always. It's lovely to hear you. How are you, and Amber?"

"Amber is wonderful, thanks. I'm recovering well, and I'm ready for work again. Joe told me he had the names and telephone numbers of a few farmers who just might be interested in a beat-up eco-farming consultant."

"Yes, he does, and I know he wants to see you himself just as soon as you're out and about. He was going to phone you, but I wouldn't let him. 'Don't you go bothering poor Adam 'til he's good and ready,' I told him. Gosh, it's so good to know that you're fit again."

"Let's not go overboard on how fit," I chuckled, "but I sure as hell am ready."

"I don't know where Joe's put the list of names, but I'll get him to phone you this evening. He'd like a chat."

"Okay, Joyce, thanks. I'll let you go now, I know you're always busy. Give my love to Mattie and the boys."

"Will do, Adam. We look forward to seeing you soon. Take good care of yourself. Bye."

"Good-bye, Joyce."

Although I still had nothing to do when I left my desk, it was no longer a problem. The resolution was at hand, and my future was looking bright again. The ongoing drought would be a problem, because it would hold physical work and land changes in abeyance until the rains came, but there was a lot I could do in the way of mentally preparing my new clients. They would need to adopt a whole new philosophy to their land, learning that nature is very forgiving, providing you explore her avenues of harmony and integration. Modern agribusiness is an imposition on the land, with an approach that is both aggressive and arrogant. When any farmer seeks only to exploit the land and its resources, trouble looms. The farm becomes a battlefield, with nature the enemy. And a vast, implacable enemy it makes.

Eco-farming requires that aggressive techniques give way to integration, and that the farmer becomes a student of nature. He or she learns to openly observe the land, and from a platform of humility, begins to use intelligence to forge a partnership with the land. The farmer learns to feel and think, instead of merely function. Some farmers are naturally good at this, and enjoy the innovative freedom that is invoked, but some unyielding types are threatened, needing the approval of the establishment. I seldom bothered with such as these. I enjoy the people who are open to change, expansion, and challenges. Flexibility and adaptability are the prime requirements of farming with nature. In no way do I deny my clients the best and latest in technology, only that it integrates rather than dominates; that it works *with* nature, rather than against. Eco-farming is cooperation with Nature, not exploitation. And the difference is immense.

Amber's call broke through my reverie. "Adaaam. Lunch is ready."

I found her out by the swimming pool, with lunch on a poolside table. "So how did it go?" she asked, as I sat down with a satisfied smirk.

I looked around. "Where's my assistant?"

"I have no idea. One moment he's here, then he's gone. A regular will-o'-the-wisp, our Selph."

"I had a chat with Joyce. They want to see me, and they have some new clients. But I'll speak to all my regulars first. They may keep me busy for a while, and I don't want to overdo things at the beginning. I intend to take it easy."

"Good heavens, sensible and cautious! What's happened?"

I looked at her seriously. "I know that I used to work myself into a lather before I got hurt, but that month with the cane bales and the wheelbarrow taught me a lot. I've learned to moderate my approach to work. And another thing, I've got a whole new appreciation of you, my darling. I used to work off my anger and frustration, but I don't have that any more. We have a relation-ship that I want to come home to, and I have a wife I love to be with."

"Don't stop. You're saying all the right things."

"Well, it's true. What you once said jokingly is more true than you realize. Some aspect of me did die at the time of the car crash, an aspect I no longer needed. I . . . ."

"I was serious, Adam, not joking," Amber cut in.

I shrugged. "So be it. Anyway, I've got a whole new approach to life now, and to people, but most particularly, to myself. I actually like me."

Amber jumped up and, plonking down onto my lap, proceeded to thoroughly kiss me. "You have no idea how happy it makes me just to hear you say that. The change is obvious to me, and everyone who knows you, but it's important that you, too, recognize it. I like you, too."

"Can anybody join the fan club?"

We laughed. "Hello Selph, just in time for lunch. What would you like?" Amber asked, sliding off my lap.

Selph held up an avocado and a plate. "I've got all the extras I need. There's plenty of salad here." He looked at me with a smile. "I like you, too."

I knew he meant it, and I nodded. "Thanks Selph. The feeling's mutual."

"Adam, how about a movie later this afternoon, and then dinner at Scoozie's? We could share a seafood pizza."

I licked my lips just thinking about it. With about eight movies on the go at the Maroochydore cinema, there was sure to be one that I would like. "How about you, Selph? Would you like to come with us?" I asked.

He surprised me by nodding. "Yes, I'd like that." He smiled at Amber. "Any film you particularly want to see?"

"Yes. I want to see *The Madness of King George.* I've read a review, and it sounds great. Besides, I like British movies. Is that okay with you two?"

Selph and I looked at each other, nodding inquiringly. "That's fine by us," I said. "Whatever you want, I want."

❖   ❖   ❖

Three hours later we entered the twilight world of the movies. Every now and then you see a peak performance by an actor, and in this film, Nigel Hawthorne reached that status. I take my movies in a fairly casual manner, but as we took our seats at Scoozie's that evening, I was enthusiastic.

Amber grinned at me. "Wasn't that better than moaning around the house about being bored, my darling?"

"You're right; it was a great movie." I glanced at the menu, then smiled at Amber. "So, how about we share a seafood pizza?"

She nodded. "Suits me."

"How about you, Selph? And the treat's on us."

Selph ordered their vegetarian lasagna, and twenty minutes later we were tucking into our food. Scoozie's makes their pizzas the good old-fashioned way, in front of a wood fire, imparting a delicious flavor.

"When is Kate due?" I asked Amber.

She looked at me reprovingly. "You don't know when your sister is expecting? Shame on you. The big event is in approximately six weeks."

"Really! So soon."

"It might be so soon for you, but she was telling me on the phone the other day that now she's so big, she swears time has slowed down. For her, the days drag."

❖  ❖  ❖

Days that drag had finished for me, and within a week Selph and I set off on the rounds of my eco-farming clients. It meant the occasional night away, but that was manageable, even though both Amber and I were reluctant to be parted.

I reveled in being active again, despite getting very tired. Resting when you want to be on the go chafes at you, but when you are physically exhausted, resting is pure luxury. I discovered that Amber was keeping tabs on my welfare with phone calls behind me as we visited my clients. But I did not mind. It was simply a reflection of her love and care. When I questioned her about it, she was unabashed.

"I just want to make sure you haven't thrown yourself and the car into any more creeks," she said.

"That's hardly likely with Selph in the car. He'd just float it up and away, rather than crash."

"True, or emerge unscathed, while you were smashed and mangled. Remember about creating your own reality?"

What could I say?

Our first call was to see Joe and Joyce, where we had arranged to spend the night with them. Their oldest boy, Tommy, was used to surrendering his bedroom to visitors. Having left home at sunrise, we had plenty of time for a catch-up chat before lunch. They were surprised to see Selph, but then they remembered meeting him at my homecoming, and learning that he was my new assistant.

Joe held out a large work-worn hand. "G'day, Ian. You're a lucky fella to get yourself a job with Adam. You listen and learn as much as you can, 'cos Adam's pretty smart at what he does. There ain't many around like him."

"I've learned that already, Joe. In fact, he's a lot more unique than he realizes."

Selph's eyes held mine while he spoke, and with an inner glow, I knew that he was not referring to my work as an eco-farming consultant.

For the next hour or so, I was besieged with questions about my health, and I answered them all as best I could.

"You look a lot better than I expected," Joyce said candidly. "You must have put a lot of work in to get yourself looking so fit."

Slipping off my T-shirt, I raised my arms dramatically.

"Do I still look a lot better?"

Joyce sucked her breath in sharply. "Christ!"

She and Joe stared at my scars in shock. I had the thin clean lines of the various operations, the large ugly scar on my chest, and other scarring over my ribs and shoulders. But thanks to Mac at the fitness center, I also had a very well developed and defined musculature.

"He's really put a lot of work in, both at the fitness center, and in his garden. Doctor Morrow is very pleased with his progress," Selph said into the silence.

Joe sat just shaking his head, speechless, but Joyce had one last comment. "My God, no wonder you nearly died. I'd no idea that you had so many injuries." Then, sensing that I had had enough, she switched her attention to Selph.

"Are you living with Amber and Adam?" she asked.

Selph fielded their questions easily, and any that would require outright lying he caused them to forget as soon as the question was asked. An enviable skill! And, of course, we both left them believing him to be Ian.

With all the chit-chat finished by the time we had eaten lunch, we were ready for the serious work to begin. I used Selph exactly as if he was an apprentice, delegating him the major share of the legwork.

Joe's cattle were looking pretty good, but it was the quality hay that accounted for it. When Dad had made ready for a long and serious drought, I had told Joe of his plans.

"If that's what your dad's doing, damned if I won't copy him. He may be an awkward old cuss, but he's smart," Joe had replied. And much to his present relief, he did. Like Dad, he had bought large quantities of hay while it was still easily affordable. Hay prices were now horrendous.

We drove as much as possible over Joe's farm, but there was also a lot of walking to do. I sent Selph out to collect a number of soil samples, because

I wanted to find out if the drought had any effect on the pH. According to the books, it should not, but books were all too often based in theory. The drought had a devastating effect on the availability of nitrogen, potassium, and most of the other major nutrients, so that in itself could trigger yet other changes.

Basically, there was little we could do about anything until it rained, and in early summer, the wet season was not yet due—if we had one! Joe's farm looked sad and battered, but most of the neighboring farms were either dying, or dead. We all knew that rain would revive and repair every farm, but the ability to extend the health and growth of the pasture well into a drought had become a critical feature in these times of walking a financial tightrope. Some of Joe's neighbors were sitting up and taking notice. Only some. There were others who refused to see the obvious differences, being too threatened by the prospect of change to consider, or accept that their time-honored techniques were no longer practical. They still looked at the thousands of young trees that Joe and Joyce had planted with cynicism and derision, unable to comprehend that the shade and nitrogen-fixing ability of these specially chosen acacias were major factors in the overall health of the soil, and the stock.

That evening, Selph met Mattie, Tommy, Jimmy, and young Liam. Mattie fell for him instantly, and I could see the heartache that awaited her. To his credit, Selph did everything he could to disenchant her, but she undoubtedly sensed that there was a hidden depth and capacity in him.

As we lay in our single beds that night, I waited for him to disappear. But he did not.

"It's time to fly. Good-bye," I chuckled.

"I'm staying with you."

"Oh, why?" I asked idly.

He hesitated. "I had to promise Amber."

"Had to?"

"Yes."

We lay there, quietly laughing.

"Mattie's a very evolved soul," he said.

"Yeah, and she's going to be a heartbroken one."

"Don't be so sure."

"Oh. How do you mean?"

"Never you mind, that's my business."

I was tired. "True enough. Good night."

Next morning, we were up and away after an early breakfast, but I noticed that Selph spent quite a while in conversation with Mattie before we left. She was smiling happily when we departed, and waving with the others.

"What did you tell her?"

"That it's still none of your business."

"As long as she's okay. I really like Mattie. She's a remarkably competent and capable girl, besides being so nice. So please, tell me or I'll pester you."

He sighed. "Okay. You do hold her best interests at heart, so I'll submit. I told her that I don't live around here, and that it's unlikely she will see me again. Then I told her that I'm a skilled palmist, and I offered to read her palm. While you where busy eating, I was telling her a touch of her future."

"I didn't know that you're a palmist."

"I'm not, but I'm good at futures." He grinned at me.

"So what did you tell her?"

"The truth. That in three years time she will meet a man ten years older than her, and they will fall in love and marry. And, of course, be very happy together."

"And that's all true?"

"I wouldn't tell her that if it wasn't her probability."

"Did she believe you?"

"Yes, she believed me because she wanted to."

"By believing you, will she create that reality?"

"What do you think?"

I thought about it carefully. "I think it doesn't matter. If she has a belief in happiness, she'll create it; whereas if she believes in a dismal future, you couldn't prevent it. And knowing Mattie, she'll have a great future."

Although I had a very good relationship with all my clients, Joe and Joyce were special to me. They had given me that first, badly needed break. Our next stop was with Billy Teams, a small, dark-haired, nuggety man in his fifties, as brown as weathered hide, and totally uneducated. I had taught him the principles of eco-farming, and he understood and practiced them, but trying to teach him about the pH of the soil, and soil fertility, was a lost cause. He survived on a feeling for the land, and a natural shrewdness. And he was very shrewd. Billy had an uncanny instinct for doing the correct thing at the right time. Billy decided to use me as a consultant because, in his words, "When there's so many farmers saying you've got to be wrong, then by the law of averages, you must be right!"

Whatever the majority did, Billy did the opposite. And, if his farm and family were anything to go by, he lived very well that way. Billy and I got along famously.

His farm was more hilly than most in the area, and using casual labor, he had planted the gullies with thousands of nitrogen-fixing trees. As we walked his land, the hilltops were dry and decimated, but deep in those gullies, the last of the moisture kept the trees growing and thriving. This was now the mainstay of his depleted herd. Rather than delimb, or cut the trees as fodder, he also fed hay in the precious shade. The gullies were many, and practically all of them were accessible for him.

"The locals reckoned I were bloody mad ter buy this 'illy place, the missus did too. I knew they'd 'ave ter be wrong." He chuckled. "Now they've changed their minds. The 'ills 'ave got their faults, mind, but when it all averages out, I reckon I'm the winner by a good length."

I glanced at Selph, grinning. "Ain't eco-farming folks just grand? I love 'em."

We had a cold lunch with Billy, and Ivy, his wife. She was a tall, slim woman, quite an intellectual, with a passion for reading. Ivy had read the books I recommended on eco-farming, and was soon convinced that Billy's shrewdness was onto another winner. She was totally supportive.

Once again, I was intensively questioned about my car smash, and Selph too had to undergo an interrogation. With his "smudging" ability, he romped home. We left with their well wishes echoing in our ears.

"Nice people," Selph said, as we drove along, "but why do they all want to know every detail of your life?"

"Country people are like that. Mostly they all know each other for a long way around them. It makes sense. If there's an emergency, they have to rely on each other. Also, what else is there for them but each other, and the land? The space out here is wide and open. It's just beautiful."

Selph looked at the stark, dried, barren land as we drove along. "How can you call this beautiful? Stark, or dramatic, or even cruel. But beautiful?"

"Yes. This is beauty in recession. Normally this is an ocean of green hills and living splendor, the waves formed by wind as it caresses the knee-high grass. By comparison, the Outback is stark, and definitely cruel by human standards, but people who live there grow to love and accept it."

We passed a couple of dead cattle near the roadside, their hides stretched tight over bare bones. And then, in a blaze of flashing color, a flock of pink-and-gray galahs swept across the road, the whole flock swinging around on outstretched wings as one, to settle on the verge ahead of us. Stopping the car, we sat and watched them as they pulled the seed from the weeds and grasses that always seem to follow the outback roads.

"Beauty is mixed and mingled with the stark and ugly in Australia. If you avoid one, you miss the other."

Selph nodded. "I see what you mean. That's also a good metaphor for life."

Because it was on my route home, I decided to call on one of the prospective clients that Joe had told me about. All I knew about him was his name, Ted. We found his farm entrance with no trouble, but as we drove into the decrepit, dirty farmyard, my heart sank.

"This won't work out. I can tell you that now."

We only had a couple of hours at the most, because I firmly intended to be home that night, but as I looked at the trio of dogs, barking and snarling at us, I knew that this would be a quick one.

Ted came ambling from the dark interior of a shed, with a grumble on his lips. "Whatever yer selling, I don't want."

"You left word that you wanted to see me. My name's Adam Baker. I'm the eco-farming consultant that Joe Steadman told you about."

Ted had the look of a human ferret—lean and mean—and he looked unwell. "Ah, yus, well I've had second thoughts about that."

"Good," I said briskly. "Come on, Ian, let's go."

As Ted spoke, his dogs were barking deafeningly around us. "Hang on a minute. Ain't you going to tell me what it is you do? I jist might change me mind."

"You'll have to speak up. I can hardly hear you over the dogs. Can't you quiet them?" I said.

"Nope. That's what they're for."

Raising one hand, thumb and forefinger making a circle, Selph said forcibly, "Sit. Quiet."

The dogs sat so abruptly they nearly collapsed, and so compelling was the command that my knees almost buckled. Ted staggered, nearly falling, then, regaining his balance, he swore. Looking from his mute, immobilized dogs to Selph, he was angry, and baffled.

"Bugger it! What the bloody hell is going on?"

Selph smiled. "What nice obedient dogs you have."

Ted stared at the bewildered, silent, dogs, each sitting as still as death, their eyes rolling wildly. Then he looked at me.

"Well you better bloody well tell me what it is you do."

I knew that he would never be a client of mine, so I decided to simply scare him off. "The first thing I would do is educate you about the soil, its microorganic life, its pH, and its cation exchange capacity, et cetera. It's really essential to understand the basis of soil fertility and the development of humus."

His eyes regarded me nastily, but before he could speak a woman came out of the nearby farm house. Like Ted, she looked sick and pale, her walk a bit shaky.

"Are you all right?" I asked, concerned.

She grinned feebly. "It's nuffin that leaving this God-forsaken land wouldn't fix. I'm wore out."

She and Ted eyed each other with scarcely concealed animosity. Then their eyes settled firmly on me.

"This here's the man what Joe told us about."

Her eyes in the thin, beaten face held a fading interest as she looked at me. "It wouldn't matter what you told us, luv," she said, "'cos Ted ain't got enough interest to make it happen. All he wants to do is play with engines in that bloody shed all day. He couldn't farm a bloody garden." She stared at the dogs. "What's wrong with them?"

"Maybe you should quit farming and get into mechanics," I said to Ted. "At least you'd be doing what you enjoy."

"When I need your bloody advice, I'll ask for it," he replied nastily.

I grinned at Selph. "You see, my instincts were right."

Walking over to the car, we got in.

"Er, what about the dogs?" I asked Selph.

He chuckled, opened his door, and, leaning out, clicked his thumb and forefinger with a loud smacking sound.

On the instant, the dogs leapt to their feet and chased barking and snarling after the car as we departed in a cloud of swirling dust.

"You sure have some neat tricks up your sleeve," I said admiringly. "You damn nearly had me sit down out there. Just as a matter of interest, how long would the dogs have stayed like that?"

Selph laughed. "I noticed. The dogs wouldn't have moved until either hunger or sleep forced them to break the command. I did think of leaving them, to teach Ted a lesson, but I guess he would only have kicked them out of it. Man, what a sick couple."

I nodded. "I've been into eco-farming for long enough to make some interesting observations. Every time I find a new client with sick land, the farmer and his family will be always be suffering from poor health. Every time. Not only that, but I've had clients go from having sick land and a sick family, to healthy soil and a healthy family. I explain to them that the farmer and the land is one unit, connected in consciousness, but while some understand and accept it, others think it doesn't make sense, or they outright reject it. I only tell them once. The rest is up to them. Another observation: in well over half my clients, it's the wife I talk to first, because invariably, it's the women who quickly understand. They are not as pragmatic as men, and far more in touch with their intuition. Once the farmer's wife is convinced, she'll mostly get her husband to give it a try."

"Do most of the men follow a similar pattern?"

"No, not by any means. You would think that a man who is a stranger to his own feelings would also be divorced from any feeling for the soil, but Ken James is just such a man, and he is an excellent custodian of the land. He has a highly developed feeling for the soil, but clearly doesn't like himself. It's odd. He's a really nice guy."

Selph chuckled. "I hear you describing yourself of about six months ago. Don't you?"

I sighed. "Yes, now that you mention it. I hadn't thought about that. Too close, I suppose."

Half an hour later, a splash of white caught my eye among some nearby gum trees, and I pulled over and stopped.

"I don't know how much you know about our fair land, but let's get out for a few moments and I'll show you something."

We had taken no more than a few paces, when a small flock of maybe fifty sulfur-crested cockatoos flapped lazily out of the trees. As they flew above us, the sun caught and seemed to magnify their snowy white plumage, so that for a brief moment they appeared as beautiful angels, then the illusion was shattered by a harsh, grating, strident cry.

"This is Oz," I said, "a land of contrast if ever there was one. Some of the greatest beauty is found in the harshest places, yet even the beauty is at odds with itself."

A couple of the cockatoos hung upside down from a branch close by, unafraid. The brilliant sulfur-yellow crests stood up on the crown of their heads, while their unblinking black eyes regarded us with casual interest. We watched them for a while, then I led Selph over to a large dry flat piece of tree bark.

"Watch."

I flipped the bark to one side, and a bearded dragon came out at a run. It stopped, unsure of where its enemy was located. Bending down, I swiftly picked it up, and it gaped at me, its jaws wide, its blue-gray beard flared out. I held it out to Selph. "You see, beautiful and bizarre."

Continuing our journey home, we were quiet for a long time. I glanced at Selph, noticing his utter stillness. It was not so much a physical thing, as an inner stillness.

"Do you think about anything at times like this, when we have three hours driving ahead of us?" I asked him.

My question seemed to bring him back, almost as though he had been someplace else.

"Not really, no. I change my focus away from a physical reality, to a nonphysical one. A bit like your altered-state journeying, only more complete."

"But your body's here. Is it aware?"

"Yes, to a degree. You could call it a filtered awareness. As you've learned when you experienced Jacob, experience is not limited to where your body resides. That's a limit that has been installed by consensus reality."

"So in moments like this, are you as fully away as I was with Jacob's experience?"

He nodded. "Yes, and even more so."

I was impressed, but he had had a lot of practice, and after all, he was my teacher.

I let him go back to wherever he went, while I continued on toward the coast. Deliberately, I let my thinking slow down, by focusing on where I was and what I was doing. It became quickly apparent that while I did this, my thoughts naturally quieted, allowing an inner silence to grow.

As I drove along, I watched the molten sun gradually sink into a golden earth, to be swallowed by the growing mystery of the night. My headlights picked out the red-eyed reflection of kangaroos along the roadside, and I drove cautiously, knowing that their light-dazzled blindness made them vulnerable to traffic at night. Unlike many inland travelers, I did not have hefty roo bars fitted to the car, preferring the cautious approach, or, to pull in at a motel and spend the evening and night in relaxed comfort. Too many vehicles with fitted roo bars were death on wheels to the unfortunate wildlife.

We arrived home about an hour earlier than I expected, so Amber was delighted. After a long and passionate kiss, she told us that a cold dinner awaited, but my first priority was a hot shower to remove the kinks and aches of driving. She and Selph were busy chattering as I entered the bathroom, and I guessed that Selph was about to be debriefed!

Amber and I had only been apart for two days and a night, but there seemed to be so much to talk about. If there is one vital link in a relationship, it must be open and clear communication. We thrived on it. I told her all about the Steadman family, and Mattie falling for Selph, and how the farm looked, et cetera. Then it was on to Billy and Ivy, and finally, an exaggerated account of Ted and his dogs, and the "sit" command that nearly felled him. Amber laughed until her sides ached.

Still chuckling, Amber switched her attention to Selph.

"How did you go as Adam's assistant? Was he bossy?"

"To be honest, I thoroughly enjoyed myself. Being with Adam when he is in engrossed with the land is like being with a different man. He really is good at what he does. With my 'inner' sight, I saw his consciousness connect with the spirit of the land. He has a gift."

He turned to me. "We haven't talked about it, but you are so attuned to the land that you 'inner' hear it, don't you? You feel an inner knowing."

I nodded. "Yes. As I walk over the land, I cease thinking, cease questioning, and an inner knowing fills me. It's as though the spirit of the land is speaking with a clear and silent voice, inaudible to the ear, but audible to the mind. It isn't even difficult. I suspect it's a latent ability within everyone, waiting for us to revive it."

"How do you know that it isn't simply your mind-talk?" Amber asked me. "The mind is certainly devious enough."

I thought about it, then shook my head. "I can't answer that. When it's happening, I 'know.' That says it. I know that I know! It's inexplicable."

Selph caught my eyes. "Has it occurred to you that if you could live without your constant thought chatter, without the constant questions, that this inner 'knowing' might expand, filling your whole day?"

I smiled wryly. "Of course, it's only logical, but doing it is something else altogether. The land is filled with silence, inviting me to become quiet, connecting, then softly whispers, whereas life is brash and noisy, shouting at me." I shrugged. "And unfortunately, I shout back. However, all things considered, I'm doing okay. The shouting is getting less, the inner silence growing. I'm getting there."

Amber leaned over and gently kissed me. "I agree. You most certainly are. Now for something completely different; I've invited Doctor Pete and Doctor Jane for dinner this Saturday, and neither of them knows about the other."

"Talk about devious! Can they make it?"

She gave me a cat smile. "Yes, they'll both be here at six o'clock. They each know that there will be one other guest, but neither knows who that person is."

Selph grinned at us. "Do I smell matchmaking?"

"If I have anything to do with it, you do," Amber said, nodding. "We intend to get two lovely, but lonely, people to notice each other if it's the last thing we do."

Selph smiled. "So this is a joint effort?"

I nodded. "Believe it or not, but it was my idea. I believe in happiness."

"You assume that they can only be happy together?"

"No. But neither do I assume that they can't. All we will do is bring them together, then it's up to them. Why?"

"It's okay, you explained it well. I just didn't want you to think that a person's happiness is up to someone else. Happiness comes from within, an investment in yourself."

"So, Adam Baker, it's Friday tomorrow. You and I will be going shopping to get all the goodies. How about you, Selph? May we be honored with your company for dinner?"

He nodded. "I'd like that, but on one condition. Let me also participate in the pleasure of cooking."

"You're in," I said promptly. I cook much more out of necessity than any real pleasure, and although I'm good at it, Selph is far and away better. He enjoys working with food; I enjoy working with the land.

My driving had made me more tired than I realized, so we went to bed early. As Amber snuggled up close to me, her kissing became more passionate, but despite my interest, each blink became longer, while my eyelids grew heavier, and I drifted away into a deep sleep.

Next day, true to her word, after breakfast she and I went down to Nambour for a stint of serious food shopping. I don't like serious shopping. Ordinary shopping is fun, but serious shopping is . . . too serious!

Soon enough, she was satisfied with our choices, and we relaxed in Holly's Coffee House. We both had an iced coffee, Oz-style, thick, sweet, and creamy.

Amber had been going through the packet of photographs she had collected from the developers. "Do you remember the photos you took of Selph? Take a look."

Looking at the photos, I gasped. Not a single photo of Selph had come out. A photo of Amber and him showed Amber alone. Even the three photos I had taken of him without his knowing were empty of his presence.

Shrugging, I grinned. "Ah well, no shadow, no photo. It's really most peculiar, but, that's Selph!"

"But how do you explain it?" Amber asked.

I gave her a fond smile. "Very simple my love, you don't! You just accept it."

I gazed up at the sky as we slurped our way though the delicious cold drink. Hardly a cloud marred the clear, intense blue sky. I sighed. When, oh when, would it rain again? Each day the unrelenting sunshine dried the land ever more, while the hopes and dreams of many outback families withered and died. Most people accepted the cyclical nature of our weather, but severe droughts like this bludgeoned the spirits of the endlessly toiling country folk.

"Oh! Adam. Did I tell you that you and I are due to attend prenatal clinic in about an hour?" Amber asked, with a look of surprise. "I think I clean forgot to tell you."

I frowned. "You did forget. Prenatal! What's that got to do with me? I don't give birth."

"Would you rather I go through it alone?" Amber's voice was hurt, subdued.

"No, of course not. It's a bit of a shock, that's all. If you told me I had a dentist appointment in an hour, you'd get the same sort of reaction." I felt contrite.

"So smile, look happy. We have a lot to learn about birthing, and I want it to be as natural as possible."

"I've seen hundreds of calves born. It's no big deal."

"Thank you Adam, but I'm not a cow!"

"I didn't mean that," I said hastily. "I meant that giving birth is natural, and should be trouble-free." I thought about it for a few moments, then shrugged. "On the other hand, I have to admit to helping many a calf into this world. And I've even had to remove the odd placenta a couple of days later with some cows. Talk about stink."

"Adam, I would rather you drop all comparison between me giving birth and a cow doing the same. We ladies certainly have our birthing problems, but they are not bovine!"

"Right, point taken. So what am I expected to do?"

"Don't worry, you'll soon find out."

She was right. An hour later we were sitting in a small room with inadequate air conditioning, along with about ten other women, all puffing to the rhythm that the instructor set. As one of only two men, I felt a bit awkward.

We had not been puffing for many moments when Sue Keen, the instructor, stopped us. She looked at me. "Mr. Baker. Instead of hovering near your wife as she pants in simulated birth, do you think you could kneel, or sit with her? You look rather like a floating spare part making only brief orbital contact."

Everyone laughed at her wit, while I scowled.

"Miss Keen," I replied, "the simple fact is I am unable to sit or kneel at my wife's head. I do, in fact, have a spare part I call a tin hip, and when I kneel, or sit on the floor, it feels as though it's losing contact altogether. So we have a choice; either I hover, or you supply me with sufficient cushions to make sitting a viable proposition."

Miss Keen scowled back. "Oh come now, I'm sure you're exaggerating the situation."

Sitting up, Amber now joined the scowl club on a level, eye-to-eye gaze with the instructor. "Miss Keen. My husband recently suffered five major, and three minor, fractures to both of his legs. He does have an artificial hip, and if he says he cannot sit or kneel, it's because he can't. I don't care whether he hovers or floats, so long as he is here with me. That's what matters. I'm the one who has the baby, not him. I want him here any way I can have him. Do we understand each other?"

The challenge was made, the gauntlet thrown, and wisely, Miss Keen decided that enough was enough.

I looked at Amber, and smiled in appreciation. "Thanks for the role reversal, my darling."

All the pregnant girls heard, and they laughed, breaking the tension. Miss Keen gathered up her tattered authority.

"Right, ladies, breathe now, one, in . . . two, out . . ."

The hour passed smoothly, and Sue Keen imparted her knowledge about childbirth and its preparation with clever articulation and a keen wit. I enjoyed her style, and at the end of it all, I told her so.

Probably only in her mid-twenties, Sue was slim and tiny, with short, bobbed dark hair, and pretty features.

"Thanks," she grinned. "I'm sorry I came on strong. I'm new at this, and because I'm so small and youthful, I was advised to take firm control of the classes. I'll learn. I hope, I'll see you both in a couple of weeks."

Amber smiled, and gave her a quick hug. "You will."

"Do you have any more surprise appointments for me?" I asked, as we drove home. "And thanks for that very spirited defense. I wasn't bothered by her, but

I really appreciate your support. You were a bit like a cow defending her bawling calf, when I used to ear-clip them."

Amber groaned. "Oh no! Not the cows and calves again! If you make one more mention of cows in relation to me, it'll be me that attacks you. And you will be bawling."

"Sitting on the horns of dilemma, I get your point," I laughed. "Don't bully me, 'cos I am truly cowed."

Amber looked at me, frowned, and then grinned. "You enjoy playing with words, don't you?"

I shrugged. "I'd rather play with you."

"Oh yes. Who fell asleep last night?"

"Not fair. I was unduly tired from driving. Just you try me tonight, oh temptress."

Happily, she did!

# Nineteen

Amber and Selph seemed to be busy all day, and whenever I dropped in to the kitchen for a friendly chat, or a mug of coffee, I was either hustled out fast, or left to my own devices. Amber is not really a party animal, but when she puts on one of her small intimate dinners, she takes it very seriously.

For me, it was a lazy day. I had more aches and twinges than I liked to admit, and my tin hip held a continuous dull throbbing that seemed to connect with my lower back ache. I spent time with the goldfish pond, swam, lazed, read, visited the Sphere of Tranquillity, wandered around the garden, gazed at my bonsai, and even dozed. However, despite having little to do, the day passed quickly, and it was early evening when Amber called to me in the swimming pool.

"Come on, Adam. Time to get dressed. I want to see you looking smart, this evening."

"Oh, don't I always?"

"No. You dress so casually that you totter on the very edge of being a sloppy dresser."

"Well, thanks a lot. I call it comfort dressing. And what about Selph? Is a bright orange T-shirt and baggy green shorts dressy enough?"

"Don't be silly, Adam. Selph looks wonderful."

I could not believe we were having this conversation until, on climbing out of the pool, I caught sight of Selph.

Goggling at him in astonishment, I gasped. Looking quite slim and suave, he was wearing a very dressy pair of white cotton lightweight pants, a pale blue silk shirt of impeccable flair and style, and woven leather sandals. With his innocent, cherubic smile firmly in place, he epitomized charm and casual elegance for a warm, subtropical evening.

He grinned at me. "Your jaw's hanging open."

Drying myself on a beach towel, I scowled at him. "Very clever. I take it that you're wearing your usual gear, and this is all an illusion?"

"Actually, no, although I could do that. No, Adam, what you see, I really am wearing."

"But . . . but I don't have any clothes like that. Where did you get them?"

It was his turn to look incredulous. "Are you kidding? You seriously think that conjuring up suitable clothing is a problem. For me!"

I shrugged. "Yeah, you're right. Silly me. For a moment there I was treating you as though you're normal." I grinned cheekily. "How about a similar outfit for me?"

His smile was all innocence. "They're on your bed."

I laughed. "Really?"

"Yes, really," he nodded. "A gift from me."

Hastening into our bedroom, I found a delightfully naked and dripping Amber emerging from the shower.

"Oh, what provocation," I murmured. "Can we?"

Wrapping a huge towel all about her, she covered all the parts that were arousing Sir Knight.

"No, Adam. Definitely not."

"You're wavering," I joked hopefully.

She shook her head vigorously, her wet auburn hair throwing droplets of water across the room. "Adam, get dressed," she said severely. "Our magical friend has very kindly conjured up a set of clothing for each of us. He insisted on giving us both a gift."

"He told me." Turning to the clothing waiting for me, I picked up a pair of lightweight pants similar to Selph's, and a silk shirt of a design and style quite new to me. I stared at it, trying to pin down the color, then, with a sudden insight, I picked up the gossamer dress lying close by. They matched! My shirt and Amber's dress were a similar swirling, elusive, sunset coloring, even though the weight of the material differed slightly.

"Wow! Is this silk, or beyond silk?"

Amber was now in her underwear and, if it were possible, looking even more provocative and desirable. "Beyond silk is a rather good description. Selph told me that this clothing comes from his frame of reality. He said that he kept it deliberately conservative so as not to arouse too much comment or attention."

Putting on the long pants, I had the feeling that I was wearing just my underwear. Lightweight did not get close! The shirt was incredible. Looking in the mirror, the shirt appeared as a fairly regular silk shirt, but with this clothing, it felt as though I had nothing on. Very sensual; it took a bit of getting used to.

I needed to look in the mirror for a while to convince myself that I was wearing clothes. The sandals that accompanied the outfit were equally odd, inasmuch as I felt as though I were barefooted while wearing them, yet with the well-shod comfort of the best fitting shoes possible.

"Incredible. What amazing material."

"What are you muttering about?" Amber asked.

"You'll see, my darling. You'll see."

Having finished with putting on whatever it is that ladies put on near-naked bodies, and smelling as tantalizing as she looked, Amber came over to the bed and, picking up the dress, wriggled into it.

I gasped. Reaching almost to the floor, her dress was the moving reflection of a summer sunset. High around her throat, and with long flared sleeves, it fitted her as though created on her slim body. Accentuating and highlighting her bouncing auburn hair, she looked stunning.

She too, stared in the mirror, and I could see the awe in her eyes. "My God! I feel naked, yet I look clothed."

"Join the club," I grinned.

She swept and swirled around the room, a beautiful rush of rippling sunset, murmuring her amazement. Compared to her dress, my shirt was subdued, yet it was the perfect foil.

There was a soft tapping on the door.

"Come in, Selph," I called out.

For once, he looked a fraction anxious. "Do you like the clothes? I selected them very carefully."

Amber swirled up to him, and hugging him, she kissed him on both cheeks. "Selph, this is the most incredible dress ever made. It's fabulous. I just adore it." She chuckled. "After a gift like this, I'm not sure that I'll ever be able to smack you again, however provoked."

"Promises, promises," Selph smiled, "all I ever get is promises. I'm glad you like it. I wondered if it was a bit too much for you, or this century. By our standards it's quite modest and, maybe just a touch understated."

"But Selph, it's seamless. How is it made?" Amber said.

Selph grinned. "It's quite simple really. You stand in front of a certain machine, visualize the person, and the image is combined with the material to become a perfect fit. It all takes about three or four minutes, your time."

"Well, I did ask," she said wryly.

Selph left us, returning to his own room, and Amber picked up her sandals. They were half-high sunset, and very elegant. Slipping them on, she whirled around the room once more. "I hope we won't be overdressed," she said.

"No, we'll be okay. Stunningly dressed, but not over-the-top. So, am I smart enough now?"

"You look very handsome, my darling."

She came over to me, and kissed me, her lips very close to my ear. "Is it just me, or are these clothes a turn-on?"

I had already experienced what she was feeling, and had figured out why. "It's the clothes. They convey an energy of nudity and sensuality. But, thank goodness, I feel certain that it's only to the people wearing them. Quite honestly, I want to throw you on the bed, right now. I hope I can last out the evening."

"I feel the same way," she confessed. "Can you imagine this clothing as commonplace in our world? It would lead to constant sexual harassment, seduction, and rape. As stupid as it seems, we're not ready for clothing of this material and energy yet." She frowned prettily. "Do you think Selph knows about this?"

Suddenly, it was very clear. "Yes, he knows. In another, very subtle way, he's testing me. He deliberately left us alone, just now. Do I give way to my base sexuality, and we have a quickie on the bed, or do I transmute it for this evening into a higher purpose. He's not implying that sex is wrong, but I bet you he's testing my timing and inner strength." I chuckled. "He's crafty. Inadvertently, you're getting tested also."

"I agree with everything you've said. I told you he's a scallywag! So, my lover, can you resist me?"

"No. But I do like to think that I'm in control of my sexuality, rather than it controlling me. Of course, that's it—control! He often says that freedom is effortless inner control. Well, I'm going to win this one."

"Effortlessly?" She smiled mockingly.

"Actually, yes. This isn't denial, it's about timing. And the right timing of anything simply makes it better."

She came into my arms and gently nipped the lobe of my ear. "And Sir Knight?" she murmured huskily, her fingers moving over his resting place.

Taking a deep breath, I stepped back and looked her in the eyes. "Like I said, I'm in control, not Sir Knight." I glanced at the bedside clock. "It's quarter to six. We better get out of here."

Amber grinned at me. "Just testing, and I'm impressed. Okay, darling, let's go."

Slipping her arm through mine, we sauntered from the bedroom and out into the warm evening air of the garden. A mischievous-looking Selph had a mild, ice-cold punch waiting for us.

Amber looked at him reprovingly. "You really are a scallywag, you know, but a very loved and special one."

He knew that we knew, and simply smiled. "Thank you, Amber. Mastery must come from all levels, and seldom the obvious." He looked at me. "It's never about rights or wrongs; they are illusions. It's about focus and timing, and knowing that you are both, constantly."

I nodded, "Yeah, I . . ." Hearing the sound of Pete's large car as it pulled up, tires crunching on the gravel, I bit off my words, and we hurried out to meet him.

"Hi, Adam. Oh, wow! Hellloo, Amber. My God, pregnancy must suit you. You look positively ravishing."

I smiled to myself. He had the correct description, no doubt about that; ravishing said it nicely. I watched as he gave her a very gentle bear hug, and a large smacking kiss.

"No chance that you've had enough of old grumpy yet, I suppose," he said in mock longing.

"No chance at all. Adam's my perfect match," a flushed Amber replied.

At that very moment another car came down the drive, and our attention was suddenly on the bright red Toyota coupe that pulled up close by. Amber was there in seconds.

"Jane, how wonderful to see you." She gave her close friend an affectionate hug, then spinning around, she called out. "Pete, come over here and meet our other guest."

Jane looked almost as good as Amber. Her long, black hair was coiled high on her head, making her look even taller than her already considerable height, while her sheath-tight, dark-blue dress, offset with white pearls, added even more to that impression. For the first time I realized that Jane was a strikingly attractive woman. I could see by the way Pete automatically pulled back his shoulders, his eyes keen and interested, that at least in one way, the chemistry was right!

He walked over in a deliberately casual way, as Amber made the introductions. "Jane, I would like you to meet our very dear friend, Doctor Peter

Morrow, the radical and brilliant man who put Adam back together again. And Pete, this beautiful lady is both my dearest friend and my gynecologist, Doctor Jane Sedgewick."

She stood back as they both stepped closer, solemnly shaking hands, while each surreptitiously appraised the other. On a sudden impulse, Pete dropped the hand he was shaking, and embraced Jane. "Any dear friend of Amber's is already overqualified to be my close friend also," he said gallantly.

"Why thank you," Jane murmured blushing. "Given a few more moments I might well come to the same conclusion." She gazed up at the huge Pete to meet his eyes, and I could see that his stature was immediately in his favor.

I felt an inward satisfaction. The chemistry was right on both sides. Great! The rest was up to them.

Jane had met Selph several times, and although puzzled by the enigma he posed, she obviously liked him. She had asked us often how a teenager could be so self-assured and worldly wise, but we always fobbed her off with, "Oh, that's just the way he is."

On cue, as usual, Selph appeared with a tray of cold drinks, and taking one, we all followed him to the casual and comfortable seats at poolside.

"Amber, darling, where in the name of all that's wonderful did you get such an incredible dress? It is just superb. Is it made of silk?" Jane asked.

Caught completely off guard, Amber looked helplessly at first me, and then Selph.

"It's something my mother came up with," Selph said with easy nonchalance. "She was a costumier, specializing in the unusual and the exotic. The fabric is a very rare type of silk. She's retired now, so this was a one-off," he smiled.

Neat, I thought admiringly. Explained and closed, all without the need of smudging.

But I had reckoned without Pete!

"Just where does your family live?" he asked.

"Oh, over the seas and far away," Selph said vaguely, and I felt the subtle "smudge, smudge" as two people either promptly forgot the question or heard it as fully answered.

Amber had also felt it, and she glanced at me with a conspiratorial grin. "Clever, huh," she whispered.

Nibbling on plates loaded with tasty appetizers, both of our guests seemed determined to learn as much about Selph as was possible. That proved to be very little! Three times in the next hour I felt Selph smudge out their deliberate attempts to learn more about him, and not once did either of them realize that it happened. Both Amber and I had to follow such a conversation carefully, for we had no idea what happened in their minds when the smudging took place. Finally, they gave up on the subject, mutually focusing their attention and interest on each other.

Before long they were deeply engrossed in each other's company, laughing and talking as an easy exchange of personal histories and stories flowed between them, while Amber and I gradually eased out of the chatter. Catching her eye, I indicated a retreat to the kitchen, where Selph was already busy with last-moment preparations.

"Excuse us, back in a minute," Amber said smiling, as, holding hands, we left them to their conversation.

"By golly, I think they really like each other," Amber said happily as we strolled into the kitchen, "but didn't Pete try hard in his attempt to interrogate Selph."

"Fat lot of good it did him," I laughed.

"When you two have finished gloating over your matchmaking abilities and my smudging, you may like to check that the table is set to your satisfaction," Selph said dryly.

Still holding hands, we went into the dining room. It was now about seven-thirty in the evening, and already our subtropical light was fading fast. While Amber checked that everything was to her liking, I lit the candles. Finally, looking pleased, she gave me the nod.

"Okay, gentle folks," I said, strolling out to Pete and Jane, "it's time to dine and wine."

Needing no encouragement, Pete was up in a heaving rush, beating me across to Jane, where he offered her his arm.

"Allow me to escort you, madam," he said.

They followed me to the dining room, where Amber seated everyone. Naturally, Pete and Jane sat on opposites sides of the table facing each other, and Amber and I likewise, while Selph insisted on sitting at the table end where he could easily slip away into the kitchen. The whole focus of the simple, but well-prepared, three-course meal was seafood, with white and/or pink wine to accompany it.

By the time we were seated, and drinks poured, Selph came in bearing a serving dish filled with piping hot fish cocktail pieces, all garnished with parsley, lemon wedges, and small bowls of tartar sauce. Pete's face took on a beatific look of deep appreciation as he gazed from the food to Selph.

"Don't tell me. Wonder boy strikes again?"

"Yeah," I grinned. "He has to earn his keep."

Several fish pieces made a swift visit and exit from Pete's plate, and there was silence while we each munched and sipped at our own particular speed.

"Delicious, Amber," Jane sighed. "Am I to understand that Selph cooked this?"

Amber nodded. "The hors d'oeuvres are all his, while the main course is my effort."

"And Adam's?" Pete rumbled, laughing.

She met his gaze levelly and seriously. "Adam is a far more than adequate cook, but it's not his joy, as it is for Selph, and me. Just take a walk around the garden, feeling its incredible energy. This is the result of his passion for nature. To each his own, Pete."

Pete held up his hands in mock surrender. "If I sounded sarcastic, I apologize. Believe me, it wasn't intended. It was no more than my poor attempt at humor."

I loved the way that Amber leapt to my defense, even though I had not felt belittled. Having made enough gaffs of my own, I recognized the misplaced humor of Pete.

"I'm not in the least bit insulted, Pete," I said, "and Amber's voiced her feelings on the matter. So forget it." I grinned at him. "Luckily, I'm almost never offensive." I clapped my hands loudly. "Hey boy," I shouted. "You there in the kitchen! Are there any more of your delicious morsels to be had? We want more."

My heavy humor rescued the moment, and Pete was chortling when Selph came out with a fresh serving dish filled with skewered prawns. A type of kebab, each skewer had prawn, bacon, mushroom, and green pepper, alternatingly, pierced onto it.

"Personally," I said, as I helped myself to a steaming hot skewer of goodies, "I happen to like living with a couple of cooks. Mind you, when it comes to making porridge, they are both rank amateurs. I've definitely got that sewn up."

"Thanks for telling me," rumbled Pete, "I'll remember to decline if I ever get a breakfast invitation from you."

The laughter and chatter continued as we demolished the skewered prawns, along with the remaining fish cocktails. When they were all eaten, Amber waited about fifteen minutes before bringing in the main course. I was reasonably full by then, but Pete was ever ready for more. He groaned in delight when she came in with a large tray of hot scallops mornay, each golden brown serving in its own large scallop shell. Even the aroma was delicious.

"Guess whose favorite meal this is," Amber chuckled.

"Adam's," Jane said quietly.

"Go to the top of the class," I said.

Pete look puzzled. "How did you know that?" he asked.

"Because I know how much Amber loves him," she replied.

The scallops mornay were bubbling hot, so we all gave close attention to our food and eating for a while. I could only eat one, and another half I shared with Amber, but Pete managed three. Luckily we had catered for his extra-large appetite. By the time that he finally sat back with a vast sigh of contentment, we had all long finished.

He held up his glass of wine. "To the cooks. Long may you invite me to share your expertise. My heartfelt and sincere thanks to you both. Cheers."

Ever since Jane's remark about Amber's love for me, Pete had been unusually quiet, almost subdued. His next words really startled me.

"I often laugh at certain things rather than reveal my sensitivity, or become vulnerable," he said softly and hesitant. "But I feel that in this present company I can come out of my protective shell, just a little bit." He paused, taking a deep breath. "When Jane spoke of how much Amber loves Adam, I felt an incredible sense of loss. Not envy, mind you, but loss. In that instant I knew that such a love was something I have never experienced, and for the first time in my life, I suddenly knew that I wanted to. For a brief moment I had an insight into how precious such a shared love is."

Silence followed this statement, as we all gazed at a slightly embarrassed Pete. He continued doggedly. "Adam told me that he came back from death because of his love for Amber. He didn't intend to tell me about it, but having let some slip out in the confusion of his pain, I wheedled the rest out of him." He shook his head, wonderingly. "I believe him. That's an incredible love these two people have, and it's all too rare. I've pondered often on what Adam and Amber are doing with their lives, not only in their love for each other, but also with their commitment to inner growth and expansion."

He chuckled. "The only real expansion I have devoted any energy to is my waistline, and that's gone far enough." He looked squarely at Amber and me. "Do you remember that you were going to teach me how to reach that inner space?"

I nodded. "Yeah, we all forgot. I'm sorry."

He shook his head. "Don't be. It's my responsibility, not yours. But, I'm ready. Would I be a party pooper if I got you to teach me the technique later this evening? You and I could perhaps sneak away for half an hour, if the others don't mind. I just don't want to keep putting it off. Putting it off is beginning to be the story of my life." He squinted at me, sighing heavily.

"I don't know what you do to me, Adam, but your energy seems to catalyze things in me. Do you remember me telling you how I wanted my own hospital?"

I nodded. "Yes, I do."

"Well, for years that was my one burning ambition, and now, all of a sudden, it seems trivial and unnecessary."

"I don't agree."

Pete grinned at me. "That's all right, my friend, you don't have to. This is my confession time. What feels of far greater importance to me right at this moment is my own growth as a human being. I've told you before, I've been thinking this way for a long time, but I've always been putting it off." He sighed. "You see, putting it off! When Jane spoke of Amber's love for you, Adam, I suddenly realized that love is the first and foremost thing in both of your lives. You've put the greatest value first in your lives, while I've put achievement and prestige before all things. Now, I . . ."

"Aw, come on Pete," I cut in, "don't you think you're being unnecessarily hard on yourself? What's wrong with a bit of prestige and achievement?"

Pete glowered at me. "Shut up, Adam, I need to get this off my chest. It's been there far too long. Achievement for the sake of prestige sucks, and you know it. Oh, I could play games and say it's all for the good of other people, my patients, but way down inside me, I know it's a lie. I also know that I'm a dedicated doctor, and that I do care very much about my patients, but, as I said, my consuming ambition is not based in love, it's based in power." He shrugged, embarrassed. "And suddenly, that's just not good enough."

He took a deep breath. "Christ! This feels like a confessional, but I need to share it with people I love, and trust. So, Adam, I'm asking you if you'll, er, sort of teach me some of the inner stuff you know about."

I had to stifle a grin. Me, a teacher! What a joke.

"If there's anything I can teach you, Pete, I'll be happy to, but the real name of the game is living your truth. That's a full-on, everyday, nitty-gritty reality, and that's where it's at."

Jane had sat listening in apparent fascination, but now she stirred, clearing her throat. "I must say that this has turned into the most extraordinary dinner party, but I rather like it." She looked levelly at Pete. "What you just shared took a lot of courage, and I would like to acknowledge that. Whereas I don't have your ambition to achieve, or have a need of prestige, I do have my own dark little secrets." She grinned rather mischievously. "Don't we all? Interestingly, love is the kicker to my own confession. When I recently met Amber, I was instantly drawn to her. In fact, this attraction was so strong that I was alarmed. I even wondered if it could be sexual, which, having once lived in a long-term relationship with a man, would have been startling, to say the least. However, I quickly realized that I loved Amber as a dear, close friend, and that she felt the same way about me. We had an instant sister relationship with a wonderful rapport, and love is the key factor.

"Whereas this is not my confessional, I realize since meeting Amber, and seeing her and Adam's relationship, that I inadvertently put love out of my life when Ken walked out on me. In hindsight, I'm well rid of him, but it's taken me five years to realize that I need to love and be loved."

"You've just described the overriding need of the whole human race; to love and be loved," Amber murmured as she hugged her friend. "And being human, we seem to reject with the most vigor that which we most need."

Jane hugged Amber, dabbing at her eyes. "The only thing I would like to add is that although I don't know what Pete means by Adam teaching him about 'inner stuff,' if it's of any benefit to my capacity to love, will you please include me?"

Shaking my head in bemusement, I chuckled. "You're right, this is one weird dinner party, but that's okay with me. I suggest we wait for another half-hour to let our food settle, and then if you want me to teach you about inner journeying, I'll be happy to."

"What about mango and peach desert?" Amber asked.

Pete patted his stomach. "How about afterward?"

Everyone, being full, agreed.

Personally, I felt a bit of a fraud, for it should be Selph who did the teaching; but I knew that he would not. It was inappropriate. Amber's and my plans for matchmaking had received a big boost, for Pete and Jane were now gazing at each other as though they were each seeing a dream come true.

Leaving the casual chatter between them, I walked out into the moonlit garden. I love full moons, even though I don't sleep as well under their influence. Crossing over to the pond, I watched the gently rippling moon at my feet.

"Some dinner party," Selph said quietly. "I'm not intruding, am I?"

"In all truth, you could never do that," I smiled. "I can never express how much I appreciate all you've done for me. But tell me one thing. Is all that has happened to Pete and Jane tonight the result of your influence?"

Selph chuckled quietly. "I knew you would ask me that, just as I know that initially you'll reject my answer. It is not I who is the catalyst in their lives, it's you. You're born to be a catalyst, and you do it very well."

"Don't be ridiculous. I'm not a catalyst, I'm just me."

"Adam, a catalyst is a person who has an energy that polarizes people and situations. People either like you very much, or they want nothing to do with you. A catalyst seems to attract change, stir passions, and ignite passivity. And, not unnaturally, many people resent this. They don't like being stirred up. You even did it with Ted in that farmyard. You open your mouth, and your words and energy stir and agitate people." He laughed. "You're a natural."

I had to concede that he was describing my effect on many of the people that I meet. Not all, but a lot. "So how do I stop it?"

"Stop it! Why would you want to stop it?"

"Because it's not the best way to win friends."

"Don't you have enough friends?"

"Of course. But you can't have too many."

"Adam, it's a gift. You may well have fewer friends, but they will all love you dearly. Would you trade quality for quantity?"

"No, but I'm damned if I can see how it's a gift."

"People like you start wars, they . . ."

"Great! That's just what I need," I interjected.

"They also end them. Catalysts are the death of stagnation, of apathy, and complacency. Catalysts promote the fresh winds of change, they are the seeds of human growth. Oh yes, it's a gift, even if a bit of a curse. It doesn't mean you are always right about things, or clever, or even wise; just the energy of ignition, movement, revolution and change. The world needs its catalysts, Adam; so as you just told Pete, you must live your truth, and honor it."

"So you're saying that what has happened at dinner tonight is my fault?"

"Fault? Why fault? There's no fault. What happened tonight is the result of what began for Pete and Jane a long time ago. Your energy has brought it to a head; shifted the blocks, created movement, allowing growth and expansion."

"Maybe it's Amber's doing?"

"Don't be obdurate. Amber isn't a catalyst, she's a healer. She is the perfect foil for you." He chuckled. "You take them apart, she puts them back together. Guess who will have most people love them?"

"Don't ask, it's always been that way. Everybody loves Amber. They walk within her ambiance, and fall at her feet."

"Like you did."

"Yeah." I laughed. "Only I fell harder than most."

"And under her healing influence you are learning how to love yourself, and other people. That's Amber's gift."

"So what do I do about being a catalyst?"

"Do! What do you mean, do? You continue being yourself just the way you are. What could be more simple than that?"

"Er, is that a subtle insult, praise, or neither?"

"Neither. It's advice. Just be yourself, Adam."

"And what about you?" I asked. "What are you?"

He grinned. "Me! I'm something else altogether."

I nodded. "Yeah, you can say that again."

"AAAAAADDAAAAAMMMM," Amber called loudly.

"COOOOMMING," I yelled back.

"Is teacher ready?" Selph chuckled.

"You should be doing this, not me."

He looked at me seriously. "Actually you're wrong. This is where it begins."

"Where what begins? What are you talking about?"

"You'll know soon enough," he said, strolling toward the house. "Timing will tell you everything."

Ten minutes later, Amber, Pete, Jane, and I were seated comfortably in the lounge, the two overhead fans turning just enough to stir the balmy evening air. Selph had disappeared to places unknown, and we were all ready.

Having explained the whole procedure to them, I told them that if they fell asleep not to be concerned, for it was rather late in the evening to be attempting this. However, they all looked remarkably bright-eyed and wide awake. I told them that when they reached the last of the twenty-one steps, they were to enter the reality and experience that awaited them. I would give them twenty minutes of silence, then I would bring them up the steps, back through the rainbow, and gently out of the experience.

And so it began. I took them into the procedure slowly, precisely, and with care. As I watched them, I could tell from their eyes and faces that without exception, they had all surrendered to the process. When we reached the last step, I closed my eyes also, easily entering my own inner experience with them.

When I opened my eyes again, exactly twenty-one minutes had elapsed. It felt to be the perfect timing to very gently bring them out of their experiences, back up the steps, and to bring the inner exercise to a close.

Still awed by my own experience, I sat quietly and waited for them to one by one, open their eyes.

Pete's eyes fluttered open first, and he smiled at me. A few minutes later Amber's eyes opened, followed immediately by Jane. We were concerned that Jane sat and quietly wept, her tears falling disregarded down her cheeks, yet despite the tears, she did not seem to be unduly distressed.

For a while we sat in a trusting, safe, silence, disturbed only by Jane's quiet sobs. Amber sat next to her, holding her in her arms.

Finally Pete shook his head like a bear. "That was just the most inexplicable and amazing experience of my life."

I smiled at him. "You're under no obligation, but if you would like to share it, we will all benefit."

He looked at Jane. "Would it disturb you if I did?"

"No," she said softly. "I think it would help."

He made a few snorting noises, clearly ill at ease, yet just as clearly keen to tell us about it. Nobody said anything, until at last he sighed heavily. "Oh, very well. You won't think me any more mad than you probably already do, so here goes. When I started off down the steps, part of me was skeptical, thinking the whole procedure was a load of bull, but another part of me was open, more receptive. As I proceeded down the steps, the cynical part seemed to diminish, and by the time we reached the last step I was feeling quite apprehensive. It's very odd. On the last step, I could see nothing, yet when I stepped away from it, to my consternation, I found myself standing in front of a private hospital. I knew immediately that it was mine. I have some carefully drawn plans at home, waiting for the big day—or they were! Anyway, this was the hospital of my own design. It was even set on the site that I have always hoped for, and landscaped beyond any ability of mine. I just stood there, gaping, staring at my dream hospital of the future.

"At first, I didn't know what to do. I walked around it, then I went in. Oddly, it was empty. Not a very big hospital, I walked through the few wards, into the operating theatre, and into the consulting rooms. Everything was just as I planned it, and without knowing how I knew, I knew that this could all happen. It was up to me. I was the key to everything. I continued aimlessly wandering around in the hospital, noting how perfect it was for what I wanted. When I first entered the place, I had felt excited, keen, but the longer I stayed there the more I began to question if this was really what I wanted. Initially, I felt a sense of achievement, victory, but this gradually faded to be replaced with a subtle feeling that I was walking around a prison. A prison of my own making."

He grinned sheepishly at us. "Crazy, huh? Just you wait, it gets even crazier! As the feeling of prison grew stronger, it gradually got darker and darker in the hospital, until finally I reached out to switch on a light. The moment I switched on the light, the interior of the hospital burst into flames, and fire alarm bells went off, making a furious din. Talk about bedlam. At first I was scared, but I got out of the building with no trouble at all. When I went outside, I saw that the fire brigade had just arrived, and as I watched, they rapidly unrolled a huge hose, twice, three times bigger than normal. I knew that they would very quickly douse the flames, and the hospital would be saved. As I watched, a couple of men took the huge hose and running to the entrance of the hospital, a massive jet of water shot out into the flames.

"I knew I had to act. In my pocket was a large sharp shut-knife, and grabbing it, I opened the blade and sprang at the hose. One deep stab and cut, and I ripped it open, the water gushing out and soaking me. The firemen turned, and seeing what I had done, rushed to stop me." He grinned. "I'm very big, and I easily held them away, letting the water from the truck all gush out uselessly onto the ground. They screamed and swore at me, telling me that the hospital would burn down, and I knew clearly that was what I wanted."

Pete shrugged. "And that's exactly what happened. As the hospital burned down, the fire engine disappeared with the flames, and soon I was alone. When the hospital reached a certain stage of destruction, it simply disappeared, and I felt the most incredible sense of release and freedom that I think I have ever experienced. I felt sad and elated, both at the same time, and I felt as though a very old and rusty chain that had long held me captive had been unshackled."

He grinned at us defiantly. "That's it, folks. Adam came in at about that time, offering us a ride home, so I turned back to the steps . . . and here I am. All I can say is that it was entirely unexpected, shockingly realistic, and unbelievably powerful." He glanced at his wrist watch. "I spent at least three hours in that hospital experience, yet less than thirty minutes has elapsed."

Jane had listened to his whole story with a look of amazement on her face. "Oh my goodness! That's incredible. But what does it all mean?"

Pete stared at her pensively, his bearded face looking surprisingly relaxed. "I knew what it meant the moment I reached into my pocket for the knife. I had the choice of keeping my lifelong dream, and really getting the hospital at some future date, or of releasing it altogether. If I had not acted, the firemen would have put the fire out, and with absolute certainty, I would have my hospital."

Jane looked baffled. "But isn't that what you wanted?"

Pete nodded. "I sure did, until this evening. When the hospital became dark—my prison—it symbolized my future. As I switched on the light, it burst into flames. I knew in that moment that I couldn't have the hospital and freedom. I chose freedom."

Pete looked at me. "Well, Adam, you promoted the whole thing. Do you agree with my summary?"

I nodded. "Absolutely. And congratulations. I would never have believed it possible for anyone to go through such a profound change in a single evening."

He looked at Amber. "And you, little lady?"

Jumping up, she went over to Pete and kissed him. "I sure do. I think you're someone very special."

Looking inordinately pleased with himself, Pete smiled at Jane. "And you, lovely madam. Will you share your inner experience with us? In all honesty, it really would help me to accept my own new, and unexpected, reality."

Jane sighed in embarrassment. "I suppose I could, if you all promise not to think me totally cuckoo."

"Jane, you don't have to. It's your choice. We love you no matter what," Amber said, an arm around Jane.

"Thank you, my dear. However, I do think that if I share it, I will be accepting it. If I go home with it all unspoken, I think I'll probably end up burying it in my subconscious. And that wouldn't be a good idea."

She reached for a wine bottle, poured some into her glass, and visibly relaxed.

"Incidentally," I said, "it might be a good idea if you both stay here tonight. It's already very late, and I don't like the idea of either of you driving home with alcohol in your system. If anything happened, Amber and I would find it very hard to live with. What do you say?"

"Damned thoughtful of you. I accept," Pete said.

"I don't have far to go," Jane murmured, "but I have had a fair bit of wine. If it's all right with Amber, I'll stay."

"Of course it's all right," Amber chuckled. "You're my dearest friend. It's always all right, any time at all."

Jane gave Amber a hug, murmuring her thanks, then she looked around the room, as though searching for an acceptable way to begin.

"Just tell it as it happened," I suggested.

She sighed. "Well, there was no drama, but, as with Pete, it was entirely unexpected. I went down the twenty-one steps totally committed, with no skepticism at all. On the way down, I could see a beautiful garden, filled with flowers of all colors. It was so enticing, I wanted to race down the steps, but I stayed with Adam's count. When I left the last step, I found that I was in the garden, having just entered through a clear and distinct doorway. I followed a path for a while that led me through a grove of golden bamboo. It was very beautiful, the leaves rustling and whispering high overhead as I walked through them. The path eventually led me out of the bamboo and onto a large, soft, green lawn. I've never seen a better lawn, and it was so irresistible I sat down. I could hear the sound of a stream nearby, and birds were singing their little hearts out. I loved being there, but I was attracted by the sound of water.

"Getting to my feet, I walked over the soft, springy grass until I reached a small hollow, fringed by a stream on one side and the golden bamboo on another. In the center of the hollow, there was a huge tree with dark green leaves and low, wide-spreading branches. Walking into the hollow, I saw a flat, comfortable rock next to the stream, so I went over to it and sat down, my bare feet dangling in the cool water. Everything I experienced seemed, somehow, more real than everyday life. Sort of . . . idyllic.

"I sat there for quite a while, when I heard a voice I recognized calling to me. Turning around, I stared in shock. Sitting on a swing hanging from a branch of the tree, was my mother. She called me again. 'Come over here, Jane, dear. We need to talk.' Not quite believing it, I went over to her, and it was definitely my mother. Considering that she died ten years ago, you can understand my shock.

"'What are you doing here?' I gasped.

"Mother smiled at me. 'I've come to see you. We've got a lot of unfinished business between us.'

"My mother died when I was twenty-five, and we had had many angry years between us. She was a dominating woman, and tried her hardest to control my career, my love life, my everything. When she died we weren't even on speaking terms. So you can imagine my shock and consternation to see her in the garden." She smiled regretfully. "But, I have to say that for the last few years, I've been wishing that she and I could have made it up. It has hurt me that we parted almost as enemies. After all, she was my mother.

"I felt a flare of anger. 'Why were you such a bossy bitch, so much into control?' I asked her.

"I know you're angry with me, and you have every right to be. I want to apologize, Jane dear. I honestly never wanted to control you; I wanted to protect you, but it all came out wrong. I was full of fear, instead of love, yet I thought it was love. I fouled up everyone with my fear; your Daddy, you, and your brother.'

"'Mum, how did you get into this garden?'

"'Oh, that. I come here often. The surprise is that you've come here. I'm so glad you did. I felt you coming.'

"'And what's happened to your fear, Mum?'

"'I've learned how not to create it. Jane, I want you to know that I love you, and to please forgive me.'

"I burst out crying then, and running over to my mother, we fell into each other's arms. It was wonderful. We sat and hugged, and shared personal stories, and reminisced, until I heard Adam begin the procedure to return. I didn't want to come back, but Mum said that it was time for her to go, also. We hugged again, shared our love for each other, and I told her that I unreservedly forgave her. Like Pete, I felt as though a heavy load had fallen from me, and I felt more free and joyous than I have in years." She smiled warmly at Amber. "So now you know why I came out of the experience crying. It was from sheer, over-whelming relief. However, the one thing that most puzzles me is time. Like Pete, I thought that I was involved for well over a couple of hours, Mum and I discussed so much, yet it was all barely half an hour." She looked at me. "How do you account for that?"

I had no intention of telling them that all time occupies the same space, with all that would involve, so I took an easier route. "It's simple. Because it wasn't a physical experience, linear time no longer applies."

Pete raised his eyebrows at me. "That's simple?"

We all looked at each other, and I could see the wonder and awe reflected in the other's eyes. The clock in the dining room struck two, its quiet chime shattering the stillness.

"At two o'clock in the morning, it's simple," I grinned. "There's nothing more to say, or do. Let's leave everything the way it is and go to bed. I'm completely pooped."

And that's exactly what we did.

# Twenty

I was standing in a deep gully, helplessly watching a huge raging torrent of water rushing directly at me. For some reason I could not move, yet I struggled desperately, aware that in moments I would be engulfed, and drowned. Suddenly, in all my terror, I knew with a total certainty that I was dreaming. I relaxed, facing the water calmly, knowing that none of this was real. In the precise moment that the main force of the water hit me, knocking me off my feet, a bell went off, clanging and jangling in my ear.

Opening my eyes groggily, sleepy and confused, my hand groped for the phone. Somehow, in all my fumbling, it abruptly stopped.

"Hello. This is Amber."

For a few minutes there was silence, punctuated only by Amber's occasional "Ah huh. Really!" And finishing with, "Oh, that's fantastic! See you soon."

I peered at the bedside clock through half-closed lids. Five o'clock! I had had less than three hours sleep. What was going on? I lay back, my eyes tightly shut, groggily contemplating the lost bliss of uninterrupted sleep.

I must have dozed immediately, for only minutes later Amber was shaking me vigorously. "Adam. Wake up. Adam."

"Wassa matta," I groaned. "Gotta sleep."

"That was Bruno. Kate's just been rushed in to the maternity hospital to have her babies. No births yet, but they are due any time now."

I sat up. "Is she okay?"

"She's fine. Bruno said we needn't rush there. He'll keep us informed."

My eyelids drooped. "Amber, my darling, please, oh please, let's get some more sleep. Another three hours and I'll be back to normal."

She tweaked my nose playfully. "Don't worry. I've no intention of rushing off just yet. I agree with you. We need more sleep. Sweet dreams."

Sweet dreams indeed! They will need to be better than the last one. I wondered what it meant. I lay back, my thoughts drifting to Kate and her twins. It seemed that I had hardly dozed off before the phone was ringing again, urging us to answer it with an insistent monotony. I left it to Amber. Feeling considerably brighter, I nevertheless had to peer disbelievingly at the bedside clock several times before I could accept that the time was now a quarter to nine.

From the squeals of delight coming from Amber, it seemed that the twins had arrived. She was chatting for nearly ten minutes, and it sounded that everything was obviously fine. When she put the phone down, Amber threw herself into my arms, hugging me with fierce passion.

"Oh, Adam. A boy and a girl! Both well and kicking. Her labor wasn't overly long, and everything went perfectly. Isn't that just wonderful, Uncle Adam?"

"It sure is, Aunty Amber. It's great."

"I told Bruno that we would be there in a few hours. Apparently, Bruno is a bit stunned by the arrival of twins, while Kate is over the moon with joy."

I felt incredibly happy for her. "I knew she would be."

We both clambered out of bed, shared the shower, and dressing quickly, went looking for our guests.

Pete was asleep in bed, gently snoring, but Jane was swimming nude in the pool. She blushed when she saw me, so I politely turned my back.

"Don't worry Jane. If it embarrasses you, I'll give you time to swim while I make some coffee."

She laughed. "It's okay, I'm not bothered, but I would love some coffee. This was a spontaneous skinny-dip, so will you ask Amber to bring me a towel, please?"

Amber took her a large towel, while I made coffee. Our cold fruit desserts from last night were untouched in the refrigerator, so I carried a couple of dishes outside.

By the time I had breakfast laid out, and coffee on the table, the sounds of household activity had roused Pete.

He came ambling outside, his hair and beard damp from the shower. "Top of the morning to you all. I say, is there some coffee ready?" He glanced at the wet Jane wrapped in her big towel, then ambled over to her. "I'm not about to unravel you, or anything rude, but you look so beautiful that my morning can't possibly begin until I've given you a hug."

Watching him hug her, and seeing the kiss they shared, I knew that it was in the bag. After their experiences of last night, with both recognizing a need for love, soon, very soon, they would be inseparable.What a way to start the day: newborn twins and a happy twosome!

Amber looked at me, and winked happily.

"As of an hour or so ago, I'm Uncle Adam," I said.

Pete disengaged with a hasty "Excuse me" and, rushing over to us, embraced Amber, then hugged me. "That's wonderful. Is Kate all right? No complications?"

I looked solemn. "Two actually." I paused, watching his growing anxiety, then I grinned. "Twins."

Jane went to get dressed, while Amber told Pete about Kate, Bruno, and the twins. "We hope to go and see her later this morning," she finished.

Pete glanced at his wrist watch. "I begin duty at midday, so I'll have to be off very soon myself."

"But not before last night's dessert, and a mug or two of coffee, I hope," I said, indicating the waiting breakfast.

"Good heavens, no," Pete grinned. "We have to get our priorities right. Food, drink, then work." He looked at me sideways. "Hmmm. I think after last night, and in view of the lovely Jane, I'm going to have to amend that. How about, true love, then food, and all the rest?"

I nodded. "Sounds good to me."

Jane had joined us, coming up behind Pete in time to catch his comment about her. She blushed as she sat down.

"It sounds pretty good to me, also," she said.

Pete was nothing if not direct. "I'm delighted to hear that, my dear, because it's with you I hope to learn about a truly loving relationship." He held her eyes for a moment, before looking away. "I'm sorry if I'm a bit up-front, but I'm inclined to say what I mean without beating around the bush. That's the way I am."

Jane was equally direct. "I like clarity and honesty. We're too old to play games." Her eyes met Pete's. "Well, word games, that is," she said boldly.

Pete chuckled. "Where have you been all my life? Madam, I get the feeling that you and I are going to enjoy each other very much."

Amber jumped up and kissed Pete, then kissed Jane.

"I'm just so happy."

"And of course, you had nothing to do with deliberately setting out to throw us together, did you?" Jane laughed.

"We knew it was a setup from the first moment," Pete added, "but we also knew it was done because you love us, so we decided to go along with it."

"But you're not faking the attraction, are you?" I asked.

"Certainly not," Pete said. "Any time you try to fix me up with a beautiful woman like Jane, you have my blessing."

"I beg your pardon?" Jane frowned.

For a moment, Pete gaped at her, then he understood. "Oh! Er, I mean, having introduced me to a beautiful woman like Jane, don't you ever dare to do such a thing again."

"Gottcha," I laughed.

"Rest assured," Amber chuckled.

The coffee and cold fruit were a perfect way to start the day. Jane was not working, so she was in no hurry; but within the hour we were waving good-bye to Pete.

I left Amber and Jane to share their women's talk. In a conversation with both men and women, there often comes a moment when men are redundant, and women need to be alone to communicate in their own unique way.

We walked into the small, private maternity hospital and went over to the reception area.

"We're here to see Kate Strickland," Amber stated.

"Ah ha," the pert and pretty girl said. "The lady with the twins. Isn't she lucky? Room three. Take the passage to your left, and it's the third door. Have a nice day."

"It's going pretty well, so far," I said to Amber as we proceeded toward Kate's room. "And it's getting better."

The door was open, and we peeped in, just in case Kate was asleep.

"Come in, Amber, and you, brother dear. Come and meet your niece and nephew."

Kate was half-sitting up in bed, a twin on each side of her. She looked tired and pale, but radiant.

"Oh! What absolute darlings," Amber gushed, her eyes devouring the two babies. "Oh, Kate, you clever Mum! They are simply adorable."

Kate chuckled. "I had a natural birth. You should have seen Bruno's face when the second baby made his presence known. He nearly collapsed he was so shocked."

"You can't say Adam the Oracle didn't tell you," I chuckled. "But did you believe me, not a bit of it." I put my arms around her and kissed her. "Congratulations, Kate, we are so very happy for you both."

Kate stared at me seriously. "Do you know, from the moment you said I was going to have twins, I had a strong premonition that you would be right." She laughed. "It was a gut feeling. I even told Bruno, but he was sure there was just the one."

"Gut feeling! I like that," I chuckled.

"Oh no, wisecracking must run in the family," Amber groaned. "Kate, dear, what are their names?"

"Tiffany Anne, and Michael Joseph. Tiffany is the oldest by about three minutes."

I have to admit, newborn babies look pretty much alike to me, and I only knew who was who because of the color coding of their wrist bands. Both were pink, wrinkled, and a bit gummy, but as babies go, they were great.

"Where's Bruno?" I asked.

"He was here at the birth. I had to come into the hospital because they thought I was going to have a whopper and I might need a Cesarean. Gosh, I was big. I feel like a deflated balloon now. About an hour after the twins were born, he had to rush off to an emergency."

"I'm glad you didn't need a Cesarean," Amber said. "I still think natural is best, if possible."

Kate grinned. "Yeah, I agree. I'm smart, instead of making one very big baby, I made two the perfect size. They each weighed just over two and a half kilograms."

Amber smiled. "That's a lot to carry around."

"Yeah, especially with about a ton of afterbirth," Kate grinned.

"I remember a cow that had twins," I said, "and wow, you should have seen how much afterbirth she had. She ate it though. Cows do that sometimes when . . ."

"Adam. Do shut up about cows and birth," Amber cut in fiercely. "If you mention them any more, I'll . . ."

"I hear you," I interjected. "I don't understand, but if that's the way you want it . . ." I let the sentence hang.

Kate laughed, wincing. "He doesn't understand, Amber. Ever since he was a little boy, he's thought things like that. He genuinely thinks that because cows are so adorable, cows and women are comparable. Especially in moments such as this. Don't worry about it."

Frowning, I listened. "Come on, Kate, that's hardly fair. Lots of cows will pick a stormy night to give birth, and I hardly expect Amber to do the same." Then I thought about that some more. "Come to think of it, she might. You never know. But she definitely won't do it outside in a field in the pouring rain. I hope. Oooooofff."

Amber's elbow caught me in the side, just below the rib cage, startling me. "Ouch, that hurt," I protested.

She glared at me fiercely. "I'll do more than hurt if you don't stop comparing me with cows giving birth. I've told you before, I don't like it."

Kate was laughing so much she was groaning in pain. "Oh stop it, you two. My laughing is pulling at the stitches where I got cut."

"Oh, so they cut you!" I exclaimed. "That reminds me of the time when I . . ." I caught the look on Amber's face. "Er, it doesn't matter. I'll tell you some other time."

Kate's shriek of laughter brought a nurse peering in through the open door. "Everything all right?"

"Yes, thanks," Kate said, giggling helplessly, "unless I suffer death by laughter."

"There must be worse ways," the nurse grinned as she departed. "It's nice to have something to laugh about."

"Are Mum and Dad coming to see you?" I asked.

"They'll be here this evening, then Dad's going to leave Mum at home with us for a week or so. Despite all protests, she insists on looking after me. If all's well, I'll only be here thirty-six hours."

"You let Mum help; she'll love it. And it will do you good to be looked after for a while. Don't knock it."

"Yeah, I think you're right. I certainly don't have much energy yet, and with the twins I may be glad of help." She yawned mightily. "Having babies is hard work."

"Right," Amber said firmly. "We're going now so you can get a chance to sleep. We'll see you again this evening. Adam and I can do some city shopping for a change."

"Some change," I groaned, "but I agree with Amber."

"I want you to stay," Kate said, "but I do badly need some sleep. Will you ask the nurse to come in as you go?"

We kissed her, and departed.

Half an hour later we were eating a late snack, just sandwiches and coffee. We planned to have a proper dinner before we went back to see Kate.

"So what do you want to buy?" I asked.

"Oh, I don't know, darling. Shopping isn't necessarily about buying any-thing, it's about the process of looking. Of course, if I find something we need, then we'll get it."

"If you don't know what you need now, how's that going to change during the afternoon?"

"Adam, don't be so pragmatic. Browsing the shops is like reading a menu: you may like what is on offer, but your appetite will determine what you order."

Our sandwiches eaten, I stood up, sighing. "Okay, lead on. Where do we begin?"

For the next couple of hours we trekked up and down the length of the Queen Street Mall in Brisbane. The place was packed with people doing the same thing, walking, looking, and, probably, buying. People jostling and being jostled. People happy. People bored. People anxious. People scared. Lonely people needing contact, and desperate people.

"Just think, Amber. Every day, every city in the world is packed with millions of stressed-out people following a mindless routine of looking and wanting. Most of them are staring into shop windows stuffed with items that they don't need, at prices they can't afford. And why? Because so many of them don't know what else to do. It's called 'pleasure.' I think that's scary."

She shook her head. "Gee, you're such wonderful company in a city, Adam. Can't you strike a more positive note?"

"Yeah. I've positively had enough. I've been jostled around until I'm limp, looking at things that I don't want, don't need, and don't interest me. Let's positively quit."

Amber looked at me, running her hand over my forehead.

"You poor darling. I've been watching your scowl getting more pronounced all afternoon." She massaged my forehead vigorously, as though to erase the wrinkles, then glanced at her wrist watch. "Okay lover, the restaurants will be serving dinner by now. Let's find a nice place, and eat."

In all fairness to Amber, we had bought several baby-type things and maternity wear that she needed, so it was not a complete waste of time. But a glance at the seafood menu indicated that the best was yet to come.

By the time we had finished our meal, I was in a very much better frame of mind.

"I've just worked out why we need cities," I announced.

"I hate to ask."

"Well, just think how terrible it would be if all the bored and lonely millions decided to go to the national parks, or the local forests for their pleasure time. Cities are a unique way of congregating huge numbers of people onto relatively small areas of concrete. Happily, this preserves nature and the wilderness."

Amber stared at me for long moments. "Are you serious?"

I grinned. "Not really, but it's a nice thought."

"Let's pay the bill and go. I think it's time to get you out of here before you do any more thinking."

When we again walked into Kate's room, Mum and Dad were already there. Enthusiastically, we hugged and greeted each other, for although we spoke often on the phone, it had been quite a while since we had all been together.

"So, how's Grandma and Granddad?" I asked.

Mum looked pleased. "Fancy that! I'm a Grandma. We're very well, Adam. And you're looking super fit."

"You should have seen me before we went shopping in the city," I quipped, grinning at Amber.

"Cities affect him mentally," Amber chuckled, "but he certainly is fit now. I know for a fact that he still has a lot of aches and pains, but he really has worked very hard at his rehabilitation. I'm proud of him. Did you know he's back at work, seeing his clients?"

Dad had said very little up to now, but he suddenly looked interested. "Is Ian, your assistant, still with you?"

I nodded. "Yeah. He does most of the legwork. It's all working out very well. How's things on the farm?"

"Bloody terrible. We're dry and parched. I honestly don't know how much more we can take."

"What's the latest long-range forecast?"

"In a nutshell, uncertainty."

"I guess that's better than knowing it'll continue."

"Maybe, but it ain't much help for long-term planning. I have to make decisions on what to do with the remaining herd. Do I sell them at sacrificial prices, or do I hang on indefinitely, hoping?"

"Okay you guys, that's enough shop talk," Kate said firmly. "You're here to look at the babies and tell me how wonderfully clever I am to produce them. Would you like to pick one up, Granddad?"

Dad walked over to the double cot alongside Kate's bed, and bending over, he gently and easily scooped Michael into his arms. "Ready for a farming career, Grandson?" he asked.

Kate laughed. "Give him fifteen years, and who knows. It'll be a pull between his Dad's doctoring, and Granddad's farming. Time will tell."

"He's born to be a farmer, and Tiffany will be a famous musician. It's all in their destiny," I said.

Kate and Amber looked at me in astonishment. "Whatever makes you think that?" Kate asked.

I shrugged. "I don't know. I heard me say it, just as you did. And yet, as I think about it, I feel a real inner certainty about it."

"How can you be so certain? We don't have musicians in our family," Kate said.

"I don't know what you're talking about," Bruno said as he walked in, "but I heard a remark about musicians in the family. Both my father, and his father, were renowned and brilliant musicians." He leaned over to Kate and kissed her. "And how's the mother of my children?"

"Fit, well, puzzled, and ready to go home," Kate said.

"Why are you puzzled?" Bruno asked her.

She told him what I had said, and Bruno laughed.

"Who knows? He was right about you having the twins, despite all my denial and objections." He grinned. "Perhaps Adam is a latent oracle."

Not liking the way that the conversation was going, I regretted my words. But why did I say them? It was as though with clear insight, I knew, but I don't know how I knew. Knowing, beyond knowledge or information! I would have to talk to Selph about it. Despite the fact that directly knowing is neither logical nor reasonable, I suspect that it is a possible reality.

"When are you going home, Kate?" I asked, successfully changing the subject.

"Midday tomorrow. Mind you, they're only letting me out because Mum will be there to look after me, and they need the bed. Seems there's a sudden flush of babies being born."

Amber looked thoughtful, then smiled at Kate. "How would it be if Adam and I stay at your place tonight, then we'll collect you tomorrow and drive you home. Mum can have everything ready for you." She glanced at Mum. "That is, of course, unless you've already made other plans."

Mum shook her head. "That's fine with me."

"Actually, I was hoping to collect Kate myself," Bruno said, "but everything at work has conspired to make that just about impossible. Personally, I would be relieved and grateful if you could pick her up."

Amber grinned happily. "Is it okay with you, Adam?"

I nodded. "Yes, as long as I get your sacred oath on a stack of Bibles that you won't drag me into the city for any more shopping."

"I do so swear," Amber intoned solemnly.

"Done," I chuckled.

We spent about an hour with Kate and the family, before departing with Mum and Dad. Bruno and Kate had a large old house in one of the older, tree-filled, green suburbs, so there was no lack of room for all of us.

Within half an hour, the kettle was boiling, a carrot cake cut up, and another snack under way.

"The twins are just beautiful," Mum said idly. "Kate and Bruno are so very fortunate."

"So how do you feel about two at a time, Dad?" I asked.

He shrugged. "It's a bit unexpected, but as a new grandfather, I intend to get it right this time. I didn't do a crash-hot job of being a father, so in some ways, I'm getting a second chance."

"I'm not complaining, Dad."

"No, not now. But you have, and with cause. I did the father bit okay, but I forgot about being your friend. I sort of thought that friendship came automatically, or that it was due to me as your father, but it doesn't work that way. I've been doing a lot of thinking about you and me, lately. I've realized that being a dad is one thing, but being a dad and a good friend is something else altogether."

"Better late than never," I quoted sincerely.

"Maybe, but you'll be a father soon, so listen and learn. The trap I fell into was of being right. I had to be right; that was everything. I now realize that being friends with your children is far more important than being right."

I nodded. "Yeah, I'll remember that."

"In any argument between us, I'd get real upset when you would not concede to being wrong. If I was right, you had to be wrong, it was that black and white."

I grinned wryly. "And every argument, whether between just two people or a whole crowd in dispute, is based on everybody believing that they are right." I laughed. "You know, Dad, you're absolutely right!"

"Being right may win you the respect of your kids, but being friends is the only way to earn their love." He looked at me seriously. "Believe me, Adam, I'm going to be a really good friend to my grandkids, and I can't wait."

I shook my head in admiration. "You're a changed man, Dad. I respect, and love you, for being able to change. For me, that's a sign of greatness. Most people hate change, and avoid it at any cost. You're something else!"

Dad gave me a sly look. "But can I change enough to give eco-farming a go?"

My heart nearly missed a beat. "Well, can you?"

"When this drought breaks, I've decided to employ the best damned eco-farming consultant in the area, and get it under way. It's never too late to learn new tricks. I reckon that if I can learn new tricks as a father, I can learn them as a farmer."

I damn near bawled, I was so overcome. For long moments I just stared at him, then I went over and hugged him. He chuckled in my ear.

"It would be worth it even if it were for nothing else than you and me to be friends, but . . ."

"We are friends, Dad," I cut in firmly.

"But as I was saying, that ain't the reason. I spoke to Joe Steadman on the phone recently, and he convinced me."

I could hardly believe my ears. "You and Joe! Gee! That's just great. You'll never regret it, I promise you."

He and I chatted about eco-farming for the next hour, and I nearly had to pinch myself to believe that we were having such a conversation. Only now did I really get a full insight into the incredible change that had affected Dad. My near death was the best thing that had ever happened to us! It had been the catalyst that precipitated the change. Catalyst! I thought of Selph and his words on that subject. It seemed that being a catalyst was an ongoing thing, as though what happened to me also had an effect on the people in my life. How odd.

Amber had been deep in conversation with Mum, so when she and I went to bed that night, I told her all that had taken place between Dad and myself.

As I told her, I watched her looking at me. Her jaw so firm it was almost pugnacious, her widely spaced green eyes holding me in that level gaze of hers, and her auburn hair falling in waves of fire over her shoulders, I felt so much awe and love for her, my words simply ceased.

"What's the matter?" she asked.

"You're so beautiful you take my breath away. I can hardly believe that I'm fortunate enough to be loved and wanted by you." I shook my head at the wonder of it.

She grinned. "Well you better believe it, lover, because it's true. I think you're every bit as wonderful as you think I am, so there!"

"I like it. I like it a lot."

We made love gently, without hurry or haste, and I savored every moment. My whole focus was on loving Amber, and sex was simply the means by which this happened. Our moods always affect our lovemaking, but the mood of wonder and awe opens up new dimensions of tenderness and touching.

Afterward, we lay entwined in each other's arms.

"Did you know that statistics indicate that couples tend to make love after there is a birth in the overall family, and after a death; most particularly when there is a death. It's as though we subconsciously try to reaffirm life," I said.

"Oh, then why do we make love after a birth?"

"Undoubtedly, to celebrate life."

"So our lovemaking was just a statistic?"

"No, my darling, it was an exploration of souls."

"Oh, Adam. Sometimes you say the nicest things."

"You mean I don't always?"

"Not when you bring cows into the discussion."

"Talking of cows, I'm glad I'm not a bull. They don't make love, they simply mate, on and off in a moment. Not much fun at all. A bit like a certain plant really."

"A certain plant?"

"Yeah. A bulrush!"

There was a few moments of silence, then Amber spoke.

"But you are a bit like a bull, you know."

"I sincerely hope not."

"You are. You're likable and adorable!"

I laughed. "Very clever. Okay, I quit. Mooove over and give me some room in the bed. It's sleepy byes time."

Amber likes to sleep close, so moving over meant that she eased her elbow out of my ribs, and her hair from my face. I wanted to protest about needing more space, but I fell asleep while thinking about it.

Next morning we were up in good time, but Mum had breakfast ready when we walked into the spacious kitchen. With the summer heat upon us, fruit and yogurt or muesli and skim milk was the usual way we started the day, along with the perennial, ever-seasonal, coffee.

"Did you sleep well?" Mum asked.

"Reasonably well, considering it's not my usual bed," I replied. In fact, I had had a repeat of my previous dream, once again standing in the steep-sided gully while a wall of water came rushing at me. Only this time it was pouring with rain as well. The dream was not scary, like the terrifying axman dream as my limbs were chopped off, but it was rather disturbing. I had no idea what it meant.

Later, I enjoyed ambling around Kate's old garden, with its aged, gnarled jacaranda trees, and the single, enormous, Morton Bay fig tree. I noticed several huge lower limbs that would easily take a swing, or two, and I knew that as soon as they were old enough, the twins would get great pleasure from climbing this tree and making friends with it. Kate was the gardener, and her rambling, rather unkempt garden showed the touch of a person who appreciated nature as it was, without overly trying to control it. Wisely, she had planted nothing under the huge fig except creeping ferns, thus the tree stood out as the dominant feature of the garden.

I sat rather uncomfortably on one of the buttress roots, just soaking in the energy of the tree. As far as the branches reached, I could feel the activity of the tree as a mystic pulse, and sitting on the high ridge of root, my hands on the bark, I felt that the tree was aware of our connection. That it had been loved by several generations of people was obvious. Some people would buy this home just to have the tree in their lives, and I suspected that my sister was just such a person. I knew that Amber and I would.

"Aaaadaaamm."

I sighed. It was time to collect Kate and the twins from the hospital. "See you again," I murmured to the tree, just as I always did. It was far too imposing a presence to ignore. Most people talk to their pets, never expecting a reply, so why not talk to a magnificent tree? In the same way that the spirit of the land can merge with our silence, so, too, can a mature tree.

Leaving the cool shade, I joined Amber.

"Sitting under the tree, huh?" she asked.

I smiled. "Where else."

She kissed me. "Time to go."

Wearing a pair of pale orange shorts, and a white singlet, she was beginning to show a clear hint that she was pregnant. I patted her small bulge. "Okay, mother to be."

Kate was ready to depart when we arrived, waiting and dressed, sitting in a chair near the bed. The twins were in their hospital cot.

"Did you bring everything I need?" she asked anxiously.

Amber kissed her. "Two carry cots, baby clothes, the lot. Relax Kate, it's all under control."

I took the vacated chair, while they did what they had to do to get the twins ready. Kate had already signed out, but the girl from reception came breezing into the room.

"Oh what a shame. You're gonna take our beautiful twins away." She leaned over them. "Hi, honey buns. Who's a gorgeous boy and girl?"

"I hope you don't expect an answer," I said seriously.

She glanced at me, and chuckled. "No, I don't. They know they're beautiful."

"They should. They're not yet two days old, and they've been told dozens of times already."

"That's what babies need to hear, silly. It's what you say to babies. You don't expect to tell them about the weather, or what's going on in politics."

I nodded. "Right. Point taken."

She looked at Kate and Amber, shaking her head in a conspiratorial way. "Geez, men! Are they dumb, or what?"

We left the hospital with the well wishes of many of the staff, as they had their last peep at the twins.

"If twins cause such a stir, imagine having quads."

"Twins will do, thank you, Adam," Kate replied.

❖　❖　❖

We spent the rest of that day, and the next, with Kate and the twins, enjoying the company of the family. It surprised me just how little we saw of Bruno, he was so busy. As expected, Mum was competent and efficient, and very careful not to take the mothering away from Kate.

Dad left the same morning that we did, eager to get back to his beloved farm, yet grateful for the break away from its parched reality.

"The next time I do my rounds, Ian and I will come and see you, Dad. My new client is very important."

"Me too," Amber said. "I'd love to see you."

She surprised me, and I kissed her. "Great."

"Will it be before or after Christmas?" Dad asked.

"It'll be January. Who knows, we may get an indication of a wet season by then. And it's only six weeks away. I had forgotten about Christmas. I guess Mum will want both the families at your place, as usual?"

"You may depend if Kate's up to it, she will."

"She will be," Amber said. "Personally, I can't wait to have another Christmas at your place. I missed them."

I thought back to the two recent Christmases when she and I were separated. Although I had spent Christmas with the family, alone, I had cried in self-pity each time, unable to join in the traditional Yuletide cheer. Christmas with Amber would be like life renewed.

"Anyway, Mother will phone you about such things in a week or so. I must go."

We all hugged, and Amber and I watched him drive away.

"I would never have believed that a man could change as much as your father. He's incredible. He's a different man."

I nodded. "I often marvel at how my nearly dying has affected a few lives so powerfully. Yours, mine, and Dad's especially."

"It goes deeper than that," Amber replied. "It reunited us, changed you, created a baby—a new life, and has changed your Dad. And how about Pete? His life has changed, and now Jane's is too. But even more, it has led to you becoming a person who will change the lives of many other people yet."

"You've lost me now."

"I've talked with Selph enough to know that, even as a eco-farming consultant, you're different. He told me that you've become a powerful catalyst: a person who brings change into people's lives. I was aware of it well before he told me; he simply confirmed it. You didn't use to be like this."

"I'm sorry, but it seems to be beyond my control."

"You silly goose. It's just you being you, and that's the way it should be. You don't have to apologize for it, or try to control it. Just be who you are. As far as I'm concerned, this is part of the potential Adam. The old you was an imprisoned, sub-Adam." Putting her arms around my neck, she kissed me passionately. "I love the new you."

We had a last coffee with Mum and Kate, hugged and kissed our farewells to everybody, and with Amber driving, we set off on our journey home.

# Twenty-One

Christmas came, was thoroughly enjoyed, and passed. We had hoped that Selph would spend Christmas with us, but he had made plans of his own. When I asked him if they had a Christmas in his reality frame, he was reluctant to be drawn on the subject. As usual, I persisted.

"For Western people in the twentieth century, I concede that Christmas is appropriate, even important. In all your worldly and personal conflict, you need a season of goodwill, but it's a celebration devoid of any true understanding of the Master's purpose," he said.

"What's that supposed to mean?" I asked defensively.

"The Master wasn't born on December the twenty-fifth, and even if he had been, one message he attempted to leave is that who you are is not born, and who you are does not die. You are spiritually immortal, while clothed in the transient guise of flesh and a persona. His apparent death, and the manner of his departure, convey this, but it has always been misunderstood and misrepresented. Christian religions celebrate his immortality, yet their sponsorship of fear and self-doubt continues to foment a flourishing denial of your own immortal truth."

I felt rather defensive about Christmas because I enjoyed it so much, but rather than get into a debate that I had no chance of winning, I went away to think over what Selph had said. It was not long before I found that I had no real argument with him, but I knew that the mass consensus reality would emphatically deny his words. However, one by one, as individuals, people are already finding this greater truth that Selph spoke of. I, however, fully intended to continue enjoying each festive season, but I would also acknowledge a new meaning within it.

Amber was now about four months pregnant, and she was happily experimenting with loose, cool clothing. The summer heat was really upon us, so all her emphasis was on cool. When she had first known she was pregnant, she told me that she had no intention of having morning sickness. I had laughed, saying that this was beyond even her control.

Now, in her fourth month, she had been sick only once, and whereas I did not believe that it was by her own command, I was delighted that she was a picture of healthy, and blossoming pregnancy.

Although I had planned to see Dad and my other eco-farming clients in January, a heat wave that had set in just after Christmas had made that impossible. Every day the temperature soared into the lower and mid-forties Celsius. On our coastal strip, this was almost unprecedented. Our garden dried up, with some well-established, but exotic shrubs and plants dying from heat stress. The plants that were the least affected were those indigenous to this sun-baked country of ours.

The heat wave was the talking point for everyone. How hot it was; how long it had lasted; how long it may last. Everybody had a story about the heat affecting either their family, pets, or the garden. The heat killed a lot of people who were elderly, or in poor health, and generally stressed just about everybody. Road surfaces melted, and tar splashes smeared the sides of most cars. And so it continued, day after sun-baked day. Even swimming pools offered little respite, for most of them had warmed to the point that they were now almost hot.

We were luckier, because ours was considered a cool pool, deep, and rather too well shaded by surrounding trees. Usually this was a disadvantage, but right now it was very welcome. Due to my insistence, Amber now had an air conditioner fitted into her studio, so during the peak heat in the afternoon, we all tended to congregate in there, idly chatting or reading.

But I was getting restless.

We had been swimming one morning, or, more correctly, simply wallowing in the cool water while conserving our energy, and as we quickly dried out in the hot air prior to getting a fruit lunch, I decided to tackle Selph on a number of issues that were bothering me.

We sat in the airy kitchen, overhead fans whirling mightily trying to cope with the heat, and as we munched on apples and bananas, I told Selph about the clarity I had felt when I had told Kate that Tiffany would be a musician and Michael a farmer.

"As I was telling her, I knew it to be true, but it's not possible to know something like that. I had a 'knowing,' beyond information or knowledge. Is this real? What is it? Can I trust it?"

Selph smiled lazily. "We've talked about this before, but for you, it was conceptual. Now it isn't. I've told you often that all time occupies the same space. That space—to give it a word—is in the moment, now. Despite the fact that people are rarely aware of the ongoing moment, we were each designed to mentally and spiritually live with a focused awareness of the moment, in the moment."

"That isn't easy."

"So you've said before. Where I come from, every person lives that way. Here, it's rare. Its power and value elude most of your twentieth-century thinking, but it's a reality that eventually you will have to embrace. When you made that statement to Kate, you were in the moment. You connected with the timelessness of a greater reality, and you spoke the truth that engaged your consciousness. It is real, and you can trust it."

"It sure ain't logical," I grinned wryly.

"Nor is polluting your air and contaminating your water, or laying your land to waste, but it persists."

"Yeah, well, so much for logic. The way we treat our environment is criminal."

"Ignorance, greed, and violence aren't crimes, they are simply the seeds of suffering, trauma, and eventually, of explosive change."

"Yeah. We call it history!"

Selph gave me a level stare. "The explosive change is yet to come. Such change has happened before, but not in your recorded or accepted history."

"Is it in yours?"

"We no longer record personal realities and call it history. There is no need, when anyone can directly 'know.' Your history is mostly an inaccurate, and biased story."

I sighed. "I don't doubt it."

We were quiet for a few minutes, sipping iced water and lime. He always gave me plenty to think about. I covertly watched him for a while, and more than ever, I was aware of how much he had changed over the months I have known him. It was something that had been nagging at my attention for several weeks. I accepted that he was an enigma, and that there was no way that I would ever understand him, but I did want to know what the changes represented. I decided to broach the subject. Who knew where it might lead?

"Don't get me wrong, but you're not the same Selph that I first met on the beach. You seemed just like a big kid then, but lately you are visibly far more mature, more how a spiritual teacher should be, apart from appearing as much too young. And yet, having said all that, it's still a lot more subtle than I can express. I'm not sure what I'm trying to say, or how to say it, except that you are somehow different from the Selph I first met."

"You mean no more bizarre McDonald's stunts, or doing things that confront and aggravate you, or where has the physical blub of adolescent immaturity gone?"

"Sort of, although it's more subtle than that."

"And you really don't know why?"

I frowned. "I wouldn't ask if I did."

He smiled his innocent smile. "All this, despite the fact I still wear my cosmic teacher's gear."

It was true that he still wore the garish orange T-shirt and baggy green shorts, but I had become used to them. They certainly did not bother me any more. He was different, although his clothing was the same. Was there supposed to be a connection?

"If there's a connection, I don't get it."

"Well you'd better tune in to the moment and find out. Who knows, you may 'get it' directly. Is there anything else bugging you while we're at it?"

I nodded. "Yes, me! You are my teacher, and I'm very happy with that, but I seem to drift and doodle along getting nowhere fast. Who I am continues to elude me, and I'm no closer to understanding the meaning of life than before. I know you've told me not to get stuck on understanding, and I probably have, but I try not to. Then I get stuck on trying not to try! Just 'doing it' is uncannily difficult. I feel that I'm stagnating, rather than continuing to expand and grow in consciousness."

"You do, huh? So what do you want me to do about it?"

"Oh, I don't know. Perhaps I need a good swift kick in the butt," I said jokingly.

"Granted," he said softly.

The next moment some force grabbed hold of me, and to my astonishment, propelled me rapidly out of the kitchen and across to the swimming pool. I felt a softly padded, yet mighty whack across my backside, throwing me far out into the pool.

I came to the surface spluttering, shocked by what had happened. As I climbed up the steps from the pool, I noticed that Selph was sitting on the corner of the kitchen table exactly as he had been while I was talking to him. I walked toward him, dripping. "My God, that's not possible."

Instantly, the same force once again grabbed me, but this time I was lifted high, and easily thrown to hurtle through the air like a basketball, unerringly splashing down in the exact center of the deepest part of the swimming pool. Once again, I came spluttering and gasping to the surface.

"Adam, darling. Are you all right?"

The humor, and the sheer bizarre impossibility of it was just too much, and I shrieked with laughter.

"I'm okay, really. Selph and I were just playing fetch, and guess what I was?"

"The ball," Amber giggled. "I saw it all the first time, but I could not believe what was happening. You seemed to stagger out of the kitchen in an uncontrolled run, and then throw yourself into the pool. But the second time was scary. You seemed to leap about ten feet high, then hurtle through the air an impossible distance, and into the pool again. That's when I came running."

"You shouldn't run in your condition," I frowned.

"And you shouldn't hurtle through the air in yours."

"Er, yes, well. That was Selph's doing."

"I guessed that. I told him that if he dares to do it again, I'll hit him."

At that, I nearly collapsed with laughing, and as Selph joined us, he too was folded up, laughing. "You should have seen your face that second time," he chortled. "Talk about a face like a stunned fish!"

By now, Amber was also laughing. "We might as well make it a party," she said, stepping into the pool fully dressed, to be followed by Selph. Together, we sat in the shallows on the wide, tiled steps, splashing each other and laughing ourselves silly.

"Did you learn the lesson in this?" Selph chuckled.

I wiped my eyes. "Yeah. Humans can't fly."

"I'm not sure I agree with that," Amber giggled, "you were doing a great job of flying."

"There was a lesson in it," Selph grinned.

"I daren't ask what it was."

"Simple enough," Selph chortled. "Never take yourself too seriously. Live with joy, have fun, play. Let the child out! Too many people take themselves so seriously. Relax. If you are on your spiritual path, loosen up. Lighten up, and you'll light up! Do you get it? You were coming on heavy about yourself. You don't need to."

I nodded, still giggling. "Yeah, you're right."

"Of course, I always am."

I laughed. "You always say that."

"Of course. I speak my truth."

"Some people would call that arrogant, or egotistical."

"Who cares what some people say? The people who make detrimental comments about others only echo their unrealized dislike of themselves."

"Yeah, I know. I used to do it all the time."

"People who speak well of others, praising them, do so because they like themselves. When your own light shines, you are able to see the light in other people."

"Of course," I grinned, "and my light is shining."

"It is, if you acknowledge that it is by living it," Selph said very seriously. "That's all it takes."

"Thanks for that spectacular lesson."

"No problem. Anytime at all," Selph chuckled.

❖　❖　❖

The new year came in baking hot, and for three weeks the temperatures steadily climbed higher, while the deaths in both human and farm-stock mounted. People were warned to stay out of the sun, and to avoid immersion in hot swimming pools, while the sales of fans, refrigerators, and air-conditioning units peaked into new records, until inevitably, the shops sold out. With the deaths of two tiny babies, an emergency was declared, and pensioners and families on low income who were unable to cool their homes were catered for in large village halls, equipped with factory-sized air conditioning. Even the deliciously cool shopping malls offered their help through the heat of the day, providing seating, and free food and cold drinks for the elderly and underprivileged.

The way the community rallied around to help each other was inspiring, soured only by the rash of house break-ins that also occurred. Bush fires became commonplace, with ten houses in one week being lost to the flames. And daily, it got worse. The landscape was dry and crisp, with even the normally green suburban areas becoming a fire hazard as the situation steadily deteriorated. A smoke haze developed over a vast area, adding respiratory problems to the harassed and besieged people. I bought a fire-fighting pump that could draw water from our swimming pool should the need arise, yet despite fires in the immediate neighborhood, not once did I feel that our place was under threat. I guess I bought it as a kind of common-sense insurance.

During this time my restlessness grew. I enjoy being active and engaged, but the heat denied all activity other than swimming in the sea, and fire-fighting. Amber was able to paint, and was in the enviable position of selling her work as fast as she could produce each painting. However, because each picture represented her love of wildlife, she was very fastidious, and they were never hurried.

Selph was with us some of the time, and abruptly missing the remainder. He seldom told us when he was going to depart, but he always seemed to turn up again at the most appropriate moment. It was as though he kept an eye on us!

Mum phoned often, and if the heat was bad for us on the coastal strip, it was far worse for those people who lived inland. Maybe it was just as well that they were better prepared than coastal people, for Mum told us that the temperature reached a staggering fifty degrees Celsius one fiendish afternoon. Cattle and sheep that were already in a semistarved condition died in the thousands daily, and the newspapers ran hot with headlines about the extraordinary heat wave that was ravaging Queensland in particular.

Oddly, or maybe not so, my physical injuries were the least painful I had known them. The little twinges seemed to dry up, and the aches all vanished. Heat was never a real bother for me, so while other people wilted from the sheer enervation of it, I was thriving. Thriving that is, so long as I did not spend time looking at our devastated garden. Because we, and many others, had to catch and store our rain water from the roof, we had little to spare. The swimming pool evaporated at an alarming rate, and I had to keep the fish pond topped up, plus the bonsai needed a daily drink. All the local water carriers were having a bonanza as they worked around the clock to keep up with the demand for water.

Late one evening, Amber and I were sitting poolside in the semicool. "Isn't it incredible how we take water for granted," Amber said, "until suddenly, it's a precious commodity. This heat and drought is a real education."

"It is for us urbanites, but the country people long ago learned to live with drought and a scarcity of water. I have to admit, this last few weeks has taught me to respect water in a way that previously, I had not. But it's a tough education for most people, and a killer for a few."

I was referring to a family who had recently been driving through a hot inland area in northern Queensland, when their car broke down. Despite the heat, the family had elected to walk along the road, hoping to either find the next township, or get picked up by a passing vehicle. Incredibly, they were carrying only two liters of water in a plastic bottle. The whole family of six, the parents and four robust teenagers, had died. Doctors estimated that they had lasted between five and eight hours in the sun and heat before dehydration began to kill them. Yet, by following the simple rules of survival that any Australian can learn, it need not have happened. The heat killed them, but as was pointed out, so also, did ignorance and foolishness.

Amber looked at me pensively. "Now that it's at least tolerably cool, how about we go inner journeying? I've got a sudden strong feeling that I need to."

Owing to the heat, I had missed the last two weeks, so I was keen. Amber was well versed in the technique, so I need not speak it. "Good idea. We'll each go on our own."

Thirty minutes later, I opened my eyes and looked at Amber. Like me, she had tear stains on her cheeks. Her eyes were still closed, but as I watched, she opened them. Taking a deep and careful breath, she sighed. "Oh, wow!"

"Oh wow, indeed," I echoed.

"You were in my experience for the first time."

I nodded. "Likewise."

"Did we share the same experience?" Amber asked.

"I rather think we did."

"You accompanied me on a journey, and you assisted me. Then something rather incredible happened."

"If what I understand is correct, you Awakened."

She nodded quietly. "We did share the experience."

"No. The experience was yours, I was only witness to some of it. I consider even that a privilege."

Amber looked at me levelly, her eyes on mine. "Be really honest, do you feel threatened by what happened to me?"

I thought about that carefully. I had just witnessed Amber go through an initiation into an Awakened state. This was what I have always wanted for me, would give my life for, but it had happened to Amber. Very definitely, the old me would have been threatened to the point of devastation. My ego would have been so overwhelmed, I would have felt totally demoralized. So what did I feel now? I definitely felt happy for Amber. More than happy, I felt thrilled for her.

Delighted. Overjoyed. But what did I feel for me? Dimly, I could feel regret, and maybe disappointment that it was not my moment, but mostly that was lost in my delight and pride in Amber. I also felt surprised. Surprised by what had happened to Amber, and surprised that I felt so good about myself, so unthreatened, so perfectly okay.

I shared my thoughts and inner speculation with her.

"So how about you? How do you feel? What's it like?"

She giggled. "First, I'm relieved about you, but not a bit surprised. Although this may sound silly, right now it's what I feel. I feel as though I have lived my whole life in a giant bottle of milk. Everything was light, and white, and ultrapositive. It was very nice, because it was all I knew. Now, suddenly, that bottle is filled with crystal-clear water. Everything is so clear, so distilled, so perfect, no longer white, or positive, or . . . labeled. Everything IS! I feel as though I am living in a vast unknown, yet *knowingly* knowing. All the rights and wrongs have ended, along with all the good and bad, and should and should nots."

She frowned thoughtfully. "It's as though I can see a view that is impossible to describe, yet I feel more human and more down to earth—while flying high—than I would have ever believed is possible. And, my darling, I love you more than you can yet realize."

I felt a sense of relief, and recognized a hidden fear.

"I guess if there was one thing within your experience that threatened me, it is that you would no longer love me in the same way."

She grinned. "In some ways, I don't love you in the same way. I can't; I'm not quite the same person. I've got a greater capacity for love and acceptance than ever I did. And with all of me, and all that I am, I love you."

The unsuspected knot of anxiety that uncoiled from my gut, was an indication of the way we hide our deepest fears. It uncoiled, and dissipated.

I smiled my relief. "I wouldn't like to think that Sir Knight was redundant," I joked.

Amber looked at me with arched eyebrows. "Redundant! You've got to be kidding."

Getting up, she came and sat in my lap, wriggling in a very provocative manner as she deliberately ran the tip of her tongue around her lips. "You can tell Sir Knight that I'm ready for some jousting, right now."

"How can you possibly feel like sex so soon after a deeply spiritual experience?"

"I feel like making love because in this moment that is exactly what I feel. Nothing to analyze, nothing to debate. Right now, I am who I am, and I want you inside me."

"Well, your experience was so profound for me just to be involved in, I'm in a mild state of shock. I don't think that Sir Knight can rise to the occasion yet."

"Oh, really?"

She wriggled some more, and I felt her hand suddenly take hold of Sir Knight in a knowing grip.

I was wrong. He could!

We made love poolside, and for the first time in my life, Sir Knight jousted in the shallow end of the swimming pool. Amber's passion was unparalleled, and intuitively, I knew that for her, this was a celebration of life, of the transcendent newness of her, and of the new life in her.

Later, when we lay in bed, exhausted, yet strangely energized, we talked about the inner journey that we had shared, albeit each in a very different way. I told her about my experience of it, and how very honored I felt.

"Do you feel like sharing your perspective?" I asked.

She nodded, and as she began talking, her voice was quiet, subdued, and tinged with wonder.

"I went through the rainbow of colors and down the twenty-one steps. When I left the last step, I found that I was on a wide road leading into a desert. At first I was a bit dubious about it, not wanting to follow this road into such a bleak terrain, but I decided to go along with it. The road in itself was unusual. It was as though some vast Being had unrolled a spool of purple ribbon across a bare, bleak landscape, and that ribbon was the road I had to follow.

"I followed it for what seemed a very long time, and I was alone. Although it was desert, I felt no heat, for the land was simply cool and bare, rather than all sand. I kept going, having made the decision that if nothing happened at all then that was fine, I would simply follow the road.

"Then, quite suddenly, I came to an oasis, and you were there. I might have known you would be somewhere near water. We talked, and I asked you how you got to the oasis, and you told me that the oasis was there, waiting for you, when you stepped off the last step."

I nodded to her. "Yes, that's true. It was."

She continued. "I pointed to the road that continued past the oasis, and asked you if you would come with me. You said you would, so together, we set off. I remember you looking back longingly at the oasis, with its abundance of trees and water, and then looking at the bare land we were heading into, but you didn't complain.

"Again, we walked for a long time, and I kept expecting that you would want to turn back to the oasis, but you just kept on walking.

"'Do you want to go back? I'll come with you,' I said.

"'I do, but I'm going to stay with you,' you replied. 'I realize that this is your road, not mine, but you need me to walk with you. You mustn't turn back.'

"'How do you know all this?' I asked.

"'Darned if I know. I just do,' you replied.

"So we kept on walking. It felt by now that I had been walking for at least half a day and I wanted to give up, but because you had made a commitment to stay with me, I knew that I was committed to following the road.

"Eventually I noticed that the endless flat horizon was no longer so distant, and that we were now walking uphill. Unlike a physical reality, it took no extra effort at all, even when the hill became very steep. It was easy. Quite soon we came to the top of the hill, and there before us was a tiny valley. We continued into the valley until we came to a huge castle with turrets and towers, but it looked as though it came out of the future, rather than the past. The whole surface was like translucent rippling water, yet when we walked up to it, and I touched it, it was as solid as rock. Was that how you saw it?"

I nodded. "Just about exactly. Strange and beautiful."

"Did it feel familiar, or did you recognize it?"

"No."

Amber continued. "Well, for me it was as though I had come home after a million years away. I nearly wept, the recognition was so powerful, yet I had no awareness of ever having seen it before. I could even feel the tears running down my cheek as I physically sat in the chair. Anyway, I knew that I had to go into the castle. I asked you if you had seen a door, or entrance, and you said you had not. Then you told me that I had to find it. You said that if I could not find the way in, then I could not enter, and I would miss the timing.

"Once again, I asked you how you knew this, but you said it simply came to you. That's why you were with me.

"Together, we walked around the whole of the castle, but there was not the remotest sign of any door, or entrance. I felt annoyed. 'How can I possibly get in without a door?'

"'Divine one,' you replied.

"I looked at you in astonishment. 'How do I do that?'

"'That's the test,' you replied. 'You are now ready to enter, but you have to divine your own way in. I cannot do it for you, nor do I know how. I can only be with you.'

"I sat down on the purple ribbon road that went right around the castle, and thought about how to get in. Nothing! I couldn't think of any way at all. Then I suggested that you wait where we were, and I would walk around on my own. I might see something that I had missed. I walked around the castle in the opposite direction to the first time, but it was just as barren of any way in. I felt annoyed."

"This is quite amazing," I said to Amber. "Everything that you have described is as it happened for me. I remember waiting while you walked around."

Amber grinned. "That's when I knew that I really had to get with it, or miss out. When I got back, you were still there, and then you gave me the vital clue. Quite honestly, I wouldn't have made it, without you."

I felt exorbitantly pleased.

"You told me that instead of seeking the entrance to the castle in its own walls, to look for the entrance within myself. So I did. I sat down, closed my eyes, and letting go of any need to enter, I visualized the castle in all its glory. Never, in any physical reality, have I been able to visualize as easily and powerfully as in that moment. It literally burst into my mind with such intense and stunning clarity that I saw the castle within the castle.

"I saw that you and I were sitting outside a castle that was a thin hollow echo of the real castle. And I knew that as it is with the castle, so it is with us. We each see ourselves as puny, limited, and mortal, whereas in truth, we are unbelievably powerful, limited only by our personal reality, and eternally immortal.

"Anyway, as I looked at the castle in my inner vision, I saw the entrance very clearly, and I knew exactly where it was, and how to enter. I opened my eyes, and the castle was just as before, seemingly impregnable. Accompanied by you, I walked around the castle a short distance until I reached the place where I knew the entrance was located. I asked you if you could see it, and you said, 'Sadly, no. But it's time for you to enter. You go now. My turn will come.'

"Although I also couldn't see the entrance, I knew that it was there, so facing the castle, I walked straight into the wall where I knew it was located. Just as I was about to collide with the wall, everything changed. I realize now that my commitment was the key. Once I had committed myself to actually walking straight into the wall, and I followed it through, it was as though I hit a switch.

"Suddenly, I was walking up a huge flight of white marble stairs of the grand and massive entrance to this incredible mystic castle. As I reached the top step, a Being of Light came toward me, and reaching out, took my hand. Close up, it was a human figure, but so illumined by light I really couldn't see any features. I was aware, however, simply by its energy that the Being, or person, was asexual, rather than male or female.

"Holding my hand, the Being accompanied me into the castle, where we walked toward a shaft of Light in the exact center of a immense room. As though coming from some celestial place on high, this Light shone through a huge crystal set in the pinnacle of the roof far above my head, pouring as a beam of intense, pure Light into the castle. As we reached the Light, I unhesitatingly stepped into it . . . and exploded.

"Nothing else can describe it. I exploded into all the Light that ever was or will be. I was all Light as countless infinite particles of Light; I was all Light as One Light. I knew that all was the same, yet different; the one and the many, simultaneously together, yet experiencing apartness."

She smiled at me dreamily. "That's it, really. I seemed to be in that state for endless infinite hours, yet when I opened my eyes; only a half hour had elapsed. Even now, I'm filled to overflowing with the experience because it's not in the past and it never will, or can be. It's happening now, this moment. Truly, it *is* All That Is."

I stared at her, almost overwhelmed by awe. "Good-bye, Amber. Hello, Supergirl," I murmured.

She sat up, and gazed at me. "Please, Adam, don't do this. You gave me the greatest gift any person can possibly give to another; you showed me how to reach my Truth. You did this because of your stature as a human being. And you know it's true, because you experienced it."

I nodded. Her experience and mine dovetailed perfectly. When she had entered the castle, she passed from my sight, and I was instantly back at the oasis. Now, abruptly, I knew with a clear certainty that the oasis was a representation of abundance, and that in my abundance I had given Amber my gift of love. There was nothing that I could or would change, not one tiny detail.

"I'm sorry I was churlish. There are no words to describe how overcome with joy I am, for you. I feel honored beyond measure that I was able to be involved."

"I wonder if Selph knows about this," Amber said.

"Don't you *know?*"

"Adam, I'm not all knowing in the terms of everyday life, or knowing the future, or things like that. I'm certainly not another Selph. I simply know who I am, and the Truth of what this means. But I don't know when the drought will end, or the heat wave, or what you will be doing tomorrow. I'm the Amber you know, except I no longer perceive myself as simply an identity. My persona is the garment that 'who I am' is wearing in this reality frame for this lifetime."

"And who are you?" I asked, knowing better.

"You know that there's no real answer to such a question, only the experience. Oh, I could speak words, but that's all they would be, meaningless, empty words. I'll tell you the only ones that have meaning, the only ones that matter. Adam, my darling, I love you."

We kissed and, cuddled in each others arms, we went to sleep. Or, should I say, perhaps, I remained asleep!

# Twenty-Two

When I woke up early next morning, Amber was asleep. For a while I lay thinking about the extraordinary event of last night. With the insight of hindsight, I realized that Amber had deliberately made love to me after her Awakening because it joined us in an act of common equality in a way that nothing else could have done. I also knew that it was a demonstration of her truth; that she does indeed love me, and not for a moment did she fake her lovemaking. Her lovemaking was the gift of normality to me; a statement that everything between us is based on the love of two people, each for the other. I also realized that although everything is the same between us, it is also utterly different. Right now, I had to focus on the sameness; the difference would present itself often enough. What an inconceivable inner journey it had turned out to be. Both of us had been under a remarkable influence. I had no doubt that it was her teacher; a Being still very active in Amber's life, even if not physically available or easily identifiable. But equally, everyone has their own guides and helpers on other planes of reality. Sadly, it is only the few who are aware of this, or even open to such a possibility. Unfortunately, we have each become our own worst enemy, locked in our little world of fears while denying any chance of a greater reality. I certainly had been, now I was enjoying being my own trusted friend, and stepping out into a finer and more friendly world.

Amber sighed, then rolled toward me, her arms sneaking out in her familiar way to hold me close. She loved physical contact, as did I. Even in this heat, Amber still wanted to be entwined in bed, but it made me too hot. With a flick of one arm, I tossed the bedsheet away, and we lay nude in the cool morning air.

"Did you sleep well, my darling?" she asked.

"Very well, thanks to the overhead fan." I watched it as it slowly rotated, stirring the cool air.

"And Sir Knight? Did he dream?"

I chuckled. Her humor was clearly unchanged. "No, he didn't dream at all. He slept the sleep of satiety."

She giggled. "So what's on the agenda for today?"

"I don't know. I'm not sure what it means, but after a few painfree weeks, I'm aware of more pain in my body this morning than I've felt in months. I ache badly, with sharp twinges all over."

"Perhaps it was the jousting in the pool last night."

I grimaced as I remembered. "Yeah. In the throes of passion I overlooked just how hard tiled steps really are. I know I collected a bruise or two, and you certainly should have. We should have gone into deeper water."

Amber giggled some more. "I was crafty. I kept you on the underneath most of the time. How cruel of me."

"Yeah, there's no doubt about that. But seriously, joking aside, the pain I'm feeling now was all too familiar a few months ago. And I'm not sure why it's come back."

Easing away from Amber, I groaned my way out of bed. Walking to the shower, I turned it on as hot as I could bear, despite really wanting a cool shower.

Amber joined me as I stepped in, but got no further than one wet foot. "Adam! That's really hot."

"I know. I'm hoping it will ease out my aches and pains. It always used to help."

But this time it did not. I was almost, not quite, alarmed by the persistence of the stabbing aches and pains. Although well used to pain, I had not felt anything like this for quite a long time.

Shuffling my way around the house, I tried in vain to get my flexibility going. When Amber laid out breakfast, I carefully sat down.

"I feel like an old man. Any ideas?"

"How about a massage? It might help."

"Good thinking. That may well do the trick."

An hour later I lay groaning as Amber really applied the pressure on my limbs and joints. She concentrated on where the bone breaks had occurred, but gave my whole body a good work-over. It definitely helped, but did not fix the problem. It did, however, ease out the kinks from the late-night session on the steps of the swimming pool.

Fifteen minutes later, as I walked carefully over to the coffee jug, the phone rang. Amber was outside somewhere, so I answered it.

"Good morning. This is Adam."

"I'm glad it's a good morning for you, Adam. It's already unbelievably bloody hot here."

"Dad! It's great to hear you. Actually, the morning's good, still cool from the sea breeze last night. But I'm not so good. I ache and twinge badly. I can't understand it."

I heard him chuckle. "No mystery to that. You've got the same problem as old Ken Parkes, next door. He fell off his horse about forty years ago, and got broke up real bad. Ever since then he aches and hurts every time the weather goes foul on us. As a matter of fact, that's why I'm phoning you. I was talking to him a couple of days ago, and he said that he's aching something terrible for the first time in three and a half years. He reckons that we're going to get the mother of all storms within the next few weeks."

A surge of pure relief swept over me. What he said made so much sense. Without a doubt, that was also my problem. Even though I was doomed to be a living barometer, it was nothing more than a change in the weather. And a massage couldn't change the weather!

"By cripes, Dad. You're right. I just know it. So you rang me to tell me about the possible storms?"

"No. I want you to come here as soon as you can, or sooner. If we've got rain coming, you can guarantee it will be with massive flooding. So I want to catch all the water that I can, and more! As my new consultant, I want you to show me all the places I can possibly put water holes and dams on the farm. This is too good an opportunity to miss."

"But suppose Ken is wrong."

"He won't be wrong; I've got a gut feeling about this. You mark my words, we're going to end this drought with some of the worst storms most of us will have ever seen. And, by God, I'm sure as hell going to be prepared."

"If we get floodwater, it'll wash away any dam walls that are not consolidated. Water holes will be okay, but we will need huge spillways for the dams, set considerably lower than usual. Better to miss catching a few feet of water than lose the lot, plus losing the dam. New dams will take a lot of careful preparation."

"You've got the idea, son. So, when are you coming? Could you make it yesterday?"

I laughed. "I'll ring you back later today, but you have my word that it'll be as soon as possible. Amber wants to come this time, so I need to discuss it with her. Don't worry, I'll ring back."

We chatted a few more minutes, then hung up. I, too, had the feeling that Ken would be right. I ached to the same tune! Pouring a mug of coffee, I went looking for Amber.

I found her in her studio, where she was in the latter stages of her latest painting, and I told her about my conversation with Dad.

"Does the new Amber have any feelings about this?" I asked playfully.

She, however, was very serious. "Yes, I do. I get an immediate knowing that we should go very soon, and an awful premonition that something terrible will happen."

My playfulness evaporated like mist in the heat. "Oh God! Not me again?"

She shook her head. "I don't know. I only know what I said. We have to go, that's certain. It can't be avoided."

"What can't be avoided?"

"Adam, I don't know. I just know that you, everyone, must be as careful as possible. What is inevitable will surely take place, but we must take care."

"Have you seen Selph?"

She shook her head. "Not recently."

I frowned. "I need him. He should be here." Jokingly I bellowed as loud as I could. "SEEEEELLLLPPHH."

The door to the studio opened, and he walked in.

"No need to shout. I heard you first time." He paused, stared at Amber, and his eyes opened wider. "Well, well. So it's happened at last. Congratulations. It's people like you two who make this teacher business so worthwhile."

Walking over to Amber, he embraced her, then, stepping back, he bowed low. As he straightened up, he was once again that ancient personage of unspeakable wisdom I had seen when I had returned from being Jacob.

Looking at Amber, he spoke. "I honor you."

He bowed again, and as he straightened, he was once more the regular Selph that we know.

"What did you mean, I heard you first time?" I asked.

Selph grinned. "You said, 'I need him. He should be here.' So I came at once. I was here before you screamed."

"I didn't scream," I said huffily. "I called, loudly."

He nodded, smiling. "Very loudly."

"How did you know what had happened to Amber, and how come you didn't know earlier?"

340

His smile became icy, mixed with a frown. "You want it both ways, and I don't owe you any explanation. Who are you to question me in a demanding manner, as though I owe you an explanation?"

I felt stupid. "You're right, and I apologize. I'm a bit overwhelmed by the sudden speed of events, beginning with Amber's Awakening last night."

I then told him about my talk with Dad, and Amber's premonition of danger. I was confused by it all.

He nodded. "Fair enough. I'll answer your question, even though it's irrelevant to all that's happening. When I am elsewhere, my focus there is nearly absolute. I keep only a thread—as it were—oriented on you. Amber's experience was not yours, so it escaped my attention. However, on arriving here, I knew immediately by her aura that she had Awakened. That is unmistakable."

"Thank you," I said contritely. "May I ask if you can throw any insight on Amber's premonition, and if it involves me in any way."

He looked at me blandly. "As long as you're being so painfully polite, the honest answer is: 'no comment.'"

"Thank you. I take that to mean, 'Yes, Buster, you're involved right up to your neck, but believe me, you wouldn't really want to know about it.'"

Selph chuckled. "Frankly, you're right. Do you feel better now?"

"No. I wish I had kept my thoughts to myself."

"Ah well, you would push. However, the lesson of the moment is very clear, but what is that lesson, Adam?"

"Live now, and focus in the moment. It just ain't easy," I grinned.

"You got the lesson right, but remember, you speak your truth. If you keep saying that it isn't easy, then it won't be. Try saying: Easy stuff, no problem at all. That will work for you, rather than against you."

I nodded. "Point taken. Thanks."

There and then I decided to dismiss the premonition. I could think about it until I was silly, and still not find any resolution, so the best thing was to forget it. I would be careful in the weeks ahead, but I was determined that it would be sensible care and precaution, not fear based.

Meanwhile, Selph had asked Amber about her experience, and she was filling him in. When she finished, he looked at her with great fondness and delight.

He swished his hand past her face. "I told you that you were that close," he chuckled, "but what a wonderful way to take that last great step." He chuckled again. "Not that it's the *last* step," he amended. "I'm not sure that we ever quite reach that." He shook his head admiringly. "Do you know, in consciousness, every human soul took a quantum leap with you. Not intellectually, nor do they know a thing about it, but in consciousness, all life is irrevocably, One."

Amber nodded. "I know. Isn't it wonderful?"

Selph turned to me. "So Mister Consultant, I take it that you'll be needing your assistant again?"

"Yes, if you don't mind."

I told them about Dad's sense of urgency, and his need to get the water holes and catchment areas in place.

"How about we go the day after tomorrow?" Amber said.

Selph and I agreed. When I suggested that we include a visit to Joe and Joyce and a short list of clients, Amber and Selph nodded their agreement.

While Amber turned back to her painting, determined to bring it to its conclusion, I returned to the house to make a few phone calls.

I began with Joe and Joyce, but there was no reply. I tried Billy Teams. Ivy, his wife, answered.

"Hello Ivy, Adam here."

"Is it hot enough for you, Adam?"

I chuckled. That remark had become so commonplace in the last few weeks that it was now a form of greeting.

"Not as hot as where you are, I bet."

"What do you think that crazy man of mine is up to now?"

"I can't even imagine."

"He's out there on the tractor, working like a maniac, digging out the water holes, and making the dams stronger. He swears that it's going to rain like crazy in a short time. As a matter of fact, he planned to phone you about it this evening. Would you believe that?"

I shook my head in admiration. "You've got a smart man, Ivy. My Dad agrees with him, and so do I. As a matter of fact, that's what I was phoning about. But he got there ahead of me. I tell you, Billy is as smart and shrewd as they come."

"Don't let him hear you say that," she laughed. "Only this morning I took him outside and asked him to show me a single cloud, or any sign of impending rain. You know what he did? He pointed to his gut. 'Listen gal,' he said, 'it's raining in my gut, so I gotta be right.'"

"A gut feeling," I chuckled.

Ivy laughed. "He is a shrewd old bugger, I'll give him that. When I told him that his neighbors wouldn't agree with his prediction, he laughed like crazy. 'That's the clincher,' he said. 'It's just gotta rain now.'"

Still chuckling, I hung up, then I phoned several other of my clients whom I knew would take my warning seriously. After thanking me with varying degrees of belief and relief, they each told me that they had their water-catchment areas ready and waiting, just as they had been for the last three empty and desolate years.

For the remainder of the day, I browsed over my notes and data on my client's farms, and within my imagination, I reflected on all the catchment areas I had long ago decided on in relation to Dad's farm. Time seemed to fly, lunch a fleeting minor distraction, and I was still lost in happy speculation and drawing up detailed plans based on aerial photographs of Dad's farm, when, many hours later, Selph called me for dinner.

I gazed at the time wonderingly. "My gosh! I can hardly believe that it's seven o'clock. Oh my God! I forgot to phone Joe again."

"Eat first," Amber said. "Then you can phone."

For a while we ate in silence, each busy in our own thoughts; or at least, I was! I wasn't sure if Selph did indulge in idle speculation; I knew he did not worry. And as for Amber, now? She looked serene and untroubled.

"Don't let it bother you if you don't see much of me tomorrow," Selph said. "I have other arrangements to make."

I glanced at him. "Six o'clock next morning, sharp."

"Sure, boss, sir," he grinned, "but there's just one little detail. I'll meet you at the entrance to the farm."

I gaped at him. "Huh! How the hell are you going to get there? Anyway, I can't tell you the precise time that we will arrive."

He gave me a look of exasperation. "Adam. I can be anywhere and anywhen I want to be, at any time I want to be there. And I can guarantee to arrive exactly thirty seconds ahead of you."

I looked at Amber. "Can you do this sort of thing?"

"Sorry," she said regretfully, "I only wish. I now have inner peace, and a joy that is beyond understanding, but I still need to travel by conventional means. I told you, I know who I am, but I'm still a normal, regular person."

"Far from normal by today's references," Selph chided, "but still a regular person by physical terms."

"Personally, I'm glad you are the way you are. It would seem daft to accompany me in the car if you could be there instantly. I'd feel that I was being patronized," I said.

"So everybody's happy," Selph chuckled.

I did not answer that, mainly because I was not fully happy. Amber's premonition hung as a threat in the distant background of my mind, and although I ignored it, it would not go away. I had an awful feeling that something big and nasty was looming, and that I would be the fall guy.

After dinner, Amber went to put the finishing touches to her painting, while Selph, with a "Cheer up, Adam," walked out of the room, and vanished. I washed the dishes, finished my plans for the water catchment, and after phoning Dad to tell him when we would be arriving, and what to get ready, I phoned Joe and Joyce.

"Hello, Adam dear," Joyce answered, "is it hot enough for you? It's been a hot 'un here today."

After a brief and cheery chat, she put Joe on, and I told him about Dad's feelings on the likelihood of flooding, and that I agreed with it.

"Thanks Adam, thanks a lot. I 'ave to admit, I can't feel any change at all, or see any of the usual signs, but if you and your Dad do, that's good enough for me. I'll be out first thing tomorrow reinforcing and repairing anything that can hold water that needs it, but it's all pretty much done. I hope you'll both call in on us, and stay the night."

"Amber will be with us this time."

"Great! Joyce will be delighted. The more the merrier. When can we expect you?"

"Within a week, or so, but I'll phone you from Dad's as soon as I know for sure."

We chatted on for a few more minutes, and hung up.

I relaxed, and watched a late-night wildlife documentary on TV. Amber came in just after midnight.

"You shouldn't have waited up for me," she reprimanded.

I smiled sleepily. "I can't sleep properly without you in the bed; besides, I don't mind. Your work is just as important to you and us, as mine is."

She smiled. "Well, it's finished darling, and already sold. Cyril Perkins has been waiting about a month, and he wants to call in for it tomorrow."

We went to bed, and I was quickly asleep, undisturbed for three hours. Then the dream came, shattering my peace.

"NOOOOOOoooooooooo," I screamed as I woke, jerking upright with such force that I almost fell out of the bed, before collapsing back with a groan.

Slowly, I realized that Amber was already awake, as though expecting this to happen. Her arms went around me, and a glass of cold water waited on the bedside table.

"It's all okay. Drink this, my darling. It's just a bad dream."

She soothed me as though I were a child, and, still held in the memory of fear and helplessness, I needed every bit of her reassurance and tenderness. I was drenched in sweat, yet Amber had anticipated that, and gently sponged me down with a cool, squeezed-out, wet towel.

"It was the axman dream, wasn't it?" she said softly.

I nodded mutely, trembling from reaction.

"It would do you good to talk about it."

Such was my reaction that for long moments I thought I was going to vomit, then it gradually subsided. I nodded.

"I will when I can," I whispered shakily.

She held me close, her swelling belly pressed up close to my body, and for the first time, I felt the strong kick of our baby. The effect was a light bursting into my darkness, and despite everything, I smiled.

"I just got kicked," I murmured wonderingly.

"I felt it too. That was the strongest movement yet, and we shared it."

"A gesture of sympathy, perhaps?"

"Of empathy, my darling," Amber said seriously.

Insight suddenly bloomed. "In your Awakened state, you know the sex of our baby, don't you."

She hesitated, then nodded. "Yes."

"So . . . what is it?"

"Adam, do you really want to know?"

And just like that, I knew I did not. By choice, I wanted the mystery of the birth to remain. For me, the moment of birth held the thrill of only then knowing the sex of the child, and I did not want to lose that. It was the same with Christmas and birthday presents; for me, the real pleasure was in the element of surprise. And the baby was not yet due to be unwrapped!

"No, I don't. Please don't tell me."

She chuckled. "I know you Adam. You would have had to drag it out of me before I would tell you. So, now that you are feeling better, tell me about the dream."

She was right. Since the baby had kicked me, my fear had dispersed with such rapidity that I was now a little bit embarrassed by the intensity of my earlier reaction.

"How did you know about my dream? You were ready to comfort me the moment I woke up, whereas last time I managed to frighten you as well." I grinned. "Perhaps you awoke ahead of me because you're already Awake," I joked.

She shrugged. "Right first time."

My eyebrows shot up. "I thought I was joking!"

"Adam, tell me about the dream."

"You're sure you don't already know?"

A frown crossed her face. "I wouldn't ask if I did."

"Well, it was more of the usual, but it was much more real, more graphic, and far more frightening. I was laying on a huge slab, and once again I knew that I had placed myself there. No one else did it to me. The axman and the ax were larger, if possible, and everything that happened was in slow motion. That made it far more scary. My legs were cut off, then my arms, and my helplessness was simply appalling. I was now completely at the mercy of the axman. When the ax slowly lifted to cut my body in half, I opened my mouth to scream, but somehow swallowed it. Then the blade flashed down and I felt the same painless cut as before, and my lower torso rolled away from the rest of my body. No blood, and no pain, but a ton of horror.

"When my torso stopped rolling, my head and upper chest was all that remained on the block, and I was staring directly up at the axman. I watched the ax slowly, so slowly raised for the last time, and I sweated my fear. Then it poised above me, and I knew that with this cut, I would cease to exist. I knew that so very clearly, and from some deep place in my consciousness, I knew that this had to happen. Then the ax began to slowly descend, and I kept my jaws clenched to keep from screaming. But at the last moment, just as the ax severed my head, it all came bursting out . . . and I woke up shrieking."

"You poor darling."

"What does it mean, Amber?"

"Did the ax actually remove your head?"

"Yes. I can remember one split instant as my vision of the axman spun sideways, and I knew it was my head rolling away from the torso, then the scream was out."

"It means that on the deepest subconscious level, you are finally ready to surrender. On a certain level of consciousness, it has already happened.

Although it might not feel like it to you, subconsciously you are ready for the final act. You are ready to know your fear."

"Final act! I don't like the sound of that. What does it mean?"

"It means that your surrender has still to reach your conscious awareness and be acted upon."

"And know your fear? What does that mean?"

"Adam, my darling, although there is an answer, I can't answer it. I know the words, but this is not the time to speak them."

"There won't be such a time, will there?" I asked with shrewd insight.

"Not from me. But you will know in the only way that has any real meaning, by the experiencing."

"And that brings us back to your premonition and all its scary implications."

"You know what Selph would say: It's your reality, Adam, and your creation. What more can I say?"

I nodded grimly. "Yeah, you're right. If I can't handle it, I should never have started it. And even if I had a chance, I would never back out, so that's it. Time now to stop taking myself so damn seriously."

Amber held my face in her cupped hands, and kissed me on the lips. Her green eyes held my blue ones, her expression serious, yet hauntingly beautiful. "My darling, you are not alone, nor will you ever be."

I met her gaze. "When the chips are down, and the dreaded moment really hits, I'll be alone. That's the way it is. It always has been."

Her eyes were very sure. "No. That's not the way it is, that's the way it *appears* to be. And the way it appears, is definitely not the way it is. Trust me."

"I do."

"But more than that, trust yourself. That's where it's really at."

"Do I have any choice?"

"You will have soon," she said enigmatically.

The new difference between us was definitely showing!

❖   ❖   ❖

The next day we each finalized our preparations. I made arrangements for Jack, our neighbor, to come in and water the bonsai while we were away, and keep the swimming pool filled and maintained, and to keep an eye on the house, and Cyril Perkins came to collect his painting from Amber. Of Selph, there was no sign.

We went to bed early that night, and despite my aches and twinges, we made love with enormous passion and energy, to finally fall asleep exhausted.

At six o'clock next morning, as we drove away from the house, the feeling in my gut was quite indescribable. Fear dominated, but a fear that was mixed and mingled with dread, anticipation, and a certain thrill. I felt much the same as I imagine a person would feel as they gazed out of an airplane at three-and-a-half thousand meters, and with their preparations finished, the countdown has just begun on their first-ever parachute jump.

I drove for the first two hours, and we chatted about trivial things while watching the early-morning wildlife. We had changed drivers, and Amber was at the wheel when we passed over the bridge at Donkey Creek. I asked her to stop, and although I had crossed it at Christmas when we went to stay at Mum's, I had very definitely not wanted to stop. Now, I was consumed by a sudden need to get out and look down at the place I had crashed all those months ago.

I had never replaced my wrecked green Nissan, and we had been using Amber's fawn-colored Mitsubishi Magna ever since. It was a larger, more powerful car, and more suitable for us. As I stepped from its air-conditioned comfort, the heat hit me as a hot blast. Accompanied by Amber, I walked to the middle of the bridge, noticing the new woodwork replacing the old where I had smashed through the side.

Looking down to the dried creek bed, I marveled that I had survived. Although they had winched the mangled car out of the creek, tiny pieces of shattered windscreen glinted and glittered in the sun, while the odd small bit of twisted bodywork lay forlorn and forgotten.

I stared in morbid fascination, trying to recapture the horror of the fall, the abrupt and shocking smash. But nothing came. Although I could relate to the smash, I had no recollection of landing in the rocky bed of the creek. I remembered the stunning impact of the truck, and the moment of breathless horror as I smashed through the railings of the bridge, but after that it was a merciful blank.

"Adam Baker died down there," I said.

Amber looked at me, smiled, and shook her head. "No. Adam Baker began the process of his dying, down there."

I blanched as I listened to her words. The difference between us was there again, and I knew that it would continue to occur over and over. She lived in a place of almost incomprehensible knowing and insight, a place that eluded me. She had found her Truth, while I still lived in the dream of my own making; a dream supported by the power and vastness of a consensus reality. And yet, in a twisted paradox, it was I who stood alone, while she, a person alone in the millions, connected with All That Is.

"You're right. The death has yet to happen."

She hugged me. "Trust yourself, Adam. Just trust."

"You could tell me so much, couldn't you?"

She looked at me, smiled wistfully, and said nothing. And by saying nothing, her lack of words spoke volumes. I gazed at her, beautiful as a fresh rose in her loose, pale-lemon dress, and marveled at the deception. She looked like a superfit, pregnant model, nothing more, yet she was a person among millions, rare beyond belief. She was an enlightened person, Awake, Self Realized, yet she looked as ordinary as any beautiful woman can look. She was a head-turner all right, but how many people would ever know the greater picture?

I thought of the irony of it all. Neither she nor I would say a thing about this to Mum and Dad, or Joe and Joyce, or to any of our friends at all. How could we? What would we even say? How many people even have a reference to what enlightenment is? How many people would ever accept that even while awake, they are asleep, dreaming a dream they call everyday life, and that there is something beyond that called Awake, or Enlightenment. Probably Jane and Pete would realize that something of great magnitude had happened to Amber, but they would never truly know, not even if I told them. Did I know? I knew that Amber was incredibly changed, but did I have the faintest idea of what that change was? I only knew what it represented. To know it, I, or any other person, would have to become it—be it.

Sighing, I released my useless speculation, and gazed blankly into the creek. Finally, realizing that I felt comfortable with the place of my devastating smash, and that my memories held no trauma, we got into the car and continued our journey. The air-conditioned rush of cold was more than welcome.

When we finally reached the entrance to the farm, Selph was there, looking as cool and nonchalant as ever.

We pulled up, and he hopped in.

"Have you been waiting long?" I asked.

He smiled cheerfully. "Exactly thirty seconds."

We all laughed, and continued along the drive across the land, toward the house. As we passed Mum's bed of roses, I gaped at them in shock. They had been looking sick and miserable at Christmas, but now there was not a single flower or leaf among them.

Mum must have seen us coming, for she was out the door and talking even before the car came to a stop. We hugged and kissed her, and I asked her where Dad was.

"He's out on the tractor somewhere, dear. He'll be back soon. Isn't it wonderful, he can't wait to see you."

"What's happened to your roses, Mum?"

She looked across at them, her face pinched and tired, and I could see the relentless heat was taking its toll.

"They looked so sick and stressed that it hurt me. I had no water to give them, so I decided to take action. I cut off every flower, bud, and leaf, and told them to go back to sleep, like it was winter. I've tried to induce a winter reaction in them. It was a gamble, I know, but I had to do something."

I looked at her in amazement. "That's brilliant, Mum. That's the smartest thing I've ever heard. And I bet you anything that it will work. But make sure to prune them when the rain comes. That will stimulate new growth."

The rose bed was deeply mulched in shredded newspaper, ruined hay that was useless for the cattle, and garden debris; a mulch that should be able to collect and hold a lot of rain without losing the soil in a heavy downpour.

When Dad came in about an hour later, I quickly learned just how prepared he was to transform his land. He had hired two medium-sized dozers, and a very large one, plus their drivers. They were here for as long as it took. After the inevitable cup of tea, he, Selph, and I went off in his Land Rover to assess the land situation, leaving Amber and Mum chatting contentedly.

Clinging to my maps, we visited one site after another, but it was my memory that turned out to be most accurate. Some of the sites that the aerial maps indicated as possible, turned out to be unsuitable, but overall, as I knew it would, the potential for water conservation was simply enormous.

The next week passed in a wonderfully happy blur of overactivity as I watched my long-held dream come true. In one area we created a catchment that would hold around five hectares of water in a super lagoon, with an average depth of three meters. Mostly, it was ready-made, as though a benign and friendly God had already set it up, and all we had to do was have the vision to turn it into a reality. I had a ball! Dad had already made an agreement with Des, Harry, and Len, the dozer drivers, that he would accommodate them, paying overtime and extras if they would put in the hours that he wanted. They were agreeable and willing. Working up to fifteen hours a day, they seemed to stop only for a fast refueling and a quick bite of food, the machines roaring up and down as they reshaped the landscape in our chosen areas. It also helped enormously that Mum cooked them a late evening meal of huge steaks, potatoes, and gravy, followed by almost unlimited cold apple pie and ice cream. Every morning at five o'clock she also had a huge breakfast of bacon and eggs, tomato and mushroom, toast and marmalade, and endless coffee, all ready and waiting for them. Having heard Dad's theory of impending rain, the three men readily got into their work, and they really excelled themselves.

I had considered it impossible to finish all the dozer work in the allotted week, but I was wrong. Dad had even hired two earth-compaction machines, and from the moment the first earth-walled dam was constructed, he and Rick, another casual man he often employed, were towing these blunt-spiked, vibrating monsters behind Dad's largest tractors, endlessly back and forth, and where possible, up and down the fresh earth on the dam walls. In his typical, methodical way, Dad left nothing to chance.

I was the designer and overall director of operations, while Selph was the person who did all the endless legwork, chasing from one place to another to keep everything smoothly coordinated in a way that did not waste either dozer power or precious time. I was quite sure that Selph made a few miraculous moves, because at one time I could see him at least a kilometer away, yet when I waved, indicating I needed him quickly, he was with me about a minute later. I also knew that nobody would ever witness such a move unless he allowed it, and there was no chance of that.

I had feared that, with all the men and dozers, we would get bogged down into a melee of confusion, but it all went as smoothly as a dream. A good dream, that is! Overall, we put in about thirty smaller water holes, all placed in such a way that we were able to connect more than half of them with a wandering watercourse. We did all this with the unavoidable loss of only three trees, but we paved the way to plant up to a thousand more when the season again became favorable.

When the earth walls that would get water pressure against them were fully compacted, I experimented by stopping the vibration motor, getting Dad to tow one of the spiked monsters across his land. Despite the fact that the land was almost iron hard, under its very heavy, water-filled weight, the spikes forced their way about a hand's depth into the ground. It was just what I wanted.

I showed the effect to Dad. "Normally I wouldn't dream of doing this to the land during a drought, but if the rain really is coming, then it's time to break the rules."

Dad looked bewildered. "I don't get it. You'll just make the soil more compact, and God knows, it's hard enough already. What's the purpose?"

I showed him the series of deep indentations in the soil. "Every spiked hole will hold water, plus over a period of time, it will deepen your topsoil. I can explain all that later, but for now, trust me. I don't want any of the rain to run off your land. We've located the water holes and lagoon so that, following the natural contours of the land, all water flow will now be directed, caught, and retained. But I want the pasture to retain all the water it can. We only want to catch the surplus. We really want the water all over the land; that's the first, and most important, area of catchment there is: the farm as a whole."

I pointed down to the spiked holes. "And that's how we will do it. I'll teach you about the refinements of all this later, right now we're assuming that we're racing the weather and therefore, the clock. So, get going. Leave all the rocky and stony places, and get as much of the farm spiked as you possibly can."

Dad stared at me, an expression of undeniable admiration and respect on his face. "Christ, son! How come I never saw any of this in you before? Was I so blind?"

Impulsively, I hugged him. "We both were, Dad. We both only saw what we wanted to see. Now, get going."

Very soon there were two tractors and the spiked soil compactors steadily working their way across the parched pasture. I knew that with the vibration motors switched off, they would not add to the compaction of the land. Nor must they, for subsoil compaction is one of the major problems of graziers the world over.

By the end of a week of prolonged and furious activity, the project was basically finished. There were still things for a small dozer to play with, and a fair bit of leveling and smoothing with a tractor and grader blade, but the heavy work and the main bulk of it all, was done. If, or when it rained now, the story on Dad's land would change dramatically. He kept at the spiking with the two tractors, until all that could be spiked was finished. A lot of land was so rocky it was impossible to work over, but as a whole, the farm had the basis laid for a transformation of the soil and the overall ecology. We needed only one more thing—the rain!

When it was all completed, one small item nearly had Dad in tears. We were standing on the compacted bank of a large dam, and I scuffed my foot in the loose topsoil.

"Do you have much hay left?" I asked him.

"Enough, hopefully. Why?"

"I want you to spread a thick layer of hay over the soil of every dam wall. We need only do the earth walls, the rest will have to make do."

Dad looked very unhappy. "I take it you're frightened that a downpour will strip the soil away. Don't you reckon it's compacted enough to handle it?"

I sighed. "Dad, you know that a heavy rain will strip it away. There's no doubt about that. If we could cut, or buy some turf and cover it that way, I would, but that's out of the question. The soil has to be covered."

Looking very unhappy at what he termed a sacrilegious waste of hay, Dad knew that it had to be done. And it was. Later, as he and I walked over it, I realized that the job had yet to be finalized.

"You need to get the spiker, and with the vibrator on the go, run it over the hay a few times. I want it plugged into the soil. I want it so secure that neither rain nor wind can shift it. And the chances are we'll get lashings of both. We've done too good a job to lose it through oversight or carelessness," I told him.

"By Christ, you're right! I hadn't thought of that. A gale before the rain, and it would peel the hay off in bloody minutes."

He turned away there and then, and half an hour later he was on the tractor, the heavy-spiked roller gradually forcing and plugging the hay into the soil. I saw immediately that I was right. The spikes were doing a super job. This was the final touch. It would take Dad the best part of another day to finish all the dams, but by then, his farm would be well and truly ready.

At last everything that could be done was finished, and my exhaustion caught up with me. For eight days I had ignored my growing aches, and the ever-increasing pains, but now I had to surrender. On the final evening, I lay back in a hot bath of their precious water, glad that I had given in to Mum's insistence. Meanwhile, Amber phoned Joyce to tell them that we would be there in one more day. When, a very soaked and soggy hour later, Amber offered to give me a massage, I readily accepted.

I crawled into our spacious bed that night, and with everything done, my mind clear, I sank into a deep sleep.

# Twenty-Three

I had no dreams that night, and despite the early-morning heat, I slept late. When I finally crawled out of bed, my aches and pains all seemed to have gathered force again, and I groaned in dismay.

I made my shower very hot, but quick, and pulling on my shorts and a T-shirt, I went down to see if I could scrounge up some breakfast. I sniffed the air, glad that it was finally rid of the smell of fried bacon. Much as I like the occasional rasher, the way the dozer drivers had been eating it had almost turned me off for life.

The house was empty, so I found some muesli and skim milk, poured them into a bowl, then sat down to eat while contemplating the new day. In my mind I went over all the work of the last week, searching for any detail that I might have overlooked. I did not expect to find anything, but I generally erred on the side of being thorough.

The back door slammed with its old familiar sound, and Mum's voice reached me. "Do you suppose he's awake yet?"

Awake, I thought ironically. I wish. Sometimes I despaired that I would ever Awaken. There was no formula, no magic incantations, just the continual daily struggle of getting there, whatever or wherever that is!

She and Amber walked into the kitchen ahead of Dad, and I knew, without knowing how I knew, that they had been talking about me. I think I came out of it rather well!

Mum smiled at me fondly. "Is there anything I can get you, dear? Would you like some bacon and eggs?"

I shuddered. "Not for at least another six months."

"I know what you mean," Amber chuckled. "I'm beginning to smell like bacon."

Dad came over and sat next to me. "I'm sure he'd like a large mug of coffee. He hasn't made any."

I smiled at them. "It's very nice to have you all so solicitous over my needs, but I'm fine, thanks. However, I would like a coffee."

Dad grinned at me, warm and friendly, and I marveled anew at our new relationship. "For the last hour I've been showing them the new dams, and the lagoon. It all looks a bit bare at the moment, but we won't have long to wait now. I'm getting the strangest feelings about the weather."

I sighed. "Well, if my aches and pains are anything to go by, they have all sharply increased."

"The air feels strange," Mum said, "as if it's getting compressed, or something. I don't like it."

And so it began. Hour by hour the atmosphere changed, becoming increasingly hostile, yet the sky remained clear of any sign of clouds. If anything, it got hotter, while the pressure of the air continued to intensify.

Dad was in and out a lot, checking on the weather.

"Damned if I know what's going on. The birds have all disappeared, and the ants are suddenly as active as all hell, but there's not a cloud to be seen. It's weird."

As best I could, I rested all day, sleeping for a couple of hours during the afternoon. Although I said nothing about it, I was feeling rotten. The aches had become so intense my whole body seemed to throb. But Amber knew.

We were alone late in the afternoon, and I was lying on the couch. Amber came and sat near me, her hand gently stroking my hair back across my head.

"You don't feel well, do you?"

"I'm okay. I just ache badly."

"Do you think you could go to your inner sphere?"

I had not been there for nearly two weeks, but when I had tried this afternoon, I fell asleep in the attempt.

"I think I could, but I've got the strangest feeling that it's not available to me, right now."

She nodded thoughtfully. "That's possible. Can you relax? Any relaxation would help."

"I'm about as relaxed as I can get. It feels as though the air is charged with high-voltage tension, and it's definitely affecting me."

For the next thirty minutes she stroked my hair, softly humming to herself, and I loved every moment of it.

Although Amber and I were aware that Selph had gone, and we had no idea when or where he would return, neither Mum nor Dad noticed, or made any comment. Undoubtedly, Selph had done a smudge job on them, so that his absence evaded their attention. Even when I deliberately made reference to him as we ate our evening meal, and it had to be totally obvious that he was missing, neither of them asked where he was. It was as if, for them, Selph had ceased to ever have existed.

Our meal finished, Dad went to the door and looked outside. "Oh hell! Look at this."

We all went outside, staring up at the sky. The light was fading in the most eerie way I had ever seen, as though some great cosmic beast were dragging it to one side. Part of the sky was a purple-and-red haze, a deep and angry bruise, while gathered around it was a blackness shot through with streaks of an ugly, sick gray.

Mum shook her head. "In all my life, I've never seen a sky like that. I don't like it one little bit."

"It's malevolent," I said. "A violence waiting to be unleashed. I pity anyone who gets caught in it."

"There's a purpose behind this," Amber murmured softly to me, her eyes dreamy, "but it's not easy to explain."

"What's that, love?" Dad asked.

"Oh nothing, Dad," she said, "I was just saying it looks very nasty. I wonder when it's going to break."

Dad gave her a canny smile. "It won't break tonight, love. It'll be sometime tomorrow. This is going to stir and stew for quite a long time yet. I feel it."

Amber and I had arranged to leave quite early the next day. Weather permitting, I wanted to be on the road by eight o'clock. But before we went to bed that night, I had to listen to Dad share his gratitude for what I had done. To me, all that mattered was the easy friendship that now existed between us. It had been hard won!

"Wait until you get my bill," I laughed. "You might retract some of those words."

In fact, I had no intention of charging him. This one was on me, a long ambition realized, a dream fulfilled. He could pay for my future work as a consultant, but I had already been paid half the account on this job. The other half would be paid as I gazed into a filled lagoon, and walked around the filled water holes and dams. I wanted nothing more than that.

Thunder woke us several times that night, and before morning the wind had gradually built up, moaning around the house as it tugged and pried at the guttering with rabid fingers, begging to be let in. I was glad that we had plugged the hay into the soil on the dam walls.

As we ate breakfast, Mum looked worried.

"Please, Adam, you really ought to stay. I don't like the idea of you both out on the road on a day like this."

"Mum, I have to go. If it's at all possible I want to check out Joe's system before the storm breaks. He was my first customer. I owe him."

"You don't owe him, he owes you," Dad grumbled. "But I know how you feel and I respect you for it."

Despite all protests, Amber and I set off just before eight o'clock, and as I glanced up at the black and angry sky, I felt a clutch of dread. Something was going to happen. I could feel it in the prickles creeping as gooseflesh over my skin, and in the empty hollow where my stomach should be. And I could feel it in the throbbing, persistent ache that had now invaded my whole body. From head to toes, I ached like a bad toothache.

Knowing how I was feeling, Amber insisted on driving. We had approximately two hours of driving ahead of us, and she chatted as she sat behind the wheel, flinching briefly when an occasional clap of thunder drowned out her words.

I kept glancing out the side window and up at the sky as she talked, hoping that the rain would hold off just a little while longer. By now, it was inky black overhead, the clouds low and menacing. Once it started, we were in for the mother and father of all storms. I hoped that Joe's farm was well prepared, because I was definitely going to be too late to check it over. The storm would not wait.

I sighed. Well, we had been blessed with luck so far, and Dad was delighted that we had finished in time.

" . . . that's why your parents are very proud of you."

I came out of my reverie in time to catch the end of what Amber had been saying.

"I'm sorry, I lost most of that. I was thinking about Joe, wondering if he got all his preparations finished."

"Don't worry. Joe will have. You know that."

It was the reassurance I needed. She was right. Both Joe and Joyce had always shown plenty of foresight. Relax!

"What were you saying?"

"I was talking about when your Dad showed Mum and me over the dams and lagoon. He was bursting proud of you, and amazed at your decisiveness and knowledge. He said that although he regretted the row that forced you apart and sent you away from the farm, it had definitely been the best thing for you. He said that it had made you grow up and develop your own independence. He said that you now had an inner strength that had not been there before."

I grunted, pleased, yet knowing that his assessment was not really very accurate. "That's his view, and I guess it's valid, for him. But we fought so much, we never really knew each other. He sees the change in me basically through my work, but you and I both know that my work simply reflects the inner changes."

Amber smiled. "Mum kept saying to me, 'My gosh, Amber, there's something different about you, but I can't put my finger on it.' I told her she was right, I'm pregnant. 'I don't think that's it, Amber,' she would say, 'but then again, what else could it be?'"

"What indeed," I chuckled. "It's sad though, isn't it? We live in a time when people are so locked into a consensus reality, and so closed to a greater reality, that if a person goes through an Awakening, experiencing that greater reality, we are unable to tell anyone. Or at least, if we do, it is highly unlikely to be our own family."

"We have our biological family, and also our spiritual family," Amber said. "It's unfortunate that only rarely are they the same people."

We continued our discussion as the road hummed beneath the wheels of our car, the vehicle quickly eating up the distance, and finally we were close to our destination.

Suddenly, I stared ahead in alarm. "My God, look!"

Ahead of us it seemed that we were about to drive into a falling wall of water, and with a shock, I realized what it was. "It's a cloudburst! Slow down. Drive really slowly."

As the crashing sheet of water swept over us, I realized that it was traveling at great speed in the direction we had come from. Dad would very soon get his dams either filled, or wiped out.

With the wiper blades going flat out, we were able to creep along at low speed. We knew we had to keep going. In a downpour like this, the road could be washed out in minutes.

"Go as fast as you dare. It's only another couple of kilometers. But be careful."

Outside the car, the world seemed to have gone crazy. The rain was so hard and heavy that all around us mud and debris was already a churned morass floating over the road. I stared at it in morbid fascination.

"There it is," Amber gasped.

The Steadman's house was only about a hundred meters off the road, and long ago Joe had put a post on each side of the entrance, painted white. Now, we gasped with relief as they loomed before us.

Amber drove between them, and a minute later we pulled up at the house. I had expected Joe to come racing out with a coat to shelter us, but there was no sign of anyone.

I looked at Amber in apprehension. "Something's wrong!"

With the onslaught of rain, the temperature had quickly plummeted, and grabbing our parkas from the back seat, I helped Amber get hers on, before struggling into mine.

Carefully opening my car door so the wind did not rip it out of my grasp, I dashed out to help Amber, and together, we ran in the lashing rain to the verandah of the house. We went up the steps, and Amber knocked on the door.

"They won't hear a thing," I shouted above the roar of rain on the tin roof. If Amber replied, it was lost in a rolling clap of thunder that shook the house.

Opening the door, I ushered Amber in, then thankfully slammed it shut in the face of the wind.

"Is anybody home?" I shouted loudly.

The house was unnaturally empty, and the hollow dread in my gut that I had felt earlier, returned in full. "I don't like this," I muttered.

We quickly searched through the house, knowing it was empty. Why? Where could they possibly be? They were expecting us. Standing in the kitchen, we were staring at each other, wondering what to do, when Joyce came bursting in through the back door. She was drenched, her face ravaged with fear and worry.

Amber shrieked. "Joyce! What's wrong?"

Joyce stared at us, her mouth opening and closing, before she dissolved into tears. "We can't find Jimmy and Liam," she wailed. "They're lost in the storm."

Amber stared at me, her face pale, her eyes aghast. "Oh God! Don't you have any idea where they might be?"

"We all went out to check on the cattle. Joe and Johnny went to Church Hill and that area, Mattie went over to North Pastures, while Jimmy came with me to South End. It hadn't started raining then. I told Liam to stay here and wait. I only expected to be gone about half an hour."

She shook her head desperately. "When Jimmy and I got back, Liam had gone. God! I didn't know what to do. I didn't know if Joe had come back, and taken him, or what. He spends so much time with Joe." She hung her head, sobbing, while Amber held her.

"Next thing, Jimmy dashed off to look for Liam before I could stop him, and I just didn't know what to do, or which way to go. A few minutes later Joe and Johnny came in, and Mattie soon after. None of them had seen hide nor hair of Liam. At that moment, the storm hit us. Christ! We thought we were going to lose the house when it hit. Joe, Mattie, and Johnny went out into the storm looking for Jimmy and Liam. I went out too, and I haven't seen any of them since."

She cried, her shoulders heaving. "Oh God, my poor little boys."

I had taken off my parka, but now I quickly put it back on, zipping it up tightly. "I'll go and look."

"No!" Joyce shouted. "You're not fit enough. You could rebreak your bones out there." Struggling to her feet, she went to the door. "I can't stop. I've gotta go and find my poor boys."

Before we could say another word, she had raced out into the storm, swallowed up as though she ceased to exist.

I glanced at Amber. "I can't sit here. I'm going, but you definitely mustn't in your state. One serious slip and you could lose the baby. Stay here so you can tell anyone who gets back what's happening. We need a coordinator."

Amber knew that she couldn't go, but she clung to me desperately. "Oh, Adam. Please, please, please, be careful. Where are you going to look? What direction?"

I stared at her blankly. "I don't know. I . . . I'll have to follow my instinct."

Kissing her, I ran out of the back door into hell.

Christ! How could a four-year-old kid survive in this? The rain came driving across the land almost horizontally, lashed and driven by the furious frenzy of a demented wind. Gritting my teeth, I bowed before it, staggering rather than running as I ploughed my way on. Where the hell should I look? Come to that, where was I? All the familiar landmarks I knew on the farm were lost in the obliteration of the storm. I stumbled, my feet flying out from under me, and I fell heavily, pain lancing through my hip and into my spine. Oh God! I was useless.

Sitting on the soaking ground, I tried to think. Where would a four-year-old boy go? Blank. What did he like doing? He loved being with his Dad on the tractor. Well, that's out. What else did he like? He was learning to ride a pony. Could he be with the pony? Christ! I don't know. The pony is probably in the stables, they were bound to have looked in there. So what else did he like? He liked me to read him stories. True, but how does that help? What are his favorite stories? Ah, yes, one's about nature.

I got the sudden feeling that I was groping toward the light. Think, Adam, think. What about nature? Anything in particular? And suddenly, it came hurtling out of my muddled thoughts. Liam was besotted with yabbies, those small lobster-like creatures that live in holes in damp or wet soil. I had told him that when it rained, he and I would go and find some.

I gritted my teeth. Young Liam could not wait! So, where the hell would he find yabbies on Joe's farm? I sighed. Come on, Adam, think. When I had read about yabbies to Liam, the story had told how yabbies come out of their holes before it rains. They smell, or sense the wet weather. So, where could there possibly be any yabbies around here? And then, with breathtaking clarity, I knew. Just off the edge of Joe's property, a deep, dried gully runs down a hillside, a gully that normally always has a trickle of water. That's where the yabbies would be, and Liam, smart little Liam, had also reasoned it out.

Scrambling to my feet, I gazed around in the eerie half light, peering through the lashing rain. Which direction? Ah, yes, this way. I tried to run, because in my mind I was seeing the water that would be cascading toward the gully, and I knew that a small boy would have no chance or hope of surviving it. Because of my slipping and sliding in the slick mud, the old familiar knives were out, stabbing and cutting into my hip and lower spine. I ran, slid, fell, got up, and kept going as fast as I could, but it seemed that I was in slow motion, as though held in some crazy demented nightmare that I could not escape. I was vaguely aware of making my painful, staggering way across three paddocks, blundering into the barbed-wire fence each time. My parka was ripped, my hands and face painfully gashed, but somehow, each time I managed to get through the fence and continue in the general direction of the gully.

Lightning arched and forked its way across the sky and into the earth, while thunder shook the air, sending it dancing and quivering until I thought that the structure of life itself would collapse. On and on I dragged myself, whimpering at the pain in my hip and back, slipping and stumbling constantly, but as horrific as the storm was, I was even more terrified by the thought of failure.

A sudden flash of lightning hit a small tree close by, and I felt the tingling crackle of electricity as it ran over my wet skin. The thunder that almost instantly followed set my ears ringing as its shocking detonation crashed into me. The very ground trembled at the violence of the storm, while icy raindrops hurtled unceasingly into my face. I was soaked, and miserable, but the effort I used just to keep going was keeping me warm. Suddenly, a stinging pain hit me across the face, and I felt the taste of blood on my lips. Shocked, I fell to my knees, my hands going to my face. Peering through my fingers, I realized that I was among the trees that surrounded the edge of the gully. One of the wildly waving branches had hit me as I ran into it, but I was almost there.

Crouched down, wiping rain and blood from my eyes, I peered ahead as I hurriedly made my way forward. My mind screamed caution, but I pressed on in a scrambling rush, terrified that I would be too late. That Liam was here I had no doubt at all. I knew it. A tree crashed to the earth with a shrieking thud close by, and I cringed in anticipation of being crushed in this terrifying storm.

Crabwise, I scrambled along, getting ever more reckless as I searched for the gully, when suddenly the world fell out from under me, and I went headfirst in a slithering, sliding rush down a steep, muddy bank. I had found it!

Gasping, I rolled over, and sat up in knee-deep water. I was shocked, dazed, and confused, trying to grasp what was happening. Liam! Oh God! Get moving. Hurry. Scrambling to my feet, I followed the surge of water down the gully, knowing that I was right at the top-end of it. Twisting and turning like a snake, the gully was strewn with rocks and boulders, while water poured down into it from all sides. Oh God! Was I in time?

It seemed that I followed the gully for long tormented hours, but it was probably only minutes later when, stumbling around a bend, I saw Jimmy and Liam ahead of me.

Each boy had managed to get onto a rock, and I wondered why they had not scrambled out. When I reached them, I saw why. Averaging three to six meters deep, at this point the bank of the gully was a smooth slick, mud slide, and one glance at their scratched and bloody hands showed me that they had given it their best. Both boys were crying, overcome by fear.

I looked back the way I had come, and with a sinking heart I knew that it was impossible to get out that way. I tried to remember what it was like further down, from the single occasion I had been here. Logic said that the gully would be deeper, and with the water rising rapidly, I knew that too could lead to disaster. Glancing up, I estimated the bank where we now were to be a little over three meters in height. I had to get the boys out of the gully right here.

With the rain lashing down, and thunder blasting around us, I shouted instructions to Jimmy.

"I'm going to get you up the bank. I'll push you as high as I can reach. Okay? Now, you're a tough kid. I want you to grab that long root up there and fight like crazy to get up the last bit of bank. Right? When you're out, I'm going to throw and push Liam as close to you as I can. I want you to grab him, and haul him out. Okay?"

Jimmy nodded, his jaw set. Now that he had an adult with him, his fear was under control. He knew that we were in great danger, but they were no longer alone.

Lifting Jimmy, I carried him to the bank, and pushing him ahead of me, I used all my strength to pitch him up the bank. Then, grabbing his feet, I pushed him higher.

"Grab the root, Jimmy," I screamed, trying to peer up through the muck and murk to his hands. He flailed about despairingly, his small hands grabbing frantically at the root that hung just out of reach. There would be no chance for a second try, it was now or never. Desperately holding him above me, I tried lifting my foot onto a slight ridge just below my knees. With my foot in place, I wobbled, then, taking a deep breath, I surged upward in a do-or-die effort.

Jimmy was suddenly gone from my hands, and as I sank back into the water, I saw him scramble nimbly up the root to the top of the bank.

I sighed, trembling. One out, one to go. Peering up at him, I shouted. "Get ready for Liam."

As I lifted Liam from his rock, he screamed in pain, and with a sinking heart I knew that he had either a badly sprained, or broken, ankle. "I've got to get you out of here, Liam. This might hurt, but you're a brave boy. Let's do it."

Liam was clearly terrified, but I had no time to comfort him. Hefting his lighter weight, I lifted him high over my head, then, transferring my grip down to his knees, I surged toward the gully bank and, desperately getting one foot on the tiny ridge, I literally jumped and threw him up to Jimmy.

I felt him leave my hands, and I waited, cringing, for him to fall back on me. But no. Standing in water creeping up my thighs, I saw, through slitted eyes, that Jimmy had him, and with grim desperation he was hauling the screaming Liam up and over the top of the bank.

I slumped back, drained, my back and hip almost seized up after the fearful abuse they had just suffered. As I peered upward, Jimmy's face appeared, staring down at me.

"What'll I do?" he screamed.

"Get Liam well back from the gully, wedge him in among some rocks, and tell him not to move. Then run as fast as you can home. Tell your Dad where we are."

He looked confused. "What about you?"

"JUST GO, JIMMY," I roared.

He stared at me, shocked, but his face disappeared, and I knew that he would do as he had been told. With the last of my flagging energy, I threw myself up the gully bank, my feet scrabbling, my hands grasping, fingernails clawing into the mud as I tried to reach the root, but I was completely exhausted. I was beaten.

Drawing on reserves of strength I did not know I had, I tried again, and again, and one last time, but finally, a terrible spasm of agony gripped me, clamping into my lower spine with a paralyzing grip. Contorted by pain, I slumped against Liam's vacated rock, when I heard a strange rumbling and roaring. Fear jerked me upright, and as I stared up the gully, I gaped in shock at the wall of muddy water that was sweeping down toward me.

Horrified, everything seemed to become slow motion, and I recognized my dream. In one awful moment I knew that I was dead. There was no way that I could survive this. I felt the most intense and terrible regret. I would never get to hold my child, never hear its laugh, and never again would I make love to Amber.

A fatalistic calm held me in its thrall, when abruptly, time was rushing along, carrying a three-meter wall of filthy water that hurtled straight at me. I had time to stagger away from the rock, but in the moment before the floodwater hit me, I collapsed, facing into the wave as it engulfed me.

A crushing pressure compressed me, forcing me ever down, while simultaneously, an enormous flowering pain filled and expanded me far beyond the confines of my body. I felt myself thrown high, hurtling forever upward, until I reached a vast, and familiar, oblivion.

# Twenty-Four

As I walked along the tunnel of silver light, I knew that I had been here before. This was the place where the Light had beckoned me; the Light I had so longed to enter.

But, looking ahead, there was no Light to be seen, and as I looked back, there was none behind me. Where was it? The tunnel was illuminated by silver light, but where was I going? And why?

I stopped, puzzled. How did I get here? The last time was when I had been in the car crash. I nearly died. Shock hit me. Nearly died! This was the place I came to when I was nearly dead. Or dead? How did I get here?

I sat down, trying to remember what had happened. I needed Selph. Selph! Of course, where was he? He bailed me out last time. No. That's not true. He gave me a choice. Would he give me a choice this time?

"SELPH," I called loudly. "I need you."

Not even an echo. I did not like this. The last time Selph had manifested a coffeehouse, with those bottomless mugs of delicious cappuccino. I had watched a movie of my car crash, and I had seen Amber at my bedside.

How come I could remember the last time, but I could not recall what had happened to put me here this time? I searched my memory, but nothing came. Okay, keep it simple. What had I been doing? Blank! Who had I been with? I sighed. My memory was blank. So what do I do? I had the feeling that I could walk down this tunnel of silver light forever, but with nowhere to go, and no reason to walk, I decided to stay where I was.

I was probably dead. That was it. But if I were dead, where were the angels? Surely an angel would come and get me? I believed in angels, so surely they would help.

As I sat on the floor of the tunnel, gazing blankly ahead, a distant movement caught my eye. Way, way ahead of me, a huge human form was very slowly coming toward me. I felt an instant apprehension. Who was it?

Rather than light around it, this figure had blackness; a cloak of darkness hugging its body. I stood up to see more easily, but what I saw and felt caused my legs to go weak. An immense, shadowy human male was approaching me, his eyes, and his whole intent fixed on me. He wore nothing but shadow, and in one large hand, he carried a huge ax.

With sudden clarity, I remembered him from my worst, most horrific nightmares. This was the axman, the man who chopped me up, limb by limb, until he reached my . . . head.

And I knew that once again, he was intent in chopping off my head. God! Am I dreaming? Is this another terrible nightmare? Can I wake up screaming?

Opening my mouth, I screamed at the top of my lungs, and then I smacked my face hard, over and over. And the axman came steadily toward me, his face grim, merciless.

Oh God! This was not a dream. Although it did not make sense, this was real. I knew it was undeniably real. It was horribly, frighteningly real. In fact, this was more real, more truly real, than anything I had ever encountered.

The axman came steadily onward, looming huge, yet he seemed not yet to reach me. As I heard a low moaning noise, I realized that it was coming from me, leaking from my mouth as though verbal spittle.

Like a mouse mesmerized by a snake, I stared at the axman in an almost paralyzed trance, and our eyes met. In that instant, I knew that the name of the axman was Fear.

I knew with startling clarity that I was facing my Fear, and that it would never go away. There was only one way out of this, and that was my death. The fact that I had yet to die told me that, physically, I still lived, but I knew that the physical me was no longer important. Bodies and identities come and go, one after another, incarnation after incarnation, but this, now, was about the real me. This was, as Selph had once said, the essential Me. On this greater, more true, level of my Being, I had endlessly carried Fear, maintaining and reinstating it lifetime after lifetime. In this incarnation, I had resolved to end it.

Selph had maneuvered and manipulated me into a place where I had to finally face the truth: to conquer Fear, I had to submit before it. To overcome Fear, Adam had to die to it. Adam had to kneel in surrender before the ax of

Fear, and lose his head; his identity. By doing so, I would most probably die physically, but the essential Me would be purged of Fear for all time.

I had to release Amber, and my unborn child. I had to release the new love and friendship with my father. I had to release everything that I most wanted and valued as Adam, because Adam had to die. Could I do this? My life as Adam would end. Who I would be when I reincarnated again, or when that would be, was irrelevant. The essential Me could not die, but Adam could. And with Adam's death, I would lose Amber. I knew that the essential Me and the essential Her would unite again, but that was in a time yet to happen.

The axman had reached me, and he stopped. I knew that he awaited my verdict. It was possible that I could elude him, running for my life though countless more incarnations, but I had had enough. To all things there comes a time. Time . . . timing! Everything has its perfect timing. This, now, was mine. Time to release Fear. Time to surrender. Regret was an unparalleled enormity, but I knew that there was nothing left but surrender. It was the moment to let go of every want, of every desire; to simply "let go."

I looked up at the gigantic form, and within the shadow, Fear sneered at me, daring me to test my resolve.

Abruptly, I knelt down, offering my neck.

"I submit."

As the axman took a careful stance, the huge ax was slowly raised higher and higher, while my calmness and resolve became ever more stabilized.

I smiled as the ax reached its zenith, and although I could not see it, I could feel it hanging there, offering me a last opportunity to scream and run.

"Do it," I whispered.

With an angry snarl, Fear brought the ax down in its final crashing blow.

I felt nothing. There was a vast explosion of LIGHT, and I clearly saw Fear disintegrate, blown apart by light into a zillion tiny pieces of shadow.

With my consciousness intact, in the brief instant before I, too, seemed to explode, I was enveloped within a glowing Golden Light, and I knew, instantly, that this is the Light Being, I Am. Only fear and isolation had maintained the illusion that I, and the Golden Light I Am, were ever separate. I was aware of myself as whole as I spun through the continuity of all the lives that the essential me had ever lived on the physical earth. Each linear lifetime was experienced simultaneously, and it seemed to take for all infinity, yet was finished in the briefest flicker of a micromoment.

Then, abruptly, I was sitting with Selph in the cosmic coffeehouse with the extraordinary mugs.

He grinned at me, a huge smile of delight plastered all over his face. "I've got to hand it to you. Drama until the very end. My God! You must love drama. Your axman almost had me trembling, and I knew the outcome."

And as I looked at him, my smile equal to his, I knew so much more than I had ever known before; not knowledge, but by directly knowing.

Adam, as a person, still lived. It was my relationship with life as an identity that had died, but my individuality continued. Although the essential me no longer related to self as Adam, the identity me had a purpose that had yet to be expressed on the physical plane. And Selph? He chose his name very carefully—Self! Selph is the essential me a whole lot more lifetimes down the track; or should I say a step through a few frames of reality. Indeed, all time does occupy the same space!

I knew now that what Selph had done for me, I had done for Jacob. The only difference was that Selph had acted from the master he knows he is, while I had acted from the victim I believed myself to be. As Selph is, so is the essential me, but timing is the governing factor.

Every thought, every revelation I had, Selph shared.

He watched me as I gazed in wonder at the Golden Light that enveloped me—and him! It seemed as though this light-body of mine came from the very essence of the Golden Light, and that time, space, and distance were meaningless to it.

"You are right, of course," he chuckled. "Your Light connects with the One Light, the All That Is, and nothing can ever separate Light from Light. Neither time nor dimensions, nor ignorance nor abuse, not even denial or hate. Love that is Light, Light that is Love, is One. And that says it: All life is One." He laughed in delight. "So, you now know the meaning of life."

I smiled at him mischievously. "In simple terms, the meaning of life is the meaning of your Self!"

He chuckled, and becoming again the older, yet ageless, sage of some future tomorrow that is also the eternal now. He bowed low before me. "I honor Self."

"Thank you. Will I see you any more?"

His reply surprised me.

"Not immediately, but I'll be back. This may well be a quantum leap, or initiation, but that's no more than the precursor to a new beginning. I've enjoyed being with you immensely. Give my love to Amber. I think you will find that she knows the rest."

"It does beg the question though, doesn't it?" I laughed. "Which comes first, the chicken or the egg?"

"And the answer is?"

"Consciousness: the expression of Love/Light/God."

"Good-bye, Self," he said.

"Good-bye, Selph," I smiled. "And thank you."

❖ ❖ ❖

I became aware of being carefully carried between two people. They had made a bush stretcher—a couple of sacks with two poles poked through the ends—and I was lying on this. I bounced gently at each step, my body throbbing and aching with pain. It was obvious that when the wall of water had hit me, it had knocked me unconscious, forcing me deep under the water, then, miraculously, it had tossed my limp body far up the bank of the gully like a discarded rag doll. I had lain there unconscious until I had been found. Beaten and battered, badly injured, but alive.

In the lashing downpour of rain, I raised my essential Self above my body, looking onto and into the physical me. I was cut and torn. My hands and face, deeply gashed by barbed wire, were running streams of blood. I looked half-drowned, mauled, and mutilated. My hip was a lancing pain that met and merged with the stabbing violence in my lower spine. I could see that one of my legs had been broken again, and an arm. All in all, I was a mess.

This won't do at all, I thought. Embracing my body with my whole and total consciousness for a one-off major healing, I focused all the Golden Light I Am on the physical me. Every cell, every molecule, was held within my consciousness of Love. My love for me—both the identity self of Adam, and the essential Self I Am—was complete, for it can only be complete when fear has been recognized for the impostor it is, and banished. Every cell, every molecule, of my physical body was illuminated and ignited by Light.

Instantly, every pain and all the aches vanished. My hip and lower spine were healed and whole, forever. My broken bones came together, mended, healed, and whole, and every cut and gash instantly healed. The anxiety that coils as a heavy steel spring of negative stress, an unrealized and malignant burden deeply established within the human psyche, was instantly released. My full and natural energy was immediately restored—my joy complete.

With crystal clarity, I knew that Joe had Gutsy, their reliable four-wheel-drive, nearby. As the rain lashed down on me, I peered through slitted eyes at Joyce, carrying the foot end of the stretcher. Our eyes met.

"It would be much easier if you let me walk."

Joe stopped as though he had hit a brick wall, and the stretcher fell from Joyce's nerveless fingers, dumping me onto the ground.

"Glory be! Adam?"

Scrambling to my feet, I faced them, grinning.

Together, they stared at me, so exhausted and frightened that they were on the point of collapse. Shock etched stark lines into their faces, before Joe's legs crumpled beneath him, and he sat down heavily. His mouth opened and closed wordlessly. In that moment, Joe was feeling just as I had felt when I witnessed a dead osprey fly.

"Adam? My God! It's a miracle," Joyce managed. "Your leg was broken!" She gaped at me, trying to comprehend. "My God! You're covered in . . . like a mist of golden light. What does . . . it's fading!"

Bending over, I put my hands under Joe's armpits, and easily lifted him upright. Then, with one arm supporting him, and one arm around Joyce, I steered them through the storm toward the four-wheel-drive vehicle that was just visible beyond the last trees.

It took about five minutes. For them, they were five stupefying minutes, where I urged them to save the questions and to just keep walking. When we reached Gutsy, I open the doors and grinned at the two pale and exhausted boys wrapped in blankets on the back seat.

"You did a great job, Jimmy. I'm proud of you."

He smiled weakly, suddenly shy. "Thanks, Adam."

I looked at Liam, and tousled his wet hair. "And you're a gutsy kid in a gutsy vehicle. How's the ankle?"

He shrugged. "All right, I guess."

I smiled at Joe. "I'll drive."

He nodded numbly, overwhelmed by events he could not understand, and clambered into the passenger seat. Her eyes wide, shocked, and uncomprehending, Joyce climbed into the back with the boys. Her words and wits were still eluding her.

It took only a few minutes to drive easily through the raging storm, whereas a short time earlier it had been the living nightmare that I had endlessly blundered through.

We reached their house, the door opened, and Amber stood framed in the doorway, with Mattie and John hovering anxiously behind her. Opening the rear door of Gutsy, I lifted Liam out and carried him into the house, while Amber helped Joyce, followed by Joe and Jimmy. Wet, bedraggled, and running with water, we stood in the room, relief like sunshine on the faces of Joe and Joyce.

I met Amber's eyes, and smiled.

"Do you know what's happened?" I asked.

She nodded, crying her relief. "Yes, but I don't know the details."

We hugged and kissed, the love between us reaching out to the stars . . . and beyond. Together, we entered the timeless realm of new beginnings.

# About the Author

In today's world, Michael J. Roads is an uncommon man. Born in England in 1937, he was delving into the hidden, silent, mysteries of nature from an early age. His background is based in farming, and after marrying the most wonderful woman he ever met, they immigrated to Australia. Here, he and Treenie raised their four—now grown—children. During a decade of farming on the island state of Tasmania, Michael went through some profound inner changes. This process of change was to take them both away from farming and Tasmania, and into a dedicated search for Self. Difficult years were to follow, but the inner search was unrelenting. To be "free" and to experience the realization of "Self" was all that had any meaning.

During this time, Michael and Treenie experienced life in an intentional community, followed by a few years of Michael working as an eco-farming consultant. Daily he focused on empowering his aware, conscious, connection with nature, eventually learning to cross the membrane separating the physical from the metaphysical, the tangible from the intangible.

Michael's life now consists of writing, playing, and giving retreats. With Treenie, he conducts the five-day Roadsway Re*treats in many countries around the world. And the number keeps growing.

He is a brilliant speaker. He is also self-realized. He speaks his truth clearly, without bias or dogma. He is funny, inspiring, and direct. Michael is many things to many people, but above all, he is simple.

For information on the Roadsway Re*treats and/or cassettes:

**United States:**
James and Carolyn Silver
The Roadsway
P.O. Box 22562
Beechwood, Ohio 44122

**Rest of the World:**
Michael and Treenie Roads
P.O. Box 778
Nambour, QLD, 4560, Australia
E-mail: roadsway@pegasus.com.au

# Hampton Roads Publishing Company

*. . .for the evolving human spirit*

Hampton Roads Publishing Company
publishes books on a variety of subjects including
metaphysics, health, complementary medicine,
visionary fiction, and other related topics.

For a copy of our latest catalog,
call toll-free, (800) 766-8009,
or send your name and address to:

Hampton Roads Publishing Company
134 Burgess Lane
Charlottesville, VA 22902